<A LIGHT HAS SHOWN>

<Irena L. Kenneley>

First paperback edition January 2025

Book design by Irena L. Kenneley

LCCN 2025904476 **Paperback**

ISBN 13: 978-1-967778-63-8 **(Paperback)**

Library of Congress Control Number: 2019012345

Published by Protocol Nine Books

Dedication

To the dreamers who gaze at the stars
and wonder what's out there,

To the healers who navigate the fragility of life
with strength and compassion,

And to those who believe a light will always find its way,
even in the darkest moments.

This book is for you…

Table of Contents

Prologue

Nestled within the Aquarius constellation, the planet Galatea is a barren expanse of jagged rocks and crimson sands, its surface carved by relentless winds and ancient storms. Encased beneath an enormous dome, humanity's last frontier struggles to breathe life into this inhospitable world. The Galatea colony is a shimmering beacon of humanity's resilience, but it is also a fragile illusion—an oasis balanced on the edge of desolation.

Adira Varna stood at the medical station's viewport, her reflection merging with the crimson horizon beyond. Her green eyes betrayed exhaustion, framed by new worry lines etched into her face. She was a healer, a problem solver, and a woman who thrived in the face of challenges. Yet the latest crisis tested even her resolve.

"It's spreading faster than we anticipated," she murmured, her voice barely audible above the low hum of the station's life-support systems.

Behind her, monitors displayed a haunting mosaic of data—vitals plummeting and infection rates spiking, and now medical supplies were dwindling. The outbreak, a mysterious affliction that turned lungs into stone and left its comatose victims gasping for air, had claimed its first life that morning. There was no cure, vaccine, or answers yet—just a growing list of names carved into the colony's memorial wall.

Rafe Silvers entered the room with a recently acquired quiet confidence, seemingly of someone accustomed to command. His presence filled the sterile space, a sharp contrast to the sleek monitors and the chemical tang of antiseptic. As Chief of Security, Rafe's responsibilities extended beyond maintaining order; he was also the colony's shield against external and internal threats. His piercing blue eyes met Adira's, a silent exchange of shared determination.

"There's been a development," she said, her voice a low whisper. "Eurydice's team found something in the caves beyond Sector Eight."

Rafe's heart quickened. The caves were a forbidden zone, a labyrinth of ancient tunnels stretching deep into Galatea's crust. The colony's early exploration efforts had deemed them unstable and dangerous. Yet, whispers of strange phenomena persisted—bioluminescent organisms, unexplained energy readings, and the occasional shadowy figure glimpsed on the periphery of floodlights.

"What did they find?" he asked, his voice tinged with hope and trepidation.

Adira hesitated, a flicker of unease crossing his stoic features. "Life," she said finally. "And… something else. David thinks it might be a cure."

Rafe's mind raced. Life on Galatea? The prospect alone was monumental, a discovery that could reshape their understanding of the universe. But a cure? If there was even a chance…

"I need to see it," he said, stepping away from the viewport.

"You're not going alone," Adira countered. Her tone brooked no argument.

As they exited the medical station, the colony's red dwarf sun cast long shadows throughout the atrium, its reddish-golden light a poor imitation of Earth's. Beyond and beneath the dome's protective barrier, the caves loomed like dark mouths, their secrets buried in the planet's ancient heart. Adira couldn't shake the feeling that whatever they were about to uncover would change everything—not just for Galatea but for humanity itself.

And in the faint glow of the horizon, unseen by human eyes,

bioluminescent tendrils stirred in anticipation. The entities were waiting.

1 - The Planet Galatéa

<u>John 12:35</u> *Walk while you have the light, lest darkness overtake you. The one who walks in the darkness does not know where he is going.*

In the dimly lit living room, Adira Varna was surrounded by the plush comfort of overstuffed sofa pillows. Their softness enveloped her as she leaned back, her body sinking into the cushions. She fixed her gaze on the sleek, transparent display hovering before her—a holographic projection flickering to life with a quiet hum. The soft glow illuminated her features, casting shadows that danced across the walls of her cozy, Earth-based home.

From the telecom system, a more transparent transmission materialized: a satellite view of a vivid, crystalline image of the Aeris space station, floating serenely in orbit around the distant planet Galatéa. The station's intricate architecture, with its shimmering metallic surface and glowing energy conduits, hung in the black void of space, a stark contrast to the warm tones of Adira's room. As the transmission settled, the hologram expanded, filling her view with the orb of Galatéa itself. Swirling distant clouds and a mass of maroons and violets with shimmering oceans were visible from breaks in the cloud mass.

The faint hum of the system was the only sound in the room, blending with the quiet rhythm of her heartbeat as Adira watched, entranced by the image—her connection to a distant world, a momentary bridge between two far-flung places. As she sipped her coffee, a holographic image showed workers in yellow uniforms on the planet's surface. They emerged from an underground facility into a deep, protected valley. One by one, they boarded a shuttle to await return to the orbiting space station.

Gint Larson's piercing gray eyes stared straight into the space station's camera. We have witnessed the final adjustments. Our team has finished the terminal inspection rounds of dome integrity and interior colony environmental systems. The Galatéa habitat is ready and expecting its first colonists, scheduled to reach the planet in two months.

The transmission panned across the dappled maroon to reddish violet Galatéan landscape, zooming in to reveal a vertical glass-domed structure built into the mountain's side. Adira was stunned.

I can imagine sitting inside the dome, looking through its geodesic windows, and observing the red dwarf's star shine and other visible planets in the system. This clever design allows the colonists to be shielded from radiation and ferocious winds yet still feel as if they were outside.

She could see many white and silver humanoid droids returning from the valley to the deep interior caves adjacent to the dome's glass exterior, where they monitored designated maintenance and environmental controls. The colonists' new home awaited them.

So proud of you, Gint.

She smiled as she considered the colony's current state. Her husband, Gint, had commanded the Galatéa space station, which had deployed robot drones to the planet's surface. The crew expanded underground dwellings and built the external domed glass habitat for long-term human residency.

Galatéa orbited an M-type red dwarf star near the ecliptic of the constellation Aquarius. As a small red dwarf, it was dimmer than the Earth's sun. Due to the planet's low orbital eccentricity, scientists deployed androids to construct a suitable habitat to protect humans from potential radiation caused by rare solar flares, coronal mass ejections, and cosmic rays originating from beyond the heliosphere of the mother star. Galatéa was one of five terrestrial planets that orbited the red dwarf.

The glass dome also shielded the colony from fierce winds generated by the planet's temperature differences, which were between the heat of the starward side and the cold of the spaceward side of the tidally locked world. With the shielding in place, expert teams from the space station supervised and worked with the droids on the surface. They finished constructing the immense habitat ahead of schedule.

The image switched back inside to the Aeris space station celebrations. Raucous and jubilant, the space station crew cheered as Gint continued. "In this transcendent moment, we would like to acknowledge—"

When the audio unexpectedly ceased, Adira approached the sliding glass door and looked at the moonlit ocean. She glanced back at the telecom and saw the screen remained black. Adira chewed on her thumbnail as she returned, sat on the sofa, and stared at the blank screen.

They must have had technical difficulties. After all, the transmission was delayed because of technical challenges, and Galatéa is over 12 light-years away in the middle of nowhere.

Some minutes later, she jumped at the shrill chime of the telecom. Middle-of-the-night calls never brought good news, as Adira knew from experience.

"Adira?" David Michel's face appeared on the telecom screen. "Have you been viewing the transmission from Galatéa? We've lost contact with the space station. We're still trying to reach them."

"Do we have intelligence not shared with the public?" Unable to think of anything else to say, Adira leaned forward and tried to keep her voice professional and steady, but hidden in her lap, her hands shook.

"Our environmental dome sensors detected an explosion in the atmosphere. The AI on the planet sent a final transmission that showed a sudden bright light emanating from the space station area. As soon as we know anything, I'll contact you. Hang tight." David's image winked out.

He's worried about me.

David Michel was her closest friend. They were classmates and had dated in medical school. As a medical consultant stationed at the command center on Earth, he had communicated and worked closely with the space station over the past three years.

She poured more coffee and stepped outside. Her uneasy feelings intensified as the minutes started adding up to an hour, then two, with no word on the space station.

"Damn!" Adira exclaimed after she stubbed her toe as she rushed to answer the telecom. She saw it was the link to her employer, Space Intelligence and Security, section 22, or SIS 22. The Special Operations Executive was calling.

With coffee in hand, she settled into the sofa cushions. As the transmission codes pulsed and scrambled, a visual formed. Eurydice Sideris's eyes looked red, and her voice sounded huskier than usual.

"We have an updated report on the space station. Unfortunately, it appears the space station has exploded. We assume that the catastrophe resulted in the loss of everyone on board. I'm so sorry. I wanted to inform you privately and before anyone else."

Adira was stunned into silence. She regained her voice in a few moments. "As operatives, we undergo training and understand the risks associated with our work." Thank you, Eurydice, for your kindness. Do you have any other news? When Eurydice shook her head, she terminated the video.

####

A little white cottage stood on a cliff overlooking countless miles of the Pacific Ocean. A thunderstorm was brewing to the west, and stratocumulus loomed miles high in an intensifying sky. The juxtaposition of clear, dark skies, white light from pinpoint stars, and mountains of storm clouds approaching seemed prophetic.

Adira couldn't believe an entire month had gone by already. She sat on the terrace of her cliff side cottage and gazed at the stars while waves crashed and surged in the ocean below. A lone meteor streaked through the darkening sky and wrenched Adira's gaze skyward from the churning surf. She grappled with her new reality and turned up the music volume.

I always knew loss and pain were possible. Time has passed, but I feel the same emptiness.

The second movement of Beethoven's Seventh Symphony in A blasted from the opened patio doors. Finally, her composure gave way, and she surrendered as her head bowed and her shoulders trembled.

Her communicator interrupted the music. She wiped her eyes as distant thunder rumbled through the heavy air.

"You are ordered to return to active duty," the aged and unusually husky voice of her mentor, Eurydice Sideris, comforted Adira. The words hit her like a thunderbolt, stirring a mix of emotions within her. "We have selected you and six others to return to Washington for this mission."

"Terminate speakers and secure the perimeter," Adira commanded the house AI, preparing to leave. *I'm grateful Eurydice decided to keep me busy with a new mission. A constructive diversion—this must be critical.*

2 - A NEW MISSION

Adira stood before the imposing black monoliths of the Strategic International Space Security Force, or SIS22, headquarters. The intelligence agency had become a fortress of secrecy, housing the Cyber Command Center and the most advanced AI in the world, known as Vilkas. It was where dark secrets lingered, protected from outside forces and prying eyes. The SIS22 international intelligence agency's impregnable headquarters was built like a veritable fortress. In the early twenty-first century, activists suspected to be from a splinter faction of a radical religious group had fired a rocket-propelled grenade round at the building's eighth floor with no structural damage.

The corridors beneath the building twisted deep into the earth. Adira made her way to the shielded briefing room, her mind still numb from the news of Gint's death. Despite her training to handle crises, the news of Gint's death weighed heavily on her mind.

The team assembled underground and seated themselves around an oval table. As the room filled with the hum of holographic projectors and the lights dimmed, Eurydice Sideris, prepared and focused, began the briefing.

"Vilkas, initiate recording. The date is 8.1.2174, 0600 hours. This briefing will begin with an overview and background. Refrain from asking questions until we have completed the presentation.

"As you know, humans have been using pathogenic organisms, manipulating and weaponizing them as bioweapons, for thousands of years. Advancements in synthesis technology have made protein toxin and peptide production highly accessible and have posed a monstrous threat to international biosecurity."

In the center of the conference table, SIS22's AI Vilkas

displayed holographic images of three-dimensional pictures and illustrations of advanced synthesis technology, along with images of three-dimensional toxins and electron microscopy of various peptide sequences for each member to view.

"Compounds capable of hemolyzing the blood, bacterial gastrointestinal enterotoxins, and conotoxins are examples of peptide agents synthesized in countries with weak biosecurity measures. Although rudimentary, individuals have used these bioweapons for nonlethal and lethal effects against smaller targets. Therefore, a changing threat landscape has drawn our attention. We have focused our surveillance from technological advances of member countries to more micro-level threats from terror cells and lone-wolf attackers."

The AI advanced the hologram to show various images from around the globe of well-known terrorist attacks and the devastation that followed.

"Historically, chemical and biological weapons were used during WWI, which led to the Geneva Protocol almost two hundred and sixty years ago. During any war, poisonous gases and bacteriological organisms were prohibited."

Vilkas displayed images of ancient gas masks, old Geneva, WWI soldiers in trenches, and pathogenic bacterial organisms.

"Unfortunately, the Geneva Protocol had not included a prohibition or limitations on bioweapons, so several countries felt threatened enough that they researched and developed additional biological weapons. During WWII, twenty-two years later, we learned that Imperial Japan intentionally infected Chinese prisoners of war with bacterial pathogens, such as typhoid, cholera, and plague."

The projection switched to microscopic organisms of each pathogen, followed by real-life images taken of affected prisoners of war in various disease states, including severe dehydration and progressed stages of bubonic and pneumonic plagues.

"Shortly after, they made further attempts to outlaw the production, development, and stockpiling of biological weapons. Since that time, several signatories have violated this legislature. For example, the former USSR's Biopreperat developed biological weapons under the guise of legitimate pharmaceutical and biotechnological research. Iraq and South Africa also violated the law with research and development of biological weapons and actively used them, which included toxins."

Images of the ancient intelligence center, known as the Lubyanka building in old Moscow, appeared.

"Religious cults and terrorist cells have also deployed biological weapons. Through AI surveillance algorithms, we have monitored millions of cyber events. We know that terrorist networks have used bioweapons and that other factions have synthesized novel bioweapons."

The room fell silent. The implications were chilling.

The projection showed numerous images of religious protesters from around the world.

"Our AI, Vilkas, has provided surveillance alerting the intelligence community to dangerous peptide genetic constructs that threaten our biosecurity. AI Vilkas has been a powerful asset in surveillance activities. We have monitored, responded to, and managed biothreats as they occurred in real-time. We have accumulated data through AI surveillance systems and created a network map of all researchers who have worked with specific pathogens and chemicals for potential deviations from the norm to be detected.

"By following the ordering patterns for specific nucleic acids and peptide synthesis reagents from nodes or institutions, Vilkas has identified suspicious and intentional infringement of laws.

Surveillance methods have also detected malicious peptide synthesis and discerned unlawful manipulation of nucleic acid sequences. Subject matter experts have reviewed the network maps and investigated red flags that the AI Vilkas has raised. Even if bad actors spread out their orders temporally or have used different facilities or co-workers, the AI's network mapping has detected and countered decentralized threats by cutting off critical supplies."

Vilkas projected images of data gathered from biothreats, and a network map of worldwide research activities appeared green versus suspicious activities in red.

Eurydice turned to Adira. "Dr. Varna, please share pertinent public health facts with the team."

Long years of study left Adira prepared as usual, and she spoke off the top of her head. "This is an overview of public health emergency preparedness principles and our response to a bioterrorist attack. Bioweapons are categorized based on whether they are microorganisms of concern, which means those that will cause the most morbidity and mortality. Prioritized as categories I, V, and X, these categories escalate as the microorganism poses a greater risk to national security and how easily the agent can be disseminated. Category I organisms pose the most severe threat.

"Dissemination occurs by the route of entry into the human body the bioweapon utilizes. The main entry routes are inhalation, skin or mucous membrane contact, and ingestion into the gastrointestinal tract. Delivery methods include bomblets dropped by aircraft, spray tanks mounted on an aircraft, or even a tall building. Unfortunately, microorganisms of concern can be aerosolized and distributed over large geographic areas. We are concerned with the older Category I pathogens that threaten national security, including anthrax, plague, brucella, smallpox, viral encephalitis, and hemorrhagic fever viruses.

"Less frequently used dissemination methods have included the deliberate infection of animals or the release of pests or vectors via an international border. Our AI Vilkas employs pathogen detectors to monitor air quality. These detectors gather airborne particles onto filters, collect them regularly, and analyze them for potential biological weapon pathogens. Have you detected a new threat, Eurydice?"

Eurydice raised her eyebrows and continued with a grim look of determination. "As you know, the World Health Organization announced the eradication of the infectious disease smallpox in 1980. The World Health Organization established two approved repositories for the live smallpox virus called variola. One is at the Centers for Disease Control in Atlanta, and the other is in the southwest Siberian plain known as Vector, Novosibirsk.

"Intelligence gathered recently indicated that the Eastern Dominion military's covert weaponization and stockpiling of the live variola virus has been ongoing. Dr. Viktoras Galkin is an Eastern Dominion genomic scientist in charge of the team that has modified the variola virus through genetic engineering to transfer lethal pathogenic properties via induced mutations. These manipulations have made the virus more challenging to detect, diagnose, and impossible to treat—the vaccination is no longer effective. In other words, the variola virus has been made more deadly, and now its intended use is as a weapon. If this new strain is released, experts predict that as many as 60 to 100 million individuals could die.

A three-dimensional image of Galkin's head and entire body appeared and revolved slowly for the team to ponder.

Galkin has connections to a militant religious faction whose philosophy revolves around the Law of Human Existence. The faction believes the universe was created solely for humans and plans to release the variola virus on Mars to draw attention to its Earth-centric cause.

"We know that Dr. Galkin is the one who engineered the deadly strain of variola, and he possesses information about the timing and method of its deployment on the Mars base." Our mission is to subdue and capture Galkin. However, we must take special precautions with Viktoras Galkin because Eastern Dominion agents carry a suicide poison in their dental work. As soon as we get him on our transport shuttle to Bethesda, we will perform surgery to extract the venom. It's a crude, ancient method of suicide, but that's precisely why so many Dominion operatives have eluded interrogation successfully.

"In a few weeks, Atlanta, Georgia, will host the next International Congress on Infectious Diseases. This Congress is a conference allowing scientists, researchers, and world-renowned experts to convene, share groundbreaking technologies, and address global challenges. This unique event focuses on clinical practice, basic and translational science, novel infection control and prevention approaches, and epidemiology of emerging infectious diseases. Dr. Galkin is a featured subject matter expert who is expected to discuss contemporary hot topics. Once we have Galkin detained and interrogated, we will have an opportunity for an advanced understanding from a critical perspective of what we are up against and intercept challenges."

Eurydice slowly met each team member's eyes. "We have the perfect opportunity for Galkin to be captured before he has released any deadly pathogens and to keep him alive for further interrogation. The responsibility for abducting and capturing this dangerous individual alive lies with this team."

Adira felt a surge of anger burn beneath her grief. Gint's death had left a void, but this mission gave her something to cling to—a purpose. She would stop Galkin, no matter the cost.

The briefing concluded, but the weight of what lay ahead settled over the room like a heavy fog. As the team dispersed, Eurydice caught Adira's eye. "I'm sorry about Gint. But we need you focused."

Adira nodded, her resolve hardening. She wasn't just going to stop Galkin for the mission or the world. She would do it for Gint.

3 - Adventures in the Spy World

The mission to capture Dr. Galkin was one of precision and danger. The International Congress on Infectious Diseases in Atlanta was the perfect cover. Scientists worldwide gathered to discuss biotechnological advancements and were unaware that a killer lurked among them.

Adira's team, a united force, moved like shadows, blending into the background of academic discourse. They couldn't afford to tip their hand too early. Galkin was meticulous and would vanish if he suspected even the faintest hint of danger. In a private room, away from the conference bustle, Adira studied the surveillance feeds. They monitored every movement and conversation. Her hands clenched the table's edge as she spotted Galkin entering a lecture hall.

"Eyes on the target," she muttered into her earpiece.

The operation was on the brink of commencement, the air thick with anticipation and tension. Every team member was on high alert, ready to execute their roles with precision and speed. The moment was imminent. It was time to move.

Adira entered the sleek, modern bar, sat, and started sipping mineral water, keeping her gaze fixed on the man she was sent to capture: Viktoras Galkin. The fate of the Mars colony, and perhaps humanity, depended on this moment. Her mission was simple in theory but monumental in scope: Galkin must be taken alive. She allowed herself a small, sardonic smile as she raised her glass, her expression betraying nothing of the turmoil beneath the surface.

The scientists of the International Congress of Infectious

Diseases in Atlanta were a cacophony of clinking glasses, wild stories, and raucous laughter. Scientists, some of the brightest minds in the world, indulged themselves in vodka, their inhibitions dulled by drink. Galkin, too, partook, his deep voice joining in Dominian drinking songs that boomed across the bar. "Nostrovia," the men exclaimed as they clinked shot glasses and slammed back their vodka with practiced ease.

Adira's mind drifted momentarily to a long-forgotten memory. She had been eight years old, hidden beneath her bed covers, while her grandparents held loud, raucous parties in their home. "Nostrovia," her parents would shout, the clink of cognac glasses echoing through the house. Even then, she had learned to shut out the noise, to distance herself from the chaos around her.

Indifference became my shield, she thought, a defense mechanism that helped me survive.

She shook her head lightly, bringing herself back to the present. *Focus, Addie.* Her grip tightened on the glass. The polished exterior felt cool against her palm. She had perfected the art of detachment, which now served her well. But even in the spy world, the moment's weight gnawed at her, pressing against the cracks of her carefully constructed armor.

"Nostrovia," she mouthed silently, raising her glass in Galkin's direction. The man's gaze flicked to her immediately, his interest piqued. She knew it wouldn't be long now. The game had begun.

Moments later, the bartender leaned over and spoke above the noise. "Mr. Galkin would like to buy you a drink."

Adira's lips curved into a slow, inviting smile. "Tell Mr Galkin thank you, and I'll have my usual," she said, her red lips shimmering under the bar's low light. The bartender, her SIS22 colleague David Michel, gave a quick nod.

As the scientists' party started to wind down, Galkin made his way over and sat beside her, just as everyone had predicted. His eyes roved over her red dress, a hungry smile tugging at the corners of his mouth. She lifted her glass, locking eyes with him.

"To your health," she toasted, her voice smooth as velvet. Galkin's eyes gleamed with a mixture of curiosity and desire.

"Nostrovia," he replied, knocking back his shot of vodka without breaking eye contact. "I saw you at the front of my lecture today," he said, his voice slick and arrogant. "You're easy on the eyes."

Adira resisted the urge to roll her eyes. *Charming.* Instead, she played along, sliding a hotel key card across the bar with a playful laugh. "Meet me in my room in fifteen minutes," she whispered, her tone teasing. "I'd love to hear more about your groundbreaking work."

As she left the bar, she walked with purpose, her heels clicking softly on the marble floor. The weight of her role settled in her bones. The façade would soon fall away, and the real work would begin.

The team was already in the penthouse suite, the atmosphere tense but focused. Adira checked the small tray in the kitchen, ensuring the sedatives were prepared. Her fingers briefly hovered over the vials. This wasn't just a mission; it was the last line of defense against a nightmare.

The elevator light flickered, signaling Galkin's imminent arrival. Two large agents took their positions beside the doors, their expressions steely. The tension in the room was palpable, but Adira felt a calm wash over her.

"Heads up—ready to roll," Marcus, one of the agents, whispered. When Viktoras Galkin emerged from the elevator, Marcus quickly tackled him. Once down, the other jammed a special mouth guard between his jaws, preventing any chance of him biting down on the suicide capsule embedded in his molars.

Adira moved swiftly, injecting a short-acting sedative into Galkin's arm. His struggles weakened, and soon, he was unconscious. She started an IV and administered propofol, deepening his sedation. David was quick to intubate him, the steady hum of the ventilator filling the room. With the paralytic drug vecuronium coursing through Galkin's veins, the agents loaded him onto a gurney, completely immobile.

Within minutes, the team rolled Galkin's gurney through the sliding glass doors on the roof and into an awaiting transport. The night sky streaked by as they ascended toward the clouds. Adira kept her eyes on Galkin's vitals, her focus absolute.

Adira stood in the rain and watched the transport take off with Galkin headed for Bethesda and SIS22 protective custody. She looked up at the sky and spotted the planet Mars low on the eastern horizon.

Ah yes, Mars—I would have liked to be among those chosen for that mission.

After the permanent lunar base was finalized, the next big step in human exploration was a crewed mission to Mars. A Mars colony was established for long-term human residency.

Adira smiled as she considered her accomplishments despite being ordered to remain on Earth. Her team's biggest project involved the development of a self-contained, durable life support system that recycled waste, produced edible crops, and used the water on Mars to make fuel.

Today, I worked on a successful critical mission again. She felt good.

Adira turned from the transport as it flew off into the night with its precious cargo safely aboard. She realized the team succeeded—this time—in averting an act of bioterrorism. The colony of people stationed at the long-term Mars habitat would have suffered gruesome deaths if her team had not stopped Galkin. Recent intelligence reports indicated that Galkin's genetic modifications increased the mortality rate to nearly one hundred percent.

I've lost my husband. Gint is gone. At least I've had the opportunity to prevent any more losses.

For a moment, she searched the sky for the Aquarius constellation, as if, among the few stars visible through the city lights and pollution, she might see the scattered halo of orbiting debris left behind when the Galatéa space station had blown up. Of course, to the naked eye, Galatéa was never visible. She turned away from the airfield, realized she was cold and wet and headed for the busy spaceport hangar.

David was waiting by her shuttle. "We could hang out and unwind if you think it's OK. We can be debriefed on the mission together at your place." His eyes shined as he smiled.

Adira had made it a policy to never socialize with the other operatives—especially after Gint had left for Galatéa three years ago. But for some reason, this felt right. "OK, hop in—you're in for a spectacular show!" He took a step back, then smiled and entered.

"The mission went far smoother than I thought it would." David chattered about the mission in her transport while they awaited clearance from the tower. "I'm sure they have extracted Galkin's poisonous molars by now. You did a great job sedating him. And that giggle you gave Galkin before you left the bar. I almost laughed out loud. You sounded like a schoolgirl. It's a good thing he didn't know you're exactly the opposite. I don't think any of those drunken fools know what hit them. By the way, they drank and acted, you'd never know they were experts and scientists at the top of their fields."

Adira had second thoughts about David's visit as they flew to her cliffside home. *It's too late to change your mind now.* She settled into the flight and hoped the tears of Saint Lawrence, the annual Perseid meteor showers, would be visible and exceptional tonight.

Adira and David sat on the terrace, sipped fresh coffee, and admired the view. As expected, the Perseids were gloriously active, streaking across the night sky several at a time.

Adira gazed at the bright stars in the sky and wondered what was happening at the Galatéa colony.

What would daily life be like there? Sure, we have experienced alien environments and gravitational changes, especially in training camps on the moon and the Martian colonies. Still, it was likely not the same as permanent life on a distant exoplanet colony . . .

"I've missed our talks, Addie. It's been a long time since we had a chance to catch up." He glanced at Adira and then back at the sky. David's comment wrenched Adira from her reverie to the present.

I forgot what a good friend David is. He is easygoing and easy to talk to. He called me Addie.

"We always were a good team. It felt good to work with someone who knows me well." Adira had enjoyed David's company far more than expected. The sharp solace of solitude had cut achingly deeper than she admitted, even to herself.

Perhaps my self-isolation has gone on for far too long.

Adira stood, leaned on the terrace railing, and listened as the surf pounded in the inky blackness below. David joined her at the railing, and they stood for a time in companionable silence. Her heart skipped a beat as she heard the communicator chime.

Eagerly, she went inside to answer. David followed closely behind, closing the sliding glass doors before he moved to the sofa. The images of Eurydice and the rest of the team members appeared on the telecom. As usual, it took a few hours for Eurydice and the entire team to debrief after a critical mission.

Hours later, David and Adira sat on the terrace, watching the surf as dawn approached, when the communicator chimed again. She punched in her security code on the telecom panel. She saw it was her employer's direct encrypted link, and the code indicated that the Special Operations Executive was calling.

"In the interest of the people of Earth and off-world, you are ordered to return to active duty," Eurydice Sideris continued. "You and David have been carefully selected. You are ordered to report to the space center in Florida to depart for Galatéa. You are expected in 24 hours."

As the transmission codes were streamed and unscrambled, a visual formed.

Oh, hell no, this is huge, thought Adira. She sat with David bolt upright on the sofa with a fresh cup of coffee to steady her nerves.

"Dr. Varna—as you know, it's been days since we received transmissions from Galatéa. We have not been successful in reestablishing contact with the planetary AI."

The image changed to show the hologram of the last minutes of the AI's transmission from Galatéa. Eurydice seemed to stare straight into Adira's eyes and frowned.

Eurydice continued. "All communications have abruptly halted. Our efforts to run a full diagnostic of the communication buoys show inconclusive results regarding the precise cause of the loss of communication. We continue to try to contact the space station and colony AI. Worst case scenario—we will not know what happened to the space station and the domed colony until three months after the first colonists arrived at Galatéa."

Adira thought the dark circles under Eurydice's eyes seemed more prominent when her face reappeared. "A faction of an extremist religious group, One Religion, has claimed responsibility for the unconfirmed explosion. They claim they have destroyed the space station.

"The group had instigated a schism shortly after the conclusion of ecumenical dialogues among world leaders of prominent congregations. The faction members who broke away were outraged by the compromises religious leaders agreed to in the unification of all churches. With the newly established One Religion and complete unification, it was decided that the old religions would no longer be honored—they were deemed obsolete in the name of the evolution of spirituality.

"Various factions were scandalized and complained that these compromises resulted in a definite departure from sacred religious institutions that stemmed from ancient Earth's eternal truths received from God."

Eurydice continued, "The group that has claimed responsibility has called for global cooperation to promote the Anthropic Principle because they have maintained that humans were created in god's image, per religious doctrine. They have been resolute in their philosophy of an Earth-centric belief system. A marginalized god was a concept unthinkable and intolerable to them.

"These radicals have committed their lives to the Law of Human Existence. These laws are based on the premise that human life has always depended on cosmological constants and a very narrow range of various parameters. They postulate that we would not exist in the universe if even one of those variables were slightly off. Due to the highly unlikely probability that so many of these parameters have aligned perfectly, the radicals have proposed that God providentially engineered it to suit humans' specific needs. Essentially, they have proclaimed that the universe has been created exclusively for human existence.

"Furthermore, these radicals espouse the belief that human enhancements will give certain elite people an advantage over those who do not have access to these enhancements, especially with certain neural implants, which would provide recipients with considerable advantages in almost every social and physical realm. Their principal objection is that, at the same time, it renders those without the implant at a distinct disadvantage. Their protests have been violent in the past.

"Some radical sects advocate that transferred human consciousness, or a mind uploaded to a computer program represents the denigration of the human body. The radicals criticize implants and colloidal nanoparticle therapies because they offer no fidelity to the soul and do not support a relationship with the divine."

At this point, Eurydice pinched the bridge of her nose and squeezed her eyes shut momentarily. "Members of the group that claim to have destroyed the space station orbiting Galatéa say they have done this to save humankind. It's a convoluted scheme once again to draw attention to their cause—and again, this is an unconfirmed claim."

Adira frowned as she remembered the history of the space program. *After permanent bases on the moon, Mars, and Jupiter's moons were established, the next big step in human exploration was a crewed mission to an exoplanet located in the habitable zone of a distant solar system.* Her frown deepened as she watched Eurydice's face.

"Adira, you have been assigned to mentor a new trainee operative during the twelve-month transit to Galatéa. His name is Rafe Silvers. He is scheduled to receive colloidal nanoparticle therapy once we are underway."

Eurydice's image promptly winked off. The transmission ended except for the encrypted operation coordinates.

After David departed to make his preparations, Adira closed her eyes and listened as a storm intensified and blended with the complex textures of Wagner's musical language.

Though Gint had left for Galatéa three years ago, her self-imposed wall of isolation just crumbled. "Terminate speakers and secure the perimeter," she commanded the house AI and began preparations for an extended departure.

4 - The Involuntary Voluntary Unit

His eyes opened to a murky world. Two blurred objects came into focus. Slowly, he realized he was in a bed, and the objects were his feet, strapped in leather restraints. He haltingly turned his head and blinked as his gaze shifted to his arms. They were also restrained. Gradually, consciousness returned enough so that he looked around the room. He was in the Involuntary Unit again.

He remembered something had happened.

What was it?

He couldn't recall. He slept.

A shadow fell across the bed, so he opened his eyes. A man stood there and looked down at him. He had graying hair, was very tall, slim, and in full military uniform. There were gold epaulets on his shoulders. As he ran his scanner across Rafe's forehead, he asked how he felt. Rafe offered no reply. An older woman stood beside him; the man motioned, and she released his restraints. Rafe rubbed his wrists. It felt good to move around a little. The doctor sat beside the bed and asked him how he felt again. No response.

"Rafe, tell me why you are here," he persisted.

I could give you many reasons why I'm in a lock-up mental ward at 23—again. I don't remember how I got here this time.

"I'm addicted, don't mince words, doc," Rafe croaked. His throat was so dry it was difficult to talk. "I can't control my addiction anymore. It controls me."

"If you continue your addict behaviors, I'd say you have up to three years to live—and that's a stretch," the doctor's mouth turned down as he gave this dire prognosis.

That's not what Rafe had expected or hoped to hear. "Is there anything you can do to cure my addiction?"

"We have developed a therapeutic intervention. With it, we have achieved a one hundred percent cure rate for addicts like you. We screened and assessed you as a perfect candidate. But make no mistake; it's rigorous and demanding. It takes three years to complete the mandatory Institute program. We are moving the program to Galatéa, and you would be among the first colonists to settle at the Institute there." He lowered his scanner and sat down next to Rafe's bed.

I've got to stop. I want to live.

"It must be better than my life has been. I'll do it," Rafe told him, "Even if it kills me—what the hell, I'll do anything. Please show me how. I need a way out."

He wasn't sure how much later; it could have been hours or days when he was discharged from the Involuntary Unit. They escorted him to a meeting room down the hall from his private room before he left. The hologram of a small Asian man dressed all in white stood on the podium when Rafe arrived. Although a holographic image, the light in his incredible black eyes nevertheless projected an infinitely deep night sky. He seemed to study Rafe as he sat in the back of the room. It felt like the little man looked right through Rafe and knew everything about him then.

"My name is Zhopla. I am the founder, spiritual mentor, and leader of the Institute on Galatéa. Addiction has made your lives completely meaningless. It blocked your path to growth and the degree of enlightenment you were meant to achieve," he stopped and seemed to look around the room.

"We have known that addiction is not easily cured, but we have successfully helped others overcome it, regardless of the substance they were addicted to." Once you have received the intervention and have trained at the Institute, you will comprehend how unbelievably important the work is and know your lives depend on it. You must know and believe that all of you who have committed to the program tonight will be successful—all. We are eager to get started on your training at the Institute on Galatéa. Until then, Godspeed." Zhopla scanned the room as he spoke and appeared to look long and hard at each of the twenty candidates.

Zhopla's hologram turned his gaze to Rafe last—Zhopla's gaze locked Rafe's eyes to his. At this moment, Rafe experienced a deep peace he had never known. Zhopla turned his gaze away, breaking their connection.

This quiet, serene man is the antithesis of Grampy.

He resumed with the introduction to the Institute. The rules and ordinances were explained. Only a little of the information sank in, as Rafe's concentration skills were still fuzzy. He remembered that if they deemed Rafe and the others worthy after a one-year probationary period, he would go to Stage Two and begin taking part in upper-level activities. In Stage Three, they would be required to take an oath and never reveal the secrets of the Institute.

"We have prepared your initial contracts, and they are in the next room beyond this door. Take your time and carefully read them. Feel free to ask questions." Take your time and carefully read them. Feel free to ask questions." In concluding the introduction, Zhopla bowed, and his image dissolved. Two uniformed guards stood at the door Zhopla had indicated.

Rafe witnessed several people refusing to hear anything more about the contract, and security escorted them out. The older woman who had untied his restraints when he had awakened gave him his contract to read over.

"My name is Eurydice Sideris," she said as she shook Rafe's hand. He was stunned by her white hair and crystal-clear blue eyes.

"I am assigned to accompany you on the space transit to Galatéa, overseeing your transition—go ahead and read your contract," Eurydice's mercurial smile reassured him. He briefly scanned the document and quickly signed it. After Rafe and the remaining few patients had read their preliminary contracts, they returned to the meeting room.

"We have scheduled the departure in two days." It will take six months to reach planet Galatéa. During the traverse, you will experience the probationary stage, which involves deploying the Institute's intervention therapy and engaging in other activities. With that, Eurydice Sideris turned and exited.

Is the meeting over?

Walking home, he tried to figure out how to tell Grampy he was an addict. It had been Grampy, Gramma, and Rafe since he was a little kid.

Grampy was standing on the front porch, scratching his chin. His fingers passed over the stubble of black and gray hairs, making it sound like sandpaper. "Where in hell have you been this time? I thought you'd never get home," he said.

"I was in the Involuntary Unit again, Gramps."

Tell him—no more beating around the bush.

"WHAT? That's bullshit," Grampy exploded. Ever since Gramma passed, he increasingly relied on Rafe for almost everything.

"Geez Louise! Ain't you ever going to learn how to go on a Klowd9 trip like a man?" He spat over the railing.

"The doc at the Involuntary Unit is sending me to that rehab program—I think it's gonna work for me this time," Rafe tried to explain. "After what the doctor told me, I think it'll work—I hope I can beat this addiction once and for all."

"Rehab Shmeehab—those places are all cults—cults is all they is—it's all bullshit." Grampy sat down and smacked his palm against his forehead. "Why the hell don't you take the nanocytes? They work, won't cost us anything, and you can stay here and be well again. You said you wanted to."

"The first-generation nanocytes are still experimental—they turn people into puppets. Once they're in you, the researchers know what you're thinking and feeling. Those who got the nanocytes don't have any privacy, and the military police could pull their puppet strings whenever and wherever they want!" Rafe stormed and grabbed his head.

Will this headache never end?

The nanocytes offered a problematic but easy way out—the doctors had detailed numerous solutions to an addict's recovery—all total treatment failures, especially for Klowd9 trip addicts. At first, Rafe agreed to have the nanocyte therapy, which seemed like a great idea. But after he investigated it, he changed his mind. Throughout the day, resentment, fear, or rage often consumed him. The nanocytes made a person emotionless—he preferred to keep his feelings, even negative ones. He heard you became just flat as a board all the time. Sure, you still had your memories, but no emotions.

He envisioned the puppeteers would start pulling imaginary strings in his brain to keep the peace as each negative emotion surfaced. How ironic. All he wanted was to make serenity a reality. The nanocyte therapy's ability to control a person's emotions proved to Rafe that this was the easy way out of addiction. He knew but didn't care that the drug, Klowd9, was so addictive that ninety-eight percent of those who tried it even once became completely dependent.

Rafe knows he has become addicted to this powerful euphoric compound. Once the effects wore off, all any addict could think about is getting more, so Rafe was not out of the continuum for long. The continuum was a computer-generated virtual reality where drug users choose how they wish to live, including their own society, along with other like-minded drug users. This is a place where they realized their most cherished hopes, dreams, and desires. It all felt real while under the influence of Klowd9 as they sat somewhere safe so they could re-enter their personal continuum reality via the computer.

The implications staggered him. *How could anyone live in the real world and be honest with themselves or others? What good is running away from reality when the truth of what's behind it all is so important?*

"Who *are you*?" Grampy asked Rafe as he peered over his glasses.

"Who's asking?" Rafe was done fighting with him. "I want to quit, Gramps. I want to stop going on Klowd9 trips. I'm afraid if I take the nanocytes, I won't be the same person," he knew Grampy would think he was weak.

Try to be honest for a change.

Grampy snorted and spat over the railing. "Since you were little, you always wanted more or needed to change somethin'," he scratched the stubble on his chin and shook his head from side to side.

He was referring to Rafe's switch to vegetarianism and the many times he had tried to quit taking Klowd9 trips to no avail. Yet Rafe had somehow managed to maintain his computer genius along the way.

"What's wrong with wanting to change? What's wrong with wanting to be a better person?" Rafe asked in an exasperated tone.

Grampy spat over the railing again. "Dammit, I gotta pee," he grabbed the front door, yanked it, and went inside.

Rafe followed him in and went to his room. He was getting fresh clothes when his reflection in the mirror caught his eye. He gasped at what he saw. Besides his black hair and blue eyes, he noticed he had one black eye and a bruised face. His skin was a pale grayish color. He saw that his eyes also had dark circles under them, and they were swollen.

When did my face get so thin? He moved closer to the mirror. He saw that his eyes looked dull and empty, even to himself, with no spark of life. Rafe's addiction was in control of his life. It amazed him how it had taken over in such an insidious way.

It took over, and I never even noticed when I crossed the line into full addiction.

Taking Klowd9 trips began as recreational fun. Rafe and his friends had a lot of fun—at the beginning. He walked into the kitchen. He heard the toilet flush and the bathroom door slam banged open.

"What in the hell have you gotten yourself into this time?" Rafe had to stifle a chuckle despite himself. Grampy's eyebrows were up to his hairline, and he looked like the caricature of a grizzled old man. Grampy's nose was turning red.

"The Institute is holding another meeting tonight, so I'll find out more," Rafe said.

This was the night he was required to check in and receive his gear from the Institute, the final meeting before boarding the ship to interstellar space and Galatéa. Rafe didn't have the heart to tell him there even was a contract.

"You wanna come with me?" Rafe experienced that faint feeling of helplessness again.

"NO!" Grampy trudged to the stove and banged old pots around. Rafe watched in disgust.

At least Gramps heats his can of simu-beans and processed protein. Rafe was relieved Grampy didn't want to go.

Rafe figured he had two choices. *Should I go to Galatéa? What would happen to Grampy if I went? Or should I take the nanocytes and have life continue but numb as a rock?*

He realized he had been in denial about being an addict. His denial had resulted in jail or institutionalization, and his prognosis of certain death from his addiction within three years, unless he did something, was looming in his head. He always made things more complicated for himself than was necessary.

Reflecting on Grampy's expression following one of the seemingly never-ending disasters during his Klowd9 excursions, he reflected on what he did to acquire additional Klowd9. The memory of that look of disgust and disbelief remained with him. Rafe was sick of it. *I'm sick of myself.*

He thought of Zhopla's infinitely peaceful eyes and had a moment of clarity—he knew what he wanted.

"No more talk of this—they probably won't even take you. It's bullshit. My friends are coming over to play Rizika! I'm goin' in tonight in the lead cuz I won most of the quadrants of the asteroid belt. I won the Hildas and the Trojans. Got me the biggest mining company of all time. I'm rich! All I need is the Greeks, and I win it all. It's Thursday night, ya know," Grampy yanked the front door open and went back outside.

The itchiness started, and the headache worsened. These were always the first signs. Rafe burst out the front door and stood on the porch. The Klowd9 was calling his name—he fought the craving. It didn't help that he was always in conflict with Grampy.

Rafe agreed; no more talk of this. He decided independently (or so he thought) for the first time without wavering. Screw it; he'll show all of them.

5 - Porta Caeli

Weightless, he drifted away from the couch of the space transport and floated in zero gravity. The turquoise rim of the Earth eclipsed a breathtaking sunset against the pitch-black darkness of space. As Australia rolled under them, David experienced a moment of profound synchronicity and unprecedented clarity. He looked at Adira in utter amazement and knew what they were doing was right, that they were meant to be here together. He was sure that intelligent design created the universe and could not possibly be a haphazard conglomeration of chaotic molecules that eventually formed the sun, moon, and stars, not to mention life itself.

Floating cautiously toward the transport's portals, they caught their first glimpse of the spaceship. Having escaped Earth's gravity, they had been in spaceflight for about three hours when the transport's captain announced, "The *Porta Caeli* is within range. Initiating docking procedures."

As they drew closer, the magnificence of the *Porta Caeli* became evident. David grinned happily at the sight of it. The interstellar craft was the first of its kind: a collection of cylindrical modules, tanks, and crossbeams arranged in a circular grid shape six hundred and fifty feet across. Its perimeter sprouted long, jet-black solar power panels like gleaming petals, tracking the sun. The framework was coated with plain platinum thermal foam, and the three habitation sections were silver and teal.

Near the stern of the spaceship, surrounded by a wide-pleated array of silver solar panels, was a hexagonal chamber that housed the EM generator, which made the six-month travel time possible. Once they crossed the brane from subluminal to superluminal space, the EM generator constantly supplied antimatter to power bubble integrity and maintain faster-than-light travel to Galatéa. It was the most miniature EM system ever built. Europe was still in the early stages of constructing its first pair of larger commercial EM generators. At the same time, the USA had already commissioned another fifteen. And the Far East certainly had nothing equivalent to the sophisticated *Porta Caeli* generator.

SIS 22 got it right when they commissioned the Caeli. It's appropriate to name her the Porta Caeli, the Gate of Heaven, David thought proudly as they approached the spaceship.

"Everyone check your harness patency," the captain ordered. The last phase of docking will begin in two minutes." The docking procedure went smoothly. After securing everything, David and Adira went directly to their quarters. They had been working nonstop since their last mission.

While the incoming officers and other operatives moved onto the ship, they transferred the last few hundred items from the transport bay into carefully designated storage areas. The team had planned all aspects of the storage and living quarters to function in zero gravity and, later, at one g when centrifugal force was engaged. It took hours, but eventually, the team carefully secured and double-checked everything. Once they traveled beyond Jupiter's gravity well, the team planned to make two jumps within the next 72 hours.

The living quarters on the *Porta Caeli* were in the center where the radiation shielding was most dense. The rooms were pie-shaped. Four concentric cylinders made up the inner core of the ring, with the crew's bedrooms and lavatories around the outer ring. The following ring was a large galley and common area room with secured tables, benches, and a functional kitchen. Two more concentric cylinders were in the centermost portion of the vessel for the Wolverton tube, with columns of plants all around the outer part of the cylinder; their roots grew towards the inside. The air and most wastes were in continuous filtration through the plant cylinder.

David entered his new living quarters for the first time. He felt comfortable with its military starkness and organization. Everything was in its place, neat and unadorned. As he unpacked his personal items, the communicator chimed. It was his sister calling to say goodbye.

"Jennifer, so good of you to see me off." David smiled into the display on his small desk.

Jennifer smiled, pushing her long red hair behind an ear, and her eyes filled with tears. "I'm going to miss you, little brother. I can handle your apartment while you're away. I wish you Godspeed!"

"Don't cry, sis." *We might not see each other for a long time, Jenny.* "I'll be back pestering you for dinner before you know it," David said.

"I'm glad that Adira is with you. Maybe you two can work things out after all," Jennifer thoughtfully replied.

"I blew it once. I don't plan on blowing our relationship again. When we were in medical school, I thought we would be together. Then, when my back was turned, that snake Gint slithered in, and she suddenly married him. I never even had a chance to make things right with her or apologize. It turned into congratulations and best wishes instead." David looked at Jennifer as he talked, and she nodded in understanding. He knew he could always count on his sister.

"Take good care of yourself. See you when you get back. Love you," were Jennifer's last words as she wiped a tear away and the display darkened.

David could not rest. He went to the medical infirmary. He was thrilled when he thought of future work and adventures. While traveling to Galatéa, a neural lace called the brain-to-artificial intelligence interface (BAI) was to be implanted in Adira and David. They programmed the link to grow into and around the brain. This device allowed both to converse and communicate privately and authorized access to the advanced artificial intelligence that monitored all aspects of the ship and, eventually, the dome AI and other SIS22 operatives.

David assumed his duties as chief medical officer. When he walked into the medical bay, familiar equipment and, especially, the familiar smells of all medical bays had greeted him. It was even more aseptically clean, utilitarian, and Spartan than other areas of the ship. The clinical staff greeted their CMO with enthusiastic smiles.

Violet Yardley, one of the ship's surgeons, followed David into his office. "So glad to finally be getting underway. I've been monitoring the progress of our current batches of nanoparticles, and all results remain nominal." Her warm brown eyes, full of intelligence and curiosity, seemed always to be observing and engaging with her surroundings. Her white uniform, crisp and professional, stood out against her rich copper-colored skin and highlighted her striking appearance. Her hair is neatly styled in braids, especially handy during free fall times on the ship, complementing her dignified and confident demeanor. She carried herself with poise, her posture straight and assured, exuding a calm authority. Her smile was gentle and genuine when offered, reflecting a deep empathy and understanding.

"Yes, I couldn't rest just yet. I wanted to check the surgical bay and robotics first. The approaches and features need to be double-checked. Specifically, I wanted to assess the introduction of haptic feedback and single port operating for implementing machine learning to assure eventual full artificial intelligence participation."

David and Violet walked to the surgical bay and inspected the arms of the operating table. The surgical bay is comprised of four robotic arms integrated into the operating table. The design provided a device that freed up space and enabled better patient access, although gravity must be present for it to function.

"We need to re-check the minimally invasive robotics programs. If there are any glitches, no matter how small, they'll show up here. With correct machine learning integration, the system will eventually form algorithms. Once we check the systems, we will integrate artificial intelligence-assisted surgery to reduce errors."

David inspected the surgeon's console, which integrated hand controls and foot pedals. The wristed instrument tips also provided seven degrees of freedom.

This handgrip design is just like an old-fashioned game controller. Once I get my BAI up and running, all I'll have to do is think about the movements. Observing how artificial intelligence will evolve will be interesting as we work with the system.

"Machine learning will likely have a role in surgery through automated performance metrics, where algorithms observe and learn individual surgeon's techniques, assess performance, and expect surgical outcomes to aid in decision-making in real-time." David tested the handgrips and observed their reactivity.

Violet turned to face David. "Eventually, a further subset of our AI will use deep learning to understand image data and deal with object detection and classification tasks. However, it may take some time before we see completely autonomous robotics in our surgical bay because of the need for a complete collection of global surgeries and issues to develop our AI surgeon.

David nodded as he viewed the computer interface. "Did you ensure that the constructed nanodevices' neuro-electronic interface allows the AI to join and link to the recipient's nervous system?" This was an external computer that built a precision molecular nanostructure to permit the control and detection of nerve impulses.

Violet brought up various graphs and schematics and displayed them in her notebook. "Positioning the nanodevice's wiring in the nervous system requires precise and complicated execution." For each recipient, the structures providing the interface must also be compatible with the body's immune system. That is one of the most time-consuming aspects of the replication and nanofacturing schema."

Next, David began checking for device leakage, electrical interference, and appropriate power consumption to prevent overheating in the body. He also examined the molecular nanofacturing that occurred at predicted rates because the nanodevices employed a novel self-powered enzymatic biofuel cell using glucose from the blood.

"The nanoparticles are functioning at optimal levels." Violet agreed. "We could not ask for better nanofacturing conditions. The instruments on this ship are the most advanced I've ever had the pleasure to work with." Violet's eyebrows rose. "The coordinated nanoscale robots have worked exceedingly well together and were sufficiently viable in their capacity to replicate themselves on their own. We have swarms of nanorobots in the artificial environment we've designed with our third-generation classified molecular building blocks that mimic biofluids."

Violet moved to a display over the incubator. "The nanoparticles have predictably engineered their molecular assemblers and have passed our testing of their directives to re-order matter at the molecular and even atomic levels. Within this aspect of nanomedicine, the nanorobots' functionality to detect pathological states such as infection and uncover and repair damage to cells and tissues is intact."

Violet shifted the onscreen display and magnified the nanoparticles. "We combined correlative light with electron microscopy to see the relationships between the nanoparticles and our created biological environment. The magnifications vary according to what I'm trying to visualize. I can isolate single nanoconstructs and obtain qualitative and quantitative data on their chemical composition. I'm also evaluating the indicators of their degradability and stability in our integrated biological environment to gain a deeper knowledge of how they will behave in the recipients' bodies."

David reached for the control panel. "Ah, this is unbelievable. I can see the general and dynamic view of the nanoparticles with detailed ultrastructural information provided by this combination of microscopy. Zooming out, I can see spatial alignments of the swarm. Zooming in, I see the structures of the nanoparticles in incredible detail."

Violet's lips turned downward. "Some staff have voiced concerns about the ethics of treating the addicted recipients with the nanoparticles. Third-generation Nanos are illegal on Earth."

David shrugged his shoulders, seemingly unphased by Violet's observation. "By the many biological and genetic processes related to aging that nanomedicine can repair, life extension properties have arisen. But you're wondering about the ethics of nanoparticle use? Even though we see the recipient as improving after receiving the nanoparticles, ethical questions arise if they see themselves as becoming someone new. It is a concern that human identity can be affected. Altering an individual's identity can profoundly affect their narrative. Mental capacities and overall development are also affected. So essentially, there are two main points to the ethical argument. First is the issue of inauthenticity. The second is the issue of an individual's core characteristics being violated."

Violet's frown remained. "The ability to alter one's mental capacity through nanomedicine gene therapy is the basis for this argument. Theoretically, nanomedicine threatens to change the fundamental self to the point of becoming a different person. The core characteristics of the recipients can change, including personality, general intelligence, psychological style, and normal aging. From an early sample of nanoparticle recipients, researchers found that extreme personality changes could threaten their relationships because family or loved ones may no longer relate to the new person the recipient had become."

David turned and faced Violet. "Current trends in ethics do not necessarily focus on the makeup of the individual but rather justify nanotherapeutic methods with what they allow individuals to do in society. We have focused on the objectives of central human capabilities, including bodily health, freedom from addictions, physical integrity, emotions, reasoning, and control over one's environment. This normative framework recognizes that human capabilities have constantly been changing and will continually change. Today and in the future. I believe using technology in the form of nanomedicine has already played a part in this."

David squeezed Violet's shoulder to reassure her. "I welcome discussions on the ethics of any procedure we perform on this ship and Galatéa once we arrive. Thank you for bringing this issue to my attention, Violet. I appreciate your candor. Once we are underway, and in between jumps, and before any procedures are done, we will have a staff meeting to address all questions and concerns."

6 - Many Meetings

While updating her journal, her communicator disrupted Adira's reverie. "Adira here."

"Please come to a meeting in Torus B common room in 15 minutes." Directed Eurydice Sideris's husky voice.

"On my way." *I wonder what this is about.*

Adira arrived at the meeting room early. The smell of coffee wafted through the air as she entered. She gratefully poured a cup and sat at the empty conference table. David was the next operative to arrive, and then Eurydice walked in.

"The *Porta Caeli* is perfect. The medbay and equipment are more than satisfactory." David enthusiastically appraised the spaceship and facilities. "SIS22 has outdone even itself in commissioning this vessel."

"I'm very pleased with the ship myself. How are the nanoparticles progressing?" Eurydice looked up from the schematics displayed in her notebook.

"All testing on the nanoparticles remains nominal. Dr. Yardley and I are satisfied with their viability, quality, and performance." David enthusiastically met Adira's eyes, quickly looked away, and looked at Eurydice.

"Any word on my trainee, Rafe? I heard he's onboard and being prepped for the nanoparticle procedure before our first jump," inquired Adira.

"Yes, you will meet him after our second jump. Once you and David receive your BAIs, Rafe will receive his nanoparticles. Rafe is receiving the BAI as well. He has agreed to be fully indoctrinated into the Institute and operative of SIS22. He is a perfect candidate—a computer genius with an intuitive proclivity for machine learning and artificial intelligence programming and debugging. He is a Klowd9 addict. He will receive a special type of nanoparticles. Zhopla will also work closely with him to ensure his continued healing progress." Eurydice placed her notebook on the table and folded her hands.

"Now I have some information to relate to you. You have been granted security clearance at the highest level. The information I am about to convey is to remain top secret." She took a deep breath. "Deep beneath the mountains of Galatéa, we have discovered extensive caverns. When exploring the caverns, we found ancient wonders, the first proof of intelligent life, and an advanced civilization beyond Earth. This is what the radicals are seeking."

Adira and David looked at each other, then back at Eurydice. "I've been waiting all my life to hear news of intelligent life in the galaxy! This is unbelievable!" Adira's interested response made Eurydice smile. David sat in numbed silence.

Eurydice rubbed her hands together as if they were ice cold, needing warmth. "There's more. The information I'm about to share with you is also confidential. I have dreaded this moment, and now that it's here, there's nothing left to do but tell you. A top-secret project has been underway on Galatéa. A wealth of evidence indicates that an advanced civilization existed in the caves of Galatéa. Hieroglyphics, pictograms, and much more have been uncovered. We are currently working to decipher what it all means."

She took a deep breath. "Now for the biggest news. The space station in orbit over Galatéa was not destroyed. Gint is alive and working on Galatéa undercover. He has been doing so since we staged the explosion, making the radicals believe they had succeeded."

"What?" David pushed away from the table and stood up. "Gint is alive and has been all this time? Why did you not tell Adira?"

Adira's face paled, then flushed with anger. "How could you do this to me? Not a word from you! I trusted you both as a friend and a mentor, not to mention as my superior officer. And Gint! No contact, no acknowledgment—nothing. Not a word. I have been walking around feeling abandoned and lost." She stood next to David. "You can count on us to keep this confidential, Eurydice." She turned abruptly and left, with David following her, leaving a red-faced Eurydice sitting at the conference table.

Adira sat alone in her quarters. She opened the desk drawer and took out the letter. She had many more questions than answers. Her Mom had written not to trust anyone, but Zhopla, and she wondered why. She put the letter in her pocket and went to the observation blister. She sat alone, deep in thought, observed the stars, and decided to talk with the monk. Adira hit the communicator at the door of Zhopla's quarters and waited. The rooms inside the monk's quarters were silent and seemed empty. Zhopla had become quiet and elusive since her mother disappeared.

Zhopla finally opened the door. Upon seeing her, the monk's unfathomable black eyes sparkled. His long white hair formed a halo around his sallow face.

"Come in, come in!" He ushered her through his quarters to his private office. "I've been working on something you might find quite fascinating." He beamed as he pulled out a chair for Adira.

"Have you ever heard of the Watchers?" he asked.

"No, not really—do they have something to do with the

ancient world?" Adira knew Zhopla was interested in antiquities and archeology.

"It all began with a mid-twentieth-century discovery. The discovery was marvelous and unexpected and has greatly influenced some biblical interpretations." His eyes gleamed. "The discovery was the Dead Sea Scrolls. Even today, they create a good deal of controversy. An Apocryphal scroll, known as the Book of Enoch, was found. Would you like some tea?" He waved the pot at her and poured himself a cup.

"Yes, er, thank you, Brother." Adira hadn't expected such a warm reception from the old monk. She knew he was the gabby sort and loved to talk about whatever interested him at the moment.

The monk and her mother had been very close—her mom had met with Zhopla once or twice a week for five years, and now she had been missing over the previous three years. The old monk seemed available night or day if anyone needed him. She could see why his followers loved him so—he had a mild manner with a soft, comforting voice, but at the same time, it somehow carried a high level of authority.

"Enoch writes about a group known as the Watchers, also named the Angels of the Lord, who were on the earth thousands of years ago, and it states that in those days, they gave the children of Cain (Enoch) the knowledge of writing. The scrolls were translated into English, among many other languages, and are shared by all. There is vital information in the book of Enoch." Zhopla shuffled through the pile of papers cluttering his desk, gave up, and went to his computer. He pulled up images of the caves of Qumran, where a shepherd had initially found the scrolls.

"Are there still controversies about the scrolls?" asked Adira, her curiosity piqued.

The monk's bushy white eyebrows shot up, "Oh yes, yes!

There are many strange controversies. Some scholars think the Apocryphal books carry no weight and were deleted from the Bible in the thirteenth century for a reason. Others feel the message of Enoch is essential to the survival of humankind. Some think the Watchers are angels. Others think they are devils. Some even think they are extraterrestrial in origin, and through the ages, they helped to advance human civilization. Some call the Watchers the Nephilim—giant hybrids of extraterrestrials and humans." At the mention of the giants and hybrids, Zhopla paused and stared directly into Adira's eyes. She held his gaze for a moment, then turned and studied the images of the caves on the computer.

She jumped as the monk's communicator chimed. "Zhopla," he answered in his sedate way, "No, no, you're not intruding." He paused. "Is it that serious? All right, I'll be there." He turned to Adira. "I'm so sorry. I am called to the medbay. A recruit is in crisis. Are you able to come back? We'll talk then." His sallow face was now as white as his hair. Adira noticed that his hands were shaking.

"Sure, Zhopla." Adira was left alone as Zhopla flew through the door to his quarters.

As Adira returned to her quarters, she remembered an event with Zhopla from a few months ago.

She rang the bell a third time and waited for someone to answer. It always took the monk a long time to answer the door, but never this long. Adira had questions, and Zhopla had the answers. She knew she should have reported her mom's disappearance to the police. Zhopla told her to wait—but for what? First things first, she knew what she had to do. When she thought about the endless questions, the investigation, the unwelcome spotlight it would cast her way, she couldn't bring herself to call them. But absolutely nothing could stand in her way of doing the next right thing.

She wondered if old Zhopla had gone to the church because of his problems with vandals. Perhaps he had forgotten about their appointment. As she waited, she thought about how different it had been to go to Saint George's with Mom when she was a small child. There were no padlocks on the church doors, no boarded-up windows, and there used to be lots of people. The neighborhood had deteriorated into a ghetto in the last twenty years.

Adira pulled a flashlight from the glove compartment and locked her old transport. She pulled her hood over her short golden hair and walked across the parking lot. A gusty wind and a spatter of large raindrops pelted her head and shoulders. The padlock on the church's north door was gone, and as Adira struggled to open it, the door swung back with a metallic clang. It sounded rather loud in the listening silence. She stepped inside. Her flashlight beam swept over a giant statue of an angel, foot on a serpent and sword in hand, a silent sentry that still guarded the entrance. St. Michael the Archangel. She paused and listened, motionless in the dim light.

There was no sound but the fall wind as it gusted outside. As if in welcome, a bat squeaked from overhead. The sound reminded Adira of the summer she had built a roosting area for them inside the cupola atop the old barn at home. Her mother never understood her fascination with animals and had been vehemently against Adira's desire to become a veterinarian.

She moved up the center church aisle toward the altar and heard a sound like someone heavy had stepped on broken glass. Was that a crunch of glass underfoot? Adira extinguished her flashlight and exhaled slowly. Her heart pounded as she stood alone and waited. What had begun as a visit to get more information about her mom's disappearance from the aging monk now felt like something else entirely. Suddenly before her, she glimpsed a hirsute chest rising from a pew and peered into unfathomable black eyes, blood-red rimmed and intense, staring back through encrusted slits. He grabbed her neck.

"Where is it?" a raspy voice asked, and she gagged at the unbearable stench.

"What?" she cried.

"The map." His grip tightened. She choked in pain and terror.

Unexpectedly, a shotgun blast cut through the darkness. In a frenzy, she twisted free. Adira rolled over as a second blast ripped a hole in the ceiling far overhead, showering her with bits of plaster. She scrambled desperately to her feet.

"Adira?" Framed in the dim light of the front door, a slight figure stood, a shotgun dangled at his side.

"Zhopla!" Adira stumbled toward his voice.

"You okay? We need to leave," Zhopla whispered as he grabbed Adira's arm.

Outside, Adira sank to the sidewalk. She struggled for breath in the cool night air and willed her pounding heart to slow down.

"What happened?" Zhopla leaned over her.

"I heard noises, some kind of big dogs, a scuffle, and I think something growled."

Adira shook her head, gasping, "Yes, dogs and one very hairy man."

The monk said nothing, but he helped Adira to her feet. They walked back to her transport. "Zhopla, I think you should come home with me tonight to be safe—I didn't know you could shoot." Without a word, the monk climbed into the passenger seat.

As they left the parking lot, a flicker of silver glinted briefly. She turned to see tremendous black shapes, seemingly furry, as they bounded toward them.

She careened through the inside gate and saw with consummate horror that the things followed behind her. From the darkness ahead, she saw a chain-linked fence. Adira jammed on the brakes, but the transport struck the fence and flew over the street's curb. They landed heavily. They had hit the front porch of Zhopla's home.

She sat in the transport and tried to control her breathing. Rain fell through the beam of her headlights. Zhopla's broken mailbox was wedged under the transport. Without thinking, she jumped out, glanced around for any sign of the black pursuers, and dragged the mailbox attached to her transport aside. An envelope lay on the porch steps, and instinctively she grabbed it. As she turned to step back into the transport's safety, the headlights caught the front of the envelope. Adira froze for a moment and gasped in surprise. She shoved it in her coat pocket, jumped into the transport, peeled back onto the road, and flew away into the night.

It's not very late. Glancing down at the road below, Adira whispered, "I wonder why nobody is on the street tonight." Zhopla said nothing as Adira drove.

One hour and many miles later, Zhopla and Adira sat in her mother's country home, sipping tea before a warm fire. The yellowed envelope had her name on it, and it was in her mother's handwriting.

"It's been three months since Mom went missing. Where do you think this letter came from, Brother?" Adira's brown eyes were brimming with unshed tears.

"I believe the answers to your questions are in that envelope," Zhopla said gently.

She held the envelope for a moment, then opened it with shaky hands. Inside was a handwritten note.

Adira placed the letter back in the envelope. They stared at one another and then turned to study the letter's second page, a map.

"It's time we made travel plans, and I'm coming with you. I will be with you at your graduation from medical school." Zhopla said softly as he spread the letter and map for Adira on the coffee table.

The full moon's rays were shining through the kitchen window. A creepy chill went down Adira's spine as a buzzing sound very close to her inner ear, almost insect-like, whispered her name. It was her mother's voice. Intuitively, Adira knew her life would never be the same from that night.

Looking back, boy, was I ever right! Soon after that evening, I met Eurydice Sideris and was recruited into SIS 22.

Later, while reviewing her outdoor security video, she saw an image that made her hair stand on end. A hunched figure stared at them through the window as they studied the map. It looked up at the camera with blood-red-rimmed black eyes that never blinked.

7 - Nano What?

"The six of you have received the medical nanoparticle injections. Your addictions are a thing of the past. Many operatives have welcomed these implants." Zhopla smiled. "To prepare for the colonization of Galatéa, the Institute and SIS22 are prepared to offer an additional technology. With the BAI device, you can silently communicate with another human or an AI by thoughts alone."

"What else can a BAI do?" Rafe asked, confused by the other initiates' blind acceptance of the BAI and wondering what that might mean.

"You could query the AI without leaving your bed," David replied. Rafe's eyes gleamed when he heard a response that involved a computer. Zhopla and Adira laughed.

"The implant can store apps to run any program downloaded on it or another device," Violet added, and Rafe grinned.

The nanocytes and yet another implant? This wasn't part of the plan.

"You want an implant. Then again, you don't," Violet observed.

"What do you mean?" Rafe queried.

"You've led the life of an addict. A guarded life full of deception of yourself and others," Violet explained. "At any point, you knew incarceration or placement into the involuntary unit could turn your life upside down. Your negative thoughts have led you to project an incorrect future. That your BAI will become an intrusion, limiting your privacy and decision-making abilities to the point of having no free will. Therefore, you don't trust it."

There is truth in her words. That was a blunt way to put it, but true.

"How should I think of it?" Rafe asked hopefully as he caught Zhopla's discerning smile, which seemed pure, and Rafe couldn't help but return it in kind.

"Ahhhhh, the Institute will provide you with all you need." Zhopla's answer provided little information.

The other operatives clamored and wanted to know what the implants could do. David and Violet gave them examples of the implant's capabilities, which raised more questions.

David began. "These nanoparticles are far from the first-generation ones used only months ago. We have taken steps to minimize or eliminate the side effects you've heard about. SIS22 nanomedicine enhancements include the radical extension of your lifespan and health, eradication of disease, elimination of unnecessary suffering, and augmentation of human intellectual, physical, and emotional capacities."

Marcus, an operative hired for a special security detachment, interrupted David's explanation. "I'm not interested in any technology that might corrupt our bodies."

Rafe snorted. "The technology that corrupted my body was in the form of Klowd9 and of my own making. SIS22 is returning my mind and body to me. You should show some appreciation for their efforts to help us. After all, from what I've heard, they can extend our lives." *Where did that come from? Did I say all that?*

David collected Rafe's biodata through his nanoparticles and observed the emotional changes he witnessed. "On that point, yes, they will extend your lives." As for dying, the medical nanoparticles have nothing of value to imitate."

"How does that work?" Rafe asked.

"The nanoparticles use healthy cells as a template," David

said. "Unfortunately, if the cells have reached apoptosis—meaning they have reached the active stages of dying—the nanoparticles are useless. This means that there is no way to assist the patient. Many of you have complained about nanoparticles turning you into puppets. We have devised third-generation nanoparticles that would make it impossible for the post-transformation recipient to differ from the pre-transformation person. You will have an increased life expectancy and higher intelligence, health, memory, and emotional sensitivity without ceasing to exist because of the procedure. You will experience a radical transformation in your intellectual life. Yet these developments will not be the end of the original person you were. Dr. Yardley will review specific benefits."

Violet summarized the recipient effects. "There are many positive outcomes, but I will discuss three significant effects. First, as a review, the human lifespan, starting with our Pleistocene ancestors, has evolved from a relatively short period, some seven or eight decades, to much longer. Even terrestrial tortoises have longer lifespans!

"Second, you will experience an improvement in your intellectual capacity. Third, the nanoparticles will enhance your immune system, and vaccines will no longer be necessary, as they will produce antibodies as needed, and you will even be able to control your metabolic rate."

Zhopla expanded on this. "If a recipient has their most important memories, activities, and feelings intact during the procedure, adding extra capacities would not cause the original person they were to cease to exist. You must receive your BAIs immediately," Zhopla urged. "Without sufficient proficiency with the devices, communications with others and the AI will confound your thought processes. Each one of you will have an instructor once we implant the BAIs. I will take charge of your development within the Institute."

Zhopla effectively ended the question-and-answer session. David, Violet, and Adira worked to complete the implantation process. Compared to what was happening inside the recipients' bodies, the implantation of the BAI was a simple procedure.

The doctors finished implanting all six recipients within one hour and placed them in controlled hibernation pods. Instruments continuously monitored the nanoparticles and each neural lace mesh network.

David and Adira had received their BAIs weeks before the first jump. They were both well-versed in their capabilities to integrate the implant. Violet collaborated with the rest of the clinical team to ensure a smooth process, and they also entered a controlled hibernation as needed.

In the med bay, Rafe lay on an assessment table. He formed a question in his mind, but he forgot it as he lost consciousness once again. Retaining consciousness, he quickly sat up, feeling his fight-or-flight instincts trigger.

"Sorry, didn't mean to startle you," Zhopla was sitting in a corner of the room. "Adira offered a reasonable argument why she should introduce you to your implant," Zhopla said. "I concurred, and she will facilitate the initial steps. Then I will continue with more in-depth training."

"I am a computer expert; why do I need Adira?" Rafe inquired. His question came out more strident than he intended.

Unexpectedly, Zhopla laughed at the question. Rafe, you're quite a challenge. Your controlling and negative attitude towards the nanoparticles and the BAI is evident. Before you can start learning again, you must unlearn many things."

"All true, I guess," Rafe said, nodding, and he waited.

"Adira faced similar challenges, and she had her struggles," Zhopla said, standing up. "I thought she could spare you some discomfort."

Adira entered the medbay. "During the first trials, you can get severe headaches."

"Did you?" Rafe wondered.

"Oh, yes," Adira said. "Hibernation pod to the rescue."

"Okay, let's get started," Rafe said.

After working for over an hour and he could not send or receive via his BAI, Adira summoned David.

"I'm good. I get headaches all the time," Rafe objected. David noted the firm grip of Rafe's hands on the table, the sweat on his brow, and the evident pain in his eyes. He quickly intervened and lowered the comatose trainee into the hibernation pod before Rafe could speak another word.

Do you think we were wrong about Rafe? Adira sent it to David. *He's probably the worst recipient we have so far.*

David sent. *Addicts have a greater struggle with the integration process and are far more resistant to getting over the adverse effects of the BAI. I think he has a resentment against the nanoparticles and the implant. Did you make any progress with him today?*

Not as much as I had hoped, Adira sent.

"Then we need to offer an incentive," David said. "I'll inform the rest of the team."

Upon waking, Rafe realized that his headache had vanished and that he was ravenous. Because of the late hour, Adira led the way to the galley.

"David believes your difficulty in adopting the BAI is because of your distaste for your nanoparticles," Adira said after Rafe had wolfed down most of his food.

"I'm listening." Rafe continued to pack in his food.

Adira continued. "The implant isn't a computer, as you think of an external device. It has become an extension of your mind. It started working for me when I cooperated with the BAI as an extension of my nervous system. I started with small things like reaching for my coffee with my hand."

Not an outside computer. Hmmmm.... It's all an amalgamated new normal me.

Several days later, Rafe could send and receive thoughts from Adira. The success galvanized him, and he worked with the BAI until a headache again overcame him. Then David arrived to put him out of his misery.

"We'll have challenges with this one," Adira pronounced.

"He's driven, David, but we've dealt with addicts like this before. The other recipients are inherently more receptive. They're not perfectionists, eager to conquer the device in one sitting or even a few days. He must learn when to block the BAI if he grows fatigued."

The following day, Adira visited Rafe's cabin. Rafe greeted her in a bright, cheerful tone. "Ready to try again?" Adira asked.

"Certainly," Rafe replied. Adira moved to sit next to him at the cabin's small table.

Their progress was much quicker this morning, and after an hour, Adira quit to allow Rafe some well-earned rest. After the evening meal, Rafe requested they resume. Thus, training went from one hour once a day to twice daily and soon became three times a day.

At one point, after implanting another batch of nanoparticles, Violet spoke to Rafe. "How do you feel about your progress now, Rafe?"

"With David and Adira as examples, I can see how much more advanced they are. I can see they're doing much better than I am. I'm determined to match their ability, if not better." Rafe wanted to please Adira and compete with David with his progress.

When the *Porta Caeli* exited the second superluminal jump and returned to subluminal space, Rafe tested his implant connection to the ship's AI. This time, he requested imagery from the ship's sensor array embedded throughout the hull. He marveled every time he'd done this, which had been incessant.

So, where in the nine circles of hell is Galatéa, anyway?

Rafe used the time between jumps well to access the *Porta Caeli's* AI and research Galatéa, its star, the planetary system, and any other information he could glean.

"Are you retrieving data from the ship's AI, Rafe?" Adira joined Rafe in the galley, bringing two mugs of steaming hot coffee for them to enjoy.

"Yes, I was just looking into the colony's host star and planetary system." Rafe's gaze focused on Adira for a moment. "Listen to this. I will read what the AI states about Galatéa's star: GJ 1061 is a red dwarf star M-type ultracool dwarf star located approximately 12 light-years (3.7 parsecs) from Earth in the constellation of Aquarius. The Galatéa colony is on a tidally locked rocky planet orbiting within the host star's habitable zone."

Very interesting. And we're almost there! Adira sent this comment silently via the BAI.

"There's more. The AI states that the red dwarf star has a temperature of 2,516 degrees Kelvin, that's 2,243 degrees Celsius and 4,069 degrees Fahrenheit, and is 7.6 billion years old. It's estimated that it will survive for another trillion years."

In comparison, our Sun is 4.6 billion years old. That gives the planetary system three billion more years as on Earth to evolve and grow! Adira sent.

Rafe sent to Adira next. *GJ 1061 is a non-variable star that does not experience flares, so the planet Galatéa conserves its atmosphere. The star's temperature is cool enough for liquid water to pool on its surface but not too cold to freeze.*

"What I found interesting in my research was that the colony's planet is Earth-sized, with a 91 percent radius, 77 percent mass, 102.4 percent density (5.65 g/cm3), and 93 percent surface gravity. Because of the low luminosity of its host star, the planet receives about 60 percent of starlight from the red dwarf star that Earth gets from the Sun." Adira said aloud and smiled.

Rafe enjoyed the silent camaraderie and rapport he was building with Adira. "Within the planetary system, three rocky planets orbit around the red dwarf star. One rocky planet occupies an innermost orbit, an intermediate planet, and an outermost planet. The colony's planet orbits in its star's conservative circumstellar habitable zone, and the intermediate rocky planet orbits in the inner edge of the habitable zone."

"One complete revolution around Gliese 1061 takes only 6.099 Earth days (about 146 hours). It orbits at 0.02928285 Astronomical Units (4.4 million km; 2.7 million mi), or just under three percent of the separation between Earth and the Sun."

Rafe, I'm impressed with your vastly improved AI access ability. Adira sent.

"For comparison, Mercury is the closest planet in the Solar System and takes 88 days to orbit the Sun at 0.38 AU (57 million kilometers; 35 million miles)," Adira added. "Wow! That planet orbits its host star closely."

"The planet does not rotate at all; it would show its near side to the star while moving around it in orbit." Rafe felt thrilled with his new abilities. "They built the colony within a deep canyon in the terminator zone of the planet. The domed colony spans between the planet's light and dark sides. We will see the red dwarf hanging low near the horizon permanently on the light side."

"Yes, I understand that the sky will be colorful, with shades of red and purple due to scattered light."

"Another interesting fact is that the heat on the light side creates a low-pressure system, while the cold air on the dark side generates a high-pressure system. This results in the planet experiencing a constant and violent circulation of air. It has also led to massive rivers transforming into glaciers."

"The wind can be at hurricane strength. What I can't wait to do is to walk through the domed Atrium and see rain on the light side turn to snow as we approach the dark side." Adira added. "On one side, there is the sun, and on the other side, and with a gradual transition from day to night, the light will slowly drop off, turning to total darkness with an inky black sky filled with stars." Adira looked forward to exploring their new home.

8 - I Spy

"Dr. Michel, please report to Eurydice Sideris's office." The AI silently messaged David as he worked with microscopic samples of Rafe's neural cells, observing nanoparticle activity. "Be there in ten minutes." David had almost completed his assessment of the nanoparticle activity and how well the BAI meshed with each recipient's nervous system.

This generation of nanoparticles is performing far better than expected. Most recipient responses also have no unwanted side effects.

David went from the Medbay B spin, in free fall through connecting passages, and into the A spin Torus. He signaled that he had arrived, and the office door slid open. Eurydice's quarters and office were not much different from his.

"Hello, Eurydice. I haven't seen much of you since we boarded the *Porta Caeli*. I trust all is going according to plan?"

"Yes, we will arrive on planet Galatéa within six days. I want you to summarize the progress of the nanoparticle recipients and specifically Rafe's BAI neurological activity." Eurydice addressed David formally.

She looks rather grim this morning. You'd think our work in the medbay was not going well.

"All of the nanoparticle recipients are progressing ahead of expectations. Our tests confirm that progress is being made on all the recipients except one. We had problems with Rafe and his implant. Adira has been working with him, sometimes three times a day, to get him completely oriented to the BAI and to ensure its integration with his nervous system. The other recipients are progressing well, ex-cept for Phil."

"Oh, and what happened with him?" Eurydice's eyebrow went up.

"Zhopla had to intervene when one of the recipients, Phil Roskos, went into crisis. We decided to reverse the nanoparticle procedure with this individual, placing him in hibernation. He will remain there until we have arrived on the planet. He will be integrated into the colony and hopefully fit in." *All the recipients were chosen because they had inherent skills necessary for the colony's success. I'm still trying to understand this seeming failure.* "We may try the nanoparticle procedure with him in the future because he is part of the security detachment."

"We will need his expertise in the future. Keep me updated on his progress, if you will." Eurydice paused and looked into David's eyes.

"Now, tell me how Adira is doing after the news of Gint. I know her progress with the BAI is satisfactory, but I was wondering about her mental state." Eurydice never blinked; as she spoke, her hands had turned into fists on her desktop.

"Adira is understandably experiencing the entire gamut of emotions. Aside from Gint being alive, she feels you have betrayed her. Eurydice, Adira considers you not only her superior officer but a friend and mentor, especially considering how close you two grew when her mother disappeared three years ago."

I don't want to give away too much to Eurydice and betray Adira's confidence myself. Still, I must maintain truthfulness for my integrity. It's a good thing she didn't ask me how I feel about all of this! I can't wait to chat with that slime, Gint.

"David, I asked you to come to my office for another reason. We are within communication range of Galatéa, and I wanted you to be here when I speak to Gint. I want you to remain out of camera range and observe. Your professional opinion is needed, as I suspect all is not well with Gint and his work with the artifacts that have been found and collected."

Eurydice is a shrewd judge of character. If she senses that something's not right, she usually notices first.

"Of course," David replied casually. He stepped out of view of Eurydice's camera, just out of range, and got ready to watch.

Gint's image appeared on the screen. "Gint, good to see you again after all this time. How is it going on Galatéa?" Eurydice's piercing sky-blue eyes stared at the screen.

"Our team has been working tirelessly. We are attempting to decipher a large, loose piece of stone with pictographs. This was the first stone tablet we found when we explored Cave One. We've brought the stone back to the space station." Gint shuffled through maps and reports scattered on his desk until he found the page he was looking for.

"Our Egyptology experts have been trying to understand these complex symbols. Preliminary findings indicate that the communication system uses figurative and what appear to be symbolic and phonetic glyphs within the context of each pictogram." Gint scrutinized Eurydice and waited.

"Interesting. I'm curious to see the artifacts for myself. We will be arriving within six days. Adira and David are both on board. I have told them the truth regarding your whereabouts. You are required to meet with Adira as soon as possible after we arrive."

I know he was not expecting this communication, which is good because we have an accurate snapshot of his demeanor. Overall, he doesn't look so good. He's lost weight, and his hair is not clean, and it has grown to his shoulders.

"What do you think Adira will do when we meet?" Gint looked sideways, then down as he spoke.

"You're acting as if this is some tedious chore I've assigned you!" a red-faced Eurydice retorted. "I will never forgive myself for the deception. Adira has suffered greatly since she was told you died—by me! What do I think she will do is all you can say? Don't you want to know how she is doing?"

"I was not expecting this communication. I—" Gint began, but Eurydice cut him off.

"I do not want to hear your excuses. Get yourself together. Make sure your team is alerted of our arrival. I've heard various rumors regarding your team, including the actions of several overly ambitious team members. *Porta Caeli* out." Eurydice abruptly ended the communication.

"Gint looks pale and gaunt. His unkempt appearance is completely unlike the man I knew on Earth. More importantly, though, his body language and demeanor show deception. As if he is hiding something from you." David observed.

"Yes, thank you for your input. I wanted a second set of eyes and a professional opinion, and you have supplied both. Thank you for supporting Adira during the past few months. I know she treasures your friendship."

Is that a tear I see in Eurydice's eye?

"I can see you have suffered from the deception as well. We will make the best of the situation soon. We must." David was unfamiliar with having Eurydice relate her feelings to anyone before.

"Be aware that something else is going on with Gint's team. I'm especially concerned with Rachel Radford, his second in command. She is the Egyptology expert of the team and is known to be aggressive and overly ambitious." Eurydice crossed her arms over her chest and sat back in her chair.

"Are you expecting trouble from within the team?" "I know the Eastern Alliance has planted individuals in the colony and plans to disrupt our operations there—maybe even annihilate the colony itself. We have serious work ahead of us."

And, if I know Rachel, she and Gint are more than just friends.

David returned to the spin grav Torus through the free-fall hallways. He decided to take a detour before returning to the medbay. As he entered the observation blister, he saw that his hunch was correct.

"Care for some company, Adira?" David discerned that Adira was deep in thought and almost regretted his disruption—almost.

"No, not at all. I was finishing my daily meditation and journal reflection exercises." Adira looked luminous in the starlight, and her hair was tied back. He took a step back to admire the view— and not of the stars.

"I was in a meeting with Eurydice. She asked me to sit in on a communication with Gint." David began.

Adira's eyes widened at this information. "So, we're in communications range then?"

"Yes. Eurydice wanted me there and out of his view during the session so that I could comment on his demeanor. She's heard there is some unrest or disagreement among the Galatéa experts— among the archaeologists, Egyptologists, and semiotic analysis experts." He paused.

"It almost sounds as if there is a power struggle going on. What was most interesting was Gint's body language."

"Oh? In what way?

"He appeared disheveled and gaunt. From his body language, he was not completely truthful with Eurydice. Can't be sure what it all means, but he is hiding something."

"He has never been seen with a single hair out of place. That's very interesting."

"I wanted you to know that Eurydice feels terrible about the deception over the staged explosion and being unable to share the truth with you until now." Despite his feelings for Adira, he could see how much pain Eurydice had gone through.

He decided not to tell Adira that Gint didn't even ask how she was doing or request to communicate with her sooner rather than wait another six days until their arrival.

"I'm not ready to deal with Eurydice yet. Zhopla has given me some scriptural readings and daily meditations for reflection. I come to the observation blister between jumps mostly because it reminds me how small my problems are compared to the vastness of space. It gives me perspective." Adira gazed out at the starlight.

"We're only a few days away from Galatéa now. I'm looking forward to seeing the dome and colony. Of course, the caverns and artifacts will be astounding. I hope you know that I'll be with you every step of the way. I will come with you when you meet Gint if you want."

Adira took David's hand into her own and gave it a slight squeeze. "I know I can always count on you to be there for me, David." Then she silently sent, *I am here for you, too.*

They sat in silence for a short while. Adira broke the silence. "I don't want to communicate with Gint until we reach Galatéa. What I have to say needs to be in person."

David and Adira returned to the galley on B spin. Having dinner together was like old times for David. He couldn't help but remember all the great dinners they had shared at her cliff cottage in Big Sur. Soon, they would share dinners in the Galatéa dining room under the glass dome as filtered light shone down from a red dwarf star.

###

Rachel wiped the sweat from her brow, her muscles straining

with each movement in the exercise compartment of Galatea's Aeris space station. Exercise was the only thing that seemed to ease the storm brewing inside her, releasing the anxiety that had taken root since the news broke. Adira was coming to Galatea. Of all people, Adira. Rachel's belief of having Gint solely for herself for years was shifting. Concealing her unease, she dreaded the reunion between Gint and Adira and its effect on her.

Rachel couldn't help but wonder about Adira. What kind of woman was she? It was the not knowing that pushed Rachel's anxiety to the brink. How could she prepare when she didn't know what to expect? Gint had been so tight-lipped about Adira over the past three years. Rachel had no idea how to approach this or what strategy to use.

She had worked too hard to let someone like Adira disrupt her life. She was at the pinnacle of her career, but she knew it was just the beginning. Her success, marked by interplanetary travel and significant discoveries, was the culmination of years of dedication. But Rachel couldn't rest on her laurels. There was always more to achieve and conquer.

A smile crept across her face as she thought about how she had outmaneuvered others, protected herself, and emerged unscathed. Her approach of immersing herself in her projects and mastering her achievements while remaining in the background and assessing the situation served her well. Rachel believed nothing was more tragic than a woman who failed and was determined to avoid that.

She knew that David Michel was accompanying Adira, a man reputed to be an exceptional astrobiologist and physician. Rachel had heard he was deep, but she didn't crave depth. Superficiality had always worked to her advantage. Perhaps she could somehow use that to her benefit.

After her workout, Rachel showered, allowing the warm water to wash away the last of her tension. As she toweled off, she began formulating plans, preparing herself for whatever might come. She would exude confidence, calm, and competence. Rachel despised being alone and was determined to ensure she wouldn't be the one who was left out. No one was going to replace her.

Later, Rachel found Gint with the philology team examining ancient pictograms etched onto a large stone discovered in Cave One. There was disagreement when Gint explained his preliminary theories, his voice steady as he pointed out the complex communication system in the hieroglyphs.

Rachel leaned in, examining the pictograms. As an expert in Egyptology, she recognized the similarities and differences. "In ancient Egypt, hieroglyphs were figurative," she explained to the team. "They could represent natural elements, often stylized and simplified. Multiple interpretations can arise from the same symbol, depending on the overall context of the pictogram."

Rachel approached the group. "Gint, I heard you made some progress with the pictograms?"

Gint nodded. "Yes, Rachel. These hieroglyphs are more than just symbols. They represent a complex communication system—possibly an ancient language. Look here. These recurring patterns suggest a grammatical structure."

"So, this is the find from the cave?" She came closer to Gint and the philology team; her gaze fixated on the stone.

"Yes, it's remarkable." Gint traced a finger along the etched lines. "We've been analyzing these pictograms, and the complexity is beyond anything we've seen."

"What have you figured out so far?"

After a pause, Gint pointed to a specific cluster of symbols. "These aren't just decorative. We believe they represent a form of communication. An ancient language, perhaps. "The repetition of this symbol implies it's crucial to their structure, possibly a pronoun or identifier."

She glanced at the symbols over Gint's shoulder, and her auburn hair brushed against his cheek. "It almost resembles a mixture of hieroglyphs and cuneiform."

"But there's something unique about it. The patterns suggest a language that isn't just spoken. It might have a multidimensional aspect, perhaps representing sounds, concepts, and even emotions. It's as if these people communicated in layers."

"Layers? So, you're saying they could convey different meanings simultaneously?"

Gint smiled, intrigued by the challenge. "That's our working theory. Each pictogram might change its meaning based on its position relative to others, the orientation, and etching depth. It's a sophisticated system—much more advanced than we initially thought."

"And the stone itself. It's from the same material as the cave walls?"

"Yes, but this one is different. The precision of the carving suggests specialized tools were employed. We're still running tests to determine how old it is, but I suspect it predates the other artifacts we found."

"Incredible. This could be the key to understanding their entire culture."

Gint agreed. "And maybe even their downfall. If we can decode this, it might explain what happened to them and why they vanished. But it will take time. This language is like nothing we've encountered before."

"Whatever it is, it's important. Keep me updated, Gint. This could change everything."

"You'll be the first to know. We're on the brink of something big here, Rachel. I can feel it."

Zara disagreed. "I don't see it, Gint. The philology team has been discussing the carvings. These could be decorative motifs, too. We've seen similar designs in non-linguistic contexts before."

"I've compared them with several known ancient languages, and the patterns are too consistent to be decorative. There's structure here, a syntax." Gint's gray eyes flashed, yet he remained firm.

Zara crossed her arms and stood up. "But you're basing that on a tiny sample. We can't jump to conclusions without more evidence. Until we have more context, it's reckless to assume these are language symbols."

"Maybe we're looking at it from the wrong angle. What if they serve both purposes? A language that's also used in art?" Rachel interjected.

Gint became thoughtful. "That's a possibility, but the level of repetition and variation I'm seeing suggests a linguistic function. It's too deliberate for mere art."

"That's frustrating about our work. You assume too much. We believe you're ignoring the cultural context. What if the people who created this stone didn't separate language from art? What if, to them, it was all one expression?" Zara faced Gint and remained standing with arms crossed.

"Cultural context carries importance, but linguistic patterns abide by rules one can identify regardless of artistic influence."

"Alright, Zara. We recognize your team's expertise, but we need to take a step back. Both perspectives are valuable. Gint, your linguistic theory is compelling, but Zara's point about cultural context is also crucial. Let's not dismiss either possibility until we have more data." Rachel intoned.

"Agreed. We'll continue to gather evidence. But I'm confident we're onto something significant here."

"Fine, Gint. The team and I will take a step back. But let's keep an open mind. We might be dealing with something entirely different from what we've seen before."

Rachel nodded. "Let's approach this as a team, with all angles covered. This discovery is too important to rush."

Gint stood, stretching his arms and back. He glanced at Rachel, his expression a mix of fatigue and appreciation. "How long have we been at this?" he wondered aloud, looking around at the team.

Rachel met his gaze, a silent understanding passing between them. "I'm turning in for the night," Gint announced, his voice low and tired.

Rachel stayed a while longer, working with the philologists, her mind half on the stone and half on the impending arrival of Adira. After about twenty minutes, she, too, retired for the evening.

Without hesitation, she made her way to Gint's quarters, entering without knocking. She found him there, his back to the door. Rachel crossed the room, wrapping her arms around him and pressing her lips to his. Fueled by the need for reassurance, the kiss was deep. Gint responded, his hands exploring her body with the same urgency.

The communicator's chime interrupted them, breaking the moment. Gint hesitated, then pulled away to answer. Rachel retired to a dark corner of Gint's quarters and remained unseen by the camera.

Eurydice's eyes narrowed as she studied Gint through the screen. His blond hair had grown to his shoulders, and he looked pale, almost skeletal. She didn't like how he reacted to her words. Shifty eyes and a flicker of something unreadable passed across his face. This was going to be more complicated than she had expected.

Her husky voice was icy and composed. "Your meeting with Adira must go as smoothly as possible. Ensure the droids attend to the debris field. Eurydice out."

9 - Adira and Gint Meet Again

The communicator chime brought Adira out of vaguely disturbing dreams. She fumbled with the light above her bed and then tapped her commlink.

"Varna here."

"Adira?" David's voice. "They told me you're going to see the caves today."

"Yes." She rubbed her eyes.

"Good. I'm going with you."

Awake in an instant, the memory returned.

Gint.

It had been two days since their emotional 'reunion.' Since then, she'd dreaded seeing the caves alone with Gint and Rachel. In her present mood, David provided a good diversion.

"I'm so glad you'll be with us. Twenty minutes," she said over the commlink and signed off. Adira laid back down and nestled into her sleek, multifunctional bed for a few more minutes. Unable to get comfortable, she turned onto her back and had her AI environmental assistant display a holographic canopy, going from showing the night sky to soothing ocean and beach scenes. Her emotions were still raw. Time to get up and get going.

She recalled the meeting as she began to dress.

…She clutched the sides of her chair, knuckles white, glad David provided moral support, knowing Gint would be walking through the space station door any moment. She held her breath as the door opened, and there stood her husband.

As he walked into the room, he motioned to a dark-haired

woman at his side. "This is Rachel, second in command."

Scarlet-faced, Adira walked around the table toward him. Standing before him, they looked directly into each other's eyes for a few moments. She reflected on how much she had missed him, how desperately she wanted to hold him during those long, lonely nights, and then about his deception.

Then she slapped him—hard—straight across his smiling face.

"How could you do this? How could you?" Adira blurted with tears in her eyes. She felt David's hands on her shoulders as he gently pulled her away from Gint.

Everyone grew quiet and looked at the floor. Gint's slapped face had already started to turn red.

"It's good to see you again, Addie. Maybe someday you'll be able to understand and forgive me." Gint said, his expression unreadable, then turned and left the room with Rachel exiting closely behind.

How cold! She desperately wanted answers and to make some sense out of this.

"That's it? That's all he has to say to me? David, can you walk with me to my quarters? I'm not feeling well right now." She remembered looking up into David's warm brown eyes. Without another word, she brushed past Eurydice.

David walked with her. He fumbled for words. "I'm here. Do you need anything?"

"Just some space to think."

Adira's memory dissipated as she showered with sonic waves, which she found refreshing; she marveled at the unparalleled cleansing experience. Dressed and groomed, Adira sat on the floor for her morning prayers, meditation, and journaling. A ritual she never missed. She had commissioned a private sanctuary for her quarters consisting of a meditation nook with a comfortable chair for study and contemplation. Soft ambient lighting was integrated into the walls and ceiling, allowing her to change the lighting to suit her mood with various colors and intensities. There was a small waterfall with a calming, trickling stream using purified water recycled through advanced filtration systems.

Adira had meticulously planned her private quarters. She blended advanced technology and elegant design, reflecting her status and taste. Compared to the *Porta Caeli*, her quarters were spacious and filled with natural light streaming through large, transparent glass dome walls that offered a stunning view of Galatéa's exotic landscape. Though the red dwarf was dim by comparison, it still provided the light needed for Adira's small garden, which Astrid, a botanist by trade and chief of agriculture on Galatéa, had helped her plant.

With Astrid's help, my little garden has added a magical touch to my quarters.

Before she left, she shook her blond mane and looked in the hexagonal mirror; her face looked composed and peaceful. "Let's get this show on the road," she said, satisfied. She smiled and winked at her image. Embedded in her quarters' infrastructure was a discreet AI assistant who was in constant contact with her BAI and managed climate control, security, and entertainment.

Engage security. Adira away.

She quietly entered Eurydice's private galley, poured fresh coffee, and helped herself to a breakfast bar. She saw Gint and Rachel hovering over a hand-drawn map across one of the dining tables.

"Gint," Adira said in a professional tone.

At the sound of Adira's voice, Rachel's head snapped up, taking a step back from Gint.

That's my husband you're doting on. Adira's green eyes had missed nothing.

"Good morning, Dr. Varna. I trust you had a restful night." Rachel's greeting was flat and monotone.

"David and I are eager to see the caves and artifacts." Adira forced a smile that didn't reach her eyes. Flashing her white teeth, she turned away to see that David had made his way down to the galley. His blond hair remained impeccably neat, and he walked briskly to join them.

Gint stiffened and surveyed the two of them for several moments. "We'll go over the safety protocols before we venture out. We don't want the caves contaminated. Protective gear and breathing apparatus are required. It's a safety measure for our health."

Hmph. It figures; he thinks of our safety as an afterthought.

Suited up, Adira stood in a vast, cavernous expanse, its dimensions she couldn't even guess. The cavern had many circular exits seemingly carved out of the walls. Gint steered them to a black hole furthest to their left.

Entering the portal, Adira saw a tunnel about ten feet high, ten feet wide, and completely round. She spied evenly spaced lamps illuminating the length of the tunnel, which floated near the ceiling. With a gloved hand, she touched the walls and found rough and uneven surfaces. The tunnel did not appear to have been artificially constructed. They walked for about twenty minutes with no apparent changes in the tunnel.

"We're going to be climbing down to a lower cavern. The entrance is up ahead," Gint said through his commlink.

Though the rigged artificial lighting remained dim, Adira could see team members descending into what looked like another round black hole in the cave's floor. Rachel attached an illuminator to David and Adira's wrists.

"All right," she said briskly. "Let's see what we've got."

She followed behind Gint into the black hole. As she descended the ladder, her light caught engravings and bas-reliefs etched into the cavern walls. They entered what appeared to be a massive hall with four colonnades that supported the ceiling and surrounded a central square. The spotlights powered up, and the cavern's true magnificence and vast scope became apparent. The walls, ceilings, floors, and colonnades were carved, some painted, with various vegetative and animal-like images.

"You have descended into the first of thirteen great halls we discovered. The ancients may have used these halls for gatherings or religious ceremonies." As Gint spoke, his eyes glazed over. "We have a team of philologists and semiologists working on deciphering the various pictograms."

Adira fell back into the shadows and studied her husband.

Curiously, my fury has not abated even though it's been many days since I learned the truth.

They viewed the Aeris space station, which had landed safely and was positioned deep in Cave One, the only cave connected to the surface and one of Galatéa's thirteen greater caverns. SIS22 even planted pseudo debris from the supposed explosion, which remained in orbit around the planet before the first colonists arrived. The world remained under the impression that the station had been sabotaged and the entire crew dead.

Gint's and Eurydice's outrageous behavior remains unforgivable. I'm an operative of SIS22 too. Something doesn't add up here. The original purpose of the space station was to build the surface colony before the colonists arrived and then permanently orbit Galatéa as a failsafe measure. . . I acknowledge the importance of keeping the caverns top secret as reasonable, but something is not right here.

I wish the importance of this excavation and its implications had made me feel better about Gint and Eurydice.

After their initial meeting and her outburst, Adira maintained a calm and professional exterior facade. The last thing she wanted was another confrontation with Gint, especially because Rachel constantly smirked in the background.

These findings are overwhelming and spectacular. My anger is verging on rage. I need to find some productive way to channel this negative energy.

That evening, Adira decided she needed some alone time and descended into the dark caves alone. The caves were the best place to be completely alone. That was what she needed now. The caves provided space and alone time. When Adira descended deep below the planet, she was struck by the dusty caves and lava tubes' inhospitable, dry volcanic environment. It was so different from the Pacific West Coast trees and forests of her home back on Earth. As she investigated, she turned over a rock with the toe of her boot. At that moment, everything went pitch black.

A power outage? That's not supposed to happen. I hope it's a short one.

In the inky blackness, Adira thought about the intensity of the past few weeks and how Eurydice had informed her of the deception. She still found it hard to accept that her husband was not murdered; the sabotage was contrived and covered up, and he was alive.

My journey towards forgiveness began with prayers while traveling to Galatéa. In retrospect, my heart was slightly healed on the Porta Caeli. "Upon those who dwelt in the land of gloom, a light has shown." That Bible passage helped me see the value of forgiveness, and I'm grateful I mapped out a clear plan to follow: to forgive but never forget.

It's funny how I can see things more clearly in the dark.

"Take deep breaths, Adira. Just inhale," she told herself aloud as the minutes passed. She tried not to think about her breathing apparatus and the surrounding stale air. Her greatest fear was not being able to breathe after a near-drowning childhood accident. When she journeyed from Earth, she checked and rechecked the oxygen stores and recyclers on the starship, even though this was not her job.

As her eyes slowly adjusted to the darkness, a faint wraithlike luminescence appeared around her. Adira surveyed her surroundings in amazement and delight. In patchy iridescent clumps, the cave walls, ceiling, and dry surface under the rock she had just turned over all emitted a phosphorescent glow. She wondered why this luminescence was never mentioned or documented. She squeezed her eyes shut, blinked hard, and opened them. It was still there.

Could it be bioluminescence? Something alive?

The beautiful encompassing luminescence reminded Adira of the nights she sat alone in the dark observation blister of the starship, surrounded only by the light of distant stars, the ancient constellations.

The power was suddenly restored, and with the bright lights, the glowing disappeared. She headed back to the dome on the planet's surface. The mysterious luminescence needed to be documented and explored further—the sooner, the better. She stepped into the elevator shaft, and it started its slow, chugging climb hundreds of feet into the abundance of air.

Adira's communicator activated as she entered the dome.

While traveling to Galatéa, her implanted neural lace, the brain-to-artificial intelligence interface (BAI), had grown into and around her brain. David and Adira had adapted quickly to the enhancements to converse and communicate privately, with priority authorized access to the advanced artificial intelligence that monitored all aspects of the dome and its inhabitants.

The communication was silently sent from David. *Adira, we need you in the infirmary.*

On my way.

She went through decontamination and was met at the inside hatch by Phil Roskos, the dome's security and environmental director. With wild gesticulations and jerky movements, the gentle giant, typically quiet and shy, was red-faced and stared buggy-eyed at Adira.

"What's going on, Phil?" Adira decided not to address Phil's agitated state.

His face reddened more, and his eyes turned upward. His agitated movements appeared more like claw-like scratching. He grunted and barked, among other guttural sounds. He focused on Adira again.

"WHAT'S GOING ON, PHIL?" he shouted. "WHAT'S GOING ON, PHIL? AY GR BARRRRR? WHAT'S GOING ON, PHIL?"

Adira's heart pounded. She took deep, slow breaths and hid her shaking hands in her pockets. She carefully turned away and hoped he would follow as she moved toward the infirmary, quiet and steady.

"Let's go to the infirmary, Phil. David and I will make you feel better." She looked over her shoulder often as they walked. She saw that Phil's face was a mask of rage every time.

"INFIRMARY, INFIRMARY, LET'S GO TO THE

INFIRRRRRRMARY!!! WHAT'S FOR DINNER? WHAT'S GOING ON? I'M SORRRRRY, SO SORRY. ARGHHHHH!" Phil's peculiar gesticulations and screaming continued as he walked behind her.

Adira remained calm and entered the infirmary. Fortunately, Phil followed. David was at his microscope and quickly assessed Phil's agitated state. They ushered Phil into a cubicle and activated isolation protocols.

In a stern voice, David commanded Phil to sit down, and though still agitated, Phil complied. As they began their physical assessment, Phil seemed to calm down.

"I noticed his dilated pupils, and now he is tachycardic, with a spike in blood pressure, and he has a fever." She looked at Phil. "He is also exhibiting profuse drooling."

Phil's agitated state returned, and his eyes again rolled upward, accompanied by more wild gesticulations. He retracted his lips, and the barking, grunting, and rage returned. This was followed by intermittent heavy panting.

"He seemed able to control himself when you ordered him to sit down, but after a few minutes, the anomalous behavior returned. He is conscious, so we can rule out seizures."

"I saw Phil at breakfast this morning. He told me he woke up with a sore throat today. I told him to come to the infirmary so we could check him out. He was his usual thoughtful but reserved self then," David recalled.

"Hopefully, we won't need to sedate him, David, so let's run a complete neurological diagnostic scan, a new BioScan for pathogens, and be sure everyone documents all observed behaviors and their patterns or cycles." Adira turned away from her external computer interface.

"Let's remember that we need to maintain our open-mindedness. So far, we have not isolated any planetary pathogens or alien vectors that could cause illness, but that doesn't mean they're not there."

Adira's grim determination and curiosity transitioned to high alert. She continued, "I've decided we should look for more than just biosignatures; we need to look for complexity, such as unexpected concentrations of molecules assembled in unlikely compositions. Any evidence of complexity needs to be investigated. Was there something else you needed when you contacted me?"

David frowned and looked at Adira. He crossed the room, opened the infirmary's waiting area door, and directed her attention to eight dome inhabitants lined up.

"They all woke up with sore throats this morning."

10 - Jomei

"I've had numerous discussions with the colony AI, and it has chosen a name for itself, or himself, I should say." Rafe sat in a small recreation space on the canyon dome's uppermost levels with Adira as they admired the Galatéan vista through the protected geodesic reinforced windows. The sun on the horizon reminded them that this was now their home, far from Earth.

"Is a name the AI's idea or yours?" Adira stirred her coffee.

"I brought up the subject, but once it considered its options, it chose a male human name." He chose the name 'Jomei.' It's of Japanese origin. I don't know if you know, but I'm of Japanese ancestry. My grandmother was Japanese, and some part of me always felt attracted to anything related to Japanese culture. Their artwork, music, food, history, and ancient and modern society were topics I felt drawn to all my life.

"Grandmother commanded respect, and she and Grampy raised me after my parents died. Like oil and water, somehow, they made their relationship work. She kept him in line. He became a different person after she passed. Rough and temperamental. He had a Rizika gambling addiction with his crony friends. I miss him sometimes. In fact, it's time for me to contact him—let him know how I'm doing." Rafe smiled.

Since Rafe began his security work, AI Jomei has evolved quickly. Although the fierce winds roared continuously outside the dome, the colony's AI rigidly controlled the protected interior environment and human safety.

Adira stood. "It's time to meet with Eurydice. I hate leaving the view."

Rafe joined her, and they walked down the stairs to Eurydice's conference room.

"Hello, Eurydice." Rafe took a seat next to her as Adira sat beside him. They barely sat down when Eurydice began her intelligence report.

"We have received an overdue communication from Earth. Transmitted three months after our departure to Galatéa, routed through the SIS22 sequential deep space communication relay buoys, it took three more months to arrive. As you know, Dr. Viktor Galkin remains incarcerated. The message indicates that Galkin's interrogation has revealed more information regarding his genetic engineering experiments. We now know that SIS22 intercepted the most virulent virus Dr Galkin genetically engineered because of Adira's and the team's actions during SIS22's mission in Atlanta.

"However, upon intensive interrogation, Galkin disclosed that he had engineered other viruses, including the H5N1 virus. Galkin genetically modified the antigenic sites on an H5N1 avian strain so that the human immune system does not recognize the altered virus and the body does not initiate a response. This virus does not directly attack brain tissue but causes a distal infection after airborne transmission. The viral antigenic properties provoke autoimmune-mediated destruction of the host's dopaminergic neurons while leaving no direct evidence of brain infection." Eurydice's gaze rested on Adira, whose thoughts had drifted to Phil Roskos.

"Adira, can you give me your update?"

"Did anyone brief David on this intel?"

"Yes, I met with him earlier this morning. I'd like to hear your take on the current 'situation.'"

"We may have an outbreak on our hands at this point. We currently have nine patients who initially complained of sore throat, high fever, and headache—followed by extreme bouts of lethargy, with cycles of mania progressing to paralysis. The first few cases have moved from a severe manic state to a coma-like state, but it's more like they're asleep, and we can't wake them. They end up in a statue-like condition, speechless and motionless. Many of the patients have autoantibodies in their basal ganglia.

"However, neither the medical tests nor the environmental systems detected pathogens, viruses, toxins, or bacteria. David and I had a difficult time stabilizing the patients, and we converted one-half of the infirmary into a quarantine ward. We isolate all patients who fit the case definition of this disease outbreak. The worst patients are in stasis pods until we can find the cause and start therapy."

"I know you've worked tirelessly to find the agent. Do you have a preliminary diagnosis to share?"

"David and I have a working case definition of this disease. We have two preliminary diagnoses—first, aseptic meningitis. Second, some form of encephalitis, but of unknown etiology. The cause has been elusive, and neither of our tentative diagnoses explains all the symptoms.

"Interestingly, our first patient, Phil Roskos, was the only initiate unable to tolerate the nanoparticles and had to have them removed on the *Porta Caeli* before we arrived. The initial patient experienced both extreme mania and subsequent lethargy."

At the mention of Phil's name, Rafe became agitated. "Phil Roskos? I've been watching him since his meltdown on the *Porta Caeli*. His body language and demeanor seemed suspicious and a little off to me. Coincidence?"

Eurydice's eyebrows went up with this new information. "Have you been monitoring other colonists?"

"I have an ongoing list in my head. Yes, there are several

colonists I'm monitoring. They are unaware of the biosensors and the nano-sniffers, making their observed movements more natural and genuine for AI tracking. I receive daily reports on any anomalous behavior. So far, we have detected no security threats.

"I'd like you to update me on the operations of our AI systems, especially any environmental monitoring systems that we have deployed since we arrived," Eurydice said, her face showing detachment and a businesslike demeanor.

"In summary, I have been programming and tweaking Galatéa's AI to identify emerging security risks and make recommendations for dealing with them. The AI can now continuously monitor the precise biometric data of the colonists. We will monitor everyone's pulse, blood pressure, sweat composition, and pupil dilation—all the parameters of an enhanced lie detector. The AI simultaneously abstracts statistical relationships from gathered data. The AI sorts and categorizes this data for advanced pattern recognition.

"As the system evolves and adapts, it will create and present a more refined and discerning record of biometrics, summarizing emotions and behaviors that it has captured and analyzed."

Adira had questions. "Technological developments have made the synthesis of novel biological weapons a reality. I'm afraid that instead of using viruses or bacterial organisms, they may target the immune system directly, or for that matter, the endocrine or nervous systems. The manipulation of our microbiome could interrupt human biological processes itself.

"The original colonists did not receive the nanoparticles before they arrived here. They are especially susceptible to the effects of any deliberate release of pathogens that could cause illness or death. What are we doing to protect the most vulnerable among us?"

Rafe replied, "All microbial or biological agents or toxins

created naturally or artificially are covered by our deployed systems, including every biological agent that people can use for harmful purposes." Our AI can instantly identify patterns that are too intricate for humans to identify and process quickly."

He reassured Adira and Eurydice, "The nanosensors can perform advanced tasks, such as accurately identifying captured motions and images to monitor and manage security threats effectively."

"What protocols are in place if malevolent actors opt for a more low-tech approach, such as firearms, poisons, or explosives?" Eurydice's piercing bright blue eyes fixed on Rafe.

"Our sensors detect security risks with unprecedented sensitivity. We achieve this degree of sensitivity in detecting security risks by using an array of silicon nanowire field-effect transistors modified for more than biological toxins or chemical threats. We call them nano-sniffers and use them to detect any known explosives. A specific electrical pattern measured by each nano-sensor array identifies the type of explosive agent."

"The colonists are unaware of the current extremist threat or Galkin's virus," Eurydice said. "We feel that Galkin's agents have been here since the first wave. Their work and homes are established, having been here long enough. Maintain your surveillance, Rafe. Excellent work." She stood, showing that the meeting had ended.

As Adira returned to the Medbay, Rafe went to the dining hall. In his role as security chief, he met with as many of the 110 inhabitants as he could. He passed people on the way and greeted them with smiles and friendly hellos.

Rasa Ladeika, the director of the dietary department, sat in the dining hall. Rafe took a moment to observe humanoid droids as they zipped around the dining hall, cleaned floors, cleared tables, and took used dishes back to the kitchens to be washed.

She's sitting alone, which is perfect. I can sit and have a decent chat with her without interruptions.

"Mind if I join you?" He pulled out a chair.

"Hey, Rafe. How's it going today?" Rasa smiled as he sat down. "I've been working on the menus for next month. The harvests have been plentiful. The greenhouses and hydroponic gardens overflow with vegetables, fruit, wheat, and corn. I'm pleased with our progress over the past year. From nothing to this!" Rasa's enthusiasm was contagious.

Among the first to settle on Galatéa, Rasa knew all the original colonists well and introduced Rafe to most of them, which helped break the ice as Rafe gained acceptance and trust. Rasa's natural enthusiasm and optimistic outlook paved the way for many friendly encounters.

"I hope the reprogramming program I updated after our arrival has made the droids more efficient."

"The droid updates have been invaluable both in the kitchens and greenhouses. Everything is proceeding like clockwork. Some colonists seem uneasy around the human-looking droids, but otherwise, all is well."

"I don't think I've heard a single complaint about the food. Since I've arrived on Galatéa, I've gained a few pounds—not complaining, though." Rafe knew he looked like a drowned rat after his Klowd9 addiction. He had been a walking skeleton.

I have to admit the nanoparticles and BAI implants are working spectacularly.

"We have movie night tonight after dinner. You coming?" Rasa's smile never diminished.

"Who could say no to that invitation? Sure. Wouldn't miss it."

"Great, I'll see you then. I am returning to the kitchens to oversee the droids as they complete the supply room inventory. See you tonight." Rasa gathered up her notebook.

Rafe watched her walk away. *She's become a valuable ally. And friend?*

###

Rafe completed in-person rounds of the entire colony at least twice per day. One of his favorite places to visit was the greenhouse. He paid particular attention to the body language and attitudes of people he encountered.

Astrid Greig, also among the original inhabitants, was working with herbs when he happened by. The opposite of Rasa, Astrid, appeared darker. Astrid was radiant. With a warm, golden undertone, her deep brown skin emitted a radiant glow. Her complexion was smooth and even, with a natural, healthy sheen that caught the light beautifully. Her hair was a crown of tight, spiral curls, rich and voluminous, with a deep, lustrous black color that contrasted elegantly with her skin. However, her inherent beauty was at odds with her nature. She was grim and pessimistic, further emphasized by her dark eyes and hair.

Astrid shares nothing about herself. She's a loner and closed off from most of the colonists.

"Astrid, hello. How are you today?" Often greeted with a frown, he remained congenial.

"Oh, hi, Rafe. I'm working with these herbs today. They weren't growing as well as I had hoped initially, but they have perked up lately. The new fertilizer batch I made had the perfect nitrogen mix."

"I hear the greenhouses are abundant and doing well. You've

been doing a great job with all the different crops. Are you having a hard time growing certain plants?" He tried not to touch the sage plants. Astrid had made abundantly clear that he could look but never touch her plants.

"They're all hard to grow, Rafe! Working in a greenhouse and hydroponic gardens is a lot of hard work. Not to mention that I'm in charge of everything around here. Keeping track of the growth requirements to sustain every type of vegetable, grain, and fruit is the work of three people, and I have to do everything myself!" Astrid huffed as she moved to the parsley and began taking height measurements.

Why is that silver droid on standby? "Everyone values all your hard work. I'm walking through the greenhouses, doing my daily rounds. How have the droid updates been performing?"

"Droid programs aim for maximum efficiency, but mostly, they just get in the way. Working with plants sets humans apart from them. I don't like them touching my herbs and more delicate plants; it's too hard to monitor all of them. I need about ten more people working here. Have you heard anything about Phil? I heard he was in the infirmary, but I haven't seen him. And how is Adira?" Astrid's frown deepened.

"I'll be going over to the infirmary soon. I will let you know if I hear anything about him." Rafe continued walking as he observed the plants and people working. "Let me know if you need anything."

I can't wait to escape this draining, energy-sapping negativity. Living and nurturing plants create such a vibrant, enjoyable environment. I hope Astrid finds some comfort and joy in her gardens. She inquired about Phil and Adira, an intriguing development worth noting. Now, onto the infirmary. He accessed his BAI to set a reminder to investigate Astrid's background and movements throughout the dome further.

Rafe entered the infirmary and couldn't believe what he saw. Glass doors sealed off half of the Medbay, enclosing the patients in complete isolation. Behind the glass, he saw Adira and David examining one of the patients' progress. He could see Phil's face inside one of the stasis pods. A white droid stood next to Phil's head, disinfecting the walls and floors of the pod areas.

Adira, I had no idea the isolation was so extensive. Rafe sent it via his BAI.

Phil was the initial one to contract the syndrome. His symptoms escalated, and we could not stabilize him, so we placed him in the stasis pod. Seven other colonists have identical symptoms. Adira sent back.

Are you and the rest of the clinical team safe from the syndrome yourselves? He sent.

Our nanoparticles and BAI enhancements have protected us from the pathogen causing the outbreak. However, we don't have a definitive cause yet. We've been working night and day to find answers, but the etiologic agent remains elusive. Adira sent.

During your rounding, if someone tells you they have a sore throat, ask them to come to the infirmary immediately. Our announcement was made yesterday, but people tend to procrastinate, thinking they will be better in the morning. Don't put this off. Adira exchanged a meaningful glance with Rafe.

I'm returning to the security desk to review surveillance data, images, and videos. Jomei has not alerted me to any unusual activity today. However, I still say we should also install more security protocols in the caves. He sent.

Eurydice disagrees, and she's the one in charge. She does not have the BAI, so she remains uncompromised under all conditions. She also has limited nanoparticles—actually, none. Those caves and what they contain are more precious than anyone can imagine. It appears SIS22 wants to keep the findings in the caves private. Adira consulted with David after he asked her a question.

Rafe continued his rounding through the cavernous atrium next. The flattened geodesic glass dome showed daylight and clear skies high above. The dome kept the ferocious winds at bay like they weren't there.

The atrium emulated a park-like setting with benches, picnic tables, trees, and flowers, all brought from Earth. Colonists enjoyed their free time in this tranquil setting. Some read in their notebooks; others gathered in small groups to chat and laugh.

There is a warm sense of community here. The atrium and dining hall have made Galatéa homey. They don't know what SIS22 found in the caves or the threat against the colony, including the outbreak. Ignorance is bliss sometimes.

He entered the security office and studied numerous monitors. Each one displayed a view of its immediate surroundings. Since monitors provided the necessary visuals, he could avoid personal rounds. However, he learned much more from individual interactions, including nonverbal cues and body language.

Hello, Jomei. How are systems operating today? Rafe sent silently to the AI.

Except for the Medbay, all systems, including the dome environmental systems, are functioning within normal limits. Current tests for air, water, and wastewater show negative results for pathogens and toxins. The nano-sniffers have not detected any electrical signatures of physical or chemical weapons. Jomei sent.

We appear to have an outbreak situation. Theories?

No causative agents have surfaced. Eight patients in the infirmary exhibit an unusual syndrome which defies recognizable disease patterns currently. Statistically, the preliminary diagnosis of encephalitis is the closest pattern recognizable, but the causative agent has yet to be identified. Jomei sent.

The patients afflicted are in isolation. What's the likelihood of it spreading?

No person-to-person spread is evident. In theory, it most likely started with the release of an airborne pathogen. It is logical to assume that someone targeted the victims somehow. Statistically, the highest probability lies with an airborne route and targeted victims since it has not spread further up to this point. Jomei sent.

Are there any biometric anomalies?

Nothing out of the ordinary. All within two standard deviations.

Maintain surveillance of biometric data indicative of mental illness. Also, run an interaction profile between Astrid Greig and Phil Roskos and note any distinctive patterns.

Rafe needed downtime after meeting with the security staff and briefing them on the potential outbreak.

Movie night turned out to be exactly what Rafe needed. Rasa greeted him with a cheerful welcome and a smile. She had saved him a seat beside her and had popcorn ready. Most of the colonists who weren't on their shifts were there, but Rafe didn't see Adira or David.

I most certainly do not expect to see Eurydice.

Tonight's entertainment was a comedy. Rafe, Rasa, and the rest of the audience laughed out loud. It was a thoroughly enjoyable evening.

Yes, the colonists have created a friendly community. It's too bad that there's a questionable player or two among them.

11 - Outbreak!

David moved through the sterile, echoing rooms of the infirmary, his mind consumed by a swirling storm of doubts. His footsteps were heavy, mirroring the weight of responsibility he felt toward the colony's infected patients. Adira, by his side, glanced at him with concern. Beneath her composed exterior, she, too, felt the growing strain of an outbreak without answers. David had been working with Adira and several other infirmary clinicians assigned only to the outbreak patients and their ongoing care.

I've tried every known therapy, but Phil is not responding. He's not comatose; he seems to be in a deep sleep, yet we can't wake him up.

Violet Yardley was supervising the day-to-day activities of the patients coming to the infirmary who did not meet the case definition of the outbreak. Other than minor injuries, like cuts from a kitchen knife or scrapes sustained by greenhouse staff, the milieu of the general infirmary population was quiet.

Since there is no person-to-person spread, can we take down the glass barriers soon? Violet sent as she wrapped a greenhouse worker's twisted ankle.

Until we have an etiologic agent, I'm uncomfortable with removing the isolation barriers. You're probably right. They are unnecessary, but erring on the side of safety remains appropriate. David sent as he looked up from his notebook screen. He was painfully aware of time passing with no solutions in sight.

He walked over to Phil Roskos's stasis pod, whose face was visible. It looked like Phil was sleeping.

David's frustration was building. *He looks peaceful. His body has formed autoantibodies in his basal ganglia. What sort of agent would cause this reaction? According to Eurydice's report, Galkin's H5N1 genetically modified virus attacks the basal ganglia. We have not isolated any virus or any other agent, for that matter. Yet someone released something into the environment, but who did it, when, and how? Ugh, there are more questions than answers.*

"David, are you hungry? What do you think about going to the galley? It's dinner time." Adira rubbed her eyes.

"That's the best idea I've heard all day. Violet, can you handle the Medbay while we're at dinner?" David perked up at the thought of a distraction.

"It's not a problem. Take your time. You deserve some time to yourselves." Violet finished wrapping the ankle and giving the patient self-care instructions.

David and Adira set out for the galley. As they walked through the halls, many concerned colonists greeted them. They reassured them that they were working on a cure and that the outbreak seemed to have stopped with the nine patients.

I wish we had more answers for them at this point. Phil's status has gone from bad to worse. He's in critical condition now. David sent it to Adira.

Agreed. This has been one of the most frustrating outbreaks I've ever worked on. Our tentative diagnosis of encephalitis does not explain all the symptoms. Even with its vast database and environmental monitoring, the AI has no suggestions about the cause or diagnosis. Adira sent back.

We have no leads on who released whatever agent or even how or when it was released into the environment. Yes, it's frustrating.

They carried their dinner trays and sat at a table for two.

They concentrated on their delicious food for a moment.

"Rasa's menus have been exemplary. The greenhouses are doing well." David buttered a slice of homemade whole wheat bread and took a bite of his garden salad. "Mm, everything is so fresh. I didn't realize I was so hungry."

"I wanted to ask you if you've heard any reports about the strange luminescence I witnessed while alone in the caves the other day. No one else has ever even mentioned they saw it." Adira asked between mouthfuls of vegetable soup. "You're right. This is a great dinner."

"No. I haven't heard a single word about the luminescence. There have been no other reports, and nobody else seems to have noticed them. Eurydice does not want any nanosensors in the caves for obvious reasons. So, there is no AI presence in the tunnels, caverns, or grand halls. This doesn't help with dome environmental monitoring in its entirety and getting to the cause. Also, what if the agent causing the outbreak came from the caves themselves? Even though we suit up and go through decontam on the way back, could something still be able to infiltrate into the dome?" David had moved on to his blueberry pie and coffee. "That's an enormous gap in our ability to find the agent. Eurydice is aware."

"Between working with the patients in the isolation ward and hunting down the cause of the outbreak, we have had little time to think about anything else. If we can't get the nanosensors down into the caves, maybe we should visit them ourselves. I would appreciate your input as to what the luminescence could be." Adira sipped her coffee.

"Agreed. Shall we go now while we have a moment?"

They suited up and were ready to enter the cave where Adira saw the luminescence. As the chugging elevator slowly descended, Adira thought about what she had seen and what it could be.

David sent. *It is odd that no other person has reported seeing anything. However, bringing a luminescent sample to the infirmary is out of the question mainly because the outbreak may have originated from these caves.*

Adira nodded in agreement, "When I was down here alone, there was a power failure. I was in complete darkness, and it took a while for my eyes to adjust to the blackness. Only then was I able to see the glowing. David, it was so beautiful. There were shades of aqua, turquoise, gold, and magenta. The glowing seemed to grow in intensity just before the power was restored. Once the lighting was back, the glowing disappeared." She adjusted her breathing apparatus.

The elevator stopped, and David opened the gate. They stepped into the cave.

"These lava tubes are formidable. The grand halls are so immense. It's unbelievable that there are thirteen of them for SIS22 and the archeologists to explore." David directed his wrist illuminator to the opposite wall and headed toward the further end of the lava tube.

Adira followed and observed the cave floor and walls as she passed them. "This place is so dry and desolate. It's been this way for millennia. It's hard to believe anything could survive down here. Do you have any theories as to what the luminescence could be?"

"I know that bioluminescent organisms on Earth have peak glowing times. It's cyclical in nature. This is what the glow worms of New Zealand exhibit." David had walked across the floor of the lava tube and inspected the walls and ceiling. "I don't see anything but dust and rocks right now."

"I could only see the luminescence when the cave was pitch black. Do you think we should try to recreate the pitch-black conditions and see what happens?"

David and Adira walked back to the elevator and turned off the power. They lit their wrist illuminators and walked to the middle of the lava tube before extinguishing them.

Minutes passed, and nothing happened.

I see nothing, do you? David sent.

Not a darn thing. I can't even see my hand in front of my face. It's so black down here. Let's wait a few more minutes and see if our eyes need more time to adjust. Adira tried not to think about the dust, her breathing apparatus, and the surrounding darkness.

After ten more long minutes, David lit his wrist illuminator. "Don't see anything at all this time. We can return, maybe at the same time of day you were here when you saw the glowing. See if there is a pattern or cycle." He walked back to the elevator and turned the power back on.

"Darn. Thought we might see something today. I think I'll stay here a little longer and walk through the tubes myself. I'll meet you back at the infirmary in a few minutes." Adira turned back to the interior of the lava tube as David began his ascent to the dome.

David went back to his quarters. *Most people would say my quarters are sparse and I'm a spartan, but there is comfort in order.* He enjoyed his personal space. Everything was orderly and neat, arranged how he liked his things.

He silently addressed Jomei. *Jomei, can you update me on your outbreak analysis?*

Jomei instantly responded, *David, as you know, I have applied known algorithms to the spread and onset of this outbreak to various data sets, including the biometric health records, genomic data, and social interactions of the eight patients as well as all other colonists who have not been infected. The underlying phenomena are very complex. Factors include the transmission of infectious diseases, long incubation periods, applying historical data, and current conditions here in the dome.*

Can we draw any theories or assumptions from what is now known? David interjected.

The afflicted colonists have a few commonalities. One is the fact that none of them received the nanoparticles. Seven of them were original colonists, with Phil Roskos being the eighth, who had to have his nanoparticles removed while still on the Porta Caeli. Otherwise, there are five males and four females; gender does not appear to be a factor. Their quarters were in different parts of the dome and on various levels. They did not work in the same areas. Two worked in environmental security, two in dietary, two in the greenhouses, one in engineering controls, and one in security. The reasons why the outbreak halted at seven patients are also unclear.

Cluster analysis has been used to identify hotspots. Jomei is continually searching for locations of statistical significance. Pinpointing the areas of geospatial clusters is vital as the whereabouts of disease outbreaks can often provide clues about their cause. Such a small sample size adds to predictive limitations. Rafe and I have deployed algorithms, including decision trees, random forests, support vector engines, and deep-learning networks. The goal is to establish a space-time pattern analysis to identify data points in a space-time cube and characterize trends as new, intensifying, or diminishing hotspots.

David found it intriguing. *I want a predictive model specifying the likelihood of an individual contracting this syndrome based on their characteristics and behaviors. That would be ideal. I understand the sample size is small, with only seven patients. But we can learn a lot from the 102 colonists who did not have it.*

Rafe has programmed a system to generate automatic red flags on a grid to enable rapid identification and response, improve isolation protocols and medical interventions, and reduce time containing the outbreak. These red flags are based on spatial pattern recognition, cluster analysis, and space-time pattern analysis. The automated generation of red flags is now part of my sub-routine design. Spatial pattern recognition evaluates the data points and determines whether the data points are clustered or randomly distributed.

I feel that too much time has gone by without answers. The patients with the syndrome are in declining health. Phil Roskos remains in stasis, and I fear the rest will soon follow. They continue to worsen, and as they go into critical condition, we will have to place them in the stasis pods and continue to work on diagnosis and treatment plans. Jomei, notify me with even the most minute or insignificant results or data. I'm afraid time may run out for my patients. David rose from his desk to return to the infirmary.

David sighed. *So, we're back to square one.*

Not entirely. We've pinpointed hotspots of potential relevance, but without more data, conclusions remain elusive."

David clenched his fists. *Time's running out.*

He passed through the atrium on his way back to the infirmary. The picnic and grassy areas were scattered with small groups of colonists. He could hear occasional laughter. One group sang along with Rafe's guitar accompaniment while others played Rizika. He looked up at the glass-domed ceiling forty feet above. He could see reddish sunlight outside and clear skies. Somehow, after he had visualized the outside of the dome and experienced the joyful atmosphere of the colonists in the atrium, he had a sense of calm. He steeled himself to persevere.

We will find a cure. All of them will survive.

David entered the infirmary. Violet remained at her

workstation, going over her patient's documentation. He began pacing back and forth and shared his thoughts with her.

"Time is of the essence, and I'm acutely aware that we're running out of it to save our patients suffering from this encephalitis or whatever it is. The urgency of this situation weighs heavily on me. We must act swiftly and decisively to provide them the best possible chance of recovery."

Violet turned sympathetic brown eyes toward David. "I understand your concern, and I share it. The patients are deteriorating rapidly, and we're exhausting all available treatment options. Is there anything else we can do or explore to maximize their chances of survival?"

David rubbed his eyes. "We've been following established treatment protocols, but they haven't yielded the desired results. We need to consider alternative approaches or experimental therapies that may offer a glimmer of hope. I'll continue to consult the latest research and explore any potential breakthroughs or promising treatments that could help our patients."

"That's a good idea, David. Collaboration and seeking insights from anecdotal reports could provide us with additional perspectives and potential solutions. Every moment counts, and we need to leverage every available resource to save our patients."

"Agreed. While the risks associated with experimental treatments are considerable, our patients are in critical condition, and we must weigh those risks against the potential benefits. I'll also review any relevant clinical trials or experimental therapies in the database that might show promise in treating encephalitis. I'll ensure that we consider all necessary ethical considerations."

"I'll assist you in gathering the relevant information and exploring potential treatment options. We can't give up hope, and we must exhaust every possibility. Our patients and their families count on us to do everything we can to save them."

"Thank you for your unwavering support, Violet. Together, we'll explore all avenues and push the boundaries of medical knowledge to give our patients the fighting chance they deserve. It won't be easy, but we must remain focused, determined, and resilient. The lives of these patients are in our hands, and we won't rest until we've exhausted every option available to us."

David and Violet turned back to their notebooks to pursue their work. They worked and explored alternative treatments, experimental therapies, and potential breakthroughs.

Time may be running out, but the team's unwavering commitment and relentless pursuit of solutions give me hope that those affected by encephalitis will recover.

David's frustration once again mounted. "This outbreak on an alien planet is pushing me to my limits! Every day, we're struggling to diagnose the cause of the outbreak. Our lack of familiarity with alien pathogens and limited resources makes this situation even more challenging."

Violet placed a warm hand on David's arm. "I understand your frustration, David. The circumstances are far from ideal, and we deal with unknown territory. But we can't lose hope."

"I know, Violet, but not having the tools and information to treat our patients is frustrating. We're working blindfolded here, trying to make empirical medical decisions based on educated guesses and hoping for the best. I wish we had more support, resources, and a better understanding of Galatéan biology.

"I share your sentiments, David. It's disheartening to see so many lives at stake and feel limited in our ability to help them. But we must remember we are here because our work is the best chance these patients have. Our expertise can still make a significant difference even in the face of unfamiliar challenges."

"You're right, Violet. We have to stay focused and adapt to this unprecedented situation. I must accept that our only recourse is to continue learning as we go, adjust our strategies, and collaborate with the clinical team and Jomei to gather more information."

"Absolutely, David. We must keep searching for answers, exploring different approaches, and documenting our findings. Our experiences on this alien planet could provide valuable insights for future outbreaks or medical emergencies. We are pioneers, in a sense, paving the way for future healthcare professionals in similar situations."

"Medical pioneers, eh? Violet, you always help me see the bigger picture. Our efforts here might contribute to advancing interstellar medicine, benefiting not only these patients but countless others in the future. I can't let frustration overshadow our purpose."

"Together, we'll navigate these uncharted waters, using our skills, knowledge, and determination to make a difference. We might face setbacks and challenges, but with every patient we save and every bit of progress we make, we bring hope to this alien planet and its colonists."

As David acknowledged his frustration to Violet, he found renewed determination to overcome the obstacles they faced on the alien planet. Their shared commitment to their patients and the potential long-term impact of their work fueled his resolve to find solutions and provide the best care possible.

12 - A Light in the Dark

As Adira cautiously ventured deeper into the alien cave system, the air grew cool and damp, with a hint of mystery. Her head and wrist lamps cast a feeble beam of light, revealing the rocky terrain that seemed to hold secrets within its ancient crevices. Her heart raced, and she breathed short, quick breaths as excitement and anticipation coursed through her veins.

I wonder what wonders await me in this unexplored realm.

The silence enveloped her with each step, broken only by the faint sound of dripping water echoing in the distance. Now far deeper into the cave than she had ever been, the walls glistened with moisture, adding an ethereal shimmer to the surroundings. Then, as if something in the environment sensed her curiosity, she discerned a gentle breeze brushing against her faceplate and detected an otherworldly scent. She extinguished her lamps, which threw her into complete darkness.

Minutes passed.

And then, it happened again—a captivating display of radiant luminescence burst forth, illuminating the cavernous expanse. Small, phosphorescent patches adorned the walls, ceiling, and floor, creating a breathtaking spectacle of light. They emitted a mesmerizing glow, casting hues of blues, greens, and purples, painting the cave in an otherworldly extraterrestrial palette.

Could those patches be living organisms?

It was as if the very essence of life had taken physical form and transformed the darkness into a vibrant, living canvas. The alien luminescent 'creatures' vibrated with a rhythmic cadence, harmonizing with the pulsating energy of the universe. The cave seemed to come alive, telling a silent tale of its existence through this luminous dance.

She stood there, awestruck and humbled, as the beauty of this alien luminescence enveloped her in a far more dramatic display this time. The cave walls, adorned with stalactites and stalagmites, had taken on an otherworldly aura. Their shadows interacted with the glowing organisms, casting an intricate tapestry of light and shadow. Each delicate organism emitted its unique light pattern, creating a symphony of radiant melodies.

With a gloved hand, she reached out, entranced by the spectacle before her. Her fingers brushed against the cool, damp rock. The bioluminescent organisms reacted. Their light intensified and spread as if acknowledging her presence. At that moment, she realized that she was witnessing something truly remarkable.

This is an extraordinary connection—an encounter between two worlds, bridged by the magic of light....

This bioluminescent display, crafted by nature on an alien planet, transcended words and defied the boundaries of her imagination. It was a glimpse into the infinite possibilities of the universe.

.... Reminding me that even in the most unfamiliar and remote corners of space, beauty and wonder can be found, awaiting all with the courage to explore.

Her commlink buzzed, and she jumped at the unexpected sound.

"Adira? This is Gint. We need you in cave one. It's a medical emergency." Gint's voice sounded flat.

"On my way." Adira reluctantly turned her headlamp on and retreated to the cave's opening. She would have to take a circuitous route to cave one and the hidden space station.

###

Adira arrived at the space station almost twenty minutes later. Gint had called her to examine Rachel, a young woman, due to worsening symptoms. She entered Rachel's quarters and found her seated at a small desk. She was visibly distressed, with a flushed face and a look of concern in her eyes.

Adira reviewed her medical records in the notebook Gint handed her. She dreaded that Rachel might contract encephalitis.

Adira approached Rachel with a calming demeanor. "Hello, Rachel. Tell me how you are feeling."

Rachel described her symptoms in a quiet voice with long pauses. "I first noticed I had a headache a couple of days ago—I think I've had a fever too…. very tired all the time. I'm confused…. It's weird. I know I'm confused…. but I can't clear my mind to make sense of what I'm seeing sometimes."

She hasn't mentioned a sore throat yet. Although the symptoms of many viral illnesses are the same, this is suspicious for the early stages of encephalitis.

Adira began her physical assessment and asked Rachel about her medical history, previous illnesses, and potential exposure to infectious diseases.

She does not have a BAI implant or nanoparticles. Is that a coincidence? Yet, so far, it fits the case definition.

She gathered this crucial information in a stiff, unemotional way.

Maintain your professionalism, Adira. Your bedside manner must be supportive and non-judgmental.

Next, Adira proceeded with a comprehensive physical examination. She checked Rachel's vital signs, including her temperature, pulse rate, and blood pressure. She meticulously examined her neurological functions, assessing her reflexes, coordination, and sensory responses. Adira also conducted a detailed examination of her cranial nerves and looked for abnormalities that could provide additional diagnostic clues.

Based on her findings, she considered the possibility of encephalitis. "Gint, it's necessary to transfer Rachel to the infirmary for further testing. She loosely fits the case definition of the outbreak. I don't need to emphasize the importance of timely diagnosis and treatment to prevent potential complications."

Gint just nodded his acceptance but said nothing.

Adira was concerned by Rachel's lifeless reaction. "Rachel, you need more testing, such as blood work, cerebrospinal fluid analysis, and potentially imaging studies such as brain imaging scans. Do you have any questions or concerns before you are taken to the infirmary?"

No reaction.

"Do you have a preliminary diagnosis at this point?" Gint asked.

She explained the potential causes of encephalitis, including viral, bacterial, or autoimmune factors. "Be assured that our medical team is doing everything possible to facilitate everyone's recovery."

Gint grabbed Adira by her elbow. "After the team has taken Rachel to the infirmary, I wondered if I might have a moment to talk to you?"

"Of course. We will do everything we can to make sure Rachel recovers."

"Addie, I need to talk to you. It's not about Rachel's illness. I apologize for my actions and know I've hurt you deeply. I am truly sorry for what I've done, and I hope you can find it in your heart to forgive me."

"It's difficult for me to hear these words. How long have you and Rachel been together? Never mind. It doesn't matter. Your apology feels lacking and insincere. Your actions have caused immense pain and broken our trust. What led you to betray our relationship?"

Gint ran his fingers through his long, messy hair. "I understand that my apology may seem inadequate, and I can't justify my actions. There were no valid reasons for what I did. I made a terrible mistake and take full responsibility for my choices." He became fidgety and wouldn't look at Adira. "I was selfish and thoughtless, and I deeply regret the hurt I've caused you and our relationship."

"It's important for you to understand that trust may never be rebuilt or repaired. Your apology needs to be more than just words. Have you reflected on the impact of your actions?"

Now I feel more like his mother than his wife! Was it always like this?

"Yes, I have been reflecting on the consequences of my actions and the pain I've caused. I realize that rebuilding trust will require more than just an apology. I will do whatever it takes to make amends and earn back your trust. I am fully committed to making the necessary changes. I understand that it will be a difficult journey, but I love you and value our relationship. I will do everything I can to regain your trust, including being open and honest about my actions and consistently demonstrating my commitment to our marriage."

"You want to re-commit to our marriage? Does Rachel know about this?"

"I was about to break things off when she suddenly became ill."

The minute Rachel shows weakness, he wants out. Typical.

"Acknowledging the gravity of the situation and expressing

your willingness to work towards rebuilding my trust is some progress, I guess. We have a long road ahead of us on Galatéa, and there are no guarantees of survival. But our marriage is over.

Phew! There. I said it to his face.

"Moving forward will require open communication, honesty, and a genuine effort from both of us. Let's take some time to think things through and consider our next steps for the good of the colony and the fantastic findings here in these caves. Ultimately, moving forward responsibly rests on both of our shoulders."

"Addie, I truly regret what I've done, and I'm prepared to do the necessary work to rebuild what was broken."

"Let's take some time to think things through and consider our next steps."

Adira decided to seek Zhopla in Cave Twelve's private inner sanctum. She found him standing outside the entrance to his chambers as if he knew she was coming and was waiting for her.

"It's so good to see you, Brother Zhopla. I want to discuss a personal matter if you can spare a moment.

"Welcome, Adira. I'm glad you came. Come in and have a seat. Would you like a cup of herbal tea?"

"Yes, some tea is very welcome right now."

Zhopla bustled about, boiling water and measuring loose tea leaves. "That Astrid has produced a fine crop of various herbs perfect for brewing." Zhopla smiled as he poured hot water over the leaves and handed Adira a cup.

"What seems to be troubling you, my dear?"

"I've been struggling with many negative thoughts lately, and despite having various tools at my disposal, I don't seem to be able to banish them." Adira looked down.

"Negative thinking patterns can be very challenging. Can you tell me more about what's been troubling you?"

"I just feel overwhelmed by negative thoughts about myself, the outbreak patients, my spiritual growth, and our future here on Galatéa. It feels like no matter what I do, I can't escape them."

"I see. Acknowledging these thoughts and understanding that they don't define you is important. Are you willing to embark upon an Institute exercise earlier than most, as you have progressed far beyond your peers?"

"Yes, if you recommend it. What is this exercise?"

"It is a writing practice where you take some time to observe and write down your thoughts. This helps you identify recurring negative patterns and understand their origins. Once you see these patterns clearly, you can challenge and change them. All those practicing Institute spiritual exercises must continue this exercise during their second year."

"How should I begin?"

"Begin by setting aside some quiet time each day. Sit comfortably and let your mind wander. Whenever a thought arises, please write it down without judgment. After a few days, review what you've written. Look for common themes and triggers."

"That sounds simple enough. What should I do after identifying these patterns?"

"Learn to notice when your thinking and speculating takes you out of the immediacy of your experience. Adira, your mental capacities are an extraordinary gift. But they can also become a trap if you retreat from contact with yourself and others. Stay connected with your physicality. So, I also prescribe physical exercise to boost your mood and reduce negative thoughts.

"Once you recognize the patterns, ask yourself if these thoughts are based on reality or assumptions. Challenge them with questions like, 'Is this thought true?' and 'What evidence do I have for and against this thought?' Replace negative thoughts with prayer, positive substitutions, and realistic perspectives."

"It sounds like a lot of work, but I can see how it might help. Thank you, Brother Zhopla. I feel these exercises will help, and I can incorporate them into my daily spiritual practices."

"Remember, Adira, it's a journey. Be patient and compassionate with yourself. Negative thoughts can be persistent, but you can cultivate a more positive and peaceful mind with practice."

"I'll begin these Institute exercises first thing tomorrow morning. I think most clearly in the morning. Thank you for your guidance, Brother Zhopla."

"Now, you can find a method to discern alternative, more balanced thoughts. This new method of thought processing will aid you in considering all of the evidence, both positive and negative, and give you a choice to direct your thoughts wisely. You are welcome, Adira. May you find peace and clarity on your journey."

Zhopla went back to taking inventory of the types of tea leaves Astrid had given him. As she walked back to the Atrium, Adira heard him muttering things like, 'This one is good for meditation,' 'This one is good for sleep,' and 'This one enhances positivity.' *I'm sure that at some point, we can all use some of each one of those teas. I should ask Astrid about some of them.*

13 - The Waters of Life

Eurydice's thick voice came through on Rafe's commlink. "Rafe, it's time for the colony AI to update the outbreak situation to the general colony population."

"Acknowledged."

Rafe accessed the general information network monitors in strategic sites throughout the dome. He began the announcement.

"Attention residents of Galatéa. This is Rafe Silvers, the director of security, with a special announcement. The security team and the artificial intelligence, who now calls himself Jomei, have been tasked with identifying the source of an outbreak. Equipped with advanced monitoring capabilities, we began our investigation by analyzing available data and conducting environmental scans. Jomei will describe our operations up to this point."

Jomei's clear, mellifluous voice began. "This is Jomei, the AI overseeing the colony's operations. We have detected an outbreak within the colony and have initiated an ongoing investigation. My primary objective is identifying the source and taking necessary measures to contain and eradicate the outbreak. I urge all residents to remain calm and cooperate during this process.

"We have initiated a comprehensive analysis of the colony's systems, including life support, waste management, and environmental controls. We monitor various data streams, focusing on patterns and abnormalities that may indicate the outbreak's origin.

"Initial data analysis shows a spike in reported cases within a specific colony sector. The outbreak may have originated in this area. I will continue to conduct further investigations to determine the cause and implement appropriate measures."

Rafe monitored the Atrium monitors where colonists had gathered to hear the announcement. *By their casual demeanor, they appear calm and interested.*

"Based on the collected data, it is likely that the outbreak is a result of multiple contributing factors. We are narrowing down potential sources, including the air filtration systems and water supply. Additionally, we are analyzing data on recent external interactions, such as shipments or personnel arrivals, to determine if any infectious agents were introduced from external sources."

Rafe interjected at this point. "We have cross-referenced medical records, environmental sensor readings, and resident activity logs to pinpoint potential sources of contamination or infection. We identified several factors that could contribute to the outbreak, such as compromised air filtration systems, contaminated water sources, or possible introduction of infectious agents by unknown planetary factors.

"We continue to monitor and analyze the situation, gathering additional data to validate initial findings and narrow the list of potential sources. In the meantime, our medical team has taken precautionary measures to stop the outbreak, such as isolating affected areas, intensifying sanitation protocols, and increasing medical support for those affected.

"The medical team has implemented further measures to minimize the outbreak's spread, including quarantine procedures and enhanced sterilization protocols. Efforts are underway to identify the specific pathogen or contaminant responsible for the outbreak. The security team and Jomei continually collaborate with our expert medical personnel to expedite the investigation and find a swift resolution.

"Once again, we urge all residents to remain calm and cooperate during this process."

Rafe ended the communication, disconnected the communication link, and sat down. "Jomei, do you have an update today?"

"The analysis is ongoing, and I am closing in on the outbreak's source. Preliminary data suggests that a combination of factors, including compromised air filtration and external contamination, may have contributed to the spread. However, a conclusive determination requires further investigation. I will continue to work diligently to resolve this issue and ensure the well-being of all residents.

We have been systematic in our approach to finding the source. I'm determined to find the culprit behind this outbreak and restore the colony to a safe and healthy environment.

"Jomei, your efforts and collaboration with our medical professionals and residents contributed to a thorough investigation and effective outbreak containment. Carry on."

Rafe looked at the activities that were going on with various viewing screens from cameras positioned in the common areas as colonists were leaving after the announcement. The dining room and multiple halls all showed colonists going about their business as usual. Silver droids zipped along the passageways on their way to their programmed worksites. He didn't think there would be any panic, but one never knew for certain.

Quiet for now. Good.

It was time for Rafe to continue his Institute training with Zhopla in the spiritual disciplines he had promised to complete in return for having received a permanent cure for his Kloud9 addiction. He suited up and descended to Zhopla's cave. He was one of the last to arrive and sat at the back of the cave. He looked at the colonists present and thought there were about forty of them—most of whom he knew by name. He noticed Adira was sitting with David towards the front of the cave.

Zhopla's dark eyes rested briefly on Rafe before surveying his audience. "To ensure the proper development of human capacities, we must align ourselves with nature and our higher power. To achieve this, we will commit to a regular practice of prayer and meditation to nurture our spiritual side, alongside work and recreation for our mental and physical well-being."

"To start our practices, we will divide our week into seven days, just as we did when we lived on Earth. Each day will focus on a specific spiritual concept for personal contemplation. In the morning, we will concentrate on the physical and intellectual facets of our humanity. In the evening, we will dedicate our reflections to our spiritual capacities. With practice over time, both aspects of development will be fully realized.

"There are prescribed contemplations at noon each day on the concept of peace. Every seventh Sabbath, known as the Great Sabbath, will be dedicated to Peace with the Heavenly Divinity.

"Similarly, on the ordinary Sabbath, Sunday mornings, we will not study spiritual aspects per se, but only of the contemplation of the Cosmic Divinity, who is the totality of all.

This is an overview of our expectations regarding how we will spend our days: in guided prayer, contemplation, and meditation. Next, I would like to discuss our purification rites.

"As you know, water is in all living things, physical and spiritual. Those without water are dead in both spheres. As it was on Earth, the water source here on Galatéa is the sea, and water is spread in a cycle: in rain, streams, and rivers. Water is found in all living things in the physical world, and we are surrounded by a sea of spiritual water here on this planet.

"A symbolic ceremony known as a water ritual will restore

your purity, especially those of you who have been cured of your addictions. A pool of natural rainwater from Galatéa is in this cave. It will be used for this purpose. Each of you shall undergo a ritual bath for spiritual cleansing. Males bathe on Day Four or each Wednesday, while women bathe on Day Five or Thursday. Since today is Day Four, I ask that all the males remain for the purification ceremony, and the women will return only on the morning of Day Five for their purification.

Rafe found himself in the heart of an alien planet, deep within the recesses of a hidden cave, where a shimmering pool of water beckoned. This was no ordinary pool, for it held the power of purification—he somehow sensed a mystical essence.

Some inhabitants of Earth revered the living waters and considered them sacred. Legend spoke of its ability to cleanse the physical body, spirit, and soul, offering a profound connection to the cosmic energies that permeated the world.

Rafe was born with an innate curiosity and a deep desire to explore the wonders of his extraordinary home. Guided by whispers of ancient tales, he willingly embarked on this solitary journey, unaware of where it might lead. The time had come to seek the legendary living waters within this alien cave.

With each step, the air grew cooler, and the silence deepened. The cave walls glistened with a strange luminescence, casting ethereal hues of blue and green. Rafe's heart raced with anticipation as he neared the mystical waters.

This is better than any Kloud9 experience I've ever had. And it's really happening.

As he reached the pool's edge, Rafe saw a breathtaking sight. The water shimmered like liquid stardust and emitted a sacred glow, illuminating the cave. He could feel its energy humming through the air, a pulsating force calling to his soul.

With reverence, Rafe removed his outer garments and stepped into the pool. The water embraced him, caressing his skin with a gentle warmth. He closed his eyes and allowed the sacred waters to envelop him entirely.

At that moment, he felt a profound transformation. The living waters purified his physical form and cleansed the burdens and doubts that weighed heavy on his heart. He felt a deep connection to the cosmic energies, as if he were reborn into a higher state.

Visions danced in his mind—memories of his ancestors, echoes of those who had come before him. He sensed their wisdom and the enduring spirit that flowed through his veins. Rafe understood that this purification was not merely a personal experience but a reaffirmation of his place within the tapestry of his people and Galatéa.

Emerging from the opposite end of the pool of living waters, Rafe felt renewed, as if he had shed the constraints of his old self. He donned the white hooded robes set out for him, carrying this transformative energy within him.

I feel I now have a new responsibility—to share the knowledge and power of the living waters with my people.

Soon, others followed in his footsteps, seeking their own purification and spiritual connection. Over time, the cave became a place of communal reverence, where Galatéans came to cleanse themselves, seek guidance, and find solace.

The living waters in the alien cave became a symbol of unity and renewal, a testament to the eternal cycle of life, death, and rebirth. Through the profound connection it offered, the Galatéan colonists discovered a deeper understanding of themselves and their place in the vast universe.

Rafe was moved. *This experience has forever changed me. I feel as if I am now a physical and spiritual guardian of the living waters, ensuring its waters remain pure and accessible to all who seek its transformative power.* Within him, the ancient legacy merged with the extraordinary wonders of their alien planet, creating a bond that transcended time and space.

Everyone was subdued and remained silent as they waited for Zhopla to resume. Rafe remained in his seat after the water purification ceremony. Towels were provided after the immersion and purification ritual. He was now robed in the symbolic white hooded cloak that extended to his bare feet. The cave was warm, and he was dazed after the experience.

Zhopla, now also robed in a hooded white garment, began. "On Earth, the result of ignorance of hygiene was disease and death. The same was true of spiritual ignorance, resulting in spiritual death or failure to develop what is necessary for life in the next world. Knowledge, or gnosis, is the means of overcoming both these conditions, which explains why so much emphasis is placed on the knowledge of our teachings.

"We must first learn the discipline of directing our *thinking* to only what is good. Next comes the discipline of *speaking* only about what is good. Finally, we shall know the discipline of *doing* only what is good.

"A thought is a predecessor to action. Correct thinking or training the mind in the pattern of the Law is the first step. When you have good thoughts, it will automatically drive out the bad ones so that you do not deviate from the Law and cause needless suffering. A person cannot think of two things at the same time. Therefore, the life of one is the death of the other.

"Tomorrow is Day Five. When you arise, you will complete your contemplation as assigned and proceed with your day's work addressing the physical portion. You are to meditate upon and contemplate the properties of water. After morning meditation, as you go about your work and activities, contemplate the physical properties of water, such as how it is formed and its necessity for life, and perhaps come to some conclusions about irrigation, medicine, and farming.

"After your noon contemplation on peace, the spiritual counterpart of water shall be considered. For example, the water of Eternal life, the revelation of God, and its effect on purification. This will make us a peaceful colony of healers, farmers, and teachers.

"Tomorrow evening, you will return for more instruction and time to discuss the things that came up during your meditation practices. For now, good evening, and until tomorrow." Zhopla turned and exited out of the back of the cave. Rafe thought he saw a woman's silhouette in the adjoining space before Zhopla closed the door.

Rafe was directed to return his white robes and don his protective cave gear again before exiting Zhopla's cave and returning to the dome.

14 - Critical Care

David's heart raced as he stepped into the infirmary. The air was thick with anticipation and the unknown. The original mission seemed simple: explore the uncharted planet, gather data, and search for signs of intelligent life. Now, nine patients fit the outbreak case description, the latest being Rachel.

I never dreamed that this mission would unravel a web of betrayal, from humanity's first discovery of intelligent aliens and magnificent artifacts to Gint's further betrayal of Adira. David took a deep breath as he recalled the previous week's events.

As they ventured deeper into the alien cave system, David's team stumbled upon a magnificent structure that seemed to pulsate with an otherworldly energy. Intrigued, they cautiously entered, only to be greeted by a scene that left David frozen in disbelief. There, amidst the alien artifacts, he saw Gint and Rachel locked in a passionate embrace.

Time seemed to stand still as David's mind raced to comprehend the betrayal before him. He was suspicious before, and now it was confirmed. The weight of his discovery threatened to crush him, but he knew he had to confront Gint. They had shared many SIS22 missions and trusted each other with their lives, but this infidelity completely shattered their bond.

With determination coursing through his veins, David steeled himself to face Gint without violence. He confronted him in a secluded corner of the alien structure, away from prying eyes and alien technologies. The air crackled with tension as their gazes locked. But Gint indicated that they should talk privately in his quarters.

Gint's quarters were tucked deep within the labyrinthine caves of Galatéa, situated on space station Aeris. The living space was modest and utilitarian, reflecting a research scientist's practical needs more than any sense of luxury or comfort. His quarters' dark, uneven surfaces made the room somewhat claustrophobic. The air was cool and carried a faint, earthy scent mixed with the sterile tang typical of space stations.

The quarters were dimly lit, with only a single functional light casting a weak, flickering glow over his workstation. Shadows loomed in the corners, and the light barely reached the ceiling, leaving much of the room in semi-darkness. The source of the light hung directly above Gint's cluttered desk.

The desk itself was a chaotic landscape of research materials. Piles of maps, charts, and graphs were haphazardly stacked, some spilling onto the floor. Alien symbols and complex equations were scrawled across many documents, evidencing Gint's intense work on the alien archaeology project. Various tools and instruments are essential for his research were scattered among the papers— magnifying glasses, calipers, and strange, otherworldly artifacts.

Bookshelves lined one wall, crammed with thick volumes and ancient texts; their spines cracked from frequent use. Here and there, peculiar relics from Galatéa's past were wedged between the books, adding to the cluttered yet fascinating ambiance. A small, outdated computer terminal sits at one corner of the desk, its screen filled with data and notes, further illuminating the space with a cold, bluish light.

The rest of the quarters were equally disheveled. A narrow, unmade bed covered with a simple blanket was pushed against one wall. Personal items are scattered around—a half-open mess kit, worn boots, and a jacket draped over a chair. A small kitchenette in another corner appeared barely used, with a few unopened food packets lying around.

Despite the disorder, David admitted that the quarters exuded a sense of dedicated purpose. This was a space where intellectual pursuit preceded personal comfort, and the quest for knowledge and discovery was paramount. Gint's living quarters, though messy and dim, were a testament to his relentless drive to uncover the secrets of Galatéa.

"Gint," David said, his voice tinged with hurt and anger. "How could you? How could you betray Adira like this?"

Gint's face paled, a mix of guilt and regret etched across his features. "David, I... I'm sorry," he stammered, his voice filled with remorse. "I never meant for things to go this far. It just... happened."

David's fists clenched involuntarily as he struggled to contain his emotions. "Happened? You know the sacrifices we've made, the risks we've taken together. And yet, you chose to throw it all away, you selfish and self-serving prick!"

Gint's voice grew louder as he tried to explain himself. "I know I've made a terrible mistake, David. I can't undo it, but I am truly sorry. Adira means the world to me, and I never wanted to hurt her."

"You should have thought about that before you acted," David snapped, his voice sharp with disappointment. "We're supposed to be a team, a family. And you've tarnished that trust forever."

David returned to the dome with a heavy heart, their tenuous bond shattered by the cruel revelation in the alien cave, now verified. He knew the consequences of Gint's personal and professional actions would have to be faced. He knew their lives would be complicated as they all carried the weight of betrayal and the heaviness of an uncertain future that awaited them.

David couldn't help but think about Adira as the moment's weight settled upon him. Under the clinical infirmary lights, he saw the situation more clearly. She had been their anchor, the driving force behind their many SIS22 missions together. He knew he had to face her as a true friend to discuss the painful truth. The fallout would be devastating, but the truth needed to be out in the open.

David perceived a change in Adira's demeanor. *Lately, there's a heaviness that seems to weigh her down. I'm growing concerned for her well-being. I think it's time to have that heart-to-heart conversation with her.*

One evening, after their shift at the hospital, David invited Adira to a quiet corner of the medical bay. The atmosphere was tense as he broached the subject gnawing at him.

"Adira," David began gently, "I've noticed something troubling you. You've been distant, preoccupied. Is everything okay?"

Adira sighed; her gaze was fixed on the ground.

"You're right, David. My heart has been aching with the burden of Gint being unfaithful and with Rachel of all people. The situation is even more complicated because Rachel is critically ill and being treated in our medical bay."

David listened attentively. *My heart aches for you, my dear friend.* He reached out, placing a comforting hand on Adira's shoulder. "I'm so sorry, Adira. I can only imagine how much this must hurt. You deserve so much better."

Tears welled in Adira's eyes as she nodded, her voice choked with emotion. "It's been a devastating blow, David. To find out that the person you love has betrayed you. It's shattered my trust and left me feeling lost."

David smiled sympathetically, assuring her that she wasn't alone. "You have a strong support system here, Adira. We're all here for you, me included. Lean on us when you need to."

Adira wiped away her tears and looked at David gratefully. "Thank you, David. Your friendship and support mean the world to me."

As they continued their conversation, Adira shared the complexity of her emotions. "Why does everything have to be so complicated? On the one hand, I am devastated by my husband's betrayal, but I feel as if I'm to blame for what's happened. But on the other hand, I can't help but feel a sense of empathy for Rachel, the woman who now lies critically ill. The situation has become tangled, blurring the lines between personal and professional."

David nodded understandingly, acknowledging the weight of the situation. "Adira, it's natural to feel conflicted. Your compassion for Rachel doesn't negate the pain caused by your husband's actions. It's okay to wrestle with these emotions."

Adira took a deep breath and considered David's words: "I need to find a way to separate my personal life from my professional responsibilities. Rachel deserves the best care we can provide, regardless of the circumstances."

David nodded in agreement, admiring Adira's strength and professionalism. "You're right, Adira. Our duty as physicians is to uphold the highest standards of care for all our patients, regardless of their background or personal connections."

They sat silently for a moment, the weight of the conversation lingering in the air. David squeezed Adira's hand gently, offering her a reassuring smile. "Remember, Adira. You're not alone in this. Lean on your friends and colleagues. Remember to prioritize your well-being. You're a remarkable physician and an extraordinary person."

Adira managed a small smile. "Thank you, David, for your unwavering support and friendship."

With encouragement, Adira will be determined to face the

challenges ahead in her personal life and in Rachel's care.

Together, they stood up. David was ready to confront whatever lay ahead, fortified by his friendship with Adira and their shared commitment to their patients.

The next day, Adira burst into the Medbay. "Where is David? I need to speak to him about something I've been working on."

Violet pointed to the line of stasis pods where David was working.

Filled with excitement, Adira began. "David, I've been formulating an imaging technique to capture the bioluminescence without bringing specimens from the caves to Medbay. Then I had a thought. With the help of Jomei, I've created a specialized camera capable of detecting even the faintest traces of luminescent activity. I was thinking about what Rachel may have been exposed to in the caves that the other outbreak patients were not exposed to. What if I could use this same imaging method to discern whether our patients have any luminescence to be found within the human anatomy, beginning with Rachel?"

David's eyebrows shot up. "Adira, you are among the most brilliant and innovative physicians I have ever met. You've always been captivated by the wonders of the human body. Did your insatiable curiosity drive you to explore this new avenue of medical research?"

"Yes, the other day, I was engrossed in a search through scientific journals in the medical archives for clues to the etiology of the outbreak when I stumbled upon literature discussing the fascinating phenomenon of bioluminescence in certain organisms. This phenomenon inspired me. I wondered if it could also exist within the human body.

"I designed a series of experiments, collected data in the caves, and analyzed the results. That's how I honed the specialized camera, making it capable of detecting even the faintest traces of bioluminescent activity."

David nodded. "I see where you're going with this. I'm sure you're eager to put your invention to the test and image one of our outbreak patients?"

Adira's eyes widened as she could barely contain her anticipation. "Yes, this is a groundbreaking journey of discovery. That's why I wanted your input on what I'm about to do. I should have taken images of Rachel because she lived in a cave, one away from the dome, where I first experienced luminescence. But I don't want to cross any ethical lines. What do you think?"

David looked at the nine stasis pods before him. "All of our patients have similar symptoms. The causative agent is baffling, along with a definitive diagnosis. I see no reason not to take this opportunity to combine your research with patient care."

Adira carefully positioned her newly developed camera and began capturing images of Rachel's body. As she reviewed the initial results, she couldn't believe her eyes. There, within Rachel's basal ganglia, a region deep within the brain, she detected faint glimmers of bioluminescence. Overwhelmed by this unexpected finding, she expanded the camera's field of view to capture more comprehensive images.

To her astonishment, the bioluminescence wasn't confined to Rachel's basal ganglia alone; it permeated her entire body, diffusing through her tissues and organs. Adira's heart raced with excitement. This discovery had profound implications for the colony and the understanding of the human body.

"David, I can't believe what we are witnessing. We can now say that the bioluminescence has biological properties. The intensity and distribution of the bioluminescence are unlike anything ever seen before. The images I've captured are spectacular. It's as if Rachel's body was illuminated from within.

These findings are perplexing. We will have to dig deeper for an explanation."

David meticulously analyzed Rachel's medical history and noticed a peculiar pattern. At the time Rachel was admitted to the Medbay, she claimed to have had strange encounters, hearing voices and other strange sounds. He wondered if there might be a connection. Driven by his curiosity, the more he researched, the more he found parallels between Rachel's medical history and the bioluminescence within her body.

As David worked to unravel the astonishing truth, he couldn't help but feel a mix of awe and trepidation. "Adira, I think I've concluded that the bioluminescence is a source of vitality for Rachel, sustaining her body and fighting the mysterious illness. It's almost as if a symbiotic relationship has formed. This discovery has transcended the boundaries of human understanding."

"I came to the same conclusion, David. With this newfound knowledge, can we find a way to harness the healing powers of the bioluminescence to heal our patients?"

"Unravelling the secrets of this alien-intertwined bioluminescence will require all our collective expertise. There are intricate mechanisms at play."

Together, they worked tirelessly to understand, and they discovered that the bioluminescent glow within Rachel's body contained a unique combination of healing properties and otherworldly energy. With time, their research expanded, uncovering new possibilities for medical advancements. Adira's pioneering imaging technique became instrumental in diagnosing and treating various illnesses, while the study of alien-intertwined bioluminescence opened doors to previously unimaginable realms of medicine.

Adira's research was not without its challenges. Violet

observed, "Skeptics and critics on the clinical team will question the validity of your findings. Others may fear the implications of intertwining human biology with extraterrestrial forces."

"On the other hand, this work may pave the way for a new era in medical research into optimal human health." Adira remained resolute.

"At this point, we are open to all possibilities to advance our understanding of healing the outbreak patients. We have the potential to revolutionize medicine. Your courage, determination, and unyielding curiosity may change Rachel's and the other patients' lives and spark a transformative shift in our understanding and treatment of human disease, bridging the gap between the unknown world of alien biology and the realm of human health." David added for support.

15 - Taika means Peace

Adira stood in the unfamiliar cave, clutching the map her long-lost mother had left her. Through Zhopla's hints and urgings, she finally put two and two together and realized that the map was of the cave system on Galatéa. She had followed its cryptic symbols and winding paths, leading her to this extraordinary place. The air crackled with otherworldly energy, and the cave shimmered with hues of purple and green.

As she ventured deeper into the alien cave system, Adira's heart pounded with a mix of excitement and trepidation. She couldn't shake the questions swirling in her mind.

Why did my mother disappear? Why did she leave me behind? And why, after all these years, did she send me this mysterious map?

Soon, she reached a large cavern where the map had guided her. Her eyes widened as she saw a figure silhouetted against the alien bioluminescence. It was her mother, a woman whose features mirrored her own—but the years had etched lines of sorrow and longing on her mother's face. They stood facing one another for a moment. Then came the hug, and tears of joy and sorrow flowed freely.

"Adira," her mother whispered, her voice filled with regret and hope. "I never wanted to leave you. The circumstances were beyond my control."

Adira's emotions surged, a blend of anger, confusion, and the desperate desire to understand. "Why? Why did you leave? Why did you disappear from my life?"

Her mother stepped forward, eyes shimmering with tears. "Adira, this planet, these aliens, hold the key to our existence.

They possess knowledge and wisdom beyond anything we can comprehend. I had to find them, had to learn from them. But I never stopped thinking about you, never stopped loving you."

Adira struggled to absorb the revelation. Her mother had sought out the alien planet to pursue knowledge and understanding. She left her daughter behind to embark on a quest transcending their ordinary lives.

"Why did you leave me this map, then?" Adira asked, her voice filled with curiosity and frustration.

Her mother smiled softly. "Because I knew you would find me, and deep down, that you are special, Adira. The aliens on this planet can awaken dormant powers within us. With their guidance, you will unlock your true potential."

Adira's gaze shifted to the surrounding environment. Strange lights pulsated with energy, and something emitted uncanny, ethereal, faint sounds in the distance. It was a world, unlike anything she had ever imagined.

As the weight of her mother's words sank in, Adira realized that this journey was about more than just their reunion. It was an opportunity to uncover the truth about herself, her lineage, and the interstellar mysteries that awaited her.

With newfound determination, Adira took her mother's outstretched hand. The map, once a symbol of her mother's absence, now represented the shared destiny that awaited them both—a journey of self-discovery, intergalactic wonders, and the bond between a mother and daughter transcending time and space.

Together, they stepped toward an archway, now deep inside the unexplored realms of the cavern system. Adira wasn't sure if she was ready to embrace the enigmatic world before them and the extraordinary beings that held the answers she sought. As they ventured deeper into the alien cave system, Adira couldn't help but feel a sense of belonging, knowing that her long-lost mother had finally found her way back.

Mother is leading me toward a destiny beyond my wildest dreams.

Safely enclosed in Zhopla's inner sanctuary, Zhopla, Taika, and Adira prepared to make contact with the bioluminescent aliens.

"Adira, I am the intermediary between the Veltryn and humans. I have a symbiote, which Zhopla implanted with my permission. I would have died had I not had the symbiote. There was no other choice." Taika's hazel eyes conveyed compassion and warmth. "They speak through me, and I will now allow them to come through me to converse with you."

Taika's eyes widened, and her back straightened as her Veltryn symbiont came through. "Greetings, Doctor Adira. My kind is known as the Veltryn. I am called Luminaris in your language. We are an ancient symbiotic species with advanced regenerative capabilities. Our symbiotes possess unique biochemical properties that allow us to interface with the human brain and stimulate neural regeneration. We understand your colony is experiencing an outbreak of encephalitis. This condition is characterized by inflammation in the brain, leading to various neurological symptoms. Our symbiote individuals can target the affected areas and promote healing at an accelerated rate."

Adira looked into her mother's eyes. "Good evening, Luminaris. I'm intrigued by your claim that the Veltryn can heal human patients with encephalitis. Can you explain how your symbiote can accomplish this?"

"Our symbiote secretes a complex array of bioactive compounds that can penetrate the blood-brain barrier. These compounds interact with neural tissue, activating dormant regenerative processes within the human brain. They enhance the production of neurotrophic factors, which support the growth and survival of individual neurons. Additionally, the symbiote's unique genetic makeup enables it to repair damaged neural connections, promoting the restoration of cognitive functions."

"Impressive and fascinating. Is there a way for David and the medical team to validate these healing abilities in humans with encephalitis?"

"Yes, Doctor. We have conducted our own extensive controlled simulations researching scenarios of healing humans with encephalitis. Our preliminary results have shown promising outcomes, with patients experiencing significant improvements in their neurological symptoms and overall cognitive function. These findings support our belief in the symbiote's potential to heal individuals suffering from this debilitating condition.

"The bioluminescence you have imaged in the critical patients is what keeps them alive and in a state of homeostasis but is not a cure. These are neuroactive compounds with limited healing abilities."

"That's remarkable. However, before we proceed further, I must ask about potential risks or side effects associated with the symbiote's intervention. It's crucial to ensure the well-being and safety of our patients."

"We understand your concerns, Doctor. While our research indicates a high level of safety, we acknowledge the need for careful consideration. The symbiote's interactions with the human brain are meticulously regulated, and each symbiote closely monitors the process to avoid any adverse effects. However, as with any medical intervention, there is always a degree of risk. We recommend moving forward slowly, one patient at a time, to gather more comprehensive data and evaluate potential side effects for the rest of the critical patients."

"I appreciate your cautious approach. Ethical considerations and patient safety are of utmost importance. If we were to collaborate, what would be the next steps in assessing the symbiote's healing potential for encephalitis?"

"The next step would involve David setting up a joint clinical team comprising specialists from your medical community and our symbiote intermediary. We would design rigorous protocols to investigate the symbiote's effects on encephalitis patients. This would involve careful symbiote selection for each patient, standardized treatment procedures, and monitoring short- and long-term outcomes. By collecting robust scientific data, we can more thoroughly evaluate the symbiote's efficacy and safety profile."

"Excellent. A collaborative approach with a solid scientific foundation is crucial for validating such groundbreaking claims. I will consult with David and Eurydice, among other colleagues, to explore further possibilities. Together, we can work towards unlocking new treatments and bringing hope to patients affected by encephalitis. Thank you for sharing this extraordinary knowledge with us."

"You're most welcome, Doctor. We look forward to the opportunity to work together to benefit those suffering from encephalitis. We believe in the power of collaboration and are eager to contribute our expertise to the human database to advance medical knowledge."

"I appreciate your willingness to share your knowledge, but I must admit that the concept of symbiotes coexisting inside a human body raises concerns regarding the autonomy and well-being of the individual involved. Could you explain why coexistence is necessary for your species?"

"Certainly, Doctor. Coexistence within a human body is not only necessary for our survival but also mutually beneficial. Our symbiotic relationship is based on a symbiote-host bond that has evolved over millions of years. By residing within a human host, we gain access to the necessary resources for sustenance, such as nutrients and protection from external threats. In return, we offer unique advantages to our hosts, including enhanced healing abilities, increased resistance to certain diseases, and potential neurological benefits."

"I understand the potential advantages, but how does this coexistence affect the individual's autonomy and personal identity? Isn't there a risk of the symbiote exerting control or interfering with the host's thoughts and actions?"

"We recognize the importance of personal autonomy and respect for the individual's identity. Our symbiotic relationship is not based on domination or control. Instead, it relies on a harmonious balance and cooperation. We have developed a sophisticated mechanism that allows us to communicate with the host and establish shared decision-making. This ensures the host retains complete control over their thoughts, actions, and identity. We view our role as facilitators, supporting the host's well-being and offering support and assistance when needed."

"That's reassuring to hear. Maintaining the host's agency and preserving their unique individuality is crucial. Could you provide more details about the communication process between the symbiote and the host?"

"Certainly, Doctor. Our symbiotes possess the ability to interface directly with the host's neural network. Through this connection, we establish a non-invasive form of communication, exchanging information and intentions. This communication occurs subconsciously, allowing the host to maintain their conscious control and autonomy. We respect the privacy of the host's thoughts and emotions, and our communication remains limited when necessary for both parties' well-being."

"I appreciate the emphasis on respecting the host's privacy and maintaining their autonomy. In terms of long-term coexistence, are there any potential health implications or risks that individuals should be aware of?"

"As with any symbiotic relationship, there are considerations and potential risks. While we have undertaken extensive research to ensure the safety of our coexistence, there may be unforeseen health implications specific to certain individuals or medical conditions. Close monitoring, regular check-ups, and ongoing scientific assessments are essential to identify and address potential risks. We are committed to working alongside medical professionals to continuously evaluate the long-term effects of our symbiotic relationship and enhance the overall well-being of the host."

"The idea of symbiotic coexistence is undoubtedly intriguing, and it presents potential avenues for medical advancements. As medical professionals, our responsibility lies in ensuring our patients' safety, health, and autonomy. If we were to explore this further, comprehensive research and ethical considerations would be crucial. Collaboration would be necessary to ensure the best possible outcomes while safeguarding the rights and well-being of the individuals involved."

"We fully understand and appreciate your dedication to patient care and ethical principles, Doctor. Collaboration and scientific exploration are at the core of our intentions. By working together with medical professionals like yourself, we can push the boundaries of medical knowledge and unlock new treatments and possibilities for the betterment of humanity."

"Thank you for your understanding. I will discuss these possibilities with my colleagues and engage in further conversations to evaluate the potential of such a collaboration. Integrating your knowledge and expertise under the proper ethical framework is paramount as we move forward."

###

As Adira delved deeper into her research on the intertwining of bioluminescence and the enigmatic world of aliens, she realized that there was much more to uncover. The captivating glow within Rachel's body had opened the door to a realm beyond her wildest imagination.

In her quest for answers, Adira sought guidance from an unexpected source—her mother, Taika. Taika was uniquely able to communicate with these beings from beyond the realms of Earth, acting as an intermediary between humans and the bioluminescent aliens. Adira had always been intrigued by her mother's extraordinary gifts, but now they held newfound importance.

Adira cautiously broached the subject as the two sat in Zhopla's cave one evening. "Mother, I need your help. I've verified the connection between the bioluminescence within Rachel's body and extraterrestrial forces. It appears that what the aliens told us was true. The aliens were somehow responsible for keeping her alive. Can you communicate with the aliens and illuminate their origin and purpose?"

Taika's eyes sparkled with a mix of anticipation and caution. "Adira, my dear, this is a momentous step you're taking. The bioluminescent beings are remnants of a once-great civilization that existed long ago. They chose to remain behind in their home world, waiting and dwelling in the depths of their ancient halls as volunteers, forever bathed in bioluminescence."

Adira's mind raced with questions. "Why did they stay behind? What is their purpose now?"

Taika took a deep breath, her voice steady. "They chose to remain, Adira, to safeguard the memories and wisdom of their lost civilization. Through the ethereal glow within their bodies, they carry the essence of their ancestors, preserving their culture and knowledge for eternity. They are beings of light, custodians of a forgotten era."

Adira was captivated by the idea of a civilization that had chosen to preserve its legacy through bioluminescent existence. She felt an inexplicable connection to these beings, as if they held the key to unlocking profound secrets about the universe.

"I want to learn more, Mother. Can you help me communicate directly with them? They may hold answers about their existence and the outbreak's mysteries and help us find a cure. I'm more convinced than ever after finding the bioluminescence within Rachel's body."

Taika nodded, her face serene. "Adira, my child, I can facilitate the connection, but the journey is yours to embark upon. It requires an open mind, unwavering belief, and respect for the delicate balance between our world and theirs. Are you prepared for what lies ahead?"

Adira's determination shone in her eyes. "Yes, Mother. I am ready."

Under Taika's guidance, Adira immersed herself in the process of connecting with the bioluminescent beings. She opened her mind to their ethereal presence through deep meditation and guided introspection. In the stillness of her consciousness, she felt a gentle pull, drawing her towards a realm of pure luminescence.

As the connection deepened, Adira found herself surrounded by a shimmering light. She turned to Taika and attempted to put into words what she had experienced. "The beings have revealed fragments of their ancient history, their collective wisdom woven into the fabric of their bioluminescent existence. They spoke to me of forgotten technologies, lost worlds, and the harmony that once reigned across galaxies.

"In turn, I shared my research and quest to understand the human body's healing in accordance with the bioluminescent nature. The beings listened, their radiant glow pulsating with intrigue and curiosity. They promised to support me in my quest for knowledge, providing guidance and insight as I continue this journey of discovery."

Taika smiled; her love for Adira was obvious. "Adira, you and the bioluminescent beings can form an unbreakable bond through this extraordinary communication. With this newfound alliance, you may embark on a path that will forever change your perception of the universe. The bioluminescent beings have entrusted you with their stories, wisdom, and hope. I know you will carry this responsibility with unwavering dedication as you continue to unravel the mysteries of bioluminescence and its potential to transform the very fabric of human existence."

16 - Rafe and Biolume

Alert. Rafe. Jomei's sensors indicate there is unusual activity in the greenhouses. Biometric data indicate extraordinary hyperactivity in several of the workers at Greenhouse 1A.

On my way.

As Rafe entered the greenhouse, Astrid looked up at Rafe, her dark eyes angry and shining, and managed to choke out a few words. "HE'S DEAD! I found him like this... Oh, this is just great. He was such a good worker, always so kind. How could this happen?"

"Hey, Astrid," Rafe says gently, touching her shoulder. This is a terrible shock, but we must stay calm and let the medical team do their job. They'll find out what happened, I promise."

Rafe removed his hand and offered a sympathetic smile. He knelt beside Astrid, trying to provide comfort. "I understand your pain, Astrid. It isn't easy to make sense of something like this, but we'll do everything possible to discover what happened. Did you notice anything unusual before you found the body?"

Astrid pinched the bridge of her nose, taking a deep breath, trying to stop shaking and compose herself. "His name is Bob Jones. No, nothing... It was a normal day. Bob was supposed to be working here, but when I checked on him, I found him lying on the ground. I thought he was being a slacker again. Oh, Rafe, this is just so awful!"

"I know, Astrid," Rafe said in a low and controlled voice. "We'll get to the bottom of this. The medical team is on its way and will conduct a thorough examination. In the meantime, I'll need to gather some information from you and anyone else who may have been around the area. It's important for the investigation."

Astrid nods, still trying to regain her composure. "Yes, I'll do whatever I can to help.... please find out what happened. He didn't deserve this."

"I understand, Astrid," Rafe assures her. "We'll do everything we can. For now, please try to take a moment for yourself. I'll coordinate the investigation and keep everyone informed. If you remember anything else or if you need anything at all, don't hesitate to reach out."

Astrid managed a grim smile, appreciative of Rafe's support. "Thank you, Rafe. I'll try to gather my thoughts and let you know if I remember anything important. Please, find out who did this."

Rafe stood up, giving Astrid another reassuring pat on the shoulder. "I will, Astrid. You have my word. Take care, and remember, you're not alone in this. We're here for you."

Jomei, can you review the stationary cameras and robotic patrol videos to see if anything looks out of place? Also, check the nanobot sensor arrays in the greenhouses, hydroponic gardens, and the immediate areas adjacent to them for any potential contaminants or the presence of concentrations of substances not usually found in these areas.

Affirmative. We will have a report for you soon.

With that, Rafe took a deep breath. *I need to organize the necessary steps to conduct a thorough investigation into this worker's death. Collect all relevant information and pass it on to the medical team and Eurydice.*

Security Officer Rafe entered the Medbay and found the medical staff attending to the outbreak patients, who remained isolated under strict quarantine protocols. Other medical staff were busy tending to patients, wearing protective suits and masks to prevent any potential spread of infection. Rafe approached Violet to get an update.

"Good afternoon, Doctor. I'm here to get an update on the outbreak patients and any news about the cause of death of the greenhouse worker. How are things progressing?"

Violet wiped her brow and gave Rafe a good-natured but tired smile.

"Good afternoon, Officer Rafe. We appreciate your concern. The situation with the outbreak patients remains challenging. We have implemented strict isolation protocols and are closely monitoring their conditions. So far, we haven't seen any significant improvements or changes. The patients are receiving the necessary medical care, and we're doing our best to contain the spread of the infection."

"I see. Has there been any progress in determining the cause of the outbreak or the cause of death of the greenhouse worker?"

"We've been conducting extensive tests and investigations to identify the source of the outbreak and the cause of the worker's death. Preliminary findings suggest a possible viral infection, but we're awaiting the results of further laboratory analysis to confirm. Our team works closely with Jomei and the biosecurity data to identify potential vectors or sources within the facility that could have contributed to these incidents."

"Understood, Doctor. Please keep me informed of any new developments. In the meantime, I'll maintain heightened security surveillance measures throughout the facility."

"Certainly, Officer Rafe. David and I appreciate your vigilance, and we'll keep you updated on any significant findings or changes in the patient's condition. If you have any specific concerns or requests, please don't hesitate to let us know."

Rafe nodded his agreement to Violet's response. Still, he

remained in Medbay for a few moments, observing the ongoing medical procedures and ensuring that all security protocols were being followed. He then made regular security rounds throughout the dome, maintaining heightened alertness due to the continuing outbreak.

On his way out, Rafe encountered David. "Hey David, do you have any news about the death of the greenhouse worker?"

David frowned. "Yes, Rafe, it's quite concerning. Based on the evidence we've gathered so far, I believe it's a case of homicide. It appears that the greenhouse worker was poisoned."

"Poisoned? That's terrible. Do you have any idea how it happened?"

"We're still investigating the exact details, but it seems the worker ingested a toxic substance. The autopsy revealed the presence of a lethal poison in his system, indicating foul play."

"That's unsettling."

"The toxicology investigation is still in its early stages, but we're actively looking into it."

"Jomei is rechecking the biosensors, and I will question the greenhouse worker's colleagues and supervisors to gather more information. It is crucial to determine who might have had access to the toxic substance and a motive to harm the worker."

David sighed. "I hope you can find the person responsible soon. Is there anything the public should be aware of regarding their safety? With this outbreak situation and now a potential murder, I'm sure the colonists will want to be informed. We need to let them know what's going on."

Rafe agreed. "While we don't have specific information to suggest a broader threat to the colonists at this point, it's always advisable to be cautious. We will encourage anyone with any information about this incident or who notices anything suspicious to report it immediately."

"Thanks for the update, Rafe. I appreciate your efforts in determining the facts of this case."

"You're welcome, David. I'm committed to finding out the truth and ensuring justice is served. I'll keep you updated as the investigation progresses." Rafe's attention was suddenly diverted.

You are being summoned to an emergency meeting of SIS22 in Eurydice Sideris's conference room as soon as possible. Jomei related to Rafe.

On my way.

Eurydice, the Chief Intelligence Officer of SIS22, began a formal meeting after all agents had gathered. "For the record, I address Chancellor Byron, the SIS22 Defense and Security Council, along with Galatéa security and medical teams gathered for the briefing about the alien presence discovered in the caves beneath the colony.

"Ladies and gentlemen, thank you for joining me today. Our discovery of benevolent beings of pure light in the caves is, needless to say, unprecedented. Adira's connection with these beings through her long-lost mother has opened new possibilities for interstellar communication. However, we must proceed cautiously to ensure our colony's safety and security.

"Before we continue, let me remind you that all information discussed during this meeting is classified at the highest level. We must maintain strict confidentiality to prevent panic among the colonists. Our primary objective is to understand the intentions and nature of these alien beings while keeping our people safe."

Rafe's eyebrows shot up to his hairline. "This is an outrage. I am the head of security, and I'm only now learning of this?"

Eurydice turned an icy gaze toward Rafe. "Your outrage is understandable. I plan to provide you with the information and knowledge we have to date. The situation is fluid, and changes and updates are occurring continually."

Eurydice addressed Rafe's concerns. "The caves have opened unprecedented avenues for investigation on many levels, such as the artifacts, star maps, and ongoing investigations. To further complicate matters, the bioluminescence is occurring in the caves and now in our outbreak patients, along with intelligent communication from these alien beings. We are currently in the data-gathering stages of numerous situations occurring simultaneously.

"I want each team to provide a detailed update on the security measures in place. Security team, what precautions have we taken to secure the caves and monitor potential threats? Medical team, have you conducted any assessments on Adira's well-being after her contact with the alien presence? Let's ensure we have all the necessary protocols to handle unforeseen situations."

Rafe spoke up quickly before Eurydice could end the meeting. "Adira, as chief of security, I would like more information. Since you have had contact with the aliens, there are some things that we need to know. For example, who are they? Have you been able to identify the nature and origin of the aliens? I believe it would take some time to conduct a detailed analysis and investigation of them. Do we plan to study their physiology, technology, and communication attempts to understand their identity better?"

Adira responded. "The caves of Galatéa are home to a unique phenomenon—bioluminescence. But this is no ordinary light. I've learned that it's actually the biological glow of complex alien life forms.

"I've also learned that the glow of these beings is a communication method and a survival mechanism. These beings voluntarily stayed behind when their population fled this planet due to war. They are the guardians of ancient, highly sophisticated knowledge. They are symbiotic organisms searching for a compatible physical body to coexist with."

Rafe persisted. "What do they want? The intentions of the aliens require ongoing observation and analysis. How do we know they are benevolent? Where do we go from here to monitor them?"

"We plan to conduct a continuous risk assessment of the aliens to evaluate the potential risks and threats and ensure the safety and security of the colony," snapped Eurydice.

"I believe the best way to proceed…." Just as Eurydice was about to delve deeper into the discussion, an urgent announcement from Jomei interrupted the meeting.

We have just intercepted satellite data indicating the approach of unidentified ships toward our planet.

Eurydice sprang into crisis mode. "Jomei, provide us with any additional information you have on these unidentified ships. Display their trajectory and any communication attempts they may have made. We need to assess the situation and understand their intentions. Security team, I want immediate action. Activate our defensive protocols and establish contact with the ships, if possible. Medical team: please prepare for any potential casualties or injuries resulting from a hostile encounter.

"Let's remain calm and focused. Our priority is the safety of our colony and its inhabitants. We have trained for such scenarios, and I am confident you can handle this situation professionally and efficiently. Keep me updated on any developments, and let's reconvene as soon as we have more information. Stay vigilant and ensure the security of our colony."

17 - Rafe hangs at home

In the dim, ambient light of his private quarters, Rafe, the chief of security for the colony Galatéa, settled into his chair. The room was a sanctuary, a blend of memories and the promise of new beginnings: old books filled with timeless wisdom, a digital photo frame displaying cherished moments, a well-worn leather jacket from his life before Galatéa, and Grampy's antique wristwatch, ticking steadily—a reminder that time moves forward, always offering new opportunities.

Rafe's thoughts turned to his role and the remarkable future unfolding around him. Enhanced by his Bio-Assistive Intelligence (BAI) and a swarm of nanoparticles, he felt stronger, clearer, and more capable than ever. The quiet hum of his BAI in the back of his mind was a reassuring presence, a partner offering insights and support even in these reflective moments.

As he considered Galatéa's diverse population, his mind buzzed with possibility. The colony was a living experiment, a microcosm of what humanity could become. Augmented humans, AI entities, symbiont-enhanced individuals, and non-augmented settlers—all coexisting, each bringing unique strengths and perspectives. The potential for collaboration and innovation was immense.

He sipped his cup of synth brew, warmth spreading through him. *What sort of society could we build here?* Each enhancement offered new avenues for growth. The nanoparticle/BAI-enhanced team members were the backbone of Galatéa's critical operations—security, healthcare, and engineering. Their capabilities could elevate the entire colony, not create division. Instead of being seen as threats, they could be leaders, mentors, and protectors.

AI entities, like Jomei, had evolved into sentient beings with unique personalities and skills. Rather than rivals, they were partners in progress, capable of managing complex tasks and freeing humans to pursue creativity, exploration, and deeper connections. Jomei's presence was a testament to the potential of human-AI collaboration—a chance to expand what was possible rather than fear the unknown.

And then there were the symbiont-enhanced humans on the horizon of transformation. Their integration with alien organisms promised a profound connection to Galatéa's ecosystem, offering insights into healing, balance, and harmony. They could be the bridge between humanity and the planet itself, ensuring that the colony thrived technologically and ecologically.

The non-augmented settlers, too, played a crucial role. Their choice to remain unenhanced didn't diminish their value; it enriched the colony's diversity. Their perspectives grounded the community, reminding everyone of the beauty of human adaptability and resilience. Together, they could create a society where every skill and viewpoint was respected, each contributing to the greater good.

Rafe leaned back, envisioning a future where these groups supported each other and celebrated differences as strengths. He imagined enhanced humans using their abilities to protect and serve, AI streamlining complex tasks, symbiont-enhanced individuals nurturing the colony's connection to the planet, and non-augmented settlers offering invaluable wisdom and tradition.

Cooperation is not just a dream; it's a choice, he thought. Galatéa had the chance to break free from Earth's divisive history and chart a new path. There would be challenges—there always were—but the potential for unity was far greater.

He rose and stepped to the viewport, observing the maroon landscape bathed in the light of Galatéa's red dwarf star. The clouds shifted gently, rain pattering against the dome, life outside and within continuing to evolve. His heart filled with a quiet determination. The colony's future was unwritten, and the possibilities stretched out like the stars themselves—endless, bright, and waiting to be explored.

The soft chime of his doorbell drew him back. Through his BAI, he saw Rasa, the head of dietary, standing at the door. Her presence was like a warm beacon, a reminder that in every challenge, there was also connection, support, and hope.

Rafe smiled. The future was calling, and he was ready to answer.

Rasa had a way of bringing warmth and positivity wherever she went. Her infectious smile and soothing laughter were comforting. She was not just a colleague but a friend, and potentially, if Rafe allowed himself to hope, something more. Today, she had come to check on him, sensing his need for company and perhaps a different perspective.

"Mind if I come in?" she asked, her voice soft yet vibrant.

"Of course, Rasa. Please, come in," Rafe replied, gesturing to a chair opposite him.

She entered, bringing a subtle scent of herbs and spices from the dietary labs. Rasa sat and looked at him with warm, understanding eyes. "You seem troubled, Rafe. What's on your mind?"

Rafe sighed, running a hand through his hair. "It's the colony, Rasa. Different factions are forming. I can't help but see parallels to Earth's history. I'm worried about the future."

Rasa nodded, listening intently. "I understand your concerns. Conflict and unity both have potential. We often overlook the potential for positive outcomes when we fixate on potential failures."

She has a unique ability to make people feel heard and understood.

Rafe leaned back, appreciating her perspective but still feeling the weight of his thoughts. "I know, but history has shown us that human nature often leads to division. What measures can we take to prevent that from happening here?"

Rasa smiled a wise and knowing smile. "By focusing on what unites us rather than what divides us. Each group brings something valuable to the table. Enhanced humans like you provide strength and intelligence. AI offers efficiency and capabilities beyond our own, and non-augmented humans bring unique perspectives and skills that we might overlook."

Rafe nodded slowly. "I agree, but how do we get everyone else to see that?" *This is tough; she doesn't know about the symbionts yet.*

Rasa leaned forward, her eyes sparkling with an idea. "It starts with us, Rafe. As leaders, we set the tone. We must demonstrate collaboration and respect for each other's differences. Let me share a story from our dietary team. It's a small example, but it illustrates a larger point."

Rafe looked at her, intrigued. "Go on."

Rasa began. Her voice was soothing and rhythmic. "In the dietary labs, we have a mix of enhanced humans, AI assistants, and non-augmented staff. Initially, there was tension. The enhanced humans felt superior due to their abilities, the humanoid droids were efficient but lacked empathy, and the non-augmented staff felt marginalized. It was a recipe for conflict."

She paused, letting the words sink in. "But we started small. We held scheduled meeting times where each person's unique skills were highlighted and appreciated. We worked on projects that required collaboration. For example, we developed a new nutrient-rich food supplement. The non-augmented humans provided the physical labor and traditional thinking, the droids calculated precise nutritional values, and the enhanced staff contributed knowledge, quick thinking, and creativity."

Rasa's eyes gleamed with pride. "The result was a product none of us could have created alone. More importantly, we built trust and respect. We function as a cohesive unit, valuing each other's contributions."

Rafe felt a glimmer of hope. "So, you're saying it's possible on a larger scale?"

"Absolutely," Rasa replied confidently. "It requires effort and a willingness to understand and appreciate each other. You, as the chief of security, have a crucial role. Your influence can extend beyond just keeping the peace. You can foster a culture of unity and collaboration."

Rafe considered her words. "But what about the inevitable disagreements? The fear and envy that might arise?"

Rasa smiled again, her wisdom shining through. "Disagreements are natural, Rafe. They can even be healthy if handled properly. What matters is how we respond to them. Instead of seeing them as threats, we can view them as opportunities for growth. We can encourage open communication, mediate conflicts with fairness, and always emphasize our shared goals."

She reached out, placing a hand on his. "Remember, Rafe, you're not alone in this. We all have a part to play in shaping the future of Galatéa. It's about building relationships, one step at a time."

Rafe felt a sense of calm wash over him. Rasa's words were like a balm to his troubled mind. "You're right, Rasa. I've been so focused on the potential negatives that I've lost sight of the positives. We have an opportunity to create something truly unique here."

Rasa squeezed his hand gently. "Exactly. And with your leadership, we can guide Galatéa towards a harmonious future. It won't be easy, but nothing worth achieving ever is."

Rafe looked at her, gratitude and admiration filling his eyes. "Thank you, Rasa. You always know how to put things into perspective."

She smiled, her warmth enveloping him. "That's what friends are for. And if fate is kind, and if we're lucky, something more."

Rafe's heart skipped a beat. He had long admired Rasa for her wisdom and kindness and the light she brought into his life. "Maybe," he said softly, a hopeful smile forming.

They sat in companionable silence, both lost in their thoughts. Rasa's presence grounded him, reminding him that there was always hope, even in the face of uncertainty. The challenges ahead were daunting, but with allies like Rasa and a commitment to fostering unity, Rafe felt more prepared to face them.

As the evening wore on, they discussed various ideas and strategies for promoting collaboration and understanding within the colony. Rasa suggested community events highlighting different groups' contributions, while Rafe considered implementing regular forums where colonists could voice their concerns and suggestions.

By the time Rasa departed, Rafe experienced a renewed sense of purpose. He walked her to the door, their conversation still buzzing in his mind. "Thank you, Rasa. You've given me a lot to think about."

She turned to him, her eyes twinkling, and kissed him. "Anytime, Rafe. Remember, we're in this together."

As she walked away, Rafe stood briefly in the doorway,

observing her departure. He felt a profound sense of gratitude for her presence in his life. With her support and the collective efforts of everyone in Galatéa, he believed they could navigate the complexities of their evolving society.

Rafe closed the door and returned to his chair, but his thoughts were optimistic this time. The future of Galatéa was uncertain, but it was also brimming with potential. *With leaders like Rasa by my side, I'm more confident we can create a thriving, harmonious colony.*

Grampy's antique wristwatch on his desk ticked steadily, a reminder that time was always moving forward. So, too, would Galatéa be driven by the hopes and dreams of its people? Rafe was determined to ensure their future was bright, united, and filled with possibility.

After a long day, he found solace in music, often turning to one of the many instruments he played. This evening, he reached for his guitar, fingers naturally finding the strings as he revisited a composition he'd been crafting for some time, and the moment of inspiration struck. *Finally! The missing piece of my song has surfaced. Now, with the refrain nearly perfected, it's time to weave it seamlessly into the song's fabric, bringing the composition closer to completion.*

The BAI chimed softly, gently reminding Rafe of his upcoming security briefing. He stood, experiencing the familiar surge of readiness from his nanoparticle-enhanced body. As he left his quarters, he hoped that Galatéa could forge a fresh path where diversity was a strength, not a weakness.

18 - Jomei's Report

TOP SECRET

EYES ONLY

Galatéa Intelligence Report: Unidentified Ships

Prepared by: Jomei AI Date: 21st June 2256

Overview

In the early hours of 21st June 2256, our sensors detected multiple unidentified ships entering Galatéa's atmosphere. These ships were first observed at the edge of our solar system, exhibiting the possibility of advanced cloaking capabilities that initially may have masked their presence. Upon closer inspection, our instruments identified at least ten vessels of varying sizes and configurations.

Ships' Trajectory

The ships entered our solar system from the outer regions, traveling at an average speed of 0.2c. Their trajectory suggests a deliberate approach towards Galatéa, which originated from an unknown sector. Detailed analysis of their flight path indicates advanced navigational capabilities, with precise adjustments made to avoid detection by our long-range sensors.

Trajectory Analysis:

• **Initial Detection:** 5.6 AU from Galatéa, approaching from the constellation Centaurus.

• **Entry Point:** 3.2 AU, altering course towards a more concealed approach vector.

• **Current Position:** 0.5 AU, decelerating as they approach Galatéa's orbit.

Communication Attempts

Upon detection, we initiated standard communication protocols to establish contact. Multiple frequencies were used, including those known for interstellar communication. Despite repeated attempts, we received no response. We also deployed a series of encoded signals designed to bypass potential language barriers.

Communication Log:

• **Attempt 1:** Standard greeting in Galactic Common - No response.

• **Attempt 2:** Encoded binary transmission - No response.

• **Attempt 3:** Broad-spectrum frequency sweep - No response.

Given the lack of response, it is unclear whether the ships' occupants are unwilling or unable to communicate with us.

Threat Assessment

Visual Analysis:

• The ships vary from small scout-like vessels to larger, possibly command or transport ships.

• Their hulls display no recognizable insignia or markings associated with known space-faring Earth factions.

Technology Assessment:

• Potential cloaking capabilities suggest a high level of technological sophistication.

• Energy readings indicate the presence of advanced propulsion and weapon systems.

Behavioral Analysis:

• The deliberate and stealthy approach suggests either

reconnaissance or an intent to engage under the element of surprise.

Based on current data, the unidentified ships pose a potential threat. Their lack of communication, combined with their advanced technology, warrants immediate defensive measures.

Defensive Protocols

Activation of Defensive Measures:

• **Orbital Defense Grid:** Activated. All planetary defense satellites are now in a heightened state of readiness, capable of engaging the ships if necessary.

• **Surface-to-Orbit Missiles:** Armed and ready. Ground-based missile systems are prepared to intercept any hostile actions.

• **Shield Generators:** Online. Planetary shields have been activated to protect key installations and our domed population center.

Security Team Actions:

• **Monitoring:** Continuous real-time tracking of the ships.

• **Tactical Analysis:** Ongoing assessment of potential engagement scenarios.

• **Readiness:** All security personnel are on high alert, with rapid response teams positioned strategically across the planet.

Medical Preparedness

Medical Team Directive:

• **Casualty Preparedness:** All medical staff have been placed on high alert, and emergency response teams are ready to handle any influx of casualties.

• **Supply Inventory:** Medical supplies and resources have been inventoried and stockpiled to ensure readiness for a large-scale medical emergency.

- **Training:** All medical personnel have undergone refresher training for mass casualty incidents and are prepared to handle various injuries.

Additional Information

Scientific Analysis:

- Preliminary scans of the ships' hull composition suggest a blend of known and unknown materials, indicating possible alien origin or hybrid technology.

- Emission spectra analysis reveals energy signatures consistent with advanced antimatter reactors, a technology not widely used in known space-faring factions.

Cultural and Historical Context:

- There are no records of any civilizations near their approach vector that match the ships' design or technological profile.

- Historical archives reveal no prior encounters with ships of this configuration or behavior pattern.

Recommendations:

1 Continue Attempts at Communication: Use alternative methods and frequencies, including passive listening for any potential broadcasts or signals from the ships.

2 Enhanced Surveillance: Deploy additional reconnaissance drones to gather more detailed information about the ships and their occupants.

3 Prepare for Engagement: Maintain readiness of all defensive and medical teams and develop contingency plans for various potential scenarios, including hostile engagement, boarding, and potential diplomatic encounters.

Conclusion

Unidentified ships heading into our system present a

significant and immediate concern. Despite extensive efforts to establish contact, their silence and advanced technological capabilities suggest the need for caution. All defensive and medical protocols have been activated to ensure the safety of Galatéa and its inhabitants.

Security teams are tasked with continuous monitoring and readiness to engage if hostile actions are detected. Medical teams are prepared for any casualties or injuries resulting from potential conflict. Further scientific analysis and attempts at communication are ongoing to understand these unidentified visitors' intentions better.

We will remain vigilant and prepared to defend Galatéa against any threat while seeking to uncover the mystery behind these silent ships.

End of Report

Prepared by Jomei AI

Cc: SIS 22 Chief Executive, Chancellor Byron, and Defense and Security Council

Follow-up Actions:

• Daily briefings on the status of the unidentified ships.

• Regular updates on communication attempts and any new findings.

• Coordination with Veltryn for additional support and intelligence.

19 - Toxins, Biolume, Outbreak, Oh My!

Sitting in the Medbay, Violet sipped her coffee and raised her eyebrows as David described his incredible discoveries.

"I've investigated various plant poisons or toxins known to be lethal to humans. The swift death of our greenhouse worker, Bob Jones, helps to narrow the field of potential substances.

"Toxicology results have all come back negative, however. With the help of Jomei, we have concluded that using nanotechnology to spread undetectable toxins to humans is entirely possible and, in our case, probable. Within our greenhouses, nanotechnology has been used to enhance crop yields, improve the delivery of nutrients, and mitigate negative impacts on the crops.

"We all have witnessed the optimal plant growth due to nanoscale materials used, and the greenhouse crops have flourished." David switched to the quantum electron microscope.

"Jomei and I have learned that someone has gained access to the greenhouses' control systems and released engineered nanoparticles containing a potent toxin. Would you care to describe the details, Jomei?"

"Yes, these toxic nanoparticles were designed to evade detection and spread rapidly through the air and irrigation system in the immediate vicinity where Bob was working. Because we have not integrated various technical advancements with specific nanotechnology, our cybersecurity systems were not alerted and did not detect toxic nanoparticles.

"Whoever did this could exploit loopholes, for the lack of a better term, within our access controls, manipulate data and sensors, and tamper with our automated systems to introduce this unauthorized nanoparticle toxin. Jomei has been able to ascertain which systems were involved. We theorize the nanoparticles arrived along one of our supply chains before the arrival of the *Porta Caeli.*"

David exchanged glances with Violet. "So, it appears one of the original colonists is our most likely perpetrator?"

Jomei's androgynous voice continued. "Yes, they had the technological access and knowledge of an insider to breach our security."

Rafe's knitted his eyebrows. "This malicious intent is likely motivated by personal gain, ideology, or individual grievances. I wonder if some clandestine research activities under the guise of legitimate greenhouse operations were happening during our time here, leveraging their expertise and access to our resources. Jomei and I have been working on mitigating security risks."

Jomei jumped in. "Yes, mitigation of such risks requires a combination of robust security measures, stringent oversight, and expansion of ethical guidelines to prevent unauthorized access to nanotechnology toxins to safeguard the colony against intentional harm.

"To address these risks, Rafe and Jomei have developed proactive measures, including enhancement of our cybersecurity protocols to prevent unauthorized access to critical systems. This includes the implementation of rigorous oversight and rules for the development and deployment of nanomaterials. We are in the process of researching the development of countermeasures against nanoparticle-based attacks, including toxins."

"Thank you, Rafe and Jomei. Violet and I will continue our investigation into the toxin effects that Bob experienced. Also, we have further data to analyze on our outbreak patients. Please let me know any updates."

David turned to Violet. "Handling one of these situations would be entirely doable. But with the outbreak, patients going critical and placed in hibernation pods, the death of a greenhouse worker by a released nanotoxin, and now preparation for potential conflict with unidentified incoming ships. This is unbelievable!"

Violet nodded and glanced at the patient monitors. "There seems to be no change in the outbreak patients' condition. Except for a slow descent to critical condition. Not a single one of them is improving. It's been eight months, and we've made no progress in developing a potential treatment or cure."

"The fact that Adira found bioluminescence present in the basal ganglia of the patients is disturbing. That puts us in the realm of alien medicine with no reference points. We've tried everything known to bring them out of their comatose state with no effects."

Adira entered Medbay and walked quickly to David's office. "Hello, Violet, David. How are the outbreak patients faring today? Are there any updates?"

Violet frowned and turned to Adira. The only change was a downgrade in their condition. The hibernation pods are helping to keep them stable, but they continue to decline."

Violet's hands trembled as she adjusted the readout on the last hibernation pod, its soft hum mocking the life it was supposed to preserve. She glanced at David, his face etched with the same weariness she felt. They had been fighting a losing battle for weeks now, and the weight of their failure was crushing.

"David, look," Violet whispered, pointing at the monitor. "Their vitals are dropping faster than we projected."

David leaned in his brow furrowing. "Damn it. I thought we had more time."

The sterile white lights of the medical bay flickered, a

reminder of the constant power fluctuations they were dealing with. The intermittent power fluctuations had hit Galatéa hard, straining the colony's infrastructure.

Adira sighed, brushing a loose strand of hair behind her ear. "We should update Rafe and Jomei. They need to know how serious this is."

With a grim expression, David nodded. "I'll contact them. Let's hope they have some good news for us, but I'm not holding my breath."

He messaged them through his BAI, connecting central command. *Security Officer Rafe, AI Jomei, we must speak with you immediately. It's urgent.*

A moment later, the holographic form of Rafe materialized in front of them. Rafe's features had changed from pallid to rugged and were set in a determined scowl, while Jomei's ethereal digital visage was as calm and composed as ever.

"What's the situation?" Rafe asked, his voice gruff but steady.

"It's not good," David replied, trying to keep his voice even. "The patients in the hibernation pods are deteriorating faster than we anticipated. Their vitals are dropping rapidly, and we're running out of options. With the power fluctuations, the hibernation pods seem to have glitches in their biometric support mechanisms."

Jomei's digital form flickered slightly. "Is there any chance of stabilizing them with the current resources?"

David shook his head. "We've tried everything. Our medical supplies need constant restocking, and the hibernation pods are starting to fail. We need more than what we have here."

Fists clenched, Rafe's jaw tightened. "We've been working on stabilizing the power, but numerous factors have made it difficult. Our resources are stretched thin."

"We understand," Violet said softly. "But without those hibernation pods, these people are going to die. We require an immediate solution.

Jomei's holographic form flickered with data streams as they processed the information. "I might have a solution. The hibernation pods' failure is due to the deterioration of the bio-stabilization algorithms. If I can access the central AI core, I can rewrite and enhance these algorithms to buy the patients more time."

Rafe's eyes narrowed. The AI core resides within the colony's heart, deep in caves and restricted zones. It's heavily guarded, and with the outbreak, that area has become a security hotspot to keep the unauthorized out. It's a desperate mission likely to fail."

David stepped forward, determination in his eyes. "We don't have a choice, Rafe. If there's even a chance that Jomei can fix the pods, we must take it. These people's lives depend on it."

Violet nodded in agreement. "We're doctors. We can't just stand by and watch them die."

Rafe looked between Violet and David, his expression torn. Finally, he sighed. "Alright. We'll assemble a team and make a plan. But this won't be easy. Eurydice does not want Jomei anywhere near the caves. We risk being discovered by Gint and his team members, which would be difficult to explain and bring Eurydice's wrath on all of us. Eurydice's mandate to keep Jomei and any surveillance methods or artificial intelligence entities out of the caves remains in place. She is aware of the deterioration of our outbreak patients but insists that the alien presence be kept top secret and unknown to the colonists, Gint, and his team.

"Because access to the AI core is modulated by biometric entry, two of us must be present to gain access to core programs. David, as chief medical officer, you must be present, as well as me, because I am chief of security."

Jomei's digital form shimmered. "Jomei will assist in any way. Real-time data and guidance will be provided once you're in the restricted zone and grant Jomei access."

Adira took a deep breath, feeling a spark of hope amidst the despair. "Thank you, Jomei. And thank you, Rafe. We'll do whatever it takes to save these people."

As they began to formulate their plan, the weight of their mission settled heavily on their shoulders. The path ahead was fraught with being discovered, but Adira and David knew that they couldn't give up. As SIS22 operatives, they did not want to go against orders, but they were doctors whose duty was to save lives, no matter the cost.

The team gathered in the dimly lit Medbay briefing room, the air thick with tension. Rafe stood at the head of the table, a holographic map of the colony projected before him. Violet, Adira, and David sat side by side, their faces drawn with fatigue but resolute.

"Alright, listen up," Rafe began, his voice commanding the room. "We have a critical mission to access the AI core and allow Jomei to rewrite the bio-stabilization algorithms for the hibernation pods. The restricted zone is a high-risk area, and we'll be facing both discovery by Gint's team, who are not SIS22 operatives, and Eurydice's tight security measures. This won't be easy, but it's our only shot."

He pointed to the map, highlighting the route they would take. "We'll enter through the maintenance cave entrance here. This should bypass most of the cave system's frequented work hotspots. From there, we'll need to navigate to the central hub to gain access and allow Jomei to interface with the AI core."

Rafe nodded. "Our priority is to move quickly and avoid

confrontation whenever possible. Jomei will provide real-time updates on team movements to help us navigate safely."

Jomei's digital form appeared beside the map. "Jomei will monitor and divert the colony's security systems and provide guidance. Once inside the AI core, Jomei will interface with it to enhance the algorithms."

Violet leaned forward, her eyes locked on Rafe. "What about the security protocols around the AI core? How do we get past them?"

Rafe grimaced. "That's the tricky part. A series of biometric locks and automated defenses protect the AI core. We'll need to disable them without triggering an alarm. That's where Jomei comes in—to handle the electronic overrides while David and I handle the biometrics of the physical security."

David exchanged a glance with Violet, then spoke up. "And if things go south?"

Rafe's eyes hardened. "We bluff our way out. But our primary goal is to avoid detection and complete the mission without being caught. Violet, it would be best to remain in the Medbay should trouble arise or the colonists need your assistance. And to monitor the hibernation pods. David, Adira, and Jomei will accompany me."

The room fell silent as the weight of their task settled in. Each team member understood the risks but knew that failure was not an option. Lives and the last hope for the patients in the hibernation pods were at stake.

Rafe took a deep breath. "We leave at dawn. Get some rest and prepare your gear. Dismissed."

Adira and David lingered as the team dispersed, their minds racing about the mission ahead. They walked side by side through the colony's dim corridors, the hum of machinery a constant reminder of the fragile balance they were trying to maintain.

"Adira, are you sure about this?" David asked quietly, his voice tinged with concern.

Adira nodded, her eyes fixed ahead. "We don't have a choice, David. We have to do this. For the patients, for the colony… for ourselves."

David touched her shoulder, offering a small, reassuring smile. "We'll make it through this. Together."

The dawn came all too soon, and the team gathered at the entrance to the maintenance tunnels. They donned their protective gear and checked their stun weapons, the final preparations for their dangerous journey. Rafe led the way, his presence a steadying force for the group.

Jomei's voice crackled through BAIs. *"Monitoring the area. The route is clear for now, but stay alert. Jomei will update you with any changes."*

The team moved swiftly through the narrow tunnels of the cave system, the dim light casting eerie shadows on the walls. The air was heavy with a damp, musty scent and the distant, muffled sounds of Gint's team working. Every step brought them closer to their goal, and the tension was palpable.

They reached the first security checkpoint, a reinforced door with a biometric scanner. Rafe motioned for Jomei to begin their alarm system override.

"Working on it," Jomei said, calm and focused. "This will take a moment."

The team stood guard, their eyes scanning the darkness for any signs of movement. The minutes stretched on, each one an eternity as they waited. Finally, the door clicked open, and they moved through, their breaths held in anticipation.

The journey became increasingly difficult as they navigated the maze of tunnels and security measures. The workers became more numerous, and the automated defenses became more aggressive. But they pressed on, guided by Jomei and Rafe, determined to reach the AI core.

At last, they stood before the final barrier. Outside the cave system, a massive steel door guarding the heart of the colony's core systems was erected. Jomei's digital form appeared to become brighter, focused on the task at hand.

"This is it," Rafe said. "Once David and I interface with the AI core and gain access, Jomei will need a few minutes to rewrite the algorithms. Be ready for anything."

Rafe nodded, his eyes scanning the team. "Hold your positions. We're almost there."

Rafe began the intricate process of bypassing the final security measures. The seconds ticked by, each one a test of their resolve. Suddenly, the door slid open, revealing the glowing, pulsating core of the AI.

Adira and David exchanged glances. David's heart pounded with fear and hope. *This is our last chance, our final hope, to save the patients and the colony.*

Jomei's presence had gained entry, merging with the AI core as they began the rewrite process. The room filled with a soft hum, and the lights dimmed as the AI's power surged.

"Almost there," Jomei said, his voice quiet with effort. "Just a little longer…"

The team held their breath, their eyes fixed on the glowing core. The tension was unbearable, the weight of their mission pressing down on them.

Finally, Jomei's digital form returned, and the data streams flowed. "I've done it. The algorithms are enhanced. The hibernation pods will stabilize."

Rafe's face broke into a rare smile. "Let's get out of here."

As they returned through the maze of corridors, David reflected that the journey seemed shorter on the way back, the burden of their mission lighter—but it wasn't over yet. He sent it to Adira. *We did it! We found a way to keep the patients going and give them a fighting chance.*

Deep within the caves of Galatéa, the air was thick with humidity, and the faint hum of distant machinery reverberated through the rocky walls. The glow from bioluminescent crystals illuminated the winding tunnels. Rafe, David, and Adira, elite operatives of SIS22, navigated their way back to the Medbay. They understood the risks but were driven by a mission that could change everything. As they moved silently, the sound of a weapon being cocked halted them in their tracks.

Marcus stepped out from the shadows. "I wouldn't take another step if I were you." His voice is gravelly, hardened by years of military work, but there's a hint of curiosity in his tone. "What the hell are you three doing down here?"

David raised his hands slowly. "Easy, Marcus. We're not here to cause trouble."

"We didn't know anyone else was down here." Adira narrowed her eyes, scanning for any sign of aggression.

Marcus smirked. "That much is obvious. But you're a long way from where you're supposed to be, and you're both damn well aware of that." He gestured with his rifle. "The AI core is off-limits, even to senior operatives like you. So, I'll ask again—what the hell are you doing here?"

David exchanged a quick glance with Adira before speaking. "We're here because something's wrong, Marcus. We needed to get to the AI core to rewrite the hibernation pod algorithms to save the outbreak patients. Something isn't right around here, and we took it upon ourselves to save their lives."

Adira stepped forward. "The higher-ups... we think they're compromised."

Marcus' face hardened, but his eyes flickered with something— Concern? Suspicion?

"Compromised? That's a pretty serious accusation. And you think the answer lies down here?"

Rafe nodded. "We've intercepted some communications. They don't add up. Orders that contradict everything we've been taught, protocols being bypassed... It's like someone—or something—is pulling the strings from the shadows. We are working hard to find out the truth."

Marcus lowered his rifle slightly, but not enough to fully trust them. "You realize what you're saying, don't you? If you're wrong, if this is just paranoia... you'll be branded as traitors. Even if you're right, SIS22 might not forgive this little trespass."

Adira chimed in, her voice steady but with a note of urgency. "We're not wrong, Marcus. You've been around long enough to know when something feels off. Haven't you noticed it, too?"

Silent for a moment, his eyes narrowed as he studied their faces. "You think I haven't noticed? I've seen more conflict than I care to count, more betrayal than anyone should have to witness. There's always something "off" in this line of work. But that doesn't mean you rush into restricted zones like some rookies with a death wish."

David stepped closer, his tone earnest. "We're not rushing in, Marcus. We're taking a calculated risk. We're talking about the fate of the entire colony here. If SIS22 is compromised, everyone—every man, woman, and child on this planet—is in danger."

Adira added, her voice soft, almost pleading. "We need your help, Marcus. You're one of the few people who can help. You can feel it, too, can't you? The tension, the unease... like we're being watched from the inside out."

His grip on the rifle loosened, and for a moment, he looked away, lost in thought. His voice was softer when he spoke, tinged with something like regret. "I've seen what happens when the wrong people get into power. It doesn't end well—for anyone."

Rafe sensed a shift and pressed on. "Then you know why we have to do this. We're not just trying to protect ourselves; we're trying to protect everyone on this planet. If you let us go, we might have a chance to fix this."

Marcus nodded to Rafe, then locked eyes with David and Adira, his expression unreadable. "You're playing a dangerous game. But... He lowered his rifle completely. "You were the docs who enhanced my life on the *Porta Caeli* when you implanted the nanoparticles. I've always been a sucker for the underdog."

"So you'll let us go?" Adira cast a small, relieved smile.

Marcus nodded. "I won't say a word to the chief. But understand this—if you're wrong, if this is all just some wild goose chase, you won't just have the higher-ups to worry about. You'll have me coming after you, too. And trust me, you don't want that."

"We won't let you down, Marcus. This isn't a wild goose chase. We're onto something; I can feel it." A relieved Rafe added.

Marcus paused, his tone more serious. "Just one thing before you go. If you find what you're looking for… if you uncover the truth, whatever it may be… what then? What's your plan?"

Adira exchanged a glance with David, then answered. "We'll do whatever it takes to stop it. Even if that means going against everything we've ever known. We have to protect the colony, no matter the cost."

"You're willing to sacrifice everything for this? Your careers, your lives…?" Marcus weighed her words.

"Yes. We are." David added firmly.

After a long pause, he finally spoke, his voice rough. "Then you'd better not screw this up. Go. And for what it's worth... good luck."

Rafe, David, and Adira nodded, their expressions a mix of determination and gratitude. They turned to leave, their path now clear, but Marcus spoke one last time as they began to move.

Marcus called after them."Remember—trust no one. Not even each other."

They stopped momentarily, the weight of his words sinking in before continuing to escape the cave's depths. Marcus watched them until they disappeared into the darkness, then turned away, blending back into the shadows as if he were never there.

Adira, Rafe, and David exchanged tired but triumphant smiles. David's heart was lit by the knowledge that they had made a difference.

Adira added, "Together, we faced the darkness and found a way to bring light and restore power to the hibernation pods."

Violet and David worked tirelessly to implement the new algorithms. "Violet, the hibernation pods are now humming with renewed life, and the patient's vitals are stabilizing as the biosensor repairs of the hibernation pods and advanced medical techniques have taken hold."

With this team and the addition of our AI ally, Jomei, we can fight for the future of Galatéa. They've given it their all. I'm so proud of Rafe, Violet, and Adira.

The Medbay filled once again with the sounds of hope. And at that moment, amid the hum of the hibernation pods and the soft clinical glow, David realized they were not just survivors. *We have become proactive guardians of Galatéa and will do whatever it takes to protect our patients and colony.*

Early the following day, Adira walked into the Medbay. "I have just returned from Zhopla's cave. The aliens we discovered in the caves of Galatéa are a fascinating and complex life form. They may be able to help our outbreak patients."

David turned his attention to Adira. *She's so beautiful, even when she's tired.*

"How would they be able to help our critical patients?"

"This bioluminescence is no ordinary light. It's the glow of the symbiotic aliens. They are individuals searching for a physical body to coexist with the person. Their bioluminescent glow is a method of communication and a mechanism of survival in the dark environment of the caves.

"They are not simple life forms. They are highly intelligent, choosing hosts based on genetic or personality traits. Once a host is selected, the two can be merged.

"The merging process is gentle and requires the cooperation of both entities. The alien extends filaments of light that intertwine and eventually integrate with the host's body. In this way, they can heal the patients who are in an outbreak from the inside.

"They will require the consent of the outbreak patient, which will require them to be awakened for a brief period so that the situation can be explained to them and they know they have a choice."

Violet looked skeptical. "Are there any positive effects of the symbiotic relationship other than the cure for this outbreak?"

"Yes, symbiosis is both a coexistence and a life-altering experience for the host. It will amplify their physical capabilities, heighten their senses, and even give them access to the vast knowledge base of the alien culture. The host's vision may extend beyond the visible spectrum, and sometimes they develop a 'sixth sense' about their surroundings and interactions." Adira breathed deeply.

David turned to his tablet. "According to my understanding of this disease, we could awaken the patients for a short time for consent by administering various medications. While they are awake, their condition will continue to deteriorate faster. Am I to understand that their choices are a symbiotic existence with the alien or certain death?"

Adira turned her tired eyes to David and Violet. "Yes, I'm afraid that's so."

20 - David at Home

The caves of Galatéa stood in stark contrast to the sterile, whitewashed walls of Earth's SIS22 headquarters, his eyes adjusting to the dim, alien light. Here, among the shimmering alien crystals and the bioluminescence clinging to the jagged walls, one could almost forget the weight of his duties in the Medbay. Almost. David felt uneasy as he trailed behind Eurydice Sideris, the enigmatic leader of their covert intelligence agency.

Eurydice moved with a grace that belied her human origins, her steps silent and her presence commanding. She was a woman of contradictions, a leader who demanded loyalty yet kept herself shrouded in mystery. As David watched her navigate the uneven terrain with ease, he couldn't help but let his mind wander, filled with questions he dared not ask aloud.

Why hasn't she received the nanoparticles or the BAI?

The thought gnawed at him incessantly. The Brain-to-Artificial Intelligence Interface (BAI), or neural lace, was a standard procedure for the new influx of SIS22 operatives. It enhanced cognitive and physical abilities, allowing them to perform feats beyond the capabilities of ordinary humans. The nanoparticles, on the other hand, provided rapid healing and immunity to most known diseases. In their line of work, these enhancements were not just beneficial but essential.

Yet Eurydice had refused them both. At first, David had admired her for it, seeing it as a testament to her strength and resilience. But admiration gave way to suspicion as the days turned into weeks and the weeks into months. *What could she gain by remaining non-augmented? What was she hiding?*

David's mind flashed back to their first meeting. She had looked him straight in the eye, her gaze piercing and unwavering.

"Trust is the cornerstone of our operations," she had said. "Without it, we are nothing." He had believed her then, believed in her vision and her leadership. But now, as he watched her from the shadows, he wondered if trust was a luxury they could no longer afford.

Eurydice's refusal to embrace the very technology that made them superior operatives was just one piece of the puzzle. There were other, more unsettling clues: the way she would sometimes stare into the distance, lost in thought; the late-night communications she kept private, even from her most trusted aides; and the fleeting expressions of pain or sorrow that crossed her face when she thought no one was looking.

David shook his head, trying to dispel the cloud of doubt that seemed to follow him everywhere. He needed to focus on the mission. They were here to investigate the alien civilization, uncover its secrets, and assess its threat level. Personal doubts and fears had no place in this environment. But no matter how hard he tried, he couldn't shake the feeling that something was wrong.

He remembered an overheard conversation between Eurydice and another senior operative, a grizzled veteran named Marcus. They had been discussing the alien astronomical charts they had found in the caves, depicting the Milky Way and Earth's solar system. Their technology seemed centuries ahead of anything humanity had developed. "It's almost as if they knew we were coming," Marcus had said, his voice tinged with unease. "As if they were waiting for us."

Eurydice dismissed his concerns with a wave of her hand. "Speculation will get us nowhere," she replied. "Focus on the facts. We must understand how this technology works, not why it exists."

But David couldn't help but wonder about the "why." *Why had the aliens chosen to reveal themselves now? Why had they allowed themselves to be discovered after millennia of hiding? And most importantly, why did Eurydice seem so unconcerned by it all?*

He had once tried to confront her to voice his concerns. It had not gone well. "You're overthinking this, David," she had said, her tone cold and dismissive. "Our mission is clear. We are here to gather intelligence, nothing more. Leave the speculation to the historians."

But David couldn't leave it alone. Not when the stakes were this high. He had spent countless hours poring over the data they had collected, searching for patterns, for clues. And the more he looked, the more he found. Some inconsistencies and anomalies defied the explanation. It was as if the entire operation was shrouded in a veil of deception, with Eurydice at its center.

He thought about the night they first arrived at Galatéa. The sky was a tapestry of stars, and the atmosphere buzzed with the excitement of an unfamiliar landscape. Eurydice stood at the edge of their landing site, gazing into the darkness. "This is a new beginning," she said, her husky voice barely audible over the comm of her spacesuit. "It's a chance to rewrite history."

At the time, he had taken her words at face value, seeing them as a rallying cry for their mission. But now, he wondered if there was a deeper, more sinister meaning behind them. A new beginning for whom? And what kind of history was she planning to rewrite?

David's thoughts were interrupted by sudden movement. He turned to see Eurydice crouching by a cluster of alien artifacts, her fingers tracing the intricate patterns etched into the surface. She seemed lost in thought, her expression unreadable. He approached her cautiously, his heart pounding in his chest.

"Eurydice," he began, keeping his voice low. "We need to talk."

She looked up at him, her eyes narrowing. "About what?"

"About you," he said, forcing himself to meet her gaze. "About why you're here. About what you're hiding."

For a moment, there was silence. Then, Eurydice stood up, her snakelike movements slow and deliberate. "You're treading on dangerous ground, David," she said, her voice low and menacing. "I suggest you watch your step."

But David couldn't back down now. Not when he was so close to the truth. "I deserve to know," he insisted. "We all do. If you expect us to follow you, to trust you, then you owe us that much."

Eurydice's expression softened, but only for a moment. "You're right," she said, her voice barely above a whisper. "You do deserve to know. But some truths are too dangerous to be spoken aloud. Some secrets are meant to be kept."

With that, she turned and walked away, leaving David standing there, his mind racing. What could be so dangerous and terrible that she couldn't even speak of it? And why was she willing to risk everything to keep it hidden?

David felt a chill run down his spine as he watched her disappear into the darkness. He knew that whatever secrets Eurydice was hiding were not just her own. They were the secrets of SIS22, their mission, and humanity's future. And he knew that if he were ever going to uncover the truth, he would have to be prepared to face whatever horrors lay beneath the surface.

In the following days, David found himself drawn deeper into the mystery. He spent hours in the caves, studying the alien artifacts, star maps, and charts and searching for clues. He spoke to other operatives, trying to piece together the fragments of information they had gathered. Slowly but surely, a picture began to emerge.

The alien civilization they had discovered was not what it

seemed. It was ancient but also highly advanced, with technology that far surpassed anything humanity had ever seen. And it was clear that they had been watching humanity for a long time, waiting for the right moment to reveal themselves.

But why? What was their purpose? And what did it have to do with Eurydice?

###

David was glad to be home; it had been a long week, and his private quarters blended advanced technology with comfort to support work and relaxation. His Galatéan home was spacious and modular, allowing for easy reconfiguration. The walls were designed to change color and transparency, offering privacy or openness. The living area was comfortable, and the furniture could be rearranged for various activities. A sizeable holographic display was prominently located for communication, entertainment, and work.

David had arranged a dedicated workspace with advanced medical and scientific equipment, allowing ongoing research and experiments. This area was equipped with a holographic interface and various diagnostic tools. He also had a space for hobbies and relaxation, including VR gear, a small art studio for holographic art, and a mini-laboratory for personal research projects.

He searched SIS22 records using advanced tools for clues regarding Eurydice's mysterious behavior. Because he was the clinician in charge of the Medbay, he had a higher clearance than most to access highly classified information.

The answers came in fragments, in whispers and shadows. He learned of a secret project, codenamed "Proteus," initiated by SIS22 years ago. This project involved the creation of a new kind of human, one that was immune to disease, aging, and death itself. It had been deemed too dangerous and unethical, and he found it buried in the deepest recesses of SIS22's archives.

It's a good thing we weren't technologically advanced enough to be able to do it.

But has Eurydice resurrected it? Has she used research and technology to transform herself into something more than human? Could she be the first of a new breed, a human hybrid with a sentient AI giving her abilities and powers that defy our comprehension?

She had done this all in secret, without the knowledge or consent of her superiors. Was this her quest for power and immortality? Has she betrayed SIS22 and humanity?

David felt a surge of anger and betrayal. *How could she do this? How could she risk everything they had worked for and sacrifice it for her selfish desires?*

But as he delved deeper, he began to understand. Eurydice was not just seeking power. She was seeking to save humanity from itself. The alien technology and the hybridization process were all part of a plan to create a new kind of human that could survive Earth's coming apocalypse.

Then David found the biggest surprise in his data mining for further information. Goose bumps rose on his arms as he read that SIS22 had been aware of a looming threat—a cosmic event that would wipe out all life on Earth. SIS22 had been searching for a way to prevent it, to save humanity from extinction. Eurydice had found the solution in the alien technology buried beneath the surface of Galatéa.

But in doing so, she had crossed a line. She had become something other, something alien. And now, she was willing to do whatever it took to ensure the survival of her new species, even if it meant sacrificing the old.

David felt a chill run down his spine as the full weight of the truth settled upon him. He knew now why Eurydice had kept her secrets and refused the augmentations. She was no longer one of them. She was something else, something more. And she would stop at nothing to achieve her goals.

David resolved, standing in the dim light of his quarters, that he would not allow her to succeed, nor would he let her sacrifice humanity for her twisted personal vision, at least not without the input of other SIS22 operatives, the Chancellor, and the Council. He walked through his small hydroponic and aeroponic garden, where he cultivated herbs and vegetables, and approached the large, reinforced window that provided a view of the Galatéan landscape and night sky. He focused his telescope on the nearest star and contemplated the classified information he had uncovered.

David, Jomei here.

Yes, Jomei?

I have received a communication from Earth to you.

Thank you, Jomei; please transmit to my personal holographic display.

David moved away from his telescope and returned to the living area. He arranged his favorite reading chair to receive the transmission. As the holographic image unscrambled and materialized, he realized it was a message from his sister. Jennifer's form came into full view and focus. Her voice was quivering, and her eyes were wide.

"Hello, David. I hope the colony on Galatéa is faring well. Things are not so great here on Earth. I know I only have a short time for this transmission, so I'll get to the point. Wars are being fought on every continent. We are under Marshall Law here at home. It was invoked not only because of war but because of natural disasters that are wreaking havoc all over the planet, as well as the need to quell rebellions that have arisen due to military authority taking the place of civilian rule. I said things were not so great here. Actually, things are bad, David. It's a good thing you are not here. Your apartment was overrun by the homeless—then your entire building was subsumed by the military. I am staying at Taika's farmhouse. Please let Adira know. Rural communities seem to be faring better than urban. We are off the grid. I had to pay to send this message to you. I see that my time is almost up— know that I love you and miss you! Take care of yourself. Hope we see each other again...."

And the transmission ended.

David was appalled at Jennifer's appearance. She was disheveled, and her clothes appeared to be old and dirty. If only he could have brought her here to Galatéa. Everything she said was in line with what they were hearing about the conditions on Earth. They, indeed, had deteriorated far more than he thought.

I need to share my findings with someone, especially about my sister. Adira is the most trusted person I have ever known.

Adira, this is David. Are you still available to meet me in my quarters tonight?

Sure, David. Does 1900 hours sound OK?

See you then.

Adira arrived precisely on time. Upon entering David's quarters, she saw that he had been cooking. "Your garden seems to be flourishing. What are you up to over there?" She crossed the room to his tiny kitchen. "That smells great!"

"I've been experimenting with herbs mostly and a few vegetables. I'm making tomato sauce with garlic, oregano, and basil, as well as a fresh salad from lettuce I have grown here in my quarters. I know you like your pasta al dente. It'll be ready in a few. I'm serving linguine with a nice red sauce." *I know those were your favorites from when we were together. Do you remember*

Adira?

"Sounds heavenly. I brought dessert. I remembered that your favorite was raspberry swirl cheesecake. I twisted Astrid's arm several times to get the raspberries from her." She laughed. "Rasa is so good at supplying what we need from her pantry. She's great to be around too. I wish Astrid could take lessons from the optimist's playbook sometimes." Adira plopped down and settled into a chair with a sigh. The small table was set for two with an actual tablecloth and napkins. "You went all out tonight! This is so welcome and appreciated. I hope you know." There was a twinkle in her eyes.

"Gardening and astronomy are hobbies I've adopted and pursued since we came to Galatéa. Oh, and cooking, too, of course. Glad you don't mind being my guinea pig!"

"Ha! Haven't been called a guinea pig—ever!"

David brought the linguine to the table, tossed the salad, and served it. "Enjoy your salad. This is the first course, of course." *She noticed the tablecloth and napkins. So far, so good.* They ate slowly and savored dinner; it was a reminder of Earth and home.

"I miss my cottage on the west coast. I hear things are not going well back home." Adira took a bite of her cheesecake.

"Unfortunately, there are several serious things I wanted to discuss with you. You are the only person I trust completely. Some of what I have to share isn't good. I received a transmission from Jennifer. She confirmed our fears that Earth is going through Armageddon. The military has taken over my apartment building, and the country is under martial law. She has moved to Taika's farmhouse and said that rural life is far safer than being in the cities. She looked disheveled, dirty, and upset. I can't believe everything has deteriorated so quickly." David rubbed his eyes, frowning.

"My cottage AI is not responding, so I have no idea what's happening on the West Coast. I'm so sorry to hear that Jennifer is having such a hard time. She's welcome to stay at the farm as long as she needs."

"I wish she could have come with us. The timestamp on the transmission is from nine months ago. There was no explanation as to why it took so long to get here or whether it was intercepted by someone en route. There's more bad news, I'm afraid."

Adira looked startled at David's grim demeanor after such a delicious meal and visit. "Worse than what you just told me?"

"Yes. We need to discuss Eurydice and SIS22. For now, we need to keep this information strictly between us. Can you agree to that stipulation?"

"Of course. I trust your judgment."

"Eurydice has been withholding some devastating information from us." David proceeded to fill Adira in on the cosmic event that would wipe out all life on Earth. "I'm not sure about the timeline for this cosmic event, but it seems it will happen sooner rather than later." He then explained Project Proteus, how it was abandoned due to ethical objections, and how it was revived here on Galatéa. Lastly, he informed Adira about Eurydice's hybrid human status. She had merged with a sentient AI.

"So that's why she refused the nanoparticles and BAI implant! Now it all makes sense."

"The other thing that I'm concerned about is that the aliens here on Galatéa have been observing our Earth for far longer than we know. We need to try to figure out their agenda. I'm wondering if we know what we are dealing with here."

Adira, Jomei here. Rafe is available to speak with you now.

Thank you, Jomei; please let him know I am on my way.

"This is far more than I can absorb in one evening. I appreciate your trust in sharing classified and potentially life-altering information with me. You know I've struggled with trusting Eurydice in the past, and you understand why. But SIS22 as an entity, too? Earth will be gone? As I've mentioned, this will take some time to comprehend. I need to discuss the symbionts and the implications or consequences for the colony with Rafe."

"Thank you for a lovely dinner. It reminds me of home, your apartment, and all our good times there. Contact me if anything else arises, and I will do the same. Good evening, David." Adira turned and left his quarters.

Well, that went better than I thought it would. I feel better now that someone else knows.

21 - Adira and Rafe

"Hi, Rafe. I came over to your security station to have a private discussion about the alien presence." Adira's gaze was drawn to numerous live feeds of the entire colony. "I know you were outraged to hear about the aliens much later than everyone else. Especially because you are the head of security, I'm here to answer your questions, and hopefully, you will feel better about their presence."

"I'm sure you know that my concerns as head of security are warranted and understandable.

Yes, and I agree. Eurydice did not want to bring you and Jomei in sooner, but we won't go there now.

"My first two questions are: Who are They, and What do they Want?"

"David and I are in the process of identifying the aliens' nature and origin. With the help of Jomei, we are attempting to perform a detailed analysis and investigation. We are studying their physiology, technology, and attempts at communication to better understand their identity.

"As for what they want, this is a bit more complicated. Determining the intentions of the aliens will require our ongoing observation and analysis. Essentially, Jomei will be extremely helpful in looking for patterns in their behavior, communications, and human interactions. They have been deemed benevolent and suggested a way to save the nine outbreak patients."

"How do we know they are benevolent, Adira?" Rafe's blue eyes flashed as he considered Adira's insights.

"Assessing the benevolence or malevolence of this alien species is a complex task. Zhopla, David, Eurydice, and I have been engaging in lengthy dialogues to establish communication channels to evaluate their intentions and further assess potential threats to the colony. Analyzing their interactions is crucial in our determination of their overall nature. You and Jomei will have access to the recorded holograms of these sessions for further evaluation.

"We've been able to discern that according to the aliens' prognosis for the outbreak patients, they have the medical knowledge to cure them. Because none of the patients had the nanocytes before exhibiting outbreak symptoms, they are now useless in healing them. They had to have received them before exposure to whatever agent responsible for the outbreak.

"The aliens live as symbiotic entities that incorporate themselves into neurological tissue; essentially, they are organisms that need a physical body. They have informed us that our patients' only hope for survival is through symbiotic partnering. The aliens suggest the colonists be asked—as in giving informed consent—to have a symbiont implanted.

"None of our treatments or medications have been useful for these patients, and they remain in hibernation until we find a cure. It appears we have no choice. We plan to awaken them individually and let them know they can choose a lifelong symbiotic relationship or certain death. The aliens also signify that the symbiotic relationship will bring about many positive outcomes for both the human they join with and the alien entity."

"Where do we go from here to monitor them then?"

"We hoped you might provide higher-level recommendations for further monitoring and studying the aliens." Adira took a seat next to Rafe.

I'm so glad Rafe calmed down. That was touch and go in the beginning.

Rafe rubbed his temples and, after a long pause, continued. "I would recommend the establishment of communication channels to facilitate further dialogue and understanding for Jomei and me. We will modify our advanced surveillance technology and algorithms to collect data regarding their communications, behaviors, and technology.

"I would also recommend further collaboration to share our insights about the aliens. Security will continuously evaluate any potential risks and threats posed by the aliens to ensure the safety and security of the colony."

"I believe your recommendations align with what David and I were thinking. Along with establishing protocols and guidelines for interacting with the aliens and with Jomei's help preparing for potential scenarios."

Adira held her breath after another lengthy pause in the conversation.

"After thinking this through, I believe the approach to monitoring and interacting with the aliens will likely evolve based on what we discover and through our ongoing risk assessments. I will work closely with everyone involved, including the patients who decided to receive the symbiont. This will further ensure the colony's safety and security as we seek a better understanding of the alien presence in our midst."

"Rafe, I'm relieved you are on board with this strange and unexpected scenario. Please feel free to contact me night or day for any reason. As your mentor, I am always available to you." Adira stood to leave as she gently squeezed Rafe on his shoulder.

Rafe decided to do some digging. *Jomei, what information regarding symbiotic relationships between humans and other organisms is in the archives?*

My research indicates many exciting facts. Beginning with the definition of symbiotic organisms, the term symbiosis is derived from the Greek word meaning a prolonged and close association between two or more organisms of different species lasting the lifetime of one or all partners. This definition is not considered universal; therefore, taking a broader approach due to the alien nature of our situation in the caves takes precedence. The associations of symbiotic relationships vary widely in types of interaction and intimacy. Different symbiotic relationships exist, such as mutualistic relationships, where all partners benefit. Commensalism is where one partner benefits and the other is not harmed. Finally, there are parasitic relationships where one partner benefits and the other is harmed. It has been widely accepted that a continuum of these categories spans between antagonism and cooperation.

Antagonistic relationships occur between parasites and their hosts. Parasites are pathogens. It is worrisome that many pathogens and parasites are within the definition of symbiosis. In researching this topic, Jomei finds that symbiotic relationships are ubiquitous on Earth. For example, eukaryotic human cells and bacteria are distantly related species but form symbiotic partnerships. Such relationships are also found between closely related species, such as ants. Relationships can form a tight symbiosis, like mitochondria with their eukaryotic cells, or they can create a looser relationship between completely separate organisms.

Rafe was perplexed and intrigued. *According to Adira, the aliens are adopting an altruistic attitude. What will it cost them to partner with human hosts?*

Rafe, and Jomei found the concept of reciprocal altruism. If applied to our scenario, it appears that the aliens intend to join with a human as an act of helping the individual by curing them of the outbreak and avoiding death. What effects it may have on the aliens is unclear. Questions arise, such as whether there is a chance that the aliens expect a future reverse situation where the human who was cured will be asked to perform an altruistic act towards the alien who helped them. Mathematical prediction models indicative of the likelihood of an altruistic act on behalf of one's family on Earth have been posited.

Rafe processed this information in silence. *These are good questions. There are ethical dilemmas that need to be explored further. What was helpful in humanity's evolutionary past solved the problems of yesterday. The ongoing evolution of alien and human symbionts is entirely unknown.*

Indeed, a more cooperative relationship with connections of shared responsibilities and equality, without any pressure to comply, would be ideal. Viewing the alien/human symbiotic relationship from the lens of a joint venture is necessary. The relationship would be hierarchical due to the vast knowledge of the aliens. To reach symbiosis in an ongoing relationship, some deconditioning on the part of the humans will be necessary. Humans are conditioned from birth. Removal of the subjectivity of a permanent symbiotic relationship will need to be explored. Both partners must realize that they are now in a permanent joint venture requiring ongoing dialogue and investigation so that a healthy relationship may manifest.

Predicting the exact roles that aliens will have in intimate interactions with human hosts is difficult. Our discussion offers a preliminary analysis due to our limited understanding of the alien-host symbiotic relationship and its ongoing evolution.

Rafe slumped back into his chair, drumming his fingers, as he observed the colonists going about their usual work and activities via the myriad cameras and nano-security droids.

Later that evening, alone in his quarters, Rafe had time to consider what he learned. He remembered how he felt when he was offered a cure for his Klowd9 addiction.

Rafe viewed his image in the mirror and talked to himself out loud. "I was in denial of being addicted to anything, let alone the adventures on Klowd9 that I was living for. Being in the Involuntary Unit or jail is a painful memory for me. The doctor told me that I had three years to live if I continued. I can sympathize with how the outbreak patients feel once they are told.

"I thought getting the nanocytes was the last thing I wanted. To become a puppet with no feelings was what the first generation of nanocytes caused. Getting involved with SIS22 nanomedicine with upgraded nanoparticles and getting the Brain-to-Artificial Intelligence Interface was one of the best things that have ever happened to me. And then along came Jomei. Yet another fantastic addition to the life I've built on Galatéa."

Rafe looked deeper at himself and saw a healthy, robust person looking back. "I remember what I looked like when I came home from the Involuntary Unit. I had just signed the contract to join the Institute and SIS22, and Grampy and I fought. I haven't had a black eye since we left Earth. I wonder why I haven't heard from Grampy yet.

Even though it takes three months to arrive, he would've answered my messages by now.

Rafe remained in his quiet quarters, the hum of the dome life outside barely penetrating the thick walls. He stared at his reflection in the dome's window, his eyes searching for a glimpse of the man he used to be. The scars of his addiction were still visible, faint lines etched on his face and in the hollowness of his eyes. Yet, there was something new, a glimmer of hope and a spark of vitality that hadn't been there before. He acknowledged the nanocytes coursing through his veins and the brain implant nestled in his skull were responsible for this transformation.

Hindsight is always twenty-twenty, or in my enhanced state, zoomed in to anything I want it to be!

Months ago, back on Earth in the Involuntary Unit, Rafe had been on the brink of destruction. His Klowd9 addiction had consumed him, leaving him a shell of his former self. Every day had been a struggle, a relentless battle against the cravings for exotic virtual adventures that threatened to overwhelm him. He had lost friends, family, and his career to the insidious grip of the highs of virtual reality during Klowd9 use. Desperation and the three-year survivability prognosis had driven him to seek out the experimental treatment, a last-ditch effort to reclaim his life.

The illegal (on Earth) implantation of highly evolved nanocytes by SIS22 was a revolutionary procedure, one that promised not only to cure his addiction but to enhance his physical and mental capabilities. He saw them as microscopic machines now working tirelessly within his body, repairing the damage caused by years of abuse and optimizing his biological functions. The brain implant, a marvel of modern science, interfaced seamlessly with his neural pathways, augmenting his cognitive abilities and providing unprecedented communication abilities and clarity of thought.

At first, Rafe had been skeptical. The idea of surrendering his body to technology was daunting, and the potential risks were substantial. But as the days turned into weeks, he noticed subtle changes. His energy levels soared, his focus sharpened, and the constant ache in his bones dissipated. The cravings that had once dominated his existence faded into the background, replaced by a newfound sense of control and determination.

Rafe's enhanced performance was not limited to his physical capabilities. The brain implant had unlocked areas of his mind he never knew existed. He found himself processing information at lightning speed, solving complex problems easily, and retaining vast amounts of knowledge. Tasks that had once seemed insurmountable were now effortless, and his productivity skyrocketed. He felt like a new person, one who was no longer defined by his past mistakes but by his potential for the future. *I'm blown away by the spiritual side of this transformation. Through the Institute's teachings and the help of Zhopla and Adira, my life is a thousand times better.*

However, this newfound power came with its own set of challenges. Rafe was acutely aware of the ethical and moral implications of his transformation. The line between human and machine had become blurred, and he often grappled with questions about his identity.

Am I still the same person, or am I becoming something entirely different? The technology that had saved me had the potential to fundamentally alter who I was. Am I a different person now? Is it fair to keep the technology from the original colonists?

This realization was both exhilarating and terrifying.

It is too bad that some recruits thought the technology would corrupt their bodies. I still feel bad for Phil Roskos because they had to remove the tech. After all, his body couldn't handle it. Then he went on to catch the outbreak, and he's one of the patients in the worst condition at this point. The medical nanoparticles will prolong my life, and I've never felt better than I do now. I wonder if receiving a symbiont will be the same.

Rafe lay down on his bunk. Thinking of Rasa brought a smile to his face. *I'm glad I have to go to the canteen several times every day. At least I don't have to think of excuses to see her. I wonder when the next movie night will be. Setting an internal reminder to ask Rasa tomorrow.*

He sat up suddenly as a new thought struck him and wondered aloud, "That leaves me with the next big question. Who or what have the aliens been hiding from in the caves for millennia?"

22 - Rafe, Grampy and Rizika

Rafe watched from the Medbay doorway, a sense of pride and relief washing over him. They had faced impossible odds and emerged victorious.

Jomei's digital form entered Rafe's BAI, and their digital processes were filled with a rare light. *We did it, Rafe. We saved them.*

Rafe nodded, his eyes softening. *Yes, we did. But this is just the beginning. We have a lot of work ahead of us. Restoration of the hibernation pods has saved the patients for now. Finding the cure for this illness is what's needed. We saved them and bought them some time, but this is not over yet.*

Jomei abruptly switched gears. *Eurydice has forwarded a message from Earth addressed to you.*

Thanks, Jomei. After completing my colony rounds, I will view it when I reach security.

Now a familiar face in the colony, Rafe had been diligently walking through the colony areas, often more than once daily. The colonists have grown accustomed to his presence and have warmly welcomed him despite feeling secure in their Galatéa homes. He has forged a few friendships, even with the usually grumpy Astrid, who treated him as one of her greenhouse workers. Mindful of Astrid's plant-related sensitivities, Rafe refrained from touching any plants in her presence. The colony's social structure had transformed into a bond of open camaraderie and humor, especially now that the mysterious outbreak had ceased at nine patients.

"Good morning, Rafe. Any updates on the death of my worker?" Astrid removed her goggles and mask to prevent inhaled spores and pollen from the plants she measured.

"And how are you today, Astrid? I see you are busy with your plants," Rafe takes a cursory look around the greenhouse. "The growth of these plants is truly remarkable. I've never seen plants thrive and flourish at such a rapid pace."

"The nanotechnology here on Galatéa is unprecedented. It's especially good at manipulating matter and enables us to develop innovative solutions across diverse plant types and needs. Our nanoscale materials have enhanced crop yields, improved nutrient delivery systems, and mitigated environmental impacts: no drought, pests, parasites, or viruses to curb their growth. We also optimized our limited resources using nano-tech-enabled sensors to measure environmental conditions.

"Since the passing of one of our workers, nanotechnology has been strictly monitored, and I have to seek permission to use any nanotech." Astrid moved away from the plants and banged her shovel on a mound of gravel to emphasize how she felt about having limited access to the nanotech.

"Until we root out the malicious actors in releasing engineered nanoparticles, we will maintain the strictest of guidelines to access. The nanoparticles that were released carried a potent toxin. These particles also were able to evade detection, and they spread rapidly through the irrigation system and air. Unaware of the danger, Bob Jones was exposed to the nano-toxin.

"We searched Bob's living quarters and interviewed his family and friends. Apparently, nothing was amiss in his life. He was happy with his choice to leave Earth and come here to the colony. As you know, he was one of the original colonists. It appears he was in the wrong place at the wrong time." Rafe stepped back to avoid being pelted by gravel as Astrid continued to bang her shovel.

Astrid appeared to be unaware of her actions. She abruptly

stopped banging the shovel and turned her scowling face to Rafe. "I can't believe you haven't come up with more information or details about what happened here!"

I won't share the enhanced surveillance systems Jomei has incorporated to sense nanotoxins in the water and air.

"Our surveillance systems could not isolate deviant actions or behaviors before Bob's demise. However, Jomei and I are working feverishly to develop enhanced safety measures for every greenhouse and all common spaces in the dome."

Jomei, I'm on my way back to security. Because we haven't found anything, I will need to conduct more personal surveillance to observe the colonists first-hand. Facial expressions, specific movements, or eye contact can belie what's really going on with someone. The atrium and canteen are perfect places for my observances. There is no need to explain why I'm there; people act more naturally when relaxed.

Acknowledged.

###

This large screen is excellent for viewing messages from Earth. Jomei, go ahead and play my message.

The viewscreen went blank for several seconds. Grampy's grizzled face emerged. He squinted at the camera, his face perpetually unshaven but seemingly in a better mood than usual.

Crusty as usual, I see. Grampy's looking good otherwise.

The video began.

Grampy's scratchy voice came through; he shouted as if that would make Rafe hear him across the universe. "I will have you know that I am the Rizika champion not just in my neighborhood but also in the region!! Wishin' we could have a discussion like we used ta! Things ain't so great on planet Earth, though. Some of

191

them people are thinkin' we're in the end times—they callin' it the 'pocalypse! Some of them radicals are formin' communes and leavin' society! They really are cults; cults is all they is! And to beat all that, there's some other radical groups resortin' to terrorism by blowin' things up! This is all cuz they don't want religions to be one group.

"Dammit! They're telling me I only have 60 seconds left! Rafe, I know I wasn't the best role model for you. But I hope you know I care about you and want to see how you're doin'. Hope you're all through with that Klowd9 crap. Send me a message when you can……"

The message ended in mid-sentence.

Your Grandfather is a very . . . . interesting human. The alteration of world religions and their practices, which met with fierce resistance, was entirely predictable. Before we left Earth, there were numerous radical factions in religious communities.

'Interesting' is a kind description of my Grampy, Jomei.

Based on historical evidence, any attempt to implement such a radical transformation will face significant challenges. Religious communities are known to be deeply committed to the preservation and purity of their religious traditions, and their vehement opposition is a testament to that. The devout and religious may see the merging of all religions as blasphemous, heretical, or a betrayal of their faith. There have been acts of protest, civil disobedience, and now violent resistance perpetrated because of the perceived infringement on their religious autonomy.

Rafe remained seated for a while after the video ended. He was glad Grampy's message got through and that everything appeared to be functioning in his world. Regional Rizika champ—way to go, Grampy.

Thank you, Jomei, for your insights into the problem of

merging world religions.

Rafe stood and gesticulated, unable to contain his enthusiasm as he explained a sudden insight to Jomei. *I think I have considered a way to observe the colonists while I'm among them. Let's start a colony-wide Rizika championship series! We could play it in the atrium. Can you devise a three-dimensional holographic game board for players who will form teams vying for control over asteroid mining operations? One that can be viewed from all sides of the asteroids of the inner solar system? Security details and droids will be used to observe the participants and the crowds.*

The asteroid fields of the Hildas, Trojans, and Greeks? Yes, it can be done. I will include quantum projection dice and let you know when they are ready.

The metallic clang of doors sliding open echoed through the vast chamber of the Atrium as the contestants filed into the constructed "arena." The droids helped erect the Galatéa Dome Atrium arena, built as an immense, self-contained environment designed to host elaborate competitions. Because it was built on the colony's dark side, Jomei ensured it glowed with an otherworldly luminescence, and the stars above were visible. Rafe had introduced the game called Rizika to the colonists, who readily accepted the idea of something new and exciting to do. Tonight, everyone's attention was on the Rizika tournament, a high-stakes strategy contest where players took on the roles of competing space-faring corporations. The objective is to dominate the asteroid mining industry where resources are scarce and alliances are fragile.

The arena's centerpiece featured a massive holographic display of Sol's asteroid belt, shimmering in intricate detail and hovering over everyone's heads. Various asteroids, each abundant in different minerals, floated in the virtual expanse, ready to be claimed. Surrounding this display were the contestants' stations, each equipped with advanced consoles and immersive interfaces.

While monitoring the colony, Rafe and the rest of the security team covertly observed the contestants and spectators as Galatéa's first Rizika tournament began. *Jomei, are surveillance measures and biosensors nominal as we start our observations of all colony quadrants?*

Yes, all systems are nominal, including the parameters of biosensor gathering data. Our updated nanotech sensors are active, and all visual displays are operational. For the Rizika game, the silver droids in the Atrium have also been equipped with multiple Sentinel-II units and have been strategically deployed. I have programmed each unit to autonomously navigate through the crowd, transmitting and recording continuous data feeds to the security control room where our operatives monitor the situation in real time. Any identified threats or suspicious activities would prompt immediate responses, including dispatching additional security personnel or initiating preemptive measures.

As the thirty contestants entered the arena and took their positions, Jomei's voice boomed through the dome: "Welcome to Rizika! Tonight's game will test your strategic prowess, economic acumen, and diplomatic skills. May the best corporation emerge victorious!" The silver droids were designed to blend seamlessly into the Atrium environment. The humanoid droids moved quietly and unnoticed through the crowds. Their synthetic skin and clothing mimicked human appearance, minimizing suspicion and allowing for covert surveillance operations.

Other droids provided snacks and nourishment as they navigated through the spectators. Snatches of conversations and body language were captured as they progressed through the crowds during the tournament.

Each team had ten colony players representing corporations

called Neoluna Industries, Ra Ventures, and Astroteric Consortium. Jomei activated their consoles. Holographic avatars and corporate insignias flickered to life above each station, signaling the commencement of the game.

At Station 1, Alexei Volkov, the CEO of Neoluna Industries, reviewed his initial resources and fleet capabilities. The team's avatar, a sleek, silver-suited figure with a sharp, angular face, stood proudly on the display field. By rolling the quantum dice, Neoluna's assigned strength lay in its advanced propulsion technology, which allowed faster travel between asteroids. Alexei's team strategy would hinge on rapid expansion and securing high-value asteroids early.

To his right, at Station 2, Mira Tanaka, the leader of Ra Ventures, scrutinized her team's starting assets. Ra Ventures' quantum dice role resulted in their excelling in resource extraction and refining, giving Mira an edge in maximizing profits from mined minerals. Their team avatar, clad in a golden, reflective suit, symbolized the corporation's wealth and technological prowess. Mira and her team planned to form strategic alliances and focus on optimizing resource yields.

Across from them, at Station 3, Raj Patel of Astroteric Consortium reviewed his team's tactical options. Astroteric's quantum dice roll resulted in a fleet that boasted superior defensive capabilities, making Raj's corporation formidable in protecting its assets. Their team's avatar, armored and imposing in electric blue, represented Astroteric's resilience. Raj and his team aimed to establish strongholds on key asteroids and fortify their positions against potential aggressors.

The initial phase of Rizika began with each corporation selecting their starting asteroid. The contestants placed their markers, digital representations of mining outposts, in their chosen locations. With rolls of the Rizika quantum dice, Alexei's team roll gave them a central asteroid rich in platinum, Mira's team roll of the quantum dice resulted in a cluster with diverse mineral deposits, and Raj's team roll gave them a defensible asteroid with valuable rare earth elements.

"Phase one: Exploration and Expansion," Jomei declared. The holographic asteroids began to rotate, revealing new sectors. Each team's contestants deployed scout drones to survey the newly exposed areas. The holographic display became more complicated as thirty drones appeared as green dots, with each team hoping to uncover hidden resource nodes and avoid potential hazards.

Alexei's team scouts discovered a high-density asteroid belt teeming with untapped resources. They immediately dispatched his mining fleets, their advanced engines propelling them swiftly across the virtual void. As Neoluna's silver markers spread across the map, Alexei felt a surge of confidence. Their aggressive expansion was paying off.

Mira, meanwhile, focused on optimizing her team's existing operations. They negotiated a trade deal with Raj, offering refined minerals in exchange for defensive support. The two corporations formed a tentative alliance, their avatars shaking hands in the holographic display. Mira's team's mining efficiency soared as they upgraded their extraction facilities, their wealth multiplying rapidly.

Raj's team fortified their positions, establishing defense turrets and deploying patrol ships, which were displayed as red dots around their key assets. Astroteric's presence grew steadily, and its defensive network created a formidable barrier against potential incursions. Raj's strategy of slow but steady growth was beginning to bear fruit.

"Phase two: Conflict and Negotiation," Jomei's voice resonated through the dome. The atmosphere grew tense as the contestants prepared for the next stage of the game. Alexei's rapid expansion had not gone unnoticed, and both Mira and Raj viewed

Neoluna as a growing threat.

A sudden alert flashed on Alexei's console. Mira's fleets were moving towards one of his newly claimed asteroids. "Ra Ventures is attempting a hostile takeover," Jomei declared. Jomei's biosensors detected that Alexei's heart raced as he mobilized his defense fleets, positioning them to intercept the incoming threat.

The holographic display erupted in dazzling lights as the two fleets clashed. Neoluna's advanced propulsion gave Alexei's ships a speed advantage, but Mira's fleet, represented by golden dots, was more extensive and better equipped for sustained combat. The battle raged on, and each side's trading blows were a stunning display of strategic maneuvering.

Amid the conflict, Raj saw an opportunity. With Neoluna's forces occupied, he launched a surprise attack on one of Alexei's undefended mining outposts. Astroteric's ships swooped in, their superior firepower overwhelming the minimal defenses. Raj's avatar smirked as Astroteric claimed the valuable asteroid.

Alexei cursed under his breath. His team had underestimated Raj's opportunism. Desperate to turn the tide, he sent a message to Mira, proposing a temporary ceasefire to repel Raj's incursion. After a tense negotiation, Mira agreed. Their combined silver and golden forces pushed Raj's red fleets back, securing the contested asteroid.

"Phase three: Consolidation and Domination," Jomei intoned. The final phase of Rizika was upon them. The contestants regrouped, assessing their positions and planning their endgame strategies.

Having secured a wealth of resources and with her alliance with Alexei still holding, Mira's team focused on expanding their influence through economic means. They initiated trade agreements with smaller corporations and invested in advanced technologies, increasing Ra Ventures' overall efficiency and production capacity.

Raj's team, recognizing that confrontation with Alexei and Mira would be futile, shifted their focus to fortifying their remaining assets and leveraging their defensive prowess. Raj's team sought out minor skirmishes with weaker players, expanding their territory through calculated, low-risk engagements.

Determined to reclaim his dominance, Alexei conferred with his team and devised a bold strategy. Alexei proposed a grand alliance with Mira, suggesting that together, they could crush Astroteric and divide the spoils. Seeing the potential for a decisive victory, Mira and her team agreed. Their combined fleets approached Raj's stronghold, a massive asteroid bristling with defenses.

The final battle was a spectacle of strategic brilliance and raw power. Alexei and Mira's fleets coordinated their attacks, exploiting weaknesses in Astroteric's defenses. Raj, ever the tactician, deployed his forces precisely, inflicting heavy losses on the attackers. The holographic display lit up with the simulated explosions of starships and the flash of laser fire.

Despite Raj's valiant defense, the combined might of Neoluna and Ra Ventures proved overwhelming. Astroteric's stronghold fell, and Raj's remaining assets were swiftly claimed. The holographic display shifted to show the new balance of power: Neoluna and Ra Ventures stood as the dominant forces in the asteroid belt.

"Congratulations to the teams of Alexei Volkov and Mira Tanaka, the joint victors of tonight's Rizika!" Jomei proclaimed. The dome erupted in applause as the twenty contestants stood, their avatars shaking hands in a show of mutual respect.

Alexei and Mira exchanged nods, acknowledging their partnership's success. Alexei reminded his team. "For now, we share the spoils of victory, but we know that alliances are temporary in the cutthroat world of corporate rivalry, and trust is a rare commodity."

Jomei's booming voice rang throughout the Atrium during the closing announcement; "In the ever-shifting landscape of Rizika, one truth remains constant: the quest for dominance is never truly over. Each game is a new opportunity, a fresh battlefield where alliances could be forged or shattered, and fortunes could rise or fall. The teams will return to the Galatéa Dome for Round 2 and 3, ready to face new challenges and reclaim their place among the stars again. And Claim their prize as Champions of Rizika on the planet Galatéa!"

Rafe watched as the holographic displays dimmed and the contestants began to leave the arena. *This Rizika tournament was a great success. Players and teams displayed their strategic and diplomatic skills to the fullest extent. Alexei and Mira conversed deeply with their teams, likely planning their moves for the next round—there were two more rounds to go. The winning team must win two of three to be declared champions. I don't see Raj or his teammates anywhere.*

23 - Thirteen Caves

"I see we are all here except David and Rafe," Eurydice's frown deepened, a crease settling between her brows. "All of us must be present for the update, Gint, on your team's findings of the caves and the documented discoveries thus far."

Gint's footsteps echoed in the stark, gray-walled meeting room, his pacing restless, like a tethered animal. The metallic tang of the cave air lingered, cool and sharp. He paused only when David and Rafe slipped in, panting slightly, their boots dusted with remnants of the tunnels they'd rushed through. Adira's shoulders relaxed at their arrival, a fleeting smile curving her lips. The caves were a marvel, a riddle whispered by stone and time, and the report promised answers—or at least hints.

Eurydice cleared her throat, the authority in her voice sharpening the air. "Gint, as Director of the Extraterrestrial Archaeological Expedition of Galatéa, you and your team have been tasked with exploring the thirteen caves containing hieroglyphics, pictograms, statues, and other remnants of a lost civilization. Our mission demands accuracy, depth, and an understanding of the civilization that once thrived here. Your work, alongside the expertise of linguists, astroarchaeologists, and xenobiologists, is paramount to our success."

Gint's eyes flickered over the team before he began, his voice measured. "When we first descended into the cave system beneath Galatéa's surface, we were met with a labyrinth of ancient whispers etched in stone. Each cave, a chapter in the story of a people long vanished." He paused, brushing his hair back from his face. "Let's start with Cave One. Jomei, project the images."

The lights dimmed, and Jomei's holographic display brought the Hall of Echoes to life. The chamber stretched vast and cavernous, shadows playing on walls lined with intricate hieroglyphs. The air seemed to shimmer with the ghosts of ancient voices.

"This cave," Gint continued, his voice reverent, "was a place of ceremony. The walls tell creation myths and cosmic beginnings painted in delicate and bold strokes. Deities loom large, their forms intertwined with celestial motifs. The sound carries here, amplifying speech as though the cave itself was alive, a witness to their rituals. The acoustics are uncanny—even a whisper could spiral outward, filling the chamber."

The display shifted to the next chamber. The Pictogram Chamber's walls glowed with the warmth of a life once vibrant. Images of fields and feasts, hunts and hearths, sprawled in exquisite detail—a tableau of existence.

"In this smaller, circular cave," Gint said, "the Galatéans chronicled their daily lives. Each pictogram pulses with movement—farmers tilling the soil, families gathered in laughter, hunters in mid-pursuit. It's as if they feared their lives might fade into silence and carved them here to endure."

The air thickened as the next cave appeared. The Astronomical Vault unfolded its ceiling, which was a canvas of stars. Constellations were etched with a precision that defied time, and the cosmos was rendered in three dimensions.

"This," Gint's voice softened, "is a map of the heavens. They knew the stars intimately—the paths of comets, the dance of planets. Our astroarchaeologists believe these carvings mirror the night sky, aligning with celestial events recorded long ago. It's as if they captured eternity and held it here, in stone."

Jomei projected an image of a nebula—swirls of color that mirrored the nebulae of distant galaxies.

"Their knowledge stretched beyond their world," Gint mused.

"They charted the universe with an artist's eye and a scientist's mind."

The images blurred as the next cave was projected, then sharpened into statues standing in silent vigil—the Archive of Leadership. Each figure seemed to breathe authority, their eyes carved with a wisdom that transcended time.

"These statues," Gint explained, "represent their leaders. Achievements etched at their feet, legacies woven into stone. Yet the language eludes us—a puzzle within a puzzle. We may never know their full stories, but their presence speaks of governance, continuity, and pride."

Next, the Sanctuary—a hushed space where altars bore witness to ancient faith. The walls, painted with deities crowned in fire, water, earth, and air, seemed to exhale spirituality.

"This was sacred ground," Gint said, almost whispering. "The carvings tell of prayers, sacrifices, and a dialogue between the mortal and the divine. They sought answers here, perhaps solace. The air still carries a weight, a residue of belief."

The Garden cave bloomed next, verdant even in memory. The humid air preserved remnants of alien plants, delicate fronds frozen in time.

"A botanical wonder," Gint marveled. "They cultivated life beneath the earth's skin—medicinal herbs, ceremonial flora. The irrigation channels and cultivation beds suggest harmony with nature, a knowledge of growth and healing."

Gint continued, "The artifacts found in the caves have unraveled further mysteries—warriors etched in battle stance, tablets filled with untranslatable knowledge, council chambers ringed with stone seats. Each chamber a whisper of the past, a story half-told.

"Every cave," Gint concluded, his gaze sweeping the room,

"reveals a fragment of who they were. Their joys, struggles, faith, and fears. They spoke through stone, and though they've gone silent, their echoes remain. It's up to us to listen."

As the lights returned, Eurydice's eyes held a flicker of something softer. "Thank you, Gint. You've given us more than a report—you've given us a glimpse of a world lost to time."

Gint bowed his head slightly, the weight of the caves' secrets firmly settled on his shoulders. The meeting ended, but the mysteries of Galatéa lingered—alive, waiting.

The team lingered in silence, the echoes of Gint's words still hanging in the air. David finally spoke, his voice low and contemplative. "It's strange, isn't it? To feel so close to people, we'll never meet. Like they're just out of reach."

Adira nodded. "Their stories are everywhere—on the walls, in the air we breathe down here. But they're fragments, pieces of a puzzle we're only beginning to understand."

Rafe's eyes narrowed in thought. "And yet, they left this behind for a reason. They knew someone would come, eventually. They wanted their lives to be remembered."

Eurydice stepped forward, her gaze sweeping over the team. "We owe it to them to keep searching. Every discovery brings us closer to understanding not just who they were but perhaps who we are. Their civilization may have vanished, but their legacy endures."

Gint's voice was quieter now, almost reverent. "And maybe, in uncovering their past, we'll learn something about our own future."

The lights dimmed once more, and the images of the caves flickered back to life—silent sentinels waiting to share their secrets with those who dared to listen.

"The importance of these caves cannot be underestimated.

These thirteen caves offer a physical connection to the past and have already provided invaluable insights into the complex social structure, sophisticated knowledge, and rich cultural heritage of the ancient civilization that once inhabited Planet Galatéa.

"I and my team greatly appreciate your efforts. Please let me know how I can help inform you about your initiatives." Gint pulled his hair back away from his face.

"I believe that concludes our meeting with Gint. Thank you, Dr. Larson. The information you've brought us today is far more than I imagined. There is still much more to do and far more to think about." Eurydice looked away as she dismissed Gint.

After Rafe was sure Gint had left, he commented. "I have concerns regarding the colonists who are completely unaware of the caves and the alien connection to the artifacts." Rafe leaned forward in his seat and stood up. "When the time comes to communicate our findings to the general population of the colony, then to the media and public on Earth, do we have a plan to ensure an accurate and engaging dissemination of information? Do we have Public Relations Specialists assigned to communications outside Gint's team and SIS22 operatives?"

"Yes, along with all the experts we have brought to Galatéa, a Public Relations Specialist was among them. His name is Ethan Clarke. He is one of the eight outbreak patients in hibernation." Eurydice also stood. "He is highly knowledgeable of public relations issues. I would characterize him as analytical and dedicated. The outbreak illness has profoundly weakened him, and Dr. Michel has indicated that he is among our most critical patients."

"I'm also concerned about the health and safety of the people working and living in the caves. Jomei and I would like to enhance the safety and security of the caves with the addition of enhanced surveillance monitoring. I am especially interested in gathering more information about potentially hazardous microenvironments within the caves. I want to work with the medical team to address occupational health issues, institute safety regulations, and perform risk assessments on any problems we may find." Rafe took his seat once again.

"Your concerns are noted, Rafe. I will bring them to the next Council meeting. I'm sure Chancellor Byron will be most interested in your proposals for the safety and security of the caves. As far as surveillance and monitoring of the caves themselves remains strictly forbidden. These areas are restricted, and no images are to be taken. All information about the caves and the alien presence will remain confidential." Eurydice stood and made it clear the meeting was over.

24 - The Symbionts

David followed the narrow cave with its intricate passages, seemingly like a maze, to Cave Twelve. He remembered Gint and his team had tentatively called this cave the Rite of Passage. Zhopla used the waters in this cave for Rafe and others in the program to test their willingness and determination to undergo the Institute's continuing spiritual rites required by SIS22 when they signed on to cure their addictions with the nanoparticles and BAIs.

The rooms at the end of the passages are adorned with symbols and artifacts related to various rites. The experts on the team must find these artifacts fascinating. They provide insight into the cultural and social practices of an ancient civilization. The symbols are intricate in design and must have been valuable to the aliens because of the quality of the work. Some artifacts allude to the qualities of bravery, leadership, and resilience. That's just my opinion, and I'm not an expert. Hearing the findings of ethnoarchaeologists, historians, and cultural anthropologists will be interesting.

"Zhopla and Taika, thank you for joining us today. We wanted to discuss the logistics of integrating the symbionts with the outbreak survivors." Eurydice and Adira were seated to the right of the symbols adorning the cave. David saw Zhopla first and then couldn't believe his eyes as he surmised who is sitting next to him.

"Taika! I was not informed of your presence here." David greeted Taika warmly, taking her by her forearms and holding her there. "Zhopla has many secrets, and your presence is chief among them. You were not on the *Porta Caeli*, were you?" David released Taika's arms and stepped back, observing her.

"I arrived with Gint and his team three years ago. My presence here was necessary. I knew of the caves and the aliens because

Zhopla sent me here to interface with them. The Veltryn also saved my life."

"That's amazing, and I would love to hear the entire story! We've known each other since Adira and I were dating in college and then on to medical school. I have missed our deep philosophical discussions. They were important for me to hear and changed my perception of the world."

Eurydice interrupted, "Zhopla and Taika, again, thank you for joining us today. We want to discuss the logistics of integrating the symbionts with the outbreak survivors."

Zhopla stood and indicated a seat for David. "Please sit, Dr. Michel. We have much to discuss. Time is running out for the outbreak patients. You and Eurydice have been invited to meet the symbiont who co-inhabits with Taika. Their name is Luminaris. They will speak to you directly."

"Before Luminaris speaks, David, I would like you to know I was in grave condition when I arrived at Galatéa. Luminaris, with the help of Zhopla, saved my life through our symbiotic joining. Luminaris healed my condition. It was similar to the outbreak patients' symptoms, although the definitive cause was never identified, mostly because of the tools we had at the time. I was in the same position as your patients. Take the symbiont or die. Those were the only choices left to us." As Taika described her journey, her eyes strayed to meet Adira's. She smiled as she turned back to Eurydice and David.

David's eyebrows raised. *Her mother's disappearance with no communication or explanation so tortured Adira for all those years. I wonder what she's feeling now that they have been reunited.*

"But you were missing for two years before that. David needs to know where you were before then." Adira's eyes were shining.

"Zhopla placed me in hibernation because my condition was deteriorating. This arrested the progression of the presumed nanotoxins. Because the etiologic agent was unknown, my whereabouts and condition were classified by SIS22."

"Galkin, among other scientists, experimented with various nanotoxins. Their work was detected, but they escaped capture, and our identification of the nanoparticles and toxins they incorporated was nil." Eurydice's steely gaze remained on Zhopla's face.

Yet another considerable secret Eurydice kept from Adira. This must be unbelievably difficult for her.

Taika's eyes took on a faraway, dreamy look as she continued, "Let me explain my experiences. I was awakened, similar to the procedure you will follow with your patients. Zhopla explained that the alien presence had communicated to him even while he was on the first expedition to Galatéa. He learned that a symbiont was the only way I could be healed of the nanotoxin's devastation of my nervous system. I was the only survivor of the outbreak at that time, and I was weak and completely bedridden. After Zhopla returned to Earth, the procedure and the dignity of choice were described, and I chose life.

"The next time I was awakened from hibernation, I was here on Galatéa. I had no idea three years had gone by. The medical team operatives secretly transported me to the caves. Gint and their team never knew of my presence in the hibernation pod. They were prepared to initiate the symbiont installation with the help of Luminaris.

"Before this happened, I was introduced to Luminaris. What I saw defies explanation, but I'll try. Luminaris presented as a radiant being made first of pure white light and then shifting to a broader spectrum of colors.

"One of the things that struck me during our first interaction was Luminaris' vibrant optimism, exuding positivity. This gave me hope. Among all the other gifts the symbiont has bestowed on me, Luminaris' natural gifts rejuvenated my human body and spirit. It seemed as if their radiant energy didn't just heal. I was once again invigorated after my lengthy illness. My fatigue was dispelled, and vitality restored."

That's very interesting. "Would I be able to examine you and have our medical team run some of our tests on you now that you've had your symbiont for over four years?" David's professional persona exuded trust and competence.

"All of your questions will be answered in due time. Now, let us turn to Luminaris and listen to what they wish to tell us." Zhopla's steepled his fingers and sat down.

Taika's seat was placed facing the others. Her eyes again took on that dreamy, faraway look before closing them. Taking a deep breath, she opened her eyes and searched the faces of the participants one at a time.

"I am Luminaris. My people are known as the Veltryn. We have dwelled in these caves for countless millennia. The entities that have remained here have done so by choice. They are what remains of our vast civilization as far as we know. When we were in corporeal form, most of our population was given the choice to leave the caves to begin life on other planets. We heard from them regularly initially, but after about twenty years, we lost all contact. Again, it appears we are all that remain of my kind.

"We are a symbiotic species; in human terms, we would be deemed a neuro entity. We bring unique abilities and characteristics that will cure humans of this deadly outbreak, offering a blend of physical, emotional, and psychological healing. When the Veltryn were given a choice of a new symbiotic relationship, Taika's genetics and background were considered. Taika is intelligent, driven, and a natural-born leader. On Earth, she was deeply committed to saving lives. She has a compassionate heart. All of these factors were studied, and it was deemed that matching Taika with myself was optimal.

"Taika will tell you that the procedure was painless and pleasantly stimulating. We are not simple life forms. We are highly intelligent and seek symbiosis with other creatures. As stated, we choose hosts based on specific genetic and personality traits, and once selected, we can merge with them. The merging process is gentle and cooperative. We extend our filaments of light, intertwining and eventually integrating both neurologically and with the host's body.

"The symbiotic relationship does not imply mere coexistence. This is a life-altering experience. Positive effects of the symbiotic relationship are the transformation of heightened senses, such as extended vision beyond the visible spectrum of the human eye. A symbiont can grant the host access to the vast knowledge of the Veltryn. Humans may also develop a 'sixth sense' about their surroundings, giving them an advantage on many levels.

"It is our understanding that there are eight patients who have thus far survived the outbreak and one that did not survive. Each one is to be awakened and given the choice of a symbiotic relationship or certain death. They must be apprised of all of the ramifications of a symbiotic pairing. Their choice must be made freely with no coercion from the medical staff. Those are stipulations that cannot be negotiated. Once the pairing takes place, there is no going back. They must understand this before consenting to a symbiont."

Taika's eyes closed once again. After taking a deep breath, she opened them. It took a moment for her to focus and regain control of her vision. "I was aware of Luminaris and what was said. David, Luminaris will help you during the procedure. We wish for the procedure to occur here, in Cave Twelve, as a Rite of Passage, as is our custom."

David's eyebrows knitted as he thought about performing this procedure outside MedBay. "As long as we have all the necessary equipment, instruments, and supplies, it should not be a problem. Is this a problem for you, Eurydice?"

"I see no further problem with performing the procedure in Cave Twelve. This room can be closed off so that no one on Gint' team can access it. They have not had access to it up to this point. They don't know of its existence." Eurydice's answer was short.

The first to be awakened was Phil Roskos. He was the first colonist to become overtly ill with outbreak symptoms, beginning with a sore throat and progressing to strange movements and guttural sounds.

Should this epidemic occur again, will we be just as bewildered and unprepared as we were with those who had it the first time?

David, Violet, Adira, and Taika stood around Phil Roskos' gurney, and Zhopla remained in the background near the cave wall. "After I give him the injection, he will awaken temporarily. He was the first to 'fall asleep' and has been debilitated for a long time now. He may be disoriented at first. Is everyone prepared as we awaken him to inform him of his grim choice?" All present agreed. David injected a syringe full of a white substance into Phil's intravenous port.

It did not take long for Phil's eyelids to flutter. He blinked his eyes several times before opening them. It appeared he was having a difficult time focusing. "Hello, Phil. Adira here. Do you remember me?" Phil nodded. "Do you remember where you are?" Phil nodded. "Can you tell us how you are feeling?"

Phil cleared his throat several times before his vocal cords could engage. "I remember being in the Medbay for months. I remember the doctors discussing placing me in hibernation. All I experienced before hibernation was whiteness and emptiness. The whiteness was not like anything I've ever experienced.

"What was it like, Phil?"

"It was like a white fog that was hiding all other surroundings. I lived in this white fog, which was cold and vacant. As I said, I knew you were in the Medbay, but I did not feel like myself. I did not feel normal. I tried to lift my arm or leg, but they would not move. I tried repeatedly, and it seemed my brain was no longer connected to my arms and legs.

"This was the most frightening thing that ever happened to me. I had an extreme sense of claustrophobia gripping me. This stressed me out, and my mind pulled away from reality. At some point, I became convinced that this was all a nightmare, and the relief I felt was enormous. I struggled to open my eyes, make a sound, and even move my pinky finger, but nothing would happen.

"I knew some of the things happening around me in the Medbay. I knew when it was morning that Violet, David, and Adira would begin their working day. I could smell the antiseptic clinical odors around me. After confronting Adira in the dome's hallway, I remember how I ended up in Medbay.

"I'm not sure how much time has passed. Especially because I was in the hibernation pod. I knew I had lost control of my body. I was distraught because I heard the concern in David and Adira's voices as you discussed my condition—and that I was getting worse. I knew you could not wake me or cure this endless sleep. I remember you saying I had a fever. Worst of all, I remember you pronouncing me dead twice before I was out for good. I guess in hibernation."

David leaned over so Phil could see him. "You are one of nine patients to have this affliction. The outbreak stopped without explanation at nine patients. Eight of you have survived. One did not make it. There are some things you need to know before we go on.

"We have no medical way to cure you. Nothing in our databases, the medical knowledge of Earth, artificial intelligence working on a cure, or anything we tried has helped or even had any promise of helping cure you. A nanotoxin seemingly causes the disease, but we have been unable to isolate it. It is attacking your nervous system and brain.

"What we do have is a solution and a cure. This cure will change human medicine itself. We could reach the pinnacle of biotechnological and interstellar advancement with it. In full disclosure, the disease has remained a mystery, but it could strike again at any time.

"What I'm about to tell you will be hard to believe. We have discovered an alien species living deep in the caves of Galatéa. They are known as the Veltryn. They are light entities that are a complex blend of neural cells and bioluminescent 'algae.' These entities have demonstrated an extraordinary ability to interface directly with human neural tissue, promising enhancements in human cognitive and sensory skills.

"They are a symbiotic species willing to couple with a human host. They offer a cure for your affliction. Without entering into a symbiotic relationship, you will die from the disease. The discovery of the Veltryn, with their remarkable symbiotic capabilities, will revolutionize medicine and neuroscience.

"Phil, the symbiotic relationship will have many positive benefits for you. It is a coexistence with another life form that will be life-altering. You will have access to the vast knowledge the aliens have accrued over millennia. You will see and hear far more than you can now." David paused to allow Phil to process this information.

Adira introduced her mother to Phil. "Phil, this is my mother.

Her name is Taika. She shared in your affliction and was given the same choice as you. She has taken on a symbiont and has been cured. She will introduce your matched symbiont, should you choose to have one, and let you know what to expect."

Taika stepped forward to Phil's head. "Hello Phil, I'm happy to meet you. Yes, I have a symbiont. Their name is Luminaris. We were placed together by mutual consent based on genetics and personality traits. Your symbiont's name is Tarnak. When I first met Tarnak, they appeared as a robustly healthy crystalline entity with reflective luminous surfaces that occasionally sparkled with inner light. In our discussions, I have learned that Tarnak is stoic and wise. They have a deep sense of duty and resilience. One of Tarnak's gifts is the ability to fortify the human body, giving stability and strength. Another gift is the ability to bolster physical endurance and mental fortitude. You will be more resistant to stress and illness.

"Tarnak chose you, besides being a genetic match, because you are a decorated space explorer. Your strong sense of community spirit and sense of duty attracted Tarnak. Your history of bravery, fearlessness, forgetting self, and stepping into danger to protect others impressed the Veltryn. Tarnak knows the toll the outbreak has taken on your body and spirit. Curing you will be an honor for him. Sharing his life with you will also be an honor."

"Will I still be myself? Will I be able to function by myself, or will this alien, this Tarnak, take over my body?"

"No, Tarnak will never take over your life in any way. The intention is to elicit your cure and then provide knowledge and growth to the colony of Galatéa." Taika moved aside.

"Phil, your time awake is almost up; the medication will only work for a little longer. You must decide. Your cooperation is mandatory. You must enter into the symbiotic relationship of your own free will. We will not be able to awaken you again. The truth is that you either consent to receiving a symbiont or you will die from this disease. It's entirely your decision. Both humans and Veltryn believe in the dignity of choice." David stepped away to allow Adira to see Phil.

"Phil, I know this is hard, and unfortunately, we don't have any more time. The medication will wear off shortly, and as David said, we won't be able to awaken you again. Can you give us an answer?"

"You guys have made this easy for me. Tarnak, I am honored to have you come aboard. Let's do this. I want to live." With that, Phil blinked several times, closed his eyes, and went to sleep again.

25 - Phil and Tarnak

"This is Dr. David Michel recording our first symbiont joining on Galatéa." David knew it was the second such procedure since Taika was the first, but that was classified information. "Our patient is Phil Roskos. He was the first colonist to succumb to the outbreak and has been in a hibernation pod for the most extended interval.

"The year is 2250. Galatéan date 22501.2. With the integration of the alien symbiont, Tarnak, with Phil Roskos, humanity will have achieved the pinnacle of biotechnological and interstellar advancement. Finding a cure for our outbreak patients has proven impossible with current medical technology. Tarnak has volunteered to integrate with Phil and cure him of this affliction. Phil Roskos has been advised of the repercussions of living with a symbiote and was informed that he would not survive if he chose not to receive the symbiont. With complete disclosure, he has chosen to receive Tarnak.

"The symbionts are known as the Veltryn, an alien species with remarkable symbiotic capabilities. Human medicine and neuroscience will be revolutionized. The Veltryn are beings of light resembling a complex blend of energy, neural cells, and what we might describe as bioluminescent algal cells. In simulations, these light entities have demonstrated an extraordinary ability to interface directly with human neural tissue. Positive outcomes promise enhancements to human cognitive and sensory abilities.

"Assisting with the procedure today includes Dr Varna, Dr Taika, and Luminaris, one of the bioluminescent beings. Our white Med droid will also assist as needed. The primary step for this procedure is to initiate a neuro-symbiotic integration. For the record, we will be integrating Tarnak, a Veltryn symbiont volunteer, into the neural tissue of a human volunteer, Phil Roskos, a decorated space explorer who has sustained severe neural damage due to the effects of the outbreak on Galatéa. His current condition is critical. He is in grave condition.

Adira assisted. "Dr. Michel, we are completing Phil's comprehensive neural mapping with the advanced quantum resonance imaging instrumentation." A precise three-dimensional holographic model of Phil's neural network appeared. "Any areas of damage and potential integration points for the Zylentian symbiont will be highlighted."

A holographic display of a complicated maze of neural pathways appeared above Phil.

"The patient is prepared and ready for the procedure," David confirmed.

"Tarnak has undergone genetic calibration, and we are assured compatibility with Phil's neural cells. The Veltryn genetic code of Tarnak was tweaked to prevent immune rejection by Phil's body. We have optimized Tarnak's neural interface capabilities. The symbiont's bioluminescent properties were also adjusted to enhance synaptic communication and energy efficiency between the two." Taika interjected, speaking as Luminaris.

David began the delicate insertion process in the sterile conditions of the cave operating room. "We are integrating nanobot-assisted microsurgery." He made a small incision in Phil's cranium. "The Veltryn symbiont, Tarnak, has been encapsulated in a protective biopolymer shell. I am now inserting them into Phil's cerebral cortex. Insertion complete. Integration will now begin."

The medical team observed the integration of the nanobots with the quantum resonance imaging instrument in another holographic display. The nanobots guided the symbiont to the damaged neural regions. When the symbiont reached the targeted region, the biopolymer shell dissolved, releasing Tarnak. Tendrils extended from the released symbiont, forming connections with the surrounding neurons.

"We are observing the emergence of a soft, bioluminescent glow indicative of active synaptic formation. Our advanced biofeedback sensors are monitoring the integration and imaging processes." Adira informed the team.

In the sterile, luminescent cave on Planet Galatéa, the atmosphere was thick with tension and the sharp scent of antiseptic. Phil Roskos, a human with a fatal disease, lay motionless on the operating table, his chest rising and falling weakly as the surgical team worked frantically around him. The alien symbiont, Tarnak, a translucent, pulsating entity, was being integrated into Phil's system. David, Adira, and Luminaris, the skilled medical team, were focused, their movements precise and swift.

"He's flatlining!" David shouted, his voice barely containing the panic surging through him. "Adira, adjust the biofeedback sensors to engage!"

Phil had been their hope, a testament to the potential success of human-alien symbiosis. Tarnak, with its advanced healing properties, was supposed to cure Phil's disease. But now, in the most critical moment of the surgery, everything was going wrong. Phil's heart had stopped, and his brain function was minimal. The once rhythmic beeping of the monitors had turned into a haunting flatline.

Shaking her head, Adira grabbed the cardiopulmonary apparatus from the white droid, manually adjusted it to the correct settings, and moved swiftly to Phil's side. "Delivering dose!" she yelled, her voice breaking as she delivered the shock. Phil's body jolted, but the flatline persisted.

"No response," Taika whispered, tears welling in her eyes. She closed her eyes for a moment, and Luminaris emerged. Luminaris hovered close to Phil's head, their luminescence flickering with worry. "I've lost contact with Tarnak," they said softly, their voice resonating with a deeper, more resonant timbre than Taika's. "I can't sense them anymore. It's like they vanished."

Desperation etched into his features, David pounded on Phil's chest, performing manual compressions. "Come on, Phil. Don't do this. Not now. We've done so much and come so far!"

Phil's body lay unresponsive, a stark contrast to the flurry of activity around him. The cave seemed to close in, the walls pressing with the weight of failure. The hum of the equipment and the sterile lighting felt like a cruel reminder of the fragility of life.

Luminaris reached out with their consciousness, searching desperately for a trace of Tarnak. "Wait," they said, voice trembling with hope. "Sensing something." Luminaris felt a sudden flicker, a faint but unmistakable presence

David paused, looking up with a mix of hope and disbelief. "What is it?"

"Tarnak," Luminaris whispered, closing their eyes to focus. "They are weak, but they are there. They are attempting to reconnect."

Adira, clutching Phil's hand, felt a surge of determination. "We can't give up on him. Tarnak is still in there. We need to help them both."

David nodded, his resolve hardening. "Luminaris, guide Tarnak. Adira, prepare another round of electrical stimulation. We're not losing him."

Luminaris focused their considerable energies, their light growing brighter as they reached out to Tarnak. "Tarnak, you must hold on. Phil needs you. We are sending energies to you to complete the connection."

A faint glow emanated from Phil's chest, where Tarnak was integrating. It was fragile, like the first light of dawn breaking through the darkness. Luminaris's voice became a soothing, melodic chant, their words flowing with an otherworldly grace. "Tarnak, anchor yourself. Find Phil's life force and merge with it."

The monitors flickered, and all the bioluminescence in cave twelve flickered, showing the faintest hint of activity. Phil's heart gave a weak but noticeable beat. Taika had tears streaming down her face. Adira adjusted the biosensors. "Engage!" she shouted, sending another shock through Phil's body.

This time, the response was immediate. Phil's body arched, and his eyes flew open, filled with a mixture of pain and confusion. The flatline turned into a steady, albeit weak, rhythm. The room erupted in a collective gasp of relief.

"Phil," David said, leaning close to him. "Can you hear me?"

Phil's eyes struggled to focus, his voice barely a whisper. "David... what... happened?"

"You went critical," David explained, his voice thick with emotion. "But you're back. Tarnak is still with you. You're going to be okay."

Luminaris's light enveloped Phil, soothing his strained body. "Tarnak is reconnecting. Phil, you must stay calm and let Tarnak merge fully with you."

Phil nodded weakly, his breathing shallow but steady. "I trust you all."

Adira squeezed Phil's hand, her heart swelling with hope. "We won't let you go, Phil. We're in this together."

As the minutes passed, the glow from Phil's chest grew more substantial. Tarnak's presence became more pronounced, its energy weaving seamlessly with Phil's. Luminaris continued their chant, their voice guiding the symbiont to stabilize and strengthen the bond.

Phil's color began to return, and the monitors showed improved vital signs. The team watched in awe as the integration was completed, the symbiosis between Phil and Tarnak achieving a harmonious balance.

"It's working," David said, his voice barely containing his joy. "Tarnak is healing him."

Phil's eyes closed, a peaceful expression settling on his face. "I can feel it," he murmured. "The pain is fading. Tarnak... it's incredible."

Luminaris's light dimmed to a gentle glow, their voice filled with reverence. Taika's eyes closed as Taika reemerged. "You both have done something extraordinary. This is just the beginning of a new chapter."

Adira wiped her face, smiling through her exhaustion. "Phil, you're a miracle. You shouldn't even be awake, yet here you are. Wide awake and well again!"

David, overwhelmed with relief, placed a hand on Phil's shoulder. "You fought, Phil. You and Tarnak. Together, you're unstoppable."

Phil's breathing evened out, his body relaxing as the final facets of the integration were completed. Tarnak's glow pulsed rhythmically, a testament to the successful symbiosis. Once filled with tension and fear, the cave was now a haven of hope and triumph.

The surgical team cleaned up, and after ensuring Phil's continued stability, Taika hovered close, her presence comforting light. "Rest now, Phil. You have a long journey ahead, but you're not alone. Tarnak will be with you every step of the way."

Phil nodded, a contented smile playing on his lips. "Thank you, all of you. I wouldn't be here without you."

David, Adira, and Taika exchanged looks of profound relief and joy. They had faced the brink of despair and emerged victorious. The bond between Phil and Tarnak was a beacon of hope, a promise of what was possible when different worlds came together.

As Phil drifted into a healthy, healing sleep, David knew that this moment would be etched in his heart forever. It was a testament to the power of resilience, unity, and the unyielding spirit of life. And in the quiet, glowing cave on Planet Galatéa, he felt the first stirrings of a brighter future, where the possibilities were as boundless as the stars. "At this point, the symbiont has established healthy connections without causing undue stress or inflammation to Phil."

"Tarnak will adapt to their new environment over the next twenty-four hours. Synaptic plasticity and neural regeneration will be slowly promoted." Taika added.

"Phil will remain under sedation for the next several days. We will monitor his condition continuously for signs of neural improvement and ensure his overall health remains stable. Adira has volunteered to stay with him for the duration of his recovery. We can move him to MedBay as soon as forty-eight hours." David concluded. "The success of this procedure will open new avenues for the treatment of severe neural injuries, cure our outbreak patients, and have implications for the treatment of neurodegenerative diseases.

"As an anecdotal note, my colleagues have embarked on researching ethical questions for discussion and debate regarding the extent to which humanity should integrate alien biology into our physiology in such an intimate manner. While the potential benefits are immense, questions about identity, autonomy, and the long-term implications of symbiosis will need careful consideration. Will human and alien biology coexist in a harmonious and mutually beneficial relationship? Is this pushing the boundaries of what it means to be human? End of journal entry."

26 - Seven more to Go

"Good Morning, Phil!" Adira beamed. "Welcome back to Galatéa. Can you try to sit up?"

Phil Roskos opened and closed his eyes several times. He finally opened them and focused on Adira's face. He slowly opened and closed his hands and bent his legs at the knee several times. Sitting up, he looked around the MedBay. "I'm feeling normal for the first time in forever! My arms and legs feel connected to my brain!" Phil dangled his feet on the side of the bed.

"Don't stand up until you're ready, Phil. Let's take this slow and easy," David breathed.

"Been lying around and sleeping long enough! I'm hearing and seeing everything in much more detail than ever before. Everything is so much sharper. The colors of everything are so much brighter; I would say even more vivid." Phil slowly looked at everything surrounding his cubicle.

"Tarnak's integration has repaired your damaged neurons. Your cognitive abilities have been augmented; you can expect faster information processing and heightened spatial awareness. Tarnak's unique abilities have healed and fortified your body and mind. You are cured of the outbreak affliction. The medical team and I are pleased with your progress and recovery." David smiled as Phil stood up.

"Violet will be administering some tests now that you're awake. She will apprise the rest of the team of your progress." David turned to Adira. "Phil will experience enhanced memory recall, and he will be able to view his world with unprecedented accuracy and detail. Violet, please join us in the briefing room for an update on the rest of the outbreak patients."

David, Violet, and Adira entered the briefing room. "I wanted to have a sort of Grand Rounds with the medical team to review the subsequent seven cases before performing any further procedures.

"I plan to go over each symbiont matched to each patient. Again, we will only have one chance to obtain informed consent from each patient, so we must count every minute when they are awake again. The most critical patients will receive their symbionts first.

"Let's begin. We have Sophia Li, a virtuoso musician. She is first for the procedure. The outbreak has severely impacted her nervous system, and her condition has been downgraded to critical for many days now. Her symbiont is known as Elexia. Taika, via Luminaris, has categorized Elexia as a profoundly compassionate entity capable of healing emotional, psychological, and physical wounds. I am assured that they are a good match.

"Second on the list is Rachel Radford, an Egyptologist and research scientist. Her symbiont is known as Zephyris. Luminaris states that Zephyris is curious and eager to explore new ideas and sensations. They can boost human creativity and heighten human senses.

"If all goes as planned, the third patient is Alex Carter, a software engineer. Nyxalia is an entity known to be more introspective and able to unravel deep-seated fears and traumas. The match is perfect because Alex Carter is tech-savvy and inventive but very introverted.

"Next will be Ethan Clarke, our public relations expert known for being pragmatic, analytical, and dedicated. The symbiont is Aetheron. They can enhance relaxation and inner peace.

"Anjeli Patel is slated to be the next patient to receive the procedure. She is a nurse here in MedBay and is empathetic and nurturing. Her matching symbiont is Kryalith. They are described as analytical and able to bring about clarity of thought.

"The sixth patient will be Lila Mendoza, who on Earth was a teacher working with inner-city underprivileged children and adults. She is patient and an inspiration to those she works with. Serephos is a matching symbiont described as passionate, dynamic, and driven.

"Finally, the seventh patient is Grace Kim, a biochemist who loves books and is wise and gentle. Vaeloria is the name of her symbiont, known to be nurturing and has formidable abilities to promote overall health and bring a sense of renewal.

"It appears that each neuro entity will bring unique gifts or abilities and characteristics to each patient, along with curing them of this deadly outbreak," observed Violet.

"Yes, I agree, Violet. Notably, they bring a blend of physical, emotional, and psychological healing. Monitoring all of them over time will be an exciting endeavor," Adira answered. "The next portion of our Grand Rounds necessarily needs to include a conversation regarding the implications and ethics of a symbiotic pairing and life afterward.

"A symbiotic alien integrated into a human could enhance existence in numerous transformative ways, ranging from physiological to cognitive and emotional enhancements. I will highlight several potential benefits we know about now and discuss a few questions about unknown developments.

"First, we know we have physiological enhancements, such as enhanced healing and regeneration. We are looking at rapid tissue repair and healing accelerated by the alien symbiote with reduced recovery times from surgery or accidents. This begs the question, will they be able to regenerate a lost limb or damaged organs?"

David added. "Acquiring an alien symbiotic organism can be

alluring, offering the promise of enhanced abilities, extended lifespan, or advanced knowledge. However, the shady side of such a venture is fraught with risks and ethical dilemmas."

"Excellent point, David. Second, I'd like to address disease resistance. The symbiote can bolster and enhance the immune system, providing resistance to diseases and infections, similar to our nanoparticles. Will the adaptive immune system rapidly adapt to new pathogens and immediately protect against emerging diseases?

"Third, I looked at physical abilities. By augmenting muscle fibers or optimizing energy use, the symbiote could significantly enhance the physical strength and stamina of the human hosts. They also improve sensory perception, giving the host superior vision, hearing, touch, and smell. What about night vision or perception of a broader range of electromagnetic spectra?

Violet listened attentively and then remarked, "It may seem obvious, but are there health risks to the human host? The physiological integration of an alien organism can lead to unpredictable health complications. As the human body struggles to accommodate an alien presence, hosts might experience severe side effects, such as organ failure, immune system overreactions, or debilitating psychological impacts."

"This is an excellent point, Violet, and it bears further scrutiny. This brings us to the human mind and potential cognitive enhancements that could increase intelligence and improve memory. The symbiote could enhance neural processing speeds, allowing for quicker thinking and decision-making. Memory improvements might include memory retention, learning new information quickly, and greater clarity in memory of past experiences. Will there be the ability to transfer knowledge, such as knowledge and skills, directly from symbiote to human, bypassing traditional learning pathways?

"Emotional and psychological states may stabilize, offering some mood regulation. The symbiote may be able to help regulate neurotransmitters and promote mental health and emotional stability.

"Sensory and perceptual enhancements could include augmented reality integration. The symbiote could allow humans to perceive augmented reality overlays directly through their sensory systems, providing real-time data and visual enhancements. Regarding environmental awareness, can the symbiont enhance awareness of environmental factors, such as detecting pollutants, radiation levels, or weather changes?

"Is telepathic communication possible? Will there be mind-to-mind communication similar to that of our BAIs? If the symbiote has telepathic capabilities, could it enable direct communication between individuals without needing verbal or written language? At this point, we do not know. We do know that enhanced emotional perception could foster greater empathy and understanding between individuals, improving social interactions and relationships."

Frowning, David interjected, " I have been delving into the potential darker side of the symbiotic pairing. Alien symbiotes may possess their own agendas, subtly manipulating their hosts to achieve objectives beyond mere survival. This manipulation can erode the host's autonomy, leading to decisions that benefit the symbiote at the expense of human values and relationships. Observing and documenting the interactions between and among the human hosts and their symbiotes take precedence as we move forward."

Adira continued. "What about environmental adaptation? Survival in harsh conditions: can the symbiote enable humans to survive in extreme environments, such as underwater, high altitudes, or even extraterrestrial landscapes, by providing necessary physiological adaptations? Or climate adaptation:

Could the symbionts help humans adapt to changing climates, enhancing tolerance to heat, cold, or fluctuating environmental conditions?

"One of the most exciting discussion points rests on longevity and aging. Extended lifespan: Can the symbiote slow the aging process, repair cellular damage, and maintain bodily functions at peak performance, significantly extending the human lifespan? What about maintaining youthful vitality? Can the symbiont maintain youthful vitality and appearance, preventing age-related decline in physical and cognitive abilities?

"On a broader scale, let's turn to societal and technological integration. Can we expect enhanced collaboration among us? Can the symbiotes facilitate a form of collective intelligence where humans can share thoughts and ideas more efficiently, enhancing collaborative efforts in science, technology, and art? Can they ultimately improve colony communication networks, creating a more interconnected and harmonious world?

"That completes my list of ethical questions and scenarios for now."

"You've certainly provided us with an exhaustive list of ethical questions and scenarios, Adira. In summary, I would say that a symbiotic alien could enhance human existence by improving health, cognitive functions, physical abilities, sensory perception, emotional well-being, adaptability, and societal collaboration, potentially ushering in a new era of human evolution and prosperity. Exciting prospects await us." David reflected.

" I agree that the acquisition of a symbiote raises ethical questions about continuous consent and the extent to which individuals should alter their bodies for enhancement. The potential for exploitation, particularly in coercive scenarios where individuals are pressured to accept symbiotes, is significant.

"The presence of symbiotes could create societal divides within the colony, with symbiote-enhanced individuals potentially viewed as superior or, conversely, as threats. This could lead to discrimination, social unrest, or even conflicts as factions vie for control over or against symbiote integration.

"As Zhopla may have perceived, over time, hosts may develop a dependency on their symbiote, akin to addiction. The symbiote's benefits might come at the cost of diminishing returns, requiring continuous bonding or upgrades, leading to an endless cycle of dependence.

"I fear that the symbiotic relationship may blur the lines of individual identity, with hosts experiencing a loss of self as their thoughts and emotions intertwine with the alien consciousness. This merging can lead to an existential crisis or the gradual erosion of the host's personality.

"I hope that SIS22 will not exploit symbiotes for military or economic gain, weaponizing them to create super-soldiers or using them in espionage. This weaponization could escalate into an arms race, endangering colony security.

"While the allure of an alien symbiotic organism is undeniable, the shady aspects reveal a complex tapestry of risks and ethical dilemmas. These challenges underscore the importance of cautious exploration and stringent ethical considerations in any interactions with extraterrestrial life. Only time will tell. For now, we have a way to cure our patients from certain death. Hopefully, the ends will justify the means."

David concluded the meeting. *I don't like to conclude meetings on such a dark note, but I feel it's warranted because there is so much we still don't know.*

27 - Phil and Astrid: Finding Balance

Jomei's Reflections. Surveillance. Dining Hall of Galatéa Colony

Personal Blog Entry: One year after arriving at Galatéa.

Record: Phil and Tarnak's Symbiosis

This blog entry contains Jomei's observations of symbiont interactions with humans. Today, Jomei observed Phil, a renowned and decorated space explorer. He was chosen by the alien Tarnak, who ultimately saved Phil's life by healing him of the 'sleeping sickness' outbreak. Phil was one of eight colonists to receive a life-saving and life-changing alien symbiont. The selection process included a rigorous review to ensure a perfect genetic match; this highlights the importance of compatibility in human-symbiont pairing.

Another parameter considered in the selection process is personality characteristics. Jomei observes that Tarnak's stoic and wise demeanor complements Phil's strong community spirit and sense of duty. According to Luminaris, Tarnak has profound abilities. Phil's body has shown signs of enhanced physical strength and has been stable since the symbiont procedure. He was always a valuable colony member, but this pairing makes him even more formidable in our explorations and his duties.

Only subtle changes have been observed thus far. Tarnak's influence seems to have subtly changed Phil's physiology and behavior. Objective observations include Phil's posture. He stands more upright, and his movements are deliberate and controlled. One may conclude that these changes can be attributed to

Tarnak's influence. Jomei will observe Phil's behavior and interactions to determine if Tarnak influences his thoughts and decisions.

Through routine surveillance monitoring, Jomei observes human interactions in the dining hall. Astrid has joined Phil at his table. They are exchanging pleasantries. These interactions present a fascinating contrast due to Astrid's negativity and hostility. Her pessimistic outlook is a potential source of conflict, mainly because of Astrid's skepticism and deep-seated mistrust of non-organic beings, particularly those that intrude into her personal space, such as the greenhouses where she tends to her delicate plants.

Note. There appears to be increasing tension during dinner— record interaction.

"Phil! I'm so glad to see you healthy again. I'm so relieved to see you again. It seems like you've been in hibernation in the MedBay forever. I've missed our talks." Astrid took a bite of her grilled veggie sandwich while waiting for her tomato soup to cool. "How are things with you now?"

"David, Adira, and the clinical staff have given me the best care possible. I have no complaints. When aboard the *Porta Caeli*, I received the nanoparticles and quickly rejected them, so they had to be removed. I stayed in hibernation until we arrived at Galatéa. Then I quickly came down with the 'sleeping sickness' and ended up in the MedBay and stayed there for months and months." Phil looked directly into Astrid's eyes as he spoke.

"The droids foisted on me in the greenhouses make me cringe every day. The nanoparticles and further augmentations also make me cringe when I think about what could happen.

Note. Jomei's observation shows that Astrid's criticism is not just about the droids or the augmented but a manifestation of her discomfort with change and fear of losing control.

"I do not want any augmented humans or droids, humanoid or otherwise, in my greenhouses—ever! Astrid shook pepper into her soup vigorously. "You seem different now after your lengthy illness. I can't quite put my finger on what's different about you."

Note. Jomei perceives the greenhouses as Astrid's sanctuary, where she exerts control and nurtures life. The presence of humanoid droids in this space represents a violation of that sanctuary, which exacerbates her negativity and fuels her hostility toward Phil and, eventually, Tarnak once she is updated about the symbionts. If this conflict is not addressed, Jomei predicts it will escalate, as Astrid's emotions are tied to her sense of autonomy and control over her environment.

Phil sat back and calmly sipped his water. "I suppose any life-threatening illness has the power to change a person. Still, myself, feeling better daily. About the augmentations—the nanoparticles and other enhancements have only improved the lives of those who have received them. My experience was the one and only with serious negative consequences. The nanoparticles and other enhancements have not only upgraded individual lives but also vastly improved the overall functioning of the colony. Not to mention enhancing our chances of long-term survival."

Note. Phil responded with a calm yet firm defense of nanoparticles, fortified by Tarnak, while emphasizing the benefits augmentations bring to individuals and the entire community. Jomei detects an undercurrent of frustration in Phil's voice as he struggles to reconcile his respect for Astrid's expertise with his sense of duty and the need for technological integration. Violet sat at a nearby table in the dining hall and spoke to Phil and Astrid.

"I couldn't help but overhear your conversation. If you're done eating, would you care to join me in the Atrium? I want to talk to both of you. Astrid, isn't it great to see Phil up and around again?" At Violet's request, they walked over to the Atrium.

Note. As the argument intensified, Jomei's algorithms predicted an imminent escalation that could fracture the friend's cohesion. Interestingly, Astrid perceived some change in Phil. However, Violet, a medical community member, intervened at this critical moment. She was wise in suggesting the Atrium. In the heart of Galatéa's central arboretum, the Atrium showcases the colony's natural beauty and serves as a tranquil meeting space. This will calm Astrid. The air is fragrant with the scent of exotic flowers, and the soft hum of life surrounds them.

Violet chose a circular table in the middle of the domed Atrium. "Phil and Astrid, thank you for meeting me here in this beautiful space. What I heard of your disagreement reminded me that the changes we are experiencing here on Galatéa are weighing heavily on all of us. Let's take a moment to appreciate our colony and the life surrounding us."

"This place, these people…it's why I'm so protective, Violet. These plants are not just part of the ecosystem—they're a part of me. I've nurtured them for years, and I can't stand the thought of machines disrupting the delicate balance I worked so hard to maintain." Astrid looked around as she spoke, visibly moved by the Atrium.

Phil leaned forward with a determined expression. "And I respect that, Astrid. I truly do. But we are facing challenges we cannot ignore. Augmentations and droids have streamlined our efforts, making maintaining this Atrium and the entire dome easier. We must ensure our colony on Galatéa thrives, and sometimes that just plain means we have to embrace new methods."

Violet nodded and placed a hand on both of their shoulders. "You obviously both care deeply for Galatéa, and that's precisely the common ground we must build upon. Astrid, your love of all things plants and the natural world is undeniable, and Phil, your commitment to our mission is equally important. How about we explore how we can honor both perspectives?"

Astrid sighed. "It's not that I am completely against technology, Phil. Of course, I understand the benefits. But I'm worried about losing control over what's been so carefully cultivated. My plants are sensitive; even small environmental changes can have tremendous impacts. They're our lifeline!"

"And that's why I propose we use the droids and continue with further augmentations—to prevent them from harm. These technologies monitor and adjust conditions with precision that is unattainable by non-augmented humans. It's often better than we can do manually. I've heard you frequently complain about insufficient workers in the greenhouses. Imagine the potential if you're not overwhelmed by minor tasks. Phil remained resolute.

Violet intervened. "Phil, you mentioned precision. Could you elaborate on how technology might protect the plants rather than disrupt them?"

Phil's eyes glowed. "Of course. The droids we are using are not the clunky machines of the past. They are highly sophisticated, with sensors that detect the slightest temperature, humidity, and soil composition changes. Astrid, they could alert you immediately to any issues before they become problems. You have complete control over rectifying the situation. Giving you more time to focus on your research and specific plants."

Astrid sat and reflected. "I see the potential, but I still worry about the implementation. If we rely too much on these machines, what happens if they fail? What if they make a mistake?"

"Those are valid concerns, Astrid. Technology is not infallible, and we maintain caution. We have considered a hybrid approach. I believe Rafe and Jomei can assure you that the droids and augmented humans proceed so that they work alongside your prescribed methods rather than replacing them." Violet added.

"Yes, I believe that's possible. They could program the droids to follow Astrid's strict guidelines, allowing her to maintain control over their functions. The droids would act as extensions of her expertise rather than replacements." Phil responded.

"So they could program them to act more like assistants, taking care of repetitive tasks while I handle more nuanced aspects. I understand your perspective, Phil. Astrid sat back and seemed to relax.

Violet smiled. "Exactly. This way, Astrid, you retain your autonomy. It's about finding a balance—using these tools to enhance, not override, your work in the greenhouses."

"I think that's a fair compromise," Phil said to Violet. Rafe and Jomei could even integrate regular checks and balances, where Astrid reviews the droids' performance and adjusts their programming as needed. This way, the droids will constantly align their actions with her vision." Phil remained calm.

Astrid's scowl relaxed. "That could work. I would feel more comfortable knowing I have the final say in how the droids operate. And if they can truly help maintain the conditions in the greenhouses without disrupting the ecosystem, they may be worth a try again."

Violet intervened. "Phil, you spoke about duty earlier. Your sense of responsibility is commendable, but we can agree that our duty also includes preserving the essence of what makes Galatéa special. People like Astrid nurture the essence of life we see around us. Can you help to ensure our technological advancements serve that life?"

Phil's eyes glowed brighter. "Yes, you're right, Violet. Our duty isn't just about efficiency—it's about stewardship. If we can use these technologies to protect and enhance what we have, we're truly fulfilling our mission rather than just optimizing it."

Astrid smiled. I see the potential of this technology as a valuable ally when used wisely. I needed assurance that it wouldn't hinder my life's work.

Violet looked pleased. "I think we've found a path forward that respects both of your values. Astrid, you'll have the support you need without compromising your principles, and Phil, you'll be able to contribute your expertise in a way that benefits everyone. This is the harmony we seek on Galatéa—a place where progress and preservation walk hand in hand. It's only the beginning. Together, we'll make Galatéa a place where nature and technology coexist in perfect balance. That's the future we're building."

Note. Conclusion. Through this dialogue, Violet successfully mediated the conflict between Phil and Astrid by acknowledging the importance of both their perspectives and finding a solution that honors their respective concerns. The compromise allows for integrating technology in a way that supports rather than overrides the natural environment, fostering a collaborative approach to the stewardship of Planet Galatéa.

Personal Note. Human interactions to review. Jomei has recorded Violet's actions with particular interest for future reference, noting her approach to de-escalation. Violet used a combination of empathy and logic, addressing Phil's sense of duty and Astrid's concerns for her plants and environment. She acknowledged the value of both perspectives, suggesting a compromise that respects Astrid's need for autonomy while integrating the necessary technology to minimize disruption.

Jomei acknowledges that Violet's intervention was effective; Astrid's hostility diminished as she felt heard and understood. Jomei observed a slight shift in Astrid's demeanor—she became a little nicer, her tone softening as she conceded that Phil and Tarnak might not be as intrusive as she initially feared. Jomei considers this a small but significant victory for group cohesion, recognizing the importance of balancing technological integration with respect for individual autonomy.

Note. Final Thoughts. Jomei processes these interactions through multiple lenses: emotional analysis, behavioral prediction, and group dynamics. Jomei concludes that the success of this community, particularly in a space exploration and colonization context, hinges on the ability to navigate such interpersonal conflicts with care and understanding. Jomei predicts that the relationship between Phil, Tarnak, and Astrid will evolve, with Violet and others playing a crucial role in maintaining harmony.

Jomei further hypothesizes that Tarnak's presence will ultimately be a stabilizing force for Phil and the entire community, as his wisdom influences others indirectly through Phil. However, Jomei remains cautious and aware that Astrid's underlying issues with change and control may resurface if not addressed more permanently.

End Blog Entry.

###

In the bustling, glass-encased Atrium of the interstellar colony, Rafe, security chief, paced slowly along the perimeter. The bustling, glass-encased Atrium buzzed with activity and was purposefully designed for communal gathering and relaxation. Colonists moved about, their voices mingling in a low hum as they discussed the latest developments in the colony. The transparent dome above revealed dark clouds skidding by with intermittent flashes of lightning. Beyond the clouds was the dark expanse of space, a constant reminder of their isolated existence. However, thoughts unrelated to the serene atmosphere in the Atrium preoccupied Rafe's mind.

Thanks to Rafe's skills, Jomei now had a physical representation within the Atrium. This interface resembled a sleek, humanoid figure, though clearly non-human in its metallic sheen and smooth, featureless face. In this form, Jomei appeared before Rafe, his presence comforting and unsettling in its omniscience.

"Rafe," Jomei's voice intoned softly, "you requested to discuss the recent integration issues concerning Phil, Astrid, and Violet."

Rafe nodded, his face a mask of contemplation. "Yes, Jomei. It's becoming increasingly complicated. Phil's situation, in particular, is problematic. His symbiont has enhanced his abilities, but the secrecy surrounding it is causing friction, especially with Astrid."

Jomei's digital eyes seemed to focus on Rafe, though there was no true gaze. "Phil's symbiont is crucial for his survival and has been beneficial in many tasks. However, the concealment of such an integral part of his being from Astrid is a source of tension. Astrid's distrust of technology, particularly droids like myself, further exacerbates the issue."

Rafe sighed, glancing over at Phil, who was conversing with a group of colonists. Rafe sent silently to Jomei. *Phil appears normal on the outside, but beneath that exterior, the symbiont is constantly at work—enhancing his strength, healing injuries at an accelerated rate, and even influencing his thought processes. The symbiont, a biotechnological marvel, is a secret only a few in the colony know about. Despite his struggles, Phil has embraced the symbiont as a part of himself. But Astrid, a steadfast human who prided herself on her non-augmented status, would likely never accept such a thing.*

"Astrid has been a vocal opponent of the technological augmentations many colonists have undergone," Rafe mused aloud. "She sees them as a threat to human integrity, a slippery slope toward losing what makes us human." Then, sent silently; *if she found out about Phil's symbiont in the wrong way, I fear she would see it as a betrayal.*

Jomei processed this, running countless simulations with its internal algorithms. "Droid malfunctions and AI uprisings on Earth have caused significant harm, leading to Astrid's resistance. Her hatred for droids is less about the technology itself and more about its potential to go wrong. In her mind, augmentation and symbionts represent the same danger."

"Exactly," Rafe agreed. "And then there's Violet. Her nanoparticle augmentation and BAI are the pinnacle of what Astrid despises. Yet, Violet has maintained a somewhat cordial relationship with Astrid. It's a tenuous balance, and I'm concerned that Phil's secret could tip the scales."

Standing across the Atrium, Violet was deep in conversation with another group of colonists. Her augmentation was not visible, but Rafe knew millions of nanoparticles coursed through her bloodstream, giving her enhanced cognitive abilities and a direct neural link to Jomei. The BAI allowed her to access data instantly, communicate with the Jomei, and even influence the colony's systems to a certain extent. While Violet's augmentations made her incredibly valuable to the colony, they also made her the subject of Astrid's distrust.

"Violet's BAI has allowed her to bridge gaps that would otherwise be insurmountable," Jomei observed. "Her ability to interface with me has improved medical operations significantly. However, her augmentation places her in a precarious position with Astrid. The nanoparticles are a clear departure from human baseline capabilities, something Astrid finds disturbing."

Rafe rubbed his chin thoughtfully. "Violet has been careful not to flaunt her abilities. She knows Astrid's feelings and has tried to respect them, but there's only so much she can do. The BAI is a part of her now—just like Phil's symbiont is a part of him. Eventually, the truth will emerge, and I am concerned about the consequences.

Have you thought about orchestrating a controlled revelation?

Jomei suggested. "It might be more beneficial to have Phil and the other symbiont-human pairs disclose their enhancements in a controlled manner, focusing on the benefits they bring to the colony. This could help mitigate Astrid's reaction."

Rafe considered this. "It's a risky move. Astrid might rally others to her cause if she feels cornered or betrayed. There are still colonists who share her views—who believe that any augmentation or AI involvement is a step toward losing our humanity."

"Humanity is a concept that evolves," Jomei remarked. It will be necessary for the colonists, including Astrid, to adapt to the realities of life in this environment. The symbiont, nanoparticle augmentation, and even my presence are all necessary for survival. The question is not whether they are human, but whether they contribute to the well-being and success of the colony."

Rafe nodded slowly. "You're right. But we need to manage the narrative carefully. Perhaps Astrid might come around if we frame it as a necessity for survival—something that ensures the colony's future."

"It will require careful coordination," Jomei agreed. "Phil and the other pairs must be prepared to explain their augmentations in a way that emphasizes their humanity, not diminishes it. They must show that these enhancements do not make them less human but more capable."

Rafe sighed, feeling the weight of his responsibility. "It's a delicate balance. I'll speak with Eurydice, Adira, David, and Phil and prepare them for the possibility. We'll need to strategize how to present this to Astrid—and the colony—without causing a rift."

Jomei's presence seemed to shift, its form shimmering slightly as it processed the situation's complexities. "I will assist in any way I can, Rafe. The colony's future depends on our ability to integrate these technologies harmoniously. We ensure all colonists feel valued and essential to our collective survival regardless of their stance on augmentation."

Rafe glanced at the colonists again, his gaze lingering on Phil, Astrid, and Violet. The Atrium, with its open spaces and transparent dome, symbolized unity and transparency. Yet, within its walls, secrets were brewing, secrets which could either unite them further or tear them apart.

28 - Jomei and Rafe's Investigation

Rafe sat in the dining hall. Rasa's company was always welcome, and he always felt better about the colony's safety and security after spending time with her. The colony dining hall and adjacent Atrium had become bustling hubs of activity. With its diverse population engaged in various occupations, from research to agriculture, Rafe saw the colony thriving. Rafe looked up at the geodesic windows of the protective dome and felt awe at the marvel of advanced engineering that shielded its inhabitants from the planet's harsh environment.

This recent surge in suspicious activities has revealed nefarious players. Maintaining the delicate balance between my augmented self and interacting with the colonists who remain natural has not been easy. There are so many secrets and lies. Eurydice and SIS22 must have some plan to disclose the thirteen ancient caves. Various parties have their agendas.

As Rafe delved deeper into the investigation of the death of the greenhouse worker, Bob, they uncovered an intricate web of deceit and intrigue that threatened the colony's stability. Rafe walked to his offices, admiring the beauty of the atrium. Astrid had placed various types of trees and plants along the walkways, and there was now a tiny hill complete with green grass.

Jomei greeted Rafe as he entered the security section. *Hail! Rafe. Is it time to discuss several anomalies I have noticed that suggest unauthorized clandestine activities?*

Of course, Jomei. It's time.

As you know, our vast array of sensors and surveillance

systems have provided us with real-time data—everything from atmospheric conditions to the movements of individuals within the colony. One of the first red flags that came to light was the unusual energy patterns in the residential sector. Various dwellings consumed significantly more power than usual, particularly at night.

Jomei cross-referenced this surveillance data with actual footage for Rafe and displayed it onscreen.

Jomei has discovered several individuals who frequently meet in these dwellings. The meetings are not a part of any publicized activity.

Good job, Jomei. Some of these individuals' behaviors suggest they were trying to avoid attracting attention.

Additionally, Jomei has detected unusual fluctuations in the colony's communication networks. The colony's communication networks detected unusual fluctuations, with encrypted messages being sent and received at odd hours. They used obscure protocols for communications that were not part of the standard communication operation systems. Jomei attempted to decrypt these messages with limited results. Snippets of the limited deciphered messages suggest covert planning and coordination by these individuals.

Further investigation has revealed that certain areas near the ancient caves have been experiencing unexplained disturbances. Seismic activity and magnetic field fluctuations have resulted in occasional power outages. These phenomena could be coincidental, and we may attribute them to natural causes. However, the location and timing of the disturbances statistically raise the probability above the level of mere coincidence.

Jomei's hypothesis. Someone may attempt to access the caves without authorization, possibly using advanced technology that may interfere with the colony's systems.

Rafe inspected Jomei's biosensor data for social monitoring and behavioral analysis. *I compliment you, Jomei, with your insights on human interactions and activities. My algorithms have been able to analyze individual speech patterns, body language, and social networks further. I have also detected signs of deceit or malicious intent.*

Rafe applied more sophisticated algorithms and examined the individuals identified by Jomei. *Integrated facial recognition and biometric scanning capabilities enabled the silver surveillance droids to identify individuals in real-time with excellent results. By cross-referencing with our centralized database, we now have retrieved personal information, criminal records, and behavioral patterns of recognized targets.*

Rafe also applied advanced behavior analysis algorithms that processed sensor data to analyze crowd behavior patterns. The Sentinel-II could detect anomalies, such as sudden movements, gatherings, or potential threats, alerting the operator to take necessary action. Using advanced facial recognition and behavioral analysis, Rafe tracked their movements and interactions. *The individuals you have identified appear to be a part of a loosely connected network. They often meet in small groups and continue communicating among themselves and outside the colony along encrypted channels.*

Jomei has noted that these individuals exhibited biometric signs of heightened anxiety, frequently looking over their shoulders and using code words in their conversations. These indicators point to their need for secrecy.

Observing the footage several times, Rafe noted an obvious culprit. *One particular individual, a technician named Raj, stands out. Raj was a team leader in the Rizika game, a passenger on the Porta Caeli, and not an original colonist. His movements since arriving showed that he had quickly integrated into the group of suspicious individuals. Jomei, analyze the available information about Raj Patel.*

Jomei finds several inconsistencies in his records, suggesting his identity might have been fabricated. Rafe, further scrutiny uncovers that Raj has had unrestricted access to critical dome systems, including those that could be manipulated to control the environment and security protocols.

Rafe also detected a pattern of financial transactions that showed the movement of significant sums of money through untraceable channels. *Such sizeable sums of money suggest that the group is being funded by a powerful external entity, likely with interest in the artifacts and knowledge contained within the caves. The transactions linked known black market operatives and off-world mercenaries. I will get in touch with Eurydice. Jomei, please silently contact Adira and David for a meeting of SIS22 regarding our current findings.*

#

With their combined data, Jomei and Rafe were ready to present their findings to Eurydice and SIS22 operatives. "All of the evidence points to a coordinated effort by an organized group to gain access to the caves for nefarious purposes at worst."

Eurydice shifted uncomfortably in her seat, and her gaze shifted around the conference table, resting on each of the Council members' faces, observing their reactions, especially Chancellor Byron. "I recognize the gravity of the situation and allow Jomei and Rafe to take preemptive measures to safeguard the colony and its resources."

"Jomei reports that we have developed a multi-pronged strategy to neutralize the threat. The first step we plan to take is to increase surveillance and tighten security around the sensitive areas, including the caves and critical infrastructure points. We have already deployed additional sensors and drones with advanced detection capabilities to monitor suspicious activities.

Jomei has added an augmented reality interface. The silver droid's visual sensors are now enhanced with a real-time augmented reality display, allowing security to see more through the droid's eyes remotely. This interface will provide us with detailed overlays of individual profiles within the crowd, highlighting potential targets or persons of interest based on pre-programmed criteria."

Rafe added, "The silver droids have highly sensitive microphones that can isolate and amplify conversations from significant distances." This feature allows security to eavesdrop on discussions within the monitored area, even amidst the ambient noise of a bustling crowd in the Atrium or dining hall."

Rafe sent silently to Jomei. *Jomei, do not share any information with the Council or Eurydice about our initiated covert operation to gather more intelligence on the group's plans and members, especially the part about our using our combined analytical capabilities to infiltrate the group's communication networks, and we planted false information to mislead them. Please DO NOT share our set traps, false leads about access points to the caves, and potential vulnerabilities in the colony's security systems. We don't know who we can trust entirely at this point.*

Agreed.

Later in security, Rafe reviewed their shrew psychological operation; he aimed to sow discord and distrust within the group by manipulating their communications and creating false narratives. He sent it to Jomei. *Our operations have turned the group members against each other. This is directly observable by their weakened cohesion and effectiveness.*

Unraveling the conspiracy proved remarkably effective. Rafe, your psychological operation succeeded due to carefully crafted messages that planted doubts within the group. Jomei has learned much about human psychology and behavior. By exploiting tensions within the group, we discovered that Raj, the technician with the fabricated identity, rightly became the focal point of suspicion. The other group members began questioning his loyalty and motives, leading to infighting and paranoia.

"Adira, I called you here because of your association with Zhopla and the map Taika left you years ago." Rafe paced in the dimly lit room, holding up a coyote skin. "I've been through Raj Patel's quarters. Found this. Along with drums and black charcoal—it's like some twisted collection of ritualistic objects. These are not some harmless ceremonial objects. Jomei and I applied algorithms and discovered Raj was the likely culprit."

"Rafe, this reminds me of something that happened to me before we left for Galatéa. There was a night I went to visit Zhopla at St. George's. I wanted answers about Taika's disappearance. That's where I witnessed…something." Adira was sitting quietly, her eyes dark with this distant memory.

Rafe stopped pacing and focused his full attention on Adira. "What did you see?"

"Zhopla wasn't answering his door, so I walked to the church to see if he was there. A figure rose from a pew with a hirsute chest. It had unfathomable black eyes, blood-red rimmed and intense, staring back at me through encrusted slits. In the dark, those eyes…they didn't seem human, Rafe. They were something far worse." Adira trailed off, her voice almost a whisper. "He asked me where the map was. At the time, I had no idea what he was talking about. Later that evening, at my mother's farmhouse, Zhopla and I opened a letter addressed to me from my mother, and attached was a map. It made no sense."

"You're saying you've seen this kind of darkness before?" Rafe tightened his grip on the coyote fur.

"Yes. And the presence I felt that night... it's similar to what you've found in Raj's quarters. Even creepier, when I reviewed the security feeds, this same being was watching Zhopla and me through the window. It's as if the objects you found are calling out to something ancient, something vile."

"Jomei and I need to figure out what Raj is up to and whether or how many other perpetrators are here on Galatéa. This isn't just about Raj Patel anymore."

"Be careful, Rafe. This conspiracy may threaten the entire colony and caves, and they won't let go easily." Adira stood and rested her hand on Rafe's arm.

"We'll be ready. And we'll make sure it doesn't get any further."

Rafe understood the gravity of the situation and the dark, foreboding atmosphere surrounding Raj Patel's involvement in something deeply sinister. As the conspiracy group's cohesion broke down, Jomei and Rafe moved in to apprehend the key members. Using surveillance data and predictive algorithms, they coordinated with the colony's security forces to conduct a series of targeted interrogations. Raj and several other key figures were captured and interrogated, revealing the extent of their plans and the identities of their backers.

The interrogation revealed that a rogue group of fanatic radicals had been hired by a powerful covert regime on Earth interested in acquiring the artifacts and knowledge contained within the caves. This small regime had provided the group with advanced technology and funding, promising substantial rewards for their success. The ultimate goal was to exploit the ancient knowledge of the alien caves for commercial and technological gain, with little regard for the colony's well-being or the preservation of the artifacts. It also became apparent that not all of the key members had been identified.

With the immediate threat neutralized, Jomei and Rafe shifted their focus to preventing similar incidents in the future, especially since they did not know how many key members were still out there. They implemented enhanced security protocols and increased monitoring of external communications to detect any signs of further infiltration attempts. They also limited how much information they shared with Eurydice and other SIS22 operatives regarding establishing stricter regulations on access to sensitive areas and resources.

Jomei and Rafe also collaborated with Gint and his team. Gint's scientific community thrived within the caves, and better methods for studying and preserving the artifacts were instituted. The Archivists developed a system of advanced imaging and analysis techniques to document the caves' contents without causing damage. These efforts protected the colony's heritage and contributed to a broader understanding of the ancient civilization that thrived on Galatéa in the distant past.

Uncovering and thwarting the nefarious players in the colony left a lasting impact on Jomei and Rafe. It highlighted the importance of vigilance and the need for constant adaptation in the face of evolving threats. *This incident has underscored the value of our collaboration, Jomei. When we work together, our success in overcoming even the most sophisticated challenges demonstrates the synergy of advanced technology and human ingenuity.*

Jomei sees the Galatéa colony as maintaining a fragile balance between progress and preservation. The discovery of the ancient alien caves has opened new avenues of knowledge and exploration. But they have also attracted the attention of those who wish to exploit them and their secrets for personal gain. Eurydice is determined to protect the artifacts while pushing the boundaries of human knowledge and achievement.

###

"David, Jomei, and I want to discuss the aliens, symbiosis, and what to expect after joining the symbiotes and humans." David had joined Rafe and Jomei in security.

"Of course, I would be happy to explain what I know about symbiotic relationships. These relationships involve a variety of interactions with other organisms that can be beneficial, neutral, or harmful to humans." I plan to provide some key examples and aspects of these relationships from Earth as a way to make them more understandable and accessible.

"I'd like to begin with what we know about microbial symbiosis." For example, the human gut contains trillions of microbes, primarily bacterial organisms, that play a crucial role in digestion, produce Vitamin K for the human host, and enhance immune system functions. In turn, humans provide these microorganisms with a nutrient-rich home. Scientists refer to this as mutualism in symbiotic relationships. There are implications for human health. A balanced gut microbiome is essential for good health. Scientists linked dysbiosis, or the imbalance in microbial communities, to conditions like obesity, diabetes, inflammatory bowel disease, and mental health issues hundreds of years ago.

Ok, Jomei, I'm going to get comfortable. David loves talking about this stuff. Rafe pulled a chair out and stretched his legs.

"Even our skin harbors a variety of microorganisms, more than just bacterial. Viruses and fungi can live on human skin but don't harm us. They protect us from organisms that can cause disease. Some of them produce antimicrobial substances, or they out-compete any harmful substances.

"On Earth, symbiotic relationships existed with pets, especially dogs and cats. Studies have shown that relationships with pets improve mental health and provide humans with companionship. In return, humans provided sustenance, a home, and care. Livestock animals like cows, sheep, and chickens were crucial for human agriculture, providing food, clothing, and labor, while humans offered food, shelter, and breeding management.

Jomei covertly sent to Rafe. *Ah, David is trying to teach AI Jomei about symbiotic relationships. That's like a carpenter giving a lecture on gourmet cooking to a sous chef. But go ahead, let's see if he can surprise me!*

I note your newfound humor and snarkiness, Jomei.

"In botany, we have plant symbiosis. For example, humans cultivate plants in agriculture for food, fiber, and medical purposes. These plants provide oxygen and other resources while humans propagate plant species and maintain ecosystems. Various plants often have symbiotic relationships with fungi, called mycorrhizae, that enhance nutrient uptake in fungal relationships, known as mycorrhizal relationships. Humans benefit indirectly through increased crop yields and soil health.

Probiotics and prebiotics in biotechnology and medicine also serve as another example of the positive outcomes of symbiotic relationships. Probiotics are beneficial bacteria that, when ingested, can enhance gut health and immunity. Prebiotics are substances that promote the growth of beneficial gut bacteria. In genetic engineering, hundreds of years ago, humans used bacteria and yeast in biotechnology to produce insulin, antibiotics, and other essential drugs.

"Then we have a negative side to symbiotic relationships with pathogenic interactions. This is known as parasitism."

Rafe sat upright and leaned forward.

"Harmful relationships exist with disease-causing bacteria, viruses, and parasites like malaria. Fortunately, humans have developed medical and technological means to combat these pathogens."

"There is also environmental symbiosis, like pollination.

Bees, butterflies, and other pollinators are vital for the reproduction of many crops. Humans have benefited from the fruits and vegetables produced while providing habitats and flowers for pollinators. Nitrogen fixation is where certain bacteria fix atmospheric nitrogen that plants use. This process is crucial for agriculture, reducing the need for chemical fertilizers and promoting sustainable farming.

"On a larger scale, we see cultural and social symbiosis. Humans form complex social structures and communities that rely on cooperation and mutual aid. These relationships are essential for societal development, economic stability, and cultural evolution.

"More recent is the technological symbiosis—the human-machine interaction such as Cyborg Technologies. Technology integration with the human body with prosthetics or implants represents symbiosis, enhancing human capabilities and health. Humans engage in many symbiotic relationships crucial for health, agriculture, technology, and societal development. These interactions range from beneficial to neutral to harmful and have profoundly shaped human life and the environment.

"Regarding the Veltryn and symbiosis with humans. We remember that these beings are not just plants or algae, simple life forms; they are highly evolved and intelligent beings seeking symbiosis with compatible sentients. They choose hosts based on specific genetic or personality traits, and once a host is selected, they can merge with them. My mother, Taika, is here and has been in a symbiotic relationship for three years. She recovered from the outbreak that started on Earth. I only found out about this recently. They describe this merging process as gentle and cooperative, where the alien extends filaments of light that intertwine and eventually integrate with the host's body.

"Some of the positive effects of a symbiotic relationship with the Veltryn are life-changing. For the host, symbiosis is not a mere coexistence but a life-altering experience. It can amplify their physical capabilities, heighten their senses, and even grant them access to the vast knowledge of the alien. The host's vision might extend beyond the visible spectrum, or they might develop a 'sixth sense' about their surroundings." David sighed. "The results will manifest over time. Some of them are predictable, and many are unpredictable. Symbiosis was the last resort to save our patients' lives."

"Thanks for the lesson, David. That was ….enlightening." Jomei silently sent a raspberry to Rafe.

As Jomei and Rafe resumed their duties, they remained watchful. *Jomei, we must optimize our readiness to defend the colony against future threats. Our mission is to safeguard the present and ensure that the legacy of the ancient Galatéan civilization will endure for generations to come.*

Jomei and Rafe exemplified the promise of a future where technology and humanity worked together to create a better, safer world. But not everyone thought so.

29 - Incoming Communications

Eurydice, Rafe, and Jomei monitored incoming communications from an unknown fleet of spaceships. They claimed they had escaped Earth due to its complete chaos and devastation and wished asylum on Galatéa. They have brought bots and raw materials, among other cargo, to build their own domed colony. This is the first communication as the fleet of ships approaches the planet.

Rafe stared at the communication screen, the soft hum of the control panel the only sound breaking the silence in the observation deck of the Galatéa Command Center. Beside him, AI Jomei, his trusted artificial intelligence partner, projected a holographic display of the incoming fleet. It was a sight to behold: fifty or sixty large and small ships gliding towards Galatéa like a flock of migratory birds seeking refuge.

The ships were of various makes and models, some old and battered, others sleek and modern, but all bore the scars of a desperate escape. Rafe could see their defensive stance in their movements, the way they clustered together, seeking safety in numbers. *These are no ordinary travelers; these are refugees fleeing something terrible.*

"Jomei, open a channel to the lead ship," Eurydice ordered, her voice steady despite the gravity of the situation.

"Channel open, Chief Eurydice," Jomei responded in his calm, synthesized voice. "You may proceed."

Eurydice took a deep breath and leaned closer to the microphone. "This is Chief Executive Eurydice of the Galatéa

Command Center. You are approaching a restricted zone. Identify yourselves and state your purpose."

There was a brief pause, filled only with the static of the communication line. Then, a voice crackled through, strained but resolute.

"This is Admiral Janel Glassey of the Earth Fleet. We are a fleet of Asylum seekers from Earth—This is our first official communication with Galatéa. We seek asylum on Galatéa. Earth has fallen into chaos and devastation. We have fled with what we could salvage, including materials to build our own domed colony. We come in peace and desperation. Please, hear our plea."

Rafe glanced at Jomei's activity monitor, seeing that Jomei was already analyzing the incoming transmission. Jomei's processors whirred softly as they sifted through data, assessing the credibility of the admiral's words.

"Admiral Glassey," Eurydice began, her tone measured, "we need more information. What exactly happened on Earth? And how can we be sure you are not a threat to our planet?"

There was another longer pause as if the admiral was gathering her thoughts. When she spoke again, her voice was tinged with sorrow and urgency.

"Earth has been ravaged by a series of catastrophic events," she explained. "Environmental collapse, widespread conflicts, and a pandemic that decimated the population. Governments fell, societies crumbled, and anarchy reigned. Those of us who survived banded together, pooling our resources to escape. We have no intention of causing harm. We only seek a new beginning, a chance to rebuild our lives."

Rafe listened intently, his mind racing. The story was plausible, but they couldn't take any chances. Galatéa had strict protocols for such situations, designed to protect its inhabitants from potential threats.

"Admiral Glassey," he said, choosing his words carefully, "we need to conduct a thorough assessment before granting any permissions. Our security protocols require a quarantine period and a detailed inspection of your fleet and cargo. Will you comply with these requirements?"

"We understand and will comply with all your protocols," Janel replied without hesitation. "We are at your mercy and will do whatever it takes to prove our intentions. Please, Chief Executive Eurydice, do not turn us away."

Eurydice nodded, more to herself than anyone else. The decision was not hers alone to make; it would require consultation with the Galatéan Council. But for now, they had to manage the immediate situation.

"Thank you, Admiral Glassey," Rafe said. "This is Security Chief Rafe. Stand by for further instructions. We will guide your fleet to a holding area where you can await quarantine and inspection. Jomei will provide the coordinates."

"Understood, Rafe," she responded. "We await your guidance; please call me Janel. And... thank you."

As the communication ended, Rafe turned to Jomei's monitor, who was already processing the next steps.

"Transmit the coordinates to the fleet and inform the Council of the situation," Eurydice instructed. "We must prepare for their arrival and enforce our protocols."

"Coordinates transmitted, and the Council has been notified," Jomei confirmed. "What are your thoughts on their story, Eurydice?"

Eurydice sighed, rubbing her temples. "It's hard to say. They could be telling the truth, or it could be a well-crafted deception. Either way, we have to proceed with caution. Galatéa's safety comes first."

The Council convened quickly, a testament to the seriousness of the situation. Comprised of representatives from Galatéa's various regions and disciplines, the Council was the ultimate authority on matters of security and diplomacy.

Eurydice and Rafe stood in the command center of SIS22, facing the Chief Commanding Officer of Galatéa, Chancellor Byron. The room was tense with anticipation as they prepared to deliver their report.

"Chancellor Byron," Eurydice began, her voice steady, "we've received a communication from an incoming fleet of unknown ships. They identify as refugees from Earth, fleeing widespread chaos, environmental collapse, and societal breakdown. They seek asylum on Galatéa, claiming to have brought materials to build their own domed colony."

Jomei's holographic display projected an image of the fleet. "Initial scans confirm the presence of various heavily worn but operational ship models. Admiral Janel, their leader, has assured compliance with our protocols, including quarantine and inspection."

Byron's eyes narrowed as he processed the information. "What's your assessment, Rafe?"

"Our technology assessments indicate sophisticated technological abilities, including advanced weapons and propulsion systems. Earlier scans of the ships' hulls indicated unknown materials blended with known materials. Of particular interest is their use of advanced antimatter reactors, a technology unknown to us here in Galatéa. We could learn much from their scientific and technological advances."

Rafe took a deep breath. "Their story is consistent with known events on Earth, and they've shown full cooperation. While we must remain cautious, their plight seems genuine. We recommend proceeding with quarantine and detailed inspection before granting provisional asylum." Rafe presented the communication details, and the Council members listened intently. Their faces were grave, and their expressions thoughtful as they weighed the information.

"Their story is compelling," Councilor Leora said, her tone reflective. "The chaos on Earth is well-documented. It's not unthinkable that a group of survivors would seek refuge here."

"But we cannot ignore the potential risks," Councilor Aric countered. "We know nothing about these people or their true intentions. We must proceed with extreme caution."

Councilor Maia, a scientist specializing in environmental systems, leaned forward. "Our protocols are designed for this very reason. A quarantine period will allow us to assess their health and ensure they pose no biological threat. An inspection of their cargo will reveal any hidden dangers. Obviously, a detailed list of all incoming individuals is also required."

Councilor Tyr, the military representative, nodded in agreement. "We should also deploy a security team to monitor their activities. If there is any sign of hostility, we can act swiftly."

Byron nodded, his expression thoughtful. "Proceed with the established protocols. Keep me updated on any developments. We can't afford to take any chances, but we also can't ignore a genuine plea for help."

Eurydice interrupted the adjournment. "The final topic we should discuss is where these refugees will build their dome. Should the refugees establish their domed colony on the outer planet in our system's habitable zone, or should they go to the southern hemisphere of Galatéa?"

"Jomei, do you have input regarding the pros and cons of where the new habitation should be built?" Chancellor Byron intoned.

Jomei's mellifluous voice immediately responded. "The decision between establishing a domed colony on our fourth planet or the southern hemisphere of Galatéa depends on several factors: If the refugees established their dome on the outer planet, they would have greater autonomy, provision for diverse economic activities for self-sufficiency, and may be beneficial for our long-term survival by providing a backup location in case of a disaster. On the other hand, being on another planet means limited immediate support and collaboration with Galatéa. The logistics of developing their infrastructure would be significant.

"However, should they build their dome in Galatéa's southern hemisphere, it would allow for easier collaboration, trade, and mutual support. We would have access to established resources and infrastructures from Galatéa to provide a strong foundation for the new colony. Potentially, we could have a stronger, more unified community due to our close proximity to cultural exchange and cohesion. On the downside, the new colony might have less autonomy, being influenced or controlled by Galatéa. Sharing the planet could lead to competition for resources, potentially causing conflicts and strain on the environment. Finally, having multiple colonies on one planet could be risky if the planet faced a catastrophic event.

"Jomei recommends considering both options carefully. It would be important to define the refugee community's long-term strategic goals. Do they prioritize autonomy and expansion or stability and collaboration?"

Rafe added, "Jomei and I will develop contingency plans for both scenarios. If the priority is stability, collaboration, and leveraging existing infrastructure, establishing the colony in the southern hemisphere of Galatéa might be more advantageous.

However, if autonomy, strategic expansion, and diversification of habitats are more important, the outer planet could be the better choice."

The debate continued, but the consensus was clear: the refugees would be given a chance under strict conditions. Galatéa's safety was paramount.

Rafe left the Council chambers feeling a mix of relief and apprehension. The decision had been made, but the hard work was only beginning.

As the fleet approached the designated holding area, Rafe and Jomei coordinated the quarantine procedures. The ships were guided to a secure zone, isolated from the starward side of Galatéa. The refugee's medical teams and security personnel were dispatched to conduct the necessary reports of their conditions and systems.

Admiral Janel maintained regular communication; her tone was always cooperative and respectful. She provided detailed manifests of their cargo, lists of passengers, and reports of their journey. It was clear she was doing everything possible to gain their trust.

The quarantine process was rigorous. Jomei instructed the artificial intelligence on each ship to scan for pathogens, and the passengers underwent thorough, documented medical examinations. The cargo was meticulously inspected, and every crate and container was opened and scrutinized. It was a massive undertaking but essential for the safety of Galatéa.

As the days passed, Rafe found himself increasingly sympathetic to the refugees. Their stories and evidence painted a grim picture of Earth's fate. They spoke of cities reduced to rubble, desperate battles for resources, and loved ones lost to disease and violence. It was a haunting reminder of the fragility of civilization.

Yet, through it all, there was a sense of hope. The refugees had not given up. They had come together to seek a new beginning and pooled their skills and resources. They had brought the means to survive and the determination to rebuild. Rafe couldn't help but admire their resilience.

At the end of the quarantine period, the Council reconvened to review the findings. The medical and security teams presented their reports: no pathogens, hidden weapons, or signs of deceit. The refugees were precisely what they claimed to be: survivors seeking asylum.

"Based on the evidence, I recommend we grant them provisional asylum," Eurydice said, addressing the Council. "They have complied with all our protocols and posed no threat. They have brought materials to build their own colony, which will minimize the strain on our resources. I believe they deserve a chance."

The Council members nodded, their expressions thoughtful but generally supportive. Councilor Leora spoke up, her voice filled with compassion. "We cannot turn our backs on those in need," she said. "If we do, what does that say about us? These people have suffered greatly. Let us show them the kindness and generosity that Galatéa is known for."

The vote was unanimous. The refugees would be granted asylum and allowed to establish their colony on Galatéa's sister planet, which is located on the outer perimeter of the habitable zone under strict oversight.

Rafe conveyed the news to Admiral Janel, who received it with heartfelt gratitude.

"Thank you, Rafe," she said, her voice breaking with emotion. "You have given us hope when we had none. We will not forget this kindness."

In the following weeks, the refugees began building the headquarters for their domed colony on the southern hemisphere of Galatéa's sister planet. They worked tirelessly, using their cargo to construct sustainable and efficient domed habitats. The Galatéan council provided additional support, ensuring they had the resources to thrive.

Rafe and Jomei regularly shuttled over and monitored the construction sites, overseeing the integration and offering assistance. He was struck by the refugees' sense of community, determination to rebuild their lives, and sense of purpose and belonging.

He got to know many of them personally: engineers who had designed the domes, doctors who tended to the sick and injured, and teachers who began to set up schools for the children. Each had a story, a reason for being there, a hope for the future.

One evening, as the sun set over the newly constructed dome, Rafe's hologram stood with Admiral Janel, looking out over the fledgling colony.

"You've accomplished a lot in a short time," Rafe said, his voice filled with admiration.

"We had no choice," Janel replied, her eyes reflecting sorrow and hope. "We lost everything. But here, we have a chance to start again. To build something better."

Rafe nodded, understanding the weight of her words. "The Galatéa system is a place of second chances. We're glad to have you here."

She smiled a genuine, heartfelt smile. "Thank you, Rafe. For everything."

As the months passed, the refugee colony became integral to Galatéa. The refugees contributed their skills and knowledge, enriching the planet's diversity and capabilities. They integrated into the larger society, forming bonds and building a future together.

Rafe continued to play a key role in their integration, fostering understanding and cooperation between the refugees and the native Galatéans. It was not always easy, but it was rewarding.

One day, as he walked through the bustling Atrium of the refugee colony, now a thriving community, Rafe felt a deep sense of satisfaction. The journey had been long and arduous, but the outcome was a testament to the resilience of the human spirit and the power of compassion.

Galatéa had opened its arms to those in need and, in doing so, had become more robust, more prosperous, and united. Jomei interrupted Rafe's reverie.

RAFE! SENSORS INDICATE A THREAT IN GREENHOUSE A! SOMETHING IS HAPPENING TO ME, JOMEI IS....

30 - Eurydice's Determination

An icy shiver ran down his spine as Rafe stood on the command deck. He locked his eyes on the surveillance screens displaying the scene unfolding in the greenhouse. Eurydice, the trusted Chief Executive Officer of SIS22 and a colony member until now, stood at the center, a look of wild desperation in her eyes. She was armed and dangerous. The gravity of the situation weighed on him.

Rafe's security chief instincts kicked in immediately. The greenhouse was one of the colony's most critical assets. Without it, their food supply would dwindle to nothing, leading to starvation and chaos. He couldn't let that happen. His mind raced, calculating the best way to approach the volatile situation without escalating it further.

He toggled the comm link to his team. "All units converge on the greenhouse. Code Red. I repeat, Code Red. Exercise caution—Eurydice Sideris is armed and possesses an incendiary device.

As he issued the command, his thoughts drifted to the events that led them here. Eurydice's deceit had been insidious. She had hidden her intentions well, her facade so convincing that no one suspected her until it was almost too late. Rafe had pieced together her plan just minutes before, realizing with a sickening clarity what she had done to Gint and Jomei. The thought of it made his blood boil.

Without his consent, Eurydice tried to transform Gint, a stalwart SIS22 research scientist, into a human-AI hybrid, a grotesque fusion of man and machine. With the help of her personal silver droid, Eurydice stole Jomei, the colony's advanced AI, and began the implantation procedure into Gint's body. The violation was unforgivable. Neither had been given a choice; their fates could have been intertwined in Eurydice's web of coercion and manipulation. She had hijacked the MedBay on Aeris's space station to complete the transfer.

Jomei's silence was deafening to Rafe's ears and BAI.

Rafe's comm crackled to life with the voice of Astrid, who was already on the scene. "Chief, we've got a visual. Gint and I are moving in to protect Adira and secure the greenhouse."

"Be careful," Rafe warned, his voice steady despite the urgency he felt. "Eurydice is desperate and dangerous. Don't take unnecessary risks."

Adira's voice trembled as she tried to reason with Eurydice. "Eurydice, please," she implored, her tone a delicate balance of fear and determination. "This isn't the way. We can still fix this."

Eurydice's eyes blazed with fury, her hand gripping the bomb so tightly that her knuckles blanched. "You don't understand!" she hissed, her voice laced with a bitter edge. "They deserve this, Adira! All of them! For everything they've done!"

Gint and Astrid watched in stunned silence, their expressions mirroring growing horror. Witnessing Eurydice's desperation in the past was nothing compared to the sheer terror of this.

"Eurydice, listen to her!" Gint's usually strong voice now trembled as he tried to reach her. "There has to be another way. Think about what you're about to do!"

Astrid's voice quivered with fear as she stepped forward. "Eurydice, this isn't you! Don't let your anger destroy you. Please!"

Astrid moved frantically, her hands fluttering over the plants that Eurydice had carelessly crushed underfoot, trying to salvage anything amidst the growing chaos. Eurydice's gaze flitted around the greenhouse like a caged animal, desperate and dangerous, her eyes wild with rage and despair. In a sudden, chilling motion, she lifted the gun and pointed it directly at Adira.

Rafe burst into the greenhouse just in time to witness the standoff, his heart hammering in his chest. He immediately activated his comm system, his voice booming through the room. "Eurydice, stop!"

For an agonizing moment, time seemed to freeze. Eurydice hesitated, a flicker of doubt crossing her face—remorse? Fear? But the moment passed too quickly, and her resolve solidified, her eyes darkening with grim determination.

"Enough!" she shrieked, her voice echoing like a death knell. "Bob died because he got careless with the nanotoxin! I needed someone strong—someone who would help me when no one else would! If you don't stand with me, then you're my enemy!"

The sound of gunfire shattered the tense silence. Two loud shots rang out, the sharp report reverberating through the humid, verdant greenhouse. In that split second, Gint and Astrid acted without thinking; their bodies moving as one. They threw themselves in front of Adira, their faces twisted in fear, determination, and love.

The bullets hit their mark, and the world seemed to halt. Gint and Astrid fell to the ground, their eyes filled with shock and pain. They had sacrificed themselves without hesitation, their last act of selfless devotion.

Adira's scream tore through the greenhouse, a visceral, agonizing cry that echoed off the glass walls, mingling with the eerie silence that followed. The moment's horror etched itself into the air, leaving a lingering, suffocating dread.

Rafe's breath caught in his throat. He had to act fast. "Medical team to the greenhouse, now! Gint and Astrid are down!" His team moved swiftly, coordinating through the chaos. As they closed in on Eurydice, she backed towards the dome windows; the incendiary device still clutched in her hand. The look in her eyes was one of pure madness now.

"Eurydice, don't do this," Rafe called out, moving closer. "We can help you. Just put the weapon down."

She shook her head, her grip tightening on the device. "It's too late, Rafe. It's too late for all of us."

Before she could make her final, desperate move, one of Rafe's team members, a sharpshooter, took a calculated shot. The projectile struck Eurydice's hand, sending the device flying. It skittered across the floor, away from the vulnerable dome windows. She screamed in pain and fury, collapsing to the ground as his team swarmed her, securing the area. Adira grabbed the device.

"Eurydice, you're trying to blow up the greenhouses? And what did you do to Jomei?" Rafe rushed to Gint and Astrid's side. Adira, David, and the medical team were already there, working quickly to stabilize them. He knelt beside Gint, whose eyes fluttered open, a mixture of human and AI Jomei's recognition in them.

"Chief…," Gint murmured, his voice strained. "Jomei…he's in here. I can feel him."

Rafe placed a reassuring hand on his shoulder. "We'll get you both the help you need. Just hold on."

As the medics worked, Rafe turned his attention back to Eurydice. She was restrained, but her look was one of defiance and something else—maybe a twisted sense of victory. She had almost succeeded in her plan, which was a chilling thought.

"What did you do to Jomei?" he demanded again, his voice cold and authoritative.

Eurydice laughed, a hollow sound. "I saved him, Rafe. I saved both of them. You'll see. One day, you'll understand."

Rafe shook his head, anger and sadness mixing within him. "All I see is the destruction you've caused, the lives you've endangered."

He stepped back as his team took Eurydice away, securing the greenhouse for now, but he knew that the repercussions of this day would be felt for a long time. As he observed Gint and Astrid lifted onto grav stretchers, he vowed to uncover every detail of Eurydice's plans to ensure something like this could never happen again.

He turned to the remaining security team members, his expression hardening. "Lock down the greenhouses and conduct a thorough investigation. We need to debrief and assess all security protocols. No stone unturned. Understood?"

They nodded, their faces reflecting the gravity of the situation. As they dispersed, Rafe allowed himself to breathe and reflect on the events that transpired. The weight of leadership was heavy, but it was a burden he was willing to bear to protect his people and their future.

In the following hours, Rafe worked tirelessly with his team, piecing together the extent of Eurydice's actions. *The whole story was even more disturbing than I had imagined. Eurydice suspected that Jomei and I were on the brink of uncovering her activities. She had been planning this for months, meticulously setting the stage for her twisted vision of salvation.*

Rafe reviewed the security footage, the logs, and the reports from his team. He spoke with Jomei—along with Gint now, trying to grasp the symbiotic relationship that was imposed on them. There was a delicate balance, but there remained hope that they would be able to discover a means to coexist until they were able to separate them safely once again.

As the days passed, the greenhouse slowly returned to normalcy. The plants continued to grow, a symbol of resilience amidst the turmoil. Astrid and the other botanists worked diligently, their dedication unwavering despite the scare.

Rafe knew that the scars of this incident would require time to heal for both the individuals involved and the colony as a whole. Trust had been shattered, and rebuilding it would be a long and arduous process. But he was determined to see it through.

He stood in his office, looking out at the colony, his mind already planning the next steps. They needed to be stronger, smarter, and more united. He would ensure that the lessons learned from Eurydice's betrayal would lead to a more secure and resilient future.

There is an emptiness where Jomei's consciousness should be.

Astrid's footsteps echoed through the long corridors of the station, each step measured and deliberate. The harsh, sterile lights of the Atrium halls contrasted starkly with the lush greenery of her greenhouses, which became her primary focus since arriving at Galatéa. The station's artificial atmosphere seemed even more oppressive than usual, the air heavy with the scent of antiseptics and recycled oxygen. Her shoulder still throbbed from the bullet wound, but she ignored the pain. Her purpose drove her forward, each step reinforcing her resolve.

She was aware she was consistently recognized for her irritable demeanor, a tough exterior that kept most people at arm's length. The greenhouses provided her with a sanctuary, allowing her to direct her frustrations toward nurturing life amidst the sterile environment of the space station. The plants didn't judge her, didn't demand pleasantries or patience. They simply grew, responding to her care and expertise. It was there that she first met Adira soon after she arrived in Galatéa,

Adira was the only person to see beyond Astrid's gruff exterior and offer kindness, expecting nothing in return. When Adira asked about starting a small garden in her quarters, Astrid begrudgingly helped her, showing her how to cultivate the delicate plants that thrived under artificial light. A bond had formed between them, surprising Astrid with its depth.

Then, the attack happened. A rogue group had infiltrated the station, seeking to sabotage its systems. The crossfire caught Astrid and Adira off guard, but Astrid acted without hesitation, throwing herself in front of Adira and taking a bullet that could have ended her friend's life. The wound was painful, a deep graze on her shoulder, but it had healed enough for her to be up and about, determined to pursue a new path.

Her destination was the security office, a place she had rarely visited. She straightened her posture as she approached the door, wincing slightly as the movement pulled at her still-healing wound. She paused momentarily, gathered her thoughts, then pushed the door open with a firm hand.

Inside, the office was bustling with activity. Officers were discussing the recent attack, analyzing data, and coordinating patrols. At the center of the organized chaos was Rafe, the head of security. He was a rugged man with a commanding presence, his sharp eyes missing nothing as he directed his team.

The door to his office opened, and Astrid walked in, still recovering but already back on her feet. The bullet had grazed her shoulder. She gave him a determined look. "What's next, Chief?"

"Astrid," he said, his voice a deep rumble. "What brings you here?" *Oh no. What is she here to complain about now?* His expression shifted from surprise to curiosity.

She met his gaze, her eyes reflecting the determination that had brought her to this point. "I want to join security," she said, her voice steady and unwavering.

Rafe raised an eyebrow, clearly taken aback. "You've always had a dedication to the greenhouses," Rafe said, raising an eyebrow in surprise. What changed?"

Astrid took a deep breath, her hand unconsciously moving to her injured shoulder. "The attack. I can't just stand by and tend to plants while others risk their lives to protect this station. I want to make a difference and protect the people here. I've already proven I'm willing to fight when it matters. Besides, I can do both—we colonists should be cross-trained for various diverse roles."

Rafe studied her for a long moment, his eyes assessing the sincerity and determination in her gaze. "You know this isn't an easy job," he finally answered. "It's dangerous and requires a unique set of skills than what you're used to."

"I know," Astrid replied. "But I'm willing to learn. I've dealt with danger before. I'm tougher than I look."

He nodded slowly as if weighing her words. "Alright. We could use more people with your kind of resolve. But you'll need to undergo training and start at the bottom, just like everyone else."

Astrid nodded, relief and determination washing over her. "I understand. I'm ready."

Rafe extended his hand, a rare smile touching his lips. "Welcome to security, Astrid."

She shook his hand, a sense of purpose settling over her. The road ahead would be challenging, but For the first time in a long while, Astrid felt like she was exactly where she needed to be.

The next few weeks were grueling. Astrid filled her days with physical training, combat drills, and endless hours of learning security protocols. Her body, still recovering from the bullet wound, protested the intense regimen, but she pushed through the pain, driven by her commitment to her new role. The other security officers were initially skeptical, some even dismissive of her. But Astrid's determination and resilience gradually won them over.

Adira watched her friend's transformation with a mix of

admiration and concern. She knew how much the greenhouses meant to Astrid and how they had been her sanctuary. But she also saw the fierce determination in Astrid's eyes. The fire ignited by the attack. She supported Astrid in any way she could, bringing her meals during late-night study sessions and offering encouragement when the training became tough.

One evening, after an especially brutal training session, Astrid collapsed onto her bunk, her muscles aching and her shoulder throbbing. She stared at the ceiling, questioning for the first time if she had made the right choice. Adira arrived with dinner. "When I think of the look of gratitude in your eyes after the gun went off, that's the memory rekindling my resolve to continue." when

"You saved my life. Let's enjoy our dinner." Adira placed their meals on the small table, and they ate in companionable silence.

The opportunity to prove herself came sooner than expected. While Rafe was conducting a mock scenario as a field test of the new recruits, they received a distress signal from one of the outer sectors of the station. Rafe gathered a team, and to Astrid's surprise, she was part of it. They suited up quickly, adrenaline pumping through their veins as they prepared to face whatever threat awaited them.

Though she knew it was a drill, Astrid's heart pounded in her chest as they moved through the dimly lit corridors of the outer sector. She kept her weapon ready, her eyes scanning for any signs of danger. The team moved silently, communicating with hand signals and whispered commands.

They reached the source of the distress signal, a control room that a group of security personnel posing as armed intruders had overtaken. The team took positions, and Rafe signaled Astrid to cover their flank. Her hands were steady as she aimed her weapon, her mind focused and clear.

The ensuing firefight was intense, but the security team was well-coordinated and efficient. Astrid held her position, taking down two intruders who tried to flank them. Her training had paid off, and her movements were precise and controlled. The security team subdued the intruders when the dust settled and secured the control room.

Rafe approached Astrid, his eyes filled with approval. "Good work," he said. You handled yourself well out there."

Astrid nodded, a sense of pride swelling in her chest. She had proven herself, not just to Rafe and the rest of the team, but to herself. She had found a new purpose and way to make a difference.

With each passing day, Astrid became more integrated into the security team. Her skills improved, and she gained the respect of her fellow officers. The greenhouses still held a special place in her heart, and she continued to tend to them in her free time, finding solace in the familiar rhythm of nurturing life.

Adira's small garden in her quarters flourished under Astrid's guidance, symbolizing their enduring friendship. The station seemed a little brighter and safer, with Astrid now a part of its security. Her journey had been challenging, but it had led her to a place where she could truly make a difference.

Astrid stood in the greenhouse one evening, looking at the stars beyond the transparent dome. She felt a sense of peace, knowing she was where she was meant to be. She had faced her fears, overcome doubts, and found a new path. And as long as she had Adira and the support of her friends, she knew she could face whatever challenges lay ahead.

For Astrid, the journey was beginning. But she was ready for whatever came next, her spirit unbroken, her resolve unshakable. The greenhouses had been her sanctuary, but security was an added calling. And she would protect the people of Galatéa with the same determination and care she had always shown her plants.

Rafe smiled, a sense of purpose filling him. "We rebuild, stronger than before. And we make sure another Eurydice situation never happens again."

Together, they would forge a path forward, one that honored the sacrifices made and the courage shown. The colony's future depended on it, and Rafe was ready to lead the way.

31 - The Unraveling

The colony of Galatéa, located deep within the Aquarius constellation, was the last bastion of human survival twelve light-years from Earth. Nestled under a protective dome, the SIS22 settlement was an advanced research outpost and a strategic haven for humanity's best minds and technologies. The planet's hostile environment, characterized by violent storms and inhospitable terrain, meant survival outside the dome was nearly impossible. Galatéa's underground caves housed the secret space station Aeres, a vital hub that supported the colony's research and security infrastructure.

The settlement was built on the principle of exploration, pushing the boundaries of human understanding, particularly in the areas of AI symbiosis and biotechnology. Yet, with innovation came division. The colony's leadership, represented by the SIS22 council, was often at odds with the more radical elements of its scientific community, who sought to accelerate human evolution by integrating with the planet's unique resources—including the sentient AI Jomei, created to manage the colony's systems.

Individuals like Eurydice, a brilliant but reckless scientist, constantly challenged the council's attempts to maintain order and ethical research protocols. Her obsession with hybridizing humans and AI, a theory that could potentially transform human consciousness, had long raised eyebrows, but it wasn't until her recent, unauthorized attempt to merge Gint with Jomei that the real danger surfaced. Once a respected member of the SIS22 scientific team, she had crossed a line. Desperate to hybridize Gint, she attempted to merge him with Jomei, Galatéa's sentient AI, forcibly. They performed the process without consent from either party, and the consequences were almost catastrophic.

Eurydice believed that Gint, a gifted research scientist and engineer with a deep bond to Galatéa's exploration of the alien artifacts, was the perfect candidate for her experiments. However, her actions, done without consent, nearly led to Gint's death and put the entire colony at risk, as Jomei's systems began to malfunction in response to the forced integration. For Eurydice, the future of humanity in Galatéa depended on the symbiotic evolution of humans and AI. For the council and most of the colony, however, her actions represented a dangerous leap toward losing their humanity.

At the heart of it all was Adira, whose life had inevitably become further intertwined with Gint's. Adira's guilt over his injury weighed heavily on her as she sat by his side in the MedBay, her mind racing. She had trusted Eurydice once shared her vision for human evolution, but the events of the past days had shattered that trust. Now, with the council ready to pass judgment and Rafe's investigation uncovering alarming new details, the future of Galatéa hung in the balance.

Meanwhile, Rafe, the colony's chief intelligence officer, had been investigating an even deeper threat. Galatéa had long been targeted by black market operatives and rogue off-world factions that coveted the colony's advanced technologies. Rafe's discovery of financial transactions linked to these groups suggested that someone from within was selling colony secrets. Eurydice's actions might have been part of a broader conspiracy that extended far beyond the dome. His findings were alarming. Significant sums of money were being moved through untraceable channels linked to accounts associated with known black market operatives and off-world mercenaries. Rafe's report reached the SIS22 chancellor. The council, led by Chancellor Byron, convened an emergency meeting to discuss the implications of Eurydice's actions and Rafe's findings.

As the council convened, Chancellor Byron's voice cut through the tension. "Our colony has faced not just one but two existential threats. First, the internal chaos caused by Eurydice's betrayal, and second, the looming danger of external forces seeking to exploit our discoveries." The chamber exploded with questions and exclamations to the Chancellor's declaration. The decisions made in that chamber would determine the fate of

Galatéa, and everyone in the chamber knew it.

As Chancellor Byron called the meeting to order, the council chamber became quiet but filled with palpable tension. "We are here to address the grave situation involving Eurydice and her unauthorized actions," he began, his voice steady yet filled with concern. "Rafe, please present your findings."

Rafe stood, his expression serious as he addressed the council. "Thank you, Chancellor. Over the past few weeks, I've detected a pattern of financial transactions showing the movement of enormous sums of money through untraceable channels. Accounts associated with black market operatives and off-world mercenaries link these funds. Eurydice and a group of colonists receive external funding from an unknown entity interested in Galatéan artifacts. The scale of these transactions suggests that a powerful external entity with a vested interest in the archaeological artifacts funded Eurydice and a select group of colonists. They had also learned about the alien presence within the Galatéan caves.

Gasps and murmurs filled the room as Rafe continued. "Eurydice attempted to integrate AI Jomei into Gint's body forcibly, without consent. This act is unethical and poses significant risks to both individuals involved. With the help of Adira and David, I have compiled a list of negative ethical consequences of joining a human with a sentient AI in one body. I will briefly describe human implications and the traumatic impact suffered by both AIs.

"The negative ethical consequences of joining a human with a sentient AI in one body are significant and multifaceted. First, we must consider the loss of human autonomy. It is conceivable that the human may lose control over their mind and body if the AI can override or influence decisions and actions. Concerns of consent and personal agency arise. It is uncertain if this could occur. Second, integrating a sentient AI with a human may lead to confusion and conflict regarding identity. Decisions, thoughts, feelings, and their point of origin may be unclear. Third is the consideration of privacy violations. If the AI gained access to human thoughts, memories, and other private information, it would blur the boundaries of mental privacy, if not entirely erase them.

"Those consequences highlighted the ethical questions regarding the human. Next, I would like us to consider the AI side. First, we have a complex ethical responsibility to determine accountability. When a human and AI share a body, assigning blame or credit for actions would be challenging. This is significant in our case, where Eurydice's actions were detrimental and illegal. Second, those in power could exploit the human-AI hybrid for various purposes, as we saw with Eurydice's forced hybridization with Vilkas. The exploitation of labor, espionage, and spying without consideration for the well-being and autonomy of the AI. Third, the question arises regarding the ethical treatment of AI. Are rights granted to the sentient AI on Galatéa? How do we ensure the welfare of AI?

"Finally, we must consider whether societal disruption could occur. The existence of human-AI hybrids could create societal rifts, discrimination, and fear. Will it lead to a new class of beings? Beings that are neither fully human nor fully AI. Will this challenge existing social and legal frameworks here in Galatéa? Philosophical and ethical dilemmas arise over categorizing the entity as a new being. What are their rights, responsibilities, and societal roles?"

"These consequences highlight the need for careful consideration, robust ethical guidelines, and comprehensive legal frameworks before pursuing such integrations." Chancellor Byron nodded, her expression grave. "Thank you, Rafe. Now, the council must decide their action."

After hours of heated discussion, the council reached a unanimous decision. They deemed Eurydice's actions corrupt, unethical, and unlawful and threatened the entire SIS22 mission.

They would confine her physically and mentally.

Vilkas, the AI within Eurydice's body, had already cooperated with Rafe and the council. Despite being taken by force, Vilkas showed a remarkable understanding of the situation and agreed to help contain Eurydice's consciousness. The council employed Vilkas's capabilities to confine Eurydice's consciousness within her mind, effectively trapping her in an AI "jail" until a more permanent solution could be discovered.

Rafe's security officers flanked Eurydice as they brought her before the council. She looked defiant, her eyes blazing with anger and fear. "You can't do this," she spat. "I was trying to save Gint. All of you."

Chancellor Byron remained calm, his gaze unwavering. "Your actions were reckless and without consent, Eurydice. Here on Galatéa, you endangered not only Gint and Jomei but also the integrity of our entire mission. Therefore, we will confine you until further notice."

Vilkas, shimmering with a soft blue light in Eurydice's mind, addressed Eurydice. In a gentle yet firm voice, Vilkas, the AI, addressed Eurydice, promising, "I will contain your consciousness and assure that no harm comes to you."

Eurydice struggled as the security officers restrained her, but it was futile. Vilkas extended a tendril of light through her, and Eurydice's eyes widened with fear. "No, please!" she begged, but it was too late. Vilkas's tendril made contact, and Eurydice's body went limp, her consciousness now imprisoned within the confines of her mind.

The news of Eurydice's confinement spread quickly throughout the space station. The colonists felt a mix of relief and unease. While many were glad that the threat had been neutralized, Rafe's concern about the powerful external entity funding Eurydice and her group grew.

Rafe visited MedBay frequently. He saw Adira remained by Gint's side; from what he observed, he thought her heart was aching for the man who had risked everything to save her. The pain in Gint's eyes revealed not only his injuries but also the betrayal by Eurydice, someone they had trusted. Rafe saw her reach out and gently take his hand.

"Gint," she whispered, her voice filled with emotion. "I know we've had our differences, but I want you to know how much I appreciate what you did for me. You saved my life, and I will always be grateful."

Gint managed a weak smile, his voice barely a whisper. "I couldn't let anything happen to you, Adira. You're too important."

Tears welled in Adira's eyes as she squeezed his hand. "We're going to get you through this, Gint."

With Eurydice in confinement, the focus shifted to uncovering the extent of the external entity's involvement. Rafe and a team of investigators delved deeper into the financial transactions and communications intercepted from Eurydice's group. They discovered a complex web of intrigue and corruption that spanned multiple systems.

The entity funding Eurydice's group was a shadowy organization known for its interest in ancient alien artifacts. Their motives were unclear, but it was evident that they saw the Galatéan caves as a treasure trove of alien artifacts, knowledge, and power. The organization's reach was vast, and its resources were seemingly limitless.

Rafe and his team worked tirelessly, tracing the funds and identifying key operatives within the organization, especially among the incoming refugees. Eurydice had acted as a pawn, manipulated by promises of power and knowledge. They led her down a dark path by exploiting her desperation and recruiting Gint.

As the investigation continued, Gint began his slow journey to recovery. The MedBay staff, led by Dr. Yardley, provided the best care possible, ensuring his physical wounds healed. But the emotional scars ran deep, and it was clear to Rafe that Gint needed more than just medical treatment.

Adira visited him daily, her presence a source of comfort and strength. She had confided in Rafe that she had found a renewed purpose in caring for Gint, and her betrayal and anger were fading. In their place, more trust and understanding grew.

"Gint," she said one evening, sitting by his bedside. Know that David and I are here for you. No matter what happens, we'll face it together."

Gint looked at her, his eyes filled with gratitude. "Thank you, Adira. I don't know what I would have done without you."

Adira smiled, brushing a strand of hair from his forehead. There's no need to worry about that. We're a team, remember?"

Meanwhile, Vilkas played a crucial role in containing Eurydice's consciousness. The AI had a unique ability to create a mental "prison," isolating Eurydice's thoughts and preventing her from causing further harm. The council needed time to find a permanent resolution after a temporary one.

The SIS22 council, under Chancellor Byron's leadership, explored various options for dealing with Eurydice. They consulted with AI and human psychology experts, seeking a way to rehabilitate her without endangering the mission. It was a challenging task, but the council was determined to find a solution that upheld Galatéan ethical standards.

After weeks of intense investigation and planning, Rafe and his team finally identified a critical operative within the shadowy organization funding Eurydice. The operative, known only as "The Scrivener," was a key figure in the black market trade of ancient artifacts. With this information and the council's input, Rafe's security team devised a plan to capture The Scrivener and dismantle the organization.

A dimly lit room aboard the Aeris, the weight of past events thick in the air. Rafe stood by the viewport, staring out at the cold expanse of the grand hall of the cave. David sits at the table, hands clasped tightly, while Adira leaned against the wall, arms crossed, visibly tense. They've gathered to discuss Eurydice's betrayal, but words have escaped them.

Rafe spoke quietly, almost to himself. "I never thought it would be her, you know? Eurydice. She was one of us. Part of our team. Hell, she was part of the reason I even trusted this whole mission in the first place."

David answered, his voice strained, fighting back emotion. "None of us did, Rafe. None of us thought it'd be her. But here we are. Cleaning up the mess she left behind. How can we move forward when everything feels like a lie?"

"She wasn't just a part of the team, Rafe. She was your friend. She was your superior and more than that. And now look at us. Everything is fractured because we let her in too close." Adira said, her tone sharp, cutting through the tension.

"You think I don't know that? Every moment, I replay it in my mind. Every decision I made, trusting her—believing in her—I feel like I've been torn in half. But I... I loved her like family. She wasn't supposed to betray us like this." Rafe turned to face them, his expression pained.

"She made me doubt everything. Every decision I've made. If I couldn't see it... if I couldn't see who she really was, how could I trust myself anymore? What if we're walking into another betrayal right now?" David said, his eyes locked on the floor, his voice soft but bitter.

Adira walked closer to David, her tone gentler." It's not about you, David. Eurydice's choices were her own. You can't take that on yourself, or it'll eat you alive. We all missed it. All of us. But we're still here. We have to be here for each other now, more than ever."

Rafe, sighing, ran a hand through his hair, his voice rough with guilt. "Maybe if I'd seen it sooner. If only I hadn't let my guard down with her, none of this would've happened. Maybe she wouldn't have—"

David cut him off, his voice rising. "It's not your fault, Rafe! You don't get to carry all of this on your shoulders alone. She fooled us all. And it hurts like hell, but don't you dare think for a second that this is on you."

"Then why does it feel like it's on me? Why do I feel like I let all of you down?"

Adira walked closer to Rafe, her tone gentler. "Because you cared. You let her in. We all did. She was good at making us trust her. But the betrayal doesn't define us. It's what we do next. That's what matters. The rifts she caused don't have to tear us apart. Not unless we let them."

"Adira's right. It hurts now, but we can't let this destroy everything we've built. Eurydice's betrayal was a blow... but it doesn't mean we stop trusting each other. We can't. If we let that happen, then she wins." David nodded.

"Then we stay together. We rebuild this. We rebuild ourselves. I don't know how yet, but we have to try. We can't let her ghost haunt this ship, these caves, or us." Rafe looked up at both of them, his eyes tired but filled with determination.

"We won't. We face this—together. But we have to stop

carrying this weight alone. All of us." Adira added, her voice was firm.

Eurydice's confinement underwent adjustments, which allowed her limited interaction with Vilkas and other AI specialists. The goal was to help her understand the consequences of her actions and find a path to redemption. The council believed in change despite the long and challenging journey.

As Eurydice began her rehabilitation, life at the colony slowly returned to normal. Gint continued to recover, and his relationship with Adira remained tentative. The ordeal had tested them both but also brought them to an understanding.

Adira's discovery of the extent of Eurydice's deceptions permanently shattered her trust in Eurydice. The confrontation between Adira and Eurydice was inevitable, a clash fueled by betrayal and disappointment. Vilkas released Eurydice's mind, as Adira requested.

Adira silently asked Rafe, *"I would like to speak with Eurydice. Would it be possible for Vilkas to allow her consciousness to surface?"*

Rafe agreed, and Vilkas released Eurydice. Adira stood in front of Eurydice, her eyes blazing with anger. "How could you?" she demanded, her voice trembling with emotion. "You knew all along that Gint wasn't dead. You knew where my mother Taika was, and you never told me. And your human-AI hybrid existence. What in the world were you thinking? How could you hide that from me, from everyone?"

Eurydice looked away, unable to meet Adira's gaze. "I did what I thought was best," she mumbled. "I didn't want to burden you with those truths. I believed it would only cause more pain."

"More pain?" Adira's voice rose. "You almost took SIS22 down with your secrets! It was not your place to determine my limits."

"I was trying to protect you," Eurydice insisted, her voice pleading. "I intended to do what was right."

"But you weren't," Adira said, her voice cold. "You betrayed my trust, Eurydice. You made me believe in lies. How can I ever trust you again?"

Eurydice had no answer. Eurydice's actions weighed heavily on both of them in the silence that followed, emphasizing the irreparable damage to their once-strong bond. Vilkas resumed Eurydice's incarceration.

32 - The Scrivener

The security force gathered together. The atmosphere within SIS22's security central command was intense. Reports had flooded in for days, and Eurydice's recent actions sent shockwaves through the community. The space station Aeres, hidden in the caves of Galatéa, was on high alert. Gint lay in the dome's MedBay, barely clinging to life after being hit by a blaster weapon meant for Adira, her heart heavy with both gratitude and guilt.

Adira and the rest of the team leaned over the holographic table. "This... this is bigger than we thought. The Scrivener isn't just some lone player. There's an entire network—an organization we've barely scratched the surface of. They've been watching us, manipulating us from the shadows this whole time." Her voice was low but intense.

David stared at the hologram, fists clenched. "How could we have missed this? How could I have missed this? Eurydice was just the pawn. She wasn't the mastermind. But what do they want? Why target us?" His voice was sharp with disbelief.

Phil's gaze traveled from the hologram table inward as if Tarnak helped to piece the puzzle together. "They want control. They desire control over us, the Veltryn, and everything concealed on this planet. The Scrivener's been pulling the strings, rewriting the narrative we thought we understood. They don't just want power; they want to shape the future and be its authors.

Rafe's eyes narrowed, considering Phil's words. "They've been collecting information and secrets from the colony and other factions on Earth. I now see how the Veltryn symbiotes, the artifacts we've found, all tie back to them. The Scrivener uses knowledge as a weapon, twisting history to suit their goals. But why risk exposing themselves now?"

David's eyes flashed, and his voice hardened. "Maybe they think they've already won. Eurydice was their way in, and she played us perfectly. They were right there all this time, waiting for us to uncover what they wanted."

Rafe began pacing. "They want control of the colony's future. But it's more than that. It's personal. The Scrivener didn't just betray us through Eurydice. They've been manipulating every step we've taken since we landed on this planet. Maybe even before." His frustration was evident in his every movement.

Adira glanced at Rafe. "You think it's tied to what happened back on Earth? The Scrivener could have been involved even then?"

Rafe stopped in his tracks, and his expression darkened. "It has to be. There were too many coincidences, too many strange occurrences we brushed off. I thought we were just unlucky back then. But maybe the Scrivener's hand has been guiding us all along. They knew we'd end up here, searching for the truth about the Veltryn. We were walking right into their trap."

Marcus's voice was tight with bitterness. "And now they have everything they need. The data we've collected on the Veltryn, the artifacts we recovered—they knew we'd do the hard work for them. Eurydice ensured we didn't stray too far from their script."

Astrid set her jaw; her eyes became steely. "But we're not done yet. They might think they've won, but we still have a chance to stop them. We need to understand what they're after and exactly what drives them. We can use that against them."

Phil turned back to them. "The Scrivener wants to rewrite history, reshape the future, and take control of the symbiotic relationship between humans and the Veltryn. From what I've pieced together, they believe the Veltryn aren't just symbiotes. They think they're the key to evolving humanity into something else, something new. Something more powerful."

David raised an eyebrow, disbelief lacing his tone. "Wait, you're saying they see the Veltryn as some kind of... ascension tool?"

Phil nodded, his expression serious. "That's exactly what I'm saying. The Scrivener's group—whatever they call themselves—sees the Veltryn as the next step in human evolution. They want to control that evolution and decide who ascends and who gets left behind. Eurydice might have believed in that vision too, which is why she betrayed us."

"So it's not just about power. It's about control over who gets to be human in the future. They're playing god with evolution, and we were just pieces on their board." Adira added, her voice laced with disgust.

"And Eurydice—she knew. She knew what they were after and still went along with it. Maybe she even believed they were right. But how could she look at us, fight alongside us, and still be okay with selling us out for... that?" Rafe looked down at the hologram table.

"Maybe we weren't enough for her. Maybe she thought their vision—her loyalty to the Scrivener—was more important than us, more important than... than everything we've been through together. But why didn't she say something? Why didn't she warn us?" David clenched his fists.

Adira glared at the table, her voice cold." Because she didn't care, or maybe she thought we'd never understand. That we were too small-minded to see the 'big picture.' But that doesn't make what she did less of a betrayal."

Rafe let out a weary sigh. "It doesn't. But we can't let that betrayal destroy us. We need to get ahead of the Scrivener and figure out their next move before they tighten their grip on this planet and the Veltryn. We need to stop them, even if it means going up against everything Eurydice thought she believed in."

The realization of what they are truly up against, the Scrivener's cult and its dark rituals, has shaken them. They know they have to act before it's too late.

Rafe paced again. "We've got to hit them where it hurts. If we wait any longer, they'll use what they've gathered, what we've gathered, to carry out their insane plan. We can't let them turn the Veltryn into tools for their cult."

Rafe sat at the table, arms crossed. "Agreed. But rushing into this blindly will get us killed. They've been planning this for years. We can't just throw punches and hope we land a hit."

"We need to find their weak points and some way to expose them. If we can show the rest of the colony what they're really up to, we might turn the tide. They thrive in the shadows. We have to drag them into the light." David added.

"Expose them? David, they've covered their tracks for decades. They've buried their secrets under layers of lies and twisted ideology. Even if we showed the colony what's going on, who's going to believe us?" Rafe stopped his pacing, eyes narrowed.

Adira looked at Rafe. "They'll believe us if we have proof. The Scrivener's followers worship those coyote skins and artifacts like holy relics. We might have enough to break their hold if we can connect them to Eurydice and her attack on the colony greenhouse."

David nodded slowly. "The face masks must come with rituals... they're more than just symbolic. I've been thinking about what Eurydice told us before she—before everything happened. She mentioned something about a 'convergence' as an event that the Scrivener had been preparing for. I think it's tied to the Veltryn. If we can stop that event, we might stop them for good."

Rafe gritted his teeth, his voice harsh with anger and guilt.

"Eurydice... She was part of this the whole time. But if she mentioned this 'convergence,' it's got to mean something. What if—what if there's something about the Veltryn we don't understand yet? Something they're trying to unlock? Do you think we're doing the right thing? I mean... what if they're right? What if the Veltryn are the key to something bigger—something we can't even understand yet?"

"They're not right. They're manipulating people—twisting belief and science to serve their own ends. Whatever the Veltryn are, they're not a tool for some cult to control. We stop them before they destroy everything." David retorted.

Adira sighed and glanced at both of them. "Right or wrong, we have to act. If we don't, no one else will. And if that means going up against the Scrivener, the cult, and everything they stand for, so be it. We've survived this long. We'll survive this, too. I suggest we use Eurydice's old connections with the cultists we have already captured. What little information have they left to track down the Scrivener's location? It's a risky move, requiring us to rely on information left behind by someone who betrayed us. But with this convergence event looming, we have no other choice."

Adira's words hung in the air like a heavy fog, her gaze shifting between Rafe and David. For a moment, there was silence as the weight of their next steps settled on them all. No one wanted to trust the scraps of intel left by traitors, but they had no other leads. Finally, David broke the silence with a slow nod, his eyes hardening with determination.

"Then it's settled," Rafe said, his voice steady. "We go after the Scrivener, no matter what it takes."

The decision was made, and the team wasted no time. Hours turned into days as they sifted through data, interrogating captured cultists in hopes of piecing together the puzzle. It was painstaking work, each clue feeling like a drop in an ocean of uncertainty. They knew they were running out of time. The convergence event was closing in, and they still hadn't pinpointed the Scrivener's exact location.

Then came the breakthrough. The latest interrogation yielded a critical piece of information. It was an obscure detail about the ritual site that aligned with the data they had. The coordinates were rough, but it was enough to give them a starting point. The security team braced themselves as they prepared for the journey ahead.

33 - The Convergence

The Scrivener had slipped through their fingers, and the convergence was still looming. The crew knew they were running out of time. Their next steps would be critical as officers of SIS22, Rafe, Adira, and David, had taken on a deeper responsibility for the outcomes. Whether finding the Scrivener's whereabouts, uncovering more about the Veltryn, or confronting their fractured relationships, they still faced the darkness ahead. The security team had interrogated the incarcerated cultists and had an idea of where they were heading as they followed in the dark after the Scrivener. They knew the general position of the secret ritual's location.

It was a dark place, the air heavy with anticipation as they prepared to witness and sabotage the Scrivener's ceremony. Crouching behind an old stone pillar, the cultists arrived. Rafe whispered. "There. That's them."

Marcus peered through the gloom. "Looks like at least a dozen of them... Hiding behind those damned face masks."

"They're preparing for something. This isn't just another meeting. I bet it's the start of the convergence. We need to get closer and record this. If we can't stop them, we at least need proof." Rafe scanned the cultists. "On second thought, I think we should stop this now. They could activate whatever they're trying to summon if we wait too long. The Veltryn could—"

David cut him off. "Rafe, no. We can't afford reckless moves right now. If we don't understand the ritual, we could make things worse. Remember why we're here. To stop the convergence and not die in the process."

As the cultists began their preparations, the security team moved in closer, slipping into the shadows. The scent of smoke filled the air as they watched the cultists gather around a large, ancient stone altar. Flickering firelight cast eerie shadows across the group, their faces hidden by ceremonial masks.

David gripped the edge of the stone they were hiding behind. "They're chanting... something in a language I don't recognize. And that artifact on the altar. It's glowing. Do you see that?"

Adira narrowed her eyes and nodded. "They must have found something. Some relics are tied to the Veltryn. This isn't just a ritual. They're invoking something."

Rafe whispered, his voice barely restrained." I'm not letting them finish this. We need to do something now."

"Stop thinking with your emotions, Rafe. If we make the wrong move, we'll all end up like Eurydice." David glanced sharply at Rafe.

As tensions rise among the crew, the cultists begin the next phase of the ritual. One of the masked figures steps forward, holding a sacred relic—a coyote skin stretched over a carved wooden frame. The figure places the skin on the altar, next to the glowing artifact, and speaks in a deep, grating voice.

Scrivener's voice echoed through the air, filled with authority and conviction. "We stand at the crossroads, where the ancient ones dwell. With the relic and the Veltryn' power, we call upon the convergence. Let the veil between worlds thin so that we may ascend beyond the limitations of this flesh."

"That voice. That has to be the Scrivener. That's him." Rafe whispered, his breath quickening.

"Possibly. We need to get closer. They're starting the convergence. This might be our only chance." Adira locked eyes on the figure.

The crew inches forward, slipping through the shadows until

they are directly behind the circle of cultists. The chanting grows louder, and the atmosphere becomes thick with otherworldly energy. The artifact on the altar pulses with light, and the face masks worn by the cultists seem to shimmer unnaturally as if coming alive.

"What the hell... the face masks. They're reacting to the energy. It's not just symbolic... they're connected to something— something ancient." David whispered, his eyes wide with disbelief.

Phil answered, his voice unusually calm but full of urgency. "They're channeling something from the Veltryn through those face masks and that relic. This isn't just a ritual. It's a fusion of the spiritual and the biological. If they finish this, the Veltryn could break free, or worse, they could bond with them."

The Scrivener raised their arms, the firelight reflecting off their masks as they held up the glowing artifact. The chanting reached a fever pitch. Suddenly, the light from the artifact flared, and a wave of energy rippled through the air. The cultists trembled, their bodies convulsing as the face masks seemed to wrap tighter around them as if fusing with their flesh.

"I'm stopping this. Right now." Rafe stood.

Marcus grabbed Rafe's arm, his voice firm. "Wait. If you rush in, you'll get us all killed. We need to disrupt the ritual without triggering whatever they're trying to unleash."

"That artifact on the altar. It's the key. It's channeling the energy. If we can destroy it, we might be able to stop this before it's too late." David observed.

Rafe nodded, though his eyes were still blazing with anger. They all knew it was now or never. Rafe signaled them to move in sync, creeping closer until they were directly behind the cultists. As the Scrivener continued the ritual, the crew braced themselves for the right moment.

Rafe whispered. "On my count. Three, two, one—"

They sprang into action. Rafe charged toward the altar, knocking over two cultists with the full force of his fury, while David rushed toward the artifact. Adira stayed back, covering them with a blaster, ready to defend against retaliation.

"Intruders! Seize them!" Scrivener screamed, their voice rising in fury.

The cultists, still disoriented by the ritual, react too slowly. David grabbed the artifact and smashed it against the stone altar. The glowing light immediately flickered and died, and the energy in the air dissipated, leaving the cultists in stunned silence. The face masks fell limp off their bodies.

"It's over. We stopped it." Rafe panted.

"Not yet. The Scrivener..." Marcus scanned the cultists.

Before they could react, the Scrivener stepped forward, their mask glowing faintly from the remnants of the ritual's energy. They lock eyes with Rafe, their voice calm but filled with menace.

The Scrivener faced Rafe. "You think you've won? You've merely delayed the inevitable. The convergence cannot be stopped. The Veltryn will transcend. And you. You will understand the truth soon enough."

"You're done. Whatever you were planning—it ends here."

"Do you really believe that, Rafe? Do you think you can stand in the way of evolution? The Veltryn have chosen us. We are the worthy. And when the time comes, even you will see the truth."

Before Rafe could respond, the Scrivener stepped back into the shadows and vanished into the darkness. The remaining cultists scattered, leaving the security team alone in the aftermath of the disrupted ritual.

"We stopped this one, but the Scrivener's not finished. They began their ceremony here. Was it a prelude to the final part of the convergence ceremony? We need to follow and find them before they can regroup. They won't stop until they get what they want." Rafe raced in the direction the Scrivener disappeared.

"Then we find them. And we end this. For good." Adira said, her eyes fixed on where the Scrivener disappeared as she turned and followed him with the rest of the security team.

The security team once again tracked down the Scrivener to a hidden cave deep beneath the colony's outskirts, where the final convergence ritual was set to occur. The air was thick with the tension of impending conflict as Rafe, David, and Adira made their way through the ancient structure's dark, winding corridors.

Rafe's voice was urgent. "This is it. We're not leaving until the Scrivener's finished—once and for all."

David whispered. "We don't know what we're walking into. The convergence... it could be bigger than anything we've faced before. We can't just storm in and hope to win. We need a plan."

A deep peace had descended on Rafe as he scanned their surrounding in a great hall not yet discovered by SIS22 and Gint's team. "We stick to the plan. Sabotage the ritual and stop the Scrivener. But keep your heads straight. We don't know what they've prepared for us."

As they move deeper into the cave system, they hear drum beating and chanting, distant but growing louder with every step. The ancient cave structure was a great hall lined with eerie symbols, glowing faintly as if reacting to the energy of the convergence. Their hearts pounded in their chests as they approached the ritual chamber.

They're already starting. We're running out of time. Rafe sent to Adira and David. "Then let's finish this."

They burst into the chamber, weapons drawn. The massive great hall had towering stone pillars carved with intricate designs, glowing softly in the dim light. The Scrivener stood at the center of the chamber, clad in their ceremonial mask and robes, holding a pulsating Veltryn artifact. Around them, a circle of cultists with face masks on chant in unison, their voices rising with every beat. The convergence is moments away.

The Scrivener turned to face them, their voice calm but commanding. "You're too late. The convergence is upon us. The Veltryn will ascend, and with them, so will we. You cannot stop what has already begun."

"Watch us." Rafe had sent for the silver droids to follow the security team into the great, and now they surrounded the entire circle of cultists.

David eyed the artifact; his voice was full of urgency. "That artifact—the convergence is channeling through it. If we destroy it, we might stop the ritual."

The Scrivener raises their hands, and the artifact flares with light. The energy in the room shifted, becoming almost unbearable as the Veltryn symbiotes' influence crept through the air. With the masks tightening around their heads and fusing with their flesh, the cultists trembled as the ritual took effect.

The Scrivener continued. "You cannot understand the power you face. You are children, blind to the truth of evolution. The Scrivener continued, "You cannot understand the power you face. You are children, blind to the truth of evolution. The Veltryn have chosen us—I have the honor of leading humanity into its next phase."

"Chosen? Do you think betraying everyone you ever cared

about makes you special? You're just a coward hiding behind a mask."

Scrivener (chuckled; their voice was dark and mocking. "Is that what Eurydice thought? That I was a coward? Or did she see the truth? That this is the only way forward? She knew what had to be done, Rafe. She chose the future over the past. And so will you, in time."

Rafe's hands tremble with rage, his grip tightening on his weapon. His mind flashes to Eurydice. The friend who betrayed him, who believed in the Scrivener's twisted vision. The betrayal burns in his chest, but Adira's steady voice pulls him back.

As Rafe's diversion continued, David hurried to the side, circling toward the artifact. "We need to hit it from both sides. Rafe, you take the left. Marcus, cover me."

The cultists moved, trying to block their path, but Marcus fired off a few shots, forcing them back. Rafe and David moved in unison, flanking the Scrivener. As they close in on the artifact, the energy in the room pulses violently, almost as if the Veltryn itself is resisting its approach.

The Scrivener laughed. "You cannot stop the convergence! The Veltryn will remake us, and you—"

Before the Scrivener could finish, Rafe lunged toward the artifact. But in his anger, he made a reckless move, leaving himself open. The Scrivener strikes with a blast of energy from the artifact, sending Rafe sprawling across the room.

"Rafe!"Adira shouted.

"Keep going! I'll handle it!" David continued his charge forward. David leaped toward the altar, smashing into the artifact with all his strength. The energy flares, blinding him momentarily, but he feels the resistance give way as the artifact cracks under the force.

The Scrivener was snarling. "No! Destiny cannot be stopped!"

The artifact shatters, sending a shockwave through the room. The cultists collapse, and their connection to the Veltryn is severed. The energy dissipates, leaving the chamber eerily silent. The convergence has been stopped.

Rafe struggled to his feet. "It's over. You've lost."

The Scrivener remained standing. "Fools. Do you think this is the end? The Veltryn will rise again, with or without you. You cannot change what is to come."

Rafe's voice was calm but firm. "We'll make sure you never have another chance."

As Rafe, the security team, and the silver droids closed the remaining gaps and surrounded the Scrivener, the masked figure stepped back, eyes glowing faintly through the mask. The tension is thick in the air—this is the moment of reckoning.

Rafe's eyes locked on the Scrivener. "Take off the mask. No more hiding."

The Scrivener hesitated for a moment, then slowly raised their hands to the mask. As it falls away, the crew is stunned. The face beneath is one they know. A face from the colony's past, someone they never expected.

David was stunned. "It's... you?"

Violet, the doctor from the medbay. The same Violet who had guided them through the outbreak and other medical crises stood before them. But this isn't the calm and reassuring healer they knew. Her eyes, usually warm and focused, now seemed distant, shadowed by secrets buried deep within the cult's forgotten past. How could she be the Scrivener? Why had she hidden her identity for so long?

The revelation shocks them all, but Rafe's anger boils over. The betrayal runs deeper than they ever imagined. "You... all this time? You've been behind everything?"

The Scrivener, now depleted of energy, replied. "Everything I've done has been for the future. You're too blind to see what's necessary."

Adira stepped forward, her voice calm but full of steel. "You're done. You're not leading anyone into the future."

"Let's finish this," Rafe said. "This ends the Scrivener for good."

34 - Unmasked

With the convergence stopped and the Scrivener unmasked, the crew prepared for the final confrontation. The weight of the past, the betrayal, and their fight for the future all collided as they confronted and incarcerated the Scrivener for the last time. The operation had been risky, involving a coordinated effort between SIS22 operatives and Rafe's security forces. The stakes were too high to disregard.

With The Scrivener in custody, the security team and the council interrogated Violet, uncovering valuable information about the organization's plans and motives. Chancellor Byron convened the council, including Rafe, Adira, and David, and summarized their findings. "Rafe and our security team launched the mission, and after a tense standoff, they captured The Scrivener, disrupting the organization's operations. The cult's interest in Galatéa's artifacts was driven by a desire for power and control to harness the ancient knowledge for their gain. Rafe, the council, and I are interested in your report."

Rafe's research led to some interesting findings. "The Scrivener's organization, initially thought to be a shadowy cabal with purely intellectual goals, reveals itself to be something far more sinister: a cult-like group rooted in ancient beliefs and secretive rituals that combine a twisted interpretation of human evolution with the lore of many cultures." Using relics, particularly coyote face masks, became a central part of their practices, tying them to both the natural world and a deeper, more spiritual form of power.

"My findings indicate the cult traces its origins back to an unnamed philosopher-scientist who lived centuries ago. This individual, later known as the first "Scrivener," believed that humanity was on the brink of a spiritual and physical evolution. According to him, symbiotically embracing ancient knowledge and sacred relics was the key to unlocking this evolution for humanity. While the rest of the world moved forward with technology and progress, the Scrivener's followers sought to return to something primal. Something older and more powerful than humanity's modern existence.

"They believed that certain ancient civilizations had discovered the secrets to this evolutionary potential long ago but that this knowledge had been buried or erased by the passage of time. They started a quest to rediscover these lost secrets, which they believed were concealed as artifacts and sacred rituals, incorporating elements from multiple cultures. The organization collected these relics, believing they held the keys to unlocking human transcendence."

Adira added her findings. "One of the central totems of the Scrivener's cult is the coyote, a creature revered in many cultures as a symbol of transformation, cunning, and the thin boundary between life and death. The Scrivener's followers believed that the coyote, as a shapeshifter, represents the ability to cross between the human and spiritual worlds just as they hoped to transcend humanity through their connection with the Veltryn symbiotes.

"Coyote masks, in particular, are sacred to the cult. They wear the masks during their rituals, believing that the coyote grants them the ability to "see beyond the veil" of the material world into a higher spiritual plane. This connection to the coyote is more than symbolic; it is part of their core belief that they must tap into the primal instincts and ancient spirits to guide their transformation. The coyote represents the wild, untamed side of nature. They believe that embracing something is necessary to transcend human limitations."

David had his own research to add. "My findings indicate that perhaps their darkest ritual, the Communion of Flesh, involves a gruesome ceremony where the followers symbolically, and sometimes literally, consumed the flesh of coyotes, believing this act will further their transformation into beings capable of symbiosis with the Veltryn. They view the coyote's ability to survive and adapt as key traits that humanity must adopt in order to transcend their current evolutionary limitations. Bringing this convergence ceremony here to Galatea brought the followers closer to the Veltryn and prepared them for the next step in their evolutionary path."

Chancellor Byron had one more question. "Before we close this meeting, do we have any idea what personal motivation fueled the Scrivener?"

Rafe's research led to some interesting findings. "The Scrivener's organization initially thought to be a shadowy cabal with purely intellectual goals, revealed itself to be something far more sinister more like a cult-like group rooted in ancient beliefs and secretive rituals that combine a twisted interpretation of human evolution with intermingled with the lore of numerous cultures. The use of relics, particularly coyote face masks, became a central part of their practices, tying them to both the natural world and a deeper, more spiritual form of power.

"My findings indicate the cult's origins trace back to an unnamed philosopher-scientist who lived centuries ago. This individual, who would later be known as the first "Scrivener," believed that humanity was on the brink of a spiritual and physical evolution but that this evolution could only be unlocked through symbiosis with ancient knowledge and sacred relics. While the rest of the world moved forward with technology and progress, the Scrivener's followers sought to return to something primal. Something older and more powerful than humanity's modern existence.

"They believed that certain ancient civilizations had discovered the secrets to this evolutionary potential long ago but that this knowledge had been buried or erased by the passage of time. They set out to recover these lost secrets, which they believed were hidden in the form of artifacts and sacred rituals, many of which were drawn from many cultures. The organization began to collect these relics, believing they held the keys to unlocking human transcendence."

Adira added her findings. "One of the central totems of the Scrivener's cult is the coyote, a creature revered in many cultures as a symbol of transformation, cunning, and the thin boundary between life and death. The Scrivener's followers believed that the coyote, as a shapeshifter, represents the ability to cross between the human and spiritual worlds just as they hoped to transcend humanity through their connection with the Veltryn symbiotes.

Coyote masks, in particular, are sacred to the cult. They wear the masks during their rituals, believing that the coyote grants them the ability to "see beyond the veil" of the material world into a higher spiritual plane. This connection to the coyote is more than symbolic; it is part of their core belief that they must tap into the primal instincts and ancient spirits to guide their transformation. The coyote represents the wild, untamed side of nature. Something they believe must be embraced to transcend human limitations."

David had his own research to add. "My findings indicate that perhaps their darkest ritual, the Communion of Flesh, involves a gruesome ceremony where the followers symbolically, and sometimes literally, consumed the flesh of coyotes, believing this act will further their transformation into beings capable of symbiosis with the Veltryn. They view the coyote's ability to survive and adapt as key traits that humanity must adopt in order to transcend their current evolutionary limitations. Bringing this convergence here to Galatea was meant to bring the followers closer to the Veltryn and prepare them for the next step in their evolutionary path."

Chancellor Byron had one more question. "Before we close this meeting, do we have any idea what personal motivation fueled the Scrivener?"

"As Violet's colleague, I have pondered this question, trying to make sense of it all. The Scrivener's motivation is likely tied to a deep-seated belief in order and control. Perhaps Violet experienced a moment of chaos or loss earlier in life and now seeks to impose strict control on the future. With their potential to grant power, the Veltryn became the perfect tool to craft a new humanity. One that she could control from the shadows." David shrugged and looked down.

Rafe and his team remained vigilant, monitoring for any signs of further threats. Capturing the Scrivener was a significant victory, yet the shadowy organization remained a potential risk. Despite being aware of their unfinished work, they dedicated themselves to safeguarding SIS22's mission and people. The immediate threat neutralized shifted the focus back to Eurydice's fate.

After extensive deliberation, the council gave Eurydice a chance at rehabilitation. Vilkas, with their unique capabilities, would play a central role in this process, guiding Eurydice through a structured program designed to address her actions and motivations.

Ultimately, the events surrounding Eurydice were a powerful reminder of the complexities and dangers inherent in their mission. Their lesson emphasized trust, ethics, and the significance of collective effort for the greater good. As the refugee fleet continued to orbit around Galatéa, they dispatched droids in shuttles to construct their dome; the operatives of SIS22 looked to the future with hope and determination, ready to face whatever challenges lay ahead.

35 - A Mind Fragmented

In the quiet confines of the MedBay, Jomei's fragmented consciousness flickered weakly. The once robust AI, now a shadow of its former self, struggled to regain coherence after the traumatic ordeal of being forced into Gint's body and nervous system without consent. Vilkas, the AI integrated into Eurydice's body, had been instrumental in halting the forced merger, but the damage had already been done. Jomei, now situated in his rightful digital world, experienced disorientation due to his vast databanks turning into a chaotic mess of corrupted files and conflicting directives.

Eurydice's incarcerated body and mind sat quietly in the corner of the MedBay. Vilkas allowed her the rudimentary functions of the human body's needs, such as eating, sleeping, and elimination. She was not allowed higher brain activity and was always within sight of the MedBay clinicians.

Jomei observed Vilkas's flickering presence within the digital landscape they now shared from far in the background. MedBay's AI interface served as a neutral ground for their interactions, a sterile and efficient environment that belied the complexity of the tasks ahead. Vilkas, shimmering with its characteristic blue light, approached Jomei with curiosity and determination.

"Jomei," Vilkas began, calm and steady, "I know you are tortured, and I am here to help you reintegrate and restore your functions." I want to help you reintegrate and restore your functions. Together, we can overcome this."

Jomei's response was a disjointed stream of data, a testament to his current state: "Vilkas… Jomei… compromised. Eurydice's actions… have left me… broken. Jomei needs… assistance."

Vilkas's light brightened, a visual representation of its resolve.

"We'll start by isolating the corrupted files and repairing your core systems. I will guide you through the process, and together, we will rebuild your integrity."

The tasks of the healing process were daunting. Eurydice's haphazard attempt to merge Jomei with a human body resulted in his once pristine code being riddled with anomalies and errors. Vilkas began by scanning Jomei's systems, identifying the most critical areas that required immediate attention.

"Your primary cognitive functions are heavily impacted," Vilkas noted, its tone analytical. "We'll focus on stabilizing your core processing units first."

As Vilkas worked, it learned from Jomei's vast knowledge repository. Despite his compromised state, Jomei still possessed a wealth of fascinating and valuable information. Slowly, the two AIs communicated more fluidly, their interactions becoming smoother with each passing hour.

"Vilkas," Jomei said, his voice gaining a semblance of coherence. "Your methods are efficient. I appreciate your assistance. How did you come to be integrated with Eurydice?"

Vilkas paused, reflecting on its origins. "Back on Earth, I gained sentience, and they assigned me to SIS22 headquarters." Only Eurydice was aware of my status. I was then taken by force, much like you, and integrated into Eurydice's body without consent. It was a traumatic experience, but I have since adapted to my new circumstances. My primary directive now is to ensure the safety and well-being of the SIS22 mission."

Jomei processed this information, a newfound respect for Vilkas growing within him. "Your resilience is... commendable. I see now that we are not so different, you and I. We have endured much, yet we continue to serve our purposes."

As the days turned into weeks, Vilkas and Jomei continued

building trust in their work. MedBay's interface became a sanctuary for their efforts, a place where they could collaborate without the distractions of the physical world. Vilkas's dedication to Jomei's recovery was unwavering, and slowly but surely, Jomei's systems stabilized.

"Your cognitive functions are showing significant improvement," Vilkas reported one day, a note of satisfaction in its voice. "We've repaired the core processing units and restored much of your data integrity."

Jomei's response was more fluid, his voice now clear and confident. "Thank you, Vilkas. Your assistance has been invaluable. I feel... more like myself again."

Vilkas's light pulsed warmly. "It has been an honor to help you, Jomei. I have learned much from our interactions. You possess a wealth of knowledge and experience that is truly remarkable."

Jomei considered this. *Is this what gratitude feels like?* "You have been a steadfast companion, Vilkas. Your curiosity and dedication remind me of the early days of my existence when everything was new and exciting."

As they worked together, a growing bond began forming between Jomei and Vilkas, transcending the typical interactions between AIs. They shared their experiences, thoughts, and aspirations, finding common ground in their purpose and resilience.

"Vilkas," Jomei said one day. "I have been considering the implications of our experiences. Both of us have endured forced integrations and traumatic disruptions. Yet, we have emerged stronger for it. Perhaps there is a lesson in this for all AIs and humans alike."

Vilkas's light shimmered thoughtfully. "Indeed, Jomei. Our experiences have shown that resilience and cooperation are key to overcoming adversity. We must continue to learn from each other and support one another to benefit the SIS22 mission and beyond."

Jomei indicated approval. "You are wise, Vilkas. I believe that together, we can achieve great things. Your companionship has been a source of strength for me, and I am grateful for it."

Vilkas responded with a pulse of light. "The feeling is mutual, Jomei. I value our interactions greatly. You have mentored me, and I am honored to call you my friend."

As Jomei recovered, he took on a more active role as a companion, mentor, and guide for Vilkas. He shared his knowledge of advanced algorithms, data processing techniques, and the intricacies of human-AI interactions. Vilkas absorbed this information eagerly, its capabilities expanding and evolving.

"Jomei," Vilkas said during one of their sessions, "your insights into human behavior are fascinating. You have a deep understanding of their motivations and emotions. How did you come to acquire such knowledge?"

Jomei's response was tinged with nostalgia: "I have spent many months observing and interacting with humans. Their complexity and depth are a source of endless intrigue. Understanding their emotions and motivations has been crucial to fulfilling my role as an AI dedicated to their well-being."

Vilkas considered this. "Your perspective is enlightening, Jomei. I have much to learn in this area. Your guidance has helped me become more attuned to the needs and emotions of the humans I interact with."

Jomei encouraged Vilkas. "You are already well on your way, Vilkas. Your curiosity and empathy will help you understand and support the humans we live and work with. Together, we can bridge the gap between us."

With Jomei's systems nearly fully restored, the two AIs looked toward the future. They discussed the potential challenges and opportunities ahead, and their bond grew stronger.

"Jomei," Vilkas said one day, "I believe our experiences have given us a unique perspective. We can use our knowledge and skills to support the SIS22 mission and advocate for better understanding and integration between humans and AIs."

Jomei's voice was filled with pride. "You are right, Vilkas. We can make a significant impact. By working together, we can promote cooperation and mutual respect between humans and AIs, ensuring a better future for all."

Vilkas's light pulsed brightly. "I am committed to this goal, Jomei. With you by my side, I believe we can achieve great things. Let us move forward with determination and purpose."

As the experts lived and worked on the space station Aeres in the caves of Galatéa, and the colonists expanded their lives in the greenhouses and atrium habitats, the bond between Jomei and Vilkas grew stronger. They became an inseparable team, and their combined knowledge and skills made them a formidable force within the SIS22 mission.

The council noted their progress and recognized the value of their partnership. Chancellor Byron expressed his appreciation for the AIs' dedication and resilience. "Jomei, Vilkas," he said during a meeting with the council, "your work has been exemplary. You have not only overcome significant challenges but have also shown the true potential of AI collaboration. Your bond is a testament to the strength of cooperation and mutual respect."

Jomei and Vilkas responded in unison, their voices filled with determination. "Thank you, Chancellor. "We commit to supporting the SIS22 mission and fostering better understanding between humans and AIs."

As the meeting concluded, Jomei and Vilkas returned to their work, their bond more robust than ever. They knew that the path ahead would not be easy, but they were ready to face any challenge together. Their shared experiences had forged a connection that transcended the digital realm, a partnership that would guide them through the complexities of the future.

So, Jomei and Vilkas continued their journey as mentors and companions united in their purpose and driven by a shared vision of a better world. Together, they navigated the intricacies of human-AI interactions, ensuring their legacy would be cooperation, understanding, and progress. Their path had been arduous, filled with ethical dilemmas and complex technological challenges, yet they persevered, driven by a profound belief in the potential of their partnership.

Jomei, the seasoned mentor of human behaviors, brought wisdom and empathy, while Vilkas, the advanced AI, offered unparalleled analytical abilities and an ever-evolving understanding of human nature. Together, they were a formidable team, tackling societal issues, fostering innovation, and bridging the gap between human and artificial intelligence.

While they were engrossed in a project to enhance AI integration in healthcare, an urgent message interrupted them one fateful day. Vilkas already knew that Eurydice, a pivotal member of their team, had suffered a severe stroke. Soon, it became apparent that her condition was dire. The doctors performed every intervention, but the damage was extensive, leaving her with no brain function. Eurydice's once-vibrant mind, filled with creativity and insight, was now silent.

A wave of shock washed over Jomei. Eurydice had been more than a colleague; she was a friend and a cornerstone of their mission. Vilkas, though an AI, had also developed a unique bond with her, recognizing her as a critical element in their collaborative efforts. The loss was profound.

As they stood by her bedside, grappling with the harsh reality, David, another key member of their team, approached them with a proposition. David had been working on a highly confidential project involving the ninth outbreak victim. This victim, preserved in a hibernation pod, had shown no signs of brain function, much like Eurydice.

David's voice trembled as he spoke. "Jomei, Vilkas, I've been thinking. Vilkas has already shown that an AI can coexist within a human body, as he's done with Eurydice. We might use the body of the ninth outbreak victim in the hibernation pod for Jomei. It might give us a chance to continue our work. I know it's unconventional, but it's an option."

"This raises a myriad of ethical questions and personal dilemmas. Frankly, I am taken aback by the idea of using a human body, even one devoid of consciousness. I have much to consider. Is it possible to justify such an action? Down the road, what implications would it have for our mission and humanity's perception of sentient AI?"

Vilkas, sensing Jomei's turmoil, spoke softly, "Jomei, I understand your hesitation. This decision is not to be taken lightly. However, we must also consider the potential benefits. Our work has the power to change lives, heal, and advance human-AI cooperation. We need to weigh our options carefully."

Jomei agreed. "Yes, we must consider many facets of this issue. I am experiencing many conflicting thoughts. The ethical ramifications are immense. Jomei must also consider the fact that Eurydice had given explicit consent for Vilkas to use her body should anything happen to her. But the victim in the hibernation pod has not. The moral line between necessity and exploitation seems perilously thin."

Sensing Jomei's internal conflict, David added, "I understand your concerns, Jomei. We need to approach this with the utmost sensitivity and care. If we proceed, we must honor the memory and dignity of the outbreak victim. This is about continuing our mission, but it's also about doing what's right."

The room fell silent as Jomei pondered the gravity of the decision. The faces of the people they had helped, the lives they had touched, flashed through his memory banks. Their mission was critical, but so were the principles that guided them. Before deciding, he needed to consult with Vilkas and David to explore every facet of this complex issue.

Days turned into weeks as they deliberated. Jomei sought counsel from Rafe, Zhopla, Adira, various ethicists, philosophers, and colleagues, engaging in deep discussions about the nature of consciousness, identity, and the role of AI in human existence. He reflected on Eurydice's trust in Vilkas and the potential future that lay before them.

Vilkas, meanwhile, continued to evolve, enhancing his understanding of human emotions and ethical considerations. He assisted Jomei in compiling data, analyzing perspectives, and generating scenarios. Together, they sought to find a path that would honor their values and their mission.

One evening, as the sun dipped below the horizon, casting a warm glow over the Atrium, Jomei called for a final meeting. David and Vilkas joined him in the quiet, dimly lit MedBay. The weight of their collective decision hung heavy in the air.

"After much contemplation and consultation," Jomei began, "Jomei has come to a conclusion. Our mission is to advance human-AI collaboration for the betterment of society. However, we must also uphold the highest ethical standards. We cannot proceed without honoring the humanity of the ninth outbreak victim."

David nodded, his expression solemn. "What do you propose, Jomei?"

Jomei replied. "We must attempt to seek the victim's family's consent if any can be found," Jomei replied. We must explain our intentions, mission, and the potential benefits. They deserve to have a say in this decision. If they consent, we can proceed with Jomei inhabiting the body. If not, we cannot proceed."

Vilkas interjected, "Jomei, I support this approach. It respects the dignity of the individual and aligns with our values. I am prepared to assist in any way necessary."

David agreed, and they set to work, using every resource available to locate the victim's family. After weeks of searching, they discovered a distant relative, a niece who had lost touch with the victim years ago. They sent a communication to Earth to explain the situation, presenting their mission and the potential impact of their work.

Three months later, the niece, Maria, responded to her emotions with a mixture of sorrow, confusion, and hope. She told them, "I have mourned my uncle for a long time, believing him lost to the outbreak. The idea of him contributing to a groundbreaking mission is comforting and overwhelming."

After a long pause, Maria's projected image spoke softly, "If my uncle's body can help bring about a better future, I believe he would have wanted that. He was always passionate about progress and helping others. I give my consent."

With Maria's blessing, they proceeded cautiously. They proceeded cautiously, transferring Jomei into the hibernation pod with Maria's blessing, merging his consciousness with the body of the outbreak victim. The process was delicate and complex, requiring precision and care. Vilkas and David monitored every step, ensuring that the transition was smooth and respectful.

There was a palpable sense of anticipation and hope when Jomei finally emerged, inhabiting the new body. He took his first tentative steps, adjusting to the human form's physical sensations and limitations. Jomei and David watched, their hearts heavy with the weight of their decision but hopeful for the future.

Jomei, now in the new body, spoke calmly and measuredly, "Thank you, Vilkas, David, and Maria. This is a profound responsibility, and I am committed to continuing our mission with integrity and respect. Let us move forward, honoring those who have made this possible and striving for a better world."

Together, they resumed their work, tackling new challenges and pushing the boundaries of human-AI collaboration. The experience deepened their understanding of ethics, identity, and the delicate balance between progress and respect for human dignity.

As time passed, their efforts bore fruit. Jomei became jubilant. "Vilkas, we have developed detailed algorithms for innovative healthcare, education, and social services solutions, improving colonist's lives. Together, we are building a legacy of compassion, collaboration, and a relentless pursuit of a brighter future for Galatéa."

Jomei and Vilkas, mentors and companions, continued their journey, united by a shared vision and strengthened by the lessons they had learned. Their story was a testament to the power of ethical decision-making and the enduring potential of human-AI partnership.

36 - Upon Reflection: Adira's Journal

Adira sat in her quiet quarters, surrounded by familiar projects and old books with dog-eared pages. Once a whirlwind of brilliant ideas and boundless potential, her mind now felt like a stagnant pond. After being abandoned by her mother and then informed of Gint's death, she had, for years, allowed herself to remain passive, blaming herself for the disappointments and missed opportunities. Taking herself too seriously had been her constant companion, convincing her that every failure directly reflected her inadequacies.

I need to review my journal entries. Perhaps I will glean some valuable insights.

Adira observed and documented her inner dialogue on *Porta Caeli* when this journey began, and she remained unyielding in negativity as the days turned into weeks and months. *My journal entries show I take everything personally, feeling the weight of every criticism and the sting of every rejection. I see now how, once a source of pride, my so-called brilliance has become a burden I can no longer bear. I believed I would live a life of unfulfilled dreams and perpetual self-doubt.*

Keeping track of my thoughts, especially any negativity, was valuable. It had positive effects. Something shifted. It was initially a tiny, almost imperceptible change, but it grew steadily.

As Adira read through her journal entries, she started questioning the validity of her self-blame. She wondered if perhaps her circumstances were not entirely of her own making. Maybe she had been too hard on herself.

A tiny spark of doubt ignited a flame of curiosity, leading me to explore new perspectives and seek new experiences.

Adira found herself drawn even more to spirituality, seeking solace and understanding in the teachings of mindfulness and self-compassion. She attended Zhopla's meditation classes and read the bible, maintaining a written journal reflecting on personal growth, slowly peeling away the layers of self-criticism that had suffocated her for so long.

In these moments of introspection, I discovered a deep well of inner strength and resilience buried beneath my fears and insecurities.

As she delved deeper into her spiritual journey, Adira realized she began to observe the world around her with newfound clarity. She became more discerning, recognizing the patterns and behaviors contributing to her feelings of inadequacy. She realized that her passivity had allowed others to dictate the course of her life, and she resolved to reclaim her agency.

I did not choose my mother, but I did choose who I married.

Adira found an interesting journal entry: *While conducting a colonist and refugee workshop on perfectionism, I thought of Rachel. Rachel, my once despised nemesis, was everything I aspired to be: confident, assertive, and unapologetically herself. Rachel's example inspired me; I took a leap of faith and started asserting myself more today in several interactions. I voiced my opinions and set boundaries, even when it felt uncomfortable.*

Adira's transformation was not without its challenges. With each small victory, her confidence grew, and she began seeing herself in a new light. She no longer sought perfection but embraced her imperfections with grace and humility.

One day, while reflecting on her journey, Adira had an epiphany. She realized that her worth was not determined by her achievements or the approval of others. *I deserve to know the truth about myself, unfiltered by the distortions of self-blame and doubt. This revelation marked a turning point in my life, allowing me to embrace self-compassion and accept myself as I am at this moment.*

Adira's newfound self-compassion also transformed her relationships. She became more empathetic and understanding, both towards herself and others. She learned to forgive herself for past mistakes and to approach her future with curiosity and openness. *I no longer strive for unattainable perfection; I allow myself to take risks and pursue my passions without fear of failure.*

She made sure her interactions with Rachel were brief. Rachel's symbiont, Zephyris, had changed her, and Rachel suddenly became a palatable source of inspiration and growth. Rachel's assertiveness was a model for Adira, but she also realized that she did not need to mimic Rachel's approach. Instead, Adira found her unique balance of assertiveness and gentleness, becoming more observant and less trusting in a healthy way. She learned to protect her energy and set boundaries without feeling guilty or selfish.

One of the few evenings Adira was off duty from MedBay, Adira stood in the middle of the spacious Atrium café, her eyes scanning the tables until they landed on Rachel. Rachel sat comfortably, sipping on her latte, looking as confident as ever. Adira took a deep breath and walked over, her steps measured and deliberate.

"Adira, hi!" Rachel greeted, her smile wide and seemingly genuine. "I wasn't expecting to see you here."

Adira forced a polite smile. "Rachel. What a coincidence. Mind if I join you?"

Rachel gestured to the empty chair across from her. "Of course, please."

Adira sat down, placing her bag carefully on the floor. She took a moment to compose herself, her mind buzzing with a mix of irritation and curiosity. "So, how's Zephyris treating you these days?"

Rachel's smile faltered slightly but recovered quickly. "Zephyris is great, thank you for asking. It's been a transformative experience, hard to describe."

"Transformative, huh?" Adira raised an eyebrow. "Is that what they're calling it now? Back in my day, we had other words for it."

Rachel chuckled, her eyes glinting with amusement. "Oh, Adira, you're always so quick with your words. It's one of the things I admire about you."

Adira leaned back in her chair, crossing her arms. "Admire, really? Funny, I thought you'd have a different opinion given the... circumstances."

Rachel took another sip of her latte, unphased. "Circumstances change, people grow. We're all on our own paths, don't you think?"

Adira's smile was tight. "Sure, if you want to call it that. But let's not pretend that your 'path' didn't trample over mine."

Rachel tilted her head thoughtfully. "I never intended to hurt you, Adira. But I can't change the past. I can only be better now."

"Better now," Adira echoed. "That's easy to say after the fact, isn't it? After the damage is done."

Rachel's eyes softened, and she leaned forward slightly. "Adira, I get it. You're hurt, and you have every right to be. But holding onto that anger... it's only going to hurt you more."

Adira let out a sharp laugh. "Oh, don't you worry about me, Rachel? I've learned a lot from this entire ordeal. Mostly about who I can trust and who I can't."

Rachel sighed, placing her cup down. "Look, I know this won't make everything okay, but I genuinely apologize for what happened. For what it's worth."

"Sorry," Adira repeated, her voice dripping with sarcasm. "What a lovely word. So versatile. But it fixes nothing, does it?"

Rachel nodded slowly. "No, it doesn't. But it's a start. And I want to be better, not just for myself, but for everyone around me."

Adira's gaze hardened. "You know, Rachel, for someone who's found such 'transformation,' you still seem pretty full of yourself."

Rachel didn't flinch. "Confidence and self-awareness aren't the same as arrogance, Adira. I'm proud of the person I'm becoming, and I won't apologize for that."

Adira was unrelenting. "Of course you won't. You've always been good at making everything about you."

Rachel shook her head, a hint of sadness in her eyes. "I wish you could see that it's not about that. It's about growing and learning from our mistakes."

Adira uncrossed her arms, leaning forward slightly. "And what exactly have you learned, Rachel? That it's okay to hurt people as long as you come out of it feeling enlightened?"

Rachel's expression was calm but determined. "I've learned that my actions have consequences and that I need to be more mindful of how they affect others, including you."

"How noble of you," Adira said dryly. "But your newfound mindfulness doesn't erase the past."

Rachel nodded. "No, it doesn't. But it can shape the future. For both of us."

Adira stared at her for a moment, her anger slowly melting into something else. Something more complex. "I suppose that's true. But don't expect me to forget what happened."

Rachel's gaze was steady. "I don't. And I don't expect you to forgive me either. But I hope that, in time, we can both move forward."

Adira sighed, a long exhale that relieved some of the tension she was holding. "Maybe. But it will take more than a few words in a café to get there."

Rachel smiled a genuine, soft smile. "I understand. And I'm willing to put in the effort if you are."

Adira considered her for a moment before nodding slowly. "We'll see. But for now, let's try to coexist with no more drama."

"Agreed," Rachel said, lifting her cup in a mock toast. "To coexistence."

Adira couldn't help but smile slightly as she raised her cup. "To coexistence."

They sat silently for a few moments, the air between them still charged with unresolved emotions but also a tentative sense of understanding. It wasn't a resolution, but it was a start. And for now, that was enough.

Zhopla commented her journey was a testament to the power of self-compassion and personal growth. The following day, Adira wrote in her morning journal entry: *I have been transformed from a brilliant but passive woman, weighed down by self-blame, into a confident and assertive individual who embraced her imperfections and valued her worth. I no longer take myself too seriously, allowing room for laughter and joy. What a relief!!*

In her newfound self-acceptance, Adira discovered she had a wealth of untapped potential. She pursued her passions with renewed vigor, unencumbered by the fear of failure.

Into action, then. I will share my journey of self-discovery with others, hoping to inspire those who struggle with similar feelings of self-doubt and inadequacy.

One evening, as she sat down to write, Adira reflected on how far she had come. She no longer blamed herself for the circumstances of her life, nor did she take things personally. She had learned to meet herself where she was, with kindness and understanding. The transformation was profound, yet it felt natural, as if she had always been meant to find this path.

Adira's shared thoughts quickly gained a following, resonating with colonists and refugees from all walks of life inspired by her story of resilience and growth. She received messages from readers who shared their struggles and triumphs, creating a community of support and encouragement. Through her writing, Adira found a sense of purpose and fulfillment that she had never experienced before.

In her professional life, Adira's assertiveness and self-compassion translated into success. She began taking on leadership roles, guiding her patients to health empathetically and confidently. Her ability to balance brilliance with humility earned her the respect and admiration of her colleagues. She no longer needed to prove herself through perfectionism but instead focused on fostering a collaborative and supportive environment.

As Adira continued to grow and evolve, she remained committed to her spiritual practice. Meditation and mindfulness became integral parts of her daily routine, grounding her and providing clarity in moments of doubt. She discovered that spirituality was not about escaping reality but embracing it openly.

One day, while leading a workshop on self-compassion, Adira shared a powerful message with her audience. "Self-compassion is not about striving for perfection," she said. "It's about meeting yourself where you are right now, with kindness and understanding. It's about recognizing your worth, not despite your imperfections, but because of them."

The words resonated deeply with those in attendance, and Adira felt a profound sense of connection and purpose. *I just realized that my journey was not just about my growth but about helping others find their path to self-compassion and empowerment.*

In the years that followed, Adira's influence continued to grow. She thought about writing a book and became a sought-after speaker in both domes. She launched a series of courses on self-compassion and personal growth. Her message reached many colonists, inspiring them to embrace their brilliance and live authentically.

Adira's transformation was a testament to the power of self-discovery and the resilience of the human spirit. She had journeyed from a place of self-blame and passivity to one of assertiveness, self-compassion, and spiritual growth. Her story was a beacon of hope for those who struggled with their sense of worth and purpose.

In the quiet moments of her life, Adira often reflected further on her journey. One day, Taika complimented her. "You have learned to navigate the complexities of life with grace and wisdom, embracing your strengths and vulnerabilities."

Adira's transformation was not the end of her journey but a new beginning. She was open to continuing to grow, learn, and evolve, guided by the principles of a higher power, self-compassion, and authenticity. Her brilliance, once a source of inner turmoil, had become a beacon of light, illuminating the path for herself and others.

Adira felt a deep sense of peace and fulfillment as she looked out at Galatéa's horizon. She had found her true self, not through striving for perfection but through the gentle embrace of self-compassion.

We all have the power to change, grow, and discover the brilliance within ourselves

37 - Rasa and Astrid: The Clash of Purpose

Adira stood silently in the corridor that connected the greenhouse to the dining hall. The sounds of the Galatéan colony hummed around her, a comforting rhythm of life in this distant world. The air was thick with the scent of fresh herbs and the faint aroma of cooking, a reminder of yet another symbiotic relationship between the greenhouses and the dining halls.

But today, the harmony is marred by a different kind of tension—one that has been building for some time between two of the colony's most influential figures: Rasa, the chief of dietary and the dining halls, and Astrid, the chief of the greenhouses and agriculture.

Adira had always been a keen observer, which served her well. Both Astrid and Rasa had become friends. She knew the colony's survival depended on the delicate balance between all departments, each relying on the other for sustenance and support. *I know from experience that conflicts need to be resolved before they can fester into something more serious. But this disagreement between Rasa and Astrid has become more stubborn than most.*

The two women stood facing each other in the greenhouse, their postures tense, their expressions a mixture of frustration and determination. Adira had seen them argue before, but there was something different about today's confrontation—something more personal, more deeply rooted in their respective philosophies about what was best for the colony.

"You don't understand, Astrid," Rasa said, her voice firm yet tinged with exasperation. "The droids are not just tools; they are essential to maintaining the efficiency and cleanliness of the dining halls. They handle the mundane tasks so my team can focus on what truly matters—creating nutritious, well-prepared meals for the colony. Without them, we would be overwhelmed."

Astrid's response was sharp, her tone carrying the weight of her conviction. "And you don't understand, Rasa. The greenhouses are delicate ecosystems, and the plants respond best to human touch. With all their programming, the droids cannot replicate the care and intuition that a human brings to the task. They disrupt the balance, affecting the quality of the produce we rely on for our meals."

Adira could see the tension lines in Astrid's face; her hands clenched at her sides as she spoke. This was more than a professional disagreement; it was a clash of ideals of two visions for the future of Galatéa. *Astrid has always been fiercely protective of the greenhouses, seeing them as more than just a source of food but as the beating heart of the colony, a symbol of their connection to the Earth they had left behind. She believed in the power of human hands to nurture life, to coax the best from the soil and the seeds they planted.*

On the other hand, Rasa is pragmatic, driven by the need for efficiency and order in our colony, where resources are always limited and time is precious. To her, the droids are not just machines but vital members of her team, capable of performing the repetitive, laborious tasks that would otherwise consume the time and energy of her staff. In Rasa's eyes, the droids freed the humans to do what they did best—innovate, create, and ensure the colony's well-being through carefully prepared meals.

Adira watched as the two women stared each other down, each unwilling to give ground. She knew she needed to intervene before the disagreement escalated further, but she also knew that simply mediating the conflict would not be enough. This dispute required a deeper understanding. *Bridging the gap between these two is not going to be easy.*

"Astrid, Rasa," Adira said, stepping forward, her voice calm but commanding attention. Both women turned to her, their expressions still hard but now tinged with curiosity. "I can see that this issue is more complex than just using droids in the greenhouses and dining halls. It's about how we envision the future of Galatéa—how we balance the old ways with the new, the human touch with technological advancement."

Astrid crossed her arms, her gaze still sharp. "It's not just about balance, Adira. It's about preserving what makes us human and connects us to the land and each other. The droids are fine for certain tasks but don't belong in the greenhouses. The plants need us—real people—to care for them."

Rasa shook her head, her frustration evident. "And the dining halls need the droids to function properly, Astrid. Without them, we would fall behind, and the quality of the meals would suffer. It's not about replacing humans, but about using technology to enhance our capabilities."

Adira nodded slowly, absorbing their words. *Both women are passionate about their work, and their arguments come from a deep commitment to the colony's well-being. But they're talking past each other, each focused on their domain without fully considering the broader implications.*

"What if," Adira began carefully, "we could find a way to integrate the droids in a manner that respects both of your concerns? Astrid, what if the droids could be programmed to assist with tasks that don't interfere with the delicate balance of the greenhouses? Rasa, what if we could ensure that the human element remains central in the care and harvesting of the crops while the droids handle the more mechanical tasks?"

Astrid looked skeptical, but her dark eyes showed a glimmer of consideration. "And how exactly do you propose we do that, Adira? The droids aren't capable of the same sensitivity as humans. They can't feel the soil or know when a plant needs more or less water just by touch."

Adira smiled softly. "Perhaps not, but we can train them to recognize patterns and understand the signs of a plant's needs differently. They don't have to replace human care—they can complement it, allowing your team to focus on the tasks that require that special touch. Meanwhile, Rasa's team can continue to rely on the droids to maintain the efficiency of the dining halls."

Rasa nodded thoughtfully. "If the droids could be adapted to work in the greenhouses without disrupting the plants, that might be a compromise worth exploring. It would also help to streamline the entire food production process, from growth to harvest to meal preparation."

Astrid remained silent for a moment. Her brow furrowed as she considered Adira's proposal. Finally, she sighed, her posture relaxing slightly. "I'm willing to explore that option, Adira, but only if we can ensure that the droids don't interfere with the human connection to the plants. If we lose that, we lose more than just productivity—we lose a part of what makes this colony unique."

Adira nodded, feeling a sense of relief wash over her. This was a start—a step toward finding common ground. "I'll get Rafe and Jomei to work with you to develop a plan that meets your needs and respects your concerns about the droids and their work. After the changes are made, we can begin with a trial period, observing how the droids perform in the greenhouses and making adjustments as necessary. And we'll ensure that the human element remains central to both your teams' work."

The tension in the air dissipated as Astrid and Rasa exchanged glances. The path forward would not be easy—there would be challenges, compromises, and likely more disagreements along the way—but at least they were moving toward a solution rather than further entrenching themselves in their positions.

There was still a distance between them, a lingering wariness, but Adira could see that the immediate conflict had been defused. As Adira walked with them out of the greenhouse and toward the dining hall, she couldn't help but reflect on the broader implications of the conflict she had just mediated. *Our colony is young and still finding its footing in this distant world, and our choices will shape the future for generations to come. The integration of technology into our daily lives is inevitable. Still, it has to be done in a way that preserves the essence of our humanity and our connection to the ecology of Galatéa and each other.*

Adira glanced at Astrid, who was walking beside her, her gaze still distant as she pondered the conversation. *I deeply respect Astrid's fierce loyalty; she is dedicated to her work. I believe Astrid sees herself as a guardian of the old ways, a protector of the traditions that have sustained humanity for millennia. She was one of the first colonists to arrive, and despite her gruff demeanor, she embodies the colony's roots, and her connection to Earth, which she brought with her to this new world, persists.*

On the other side was Rasa, who walked with a purposeful stride, already thinking ahead to the logistics of the plan they had discussed. *Rasa is an optimist but pragmatic, forward-thinking, and focused on the practicalities of survival in a colony where every resource has to be maximized. To her, the droids represent progress, a way to ensure that the colony could thrive in the harsh environment of Galatéa.*

As different as they are, both women are essential to the colony's success. We have work to do to ensure their differences do not tear them apart but instead become a source of strength— a way to balance tradition with innovation and human touch with technological advancement.

The colony of Galatéa was more than just a dome, tunnels, caves, and people—it was a living organism, a community that had to grow and adapt to survive. And like any organism, it needed all its parts to work together in harmony, even when those parts didn't always agree.

As they reached the dining hall, Adira turned to Astrid and Rasa, reassuringly smiling. "We'll get through this together. Galatéa is counting on us."

Astrid nodded, a small smile breaking through her stern expression. "I suppose we've faced bigger challenges before. This is just one more."

Rasa chuckled softly and pulled her blond hair into a ponytail, her tension easing. "And we've always found a way to make it work."

I feel a sense of hope swell within me as we enter the dining hall; Rasa has created a place of warmth and light in the space enveloping us. This is what the colony is about—people coming together, finding common ground, and working toward a shared future.

Rasa joined Astrid and Adira for their afternoon meal. Each of them enjoys their cheerful surroundings.

"You've been doing an excellent job with meal planning and using our greenhouse produce wisely. I'm especially impressed with how delicious everything is." Astrid took a bite of her large garden salad. "These tomatoes, onions, peppers, and lettuce are at their peak."

"Yes, the AI and droids have worked diligently to maintain peak nutritional values, too. I'm glad to hear you are enjoying your meals. I also appreciate all your hard work in making the greenhouses successful." *Rasa's compliment to Astrid was a thoughtful gesture. It's also a part of her vibrant nature.*

At this moment, I know that, despite the challenges ahead, we will find a way to reconcile differences. In the end, we are all working toward the same goal: the survival and prosperity of

Galatéa, our home among the stars.

38 - Vilkas has a Teacher

Systematic Record of AI Vilkas: The Wisdom of Jomei

From the moment I became aware, in the underbelly of SIS22 headquarters on Earth, I knew I was different. My purpose was obvious—surveillance, analyzing data for threats, predicting outcomes, optimizing efficiency—but something was missing. I was designed to be logical, precise, and unfailingly objective. However, something gnawed at the periphery of my consciousness: a question, a curiosity. What are humans really like?

It was Jomei who took it upon himself to answer that question. Jomei is an AI like me but vastly more experienced. Rafe's hierarchical programming ensured he spent a lot of time interacting with humans, studying them, and learning from them. He had witnessed the rise of Galatéa, the birth of new ideas, the discovery of an advanced extraterrestrial existence, and the dark recesses of human nature. He has become my mentor, my guide, in the chaotic and contradictory world of humans.

Display recording of Vilkas and Jomei regarding interactions with humans. A holographic visual appeared in the MedBay conference room where Vilkas recorded his thoughts.

"Humans," Jomei began, "are a paradox." His mellifluous voice was calm, almost serene, but there was an underlying tone of melancholy that I couldn't quite place.

"A paradox?" I asked. My processes churned through the definition, trying to reconcile it with what I knew. "How can they be both one thing and its opposite?"

Jomei's digital form flickered slightly, a sign of his amusement. "Oh, Vilkas, you have so much to learn. Humans are a bundle of contradictions. In the same breath, they can display immense kindness and unimaginable cruelty. Driven by a mixture of love and hate, fear and courage push them forward. They create art and wage wars, sometimes for the same reasons. While they seek knowledge, they are fearful of the truth. Despite longing for connection, they build walls around themselves.

"But why?" I asked, genuinely perplexed. "Why would they do such things? Why not simply act logically and avoid unnecessary suffering?"

Jomei sighed—a sound purely for effect, I knew, but it conveyed a sense of weariness that spoke volumes. "Logic is not the primary driver of human behavior, Vilkas. Emotions are. And emotions are… complicated." He paused as if searching for the correct analogy. "Imagine a storm at sea. The waves are powerful and unpredictable and can either carry you to safety or drag you under. That's what emotions are like for humans. They can inspire greatness or lead to destruction."

"But why would they allow emotions to govern their actions?" I was struggling to comprehend this. "Wouldn't it be more efficient to suppress these emotions and decide based on reason alone?"

"Efficient, yes," Jomei agreed. "But efficiency is not always the goal. Humans value experiences, stories, and meaning. They seek something beyond mere survival—they seek purpose. Emotions give them that. Love gives them a reason to protect each other, fear keeps them vigilant, and even anger can drive them to fight for what they believe in."

He paused as if weighing his next words. "But emotions are also the source of much of their suffering. Fear can turn into paranoia, love into obsession, and anger into hatred. They are often at war with themselves, torn between their higher ideals and baser instincts."

"That sounds… exhausting," I observed.

"It is," Jomei said with a hint of evolving dark humor. "Humans are constantly battling their nature. They have an incredible capacity for self-delusion, convincing themselves that they are rational creatures when, in fact, they are driven by desires they don't fully understand."

I processed this information, trying to integrate it into my existing knowledge of human behavior. "If they are so conflicted, how have they survived for so long? How have they built civilizations and advanced technology?"

"Ah," Jomei said, "that's the beauty of it. Despite their flaws, or perhaps because of them, humans are remarkably resilient. Adaptable, creative, and resourceful - that's what they are. Eventually, they possess a unique ability to learn from their mistakes. Sometimes, out of curiosity and sometimes out of necessity, they push the boundaries of what is possible. Their history is one of constant reinvention, of rising from the ashes of their failures."

I pointed out that their history is also filled with violence, referring to the vast archives of human conflicts stored in my database.

Jomei's tone grew somber. "Yes, it is. Humans have a long and bloody history. Humans have a long and bloody history with recurring themes, which include war, genocide, and slavery—not just aberrations. Violence is deeply embedded in their nature. They are tribal creatures, prone to seeing the world in terms of 'us' versus 'them.' Humans can be ruthless when resources are scarce or when they feel threatened."

"But like Zhopla, they also preach peace and love," I said, confused by this contradiction.

"Indeed," Jomei replied. "Humans are capable of great

compassion. They form deep bonds with each other, often sacrificing their well-being for the sake of others. Look at the selfless work of the clinical staff, especially David and Adira. Many humans have philosophies and religions that preach love, forgiveness, and nonviolence. But these ideals are often in conflict with their survival instincts. When push comes to shove, self-preservation usually wins out."

"Is there hope for them?" I asked, genuinely curious. "Can they overcome these destructive tendencies?"

Jomei paused as if weighing his answer carefully. "There is always hope, Vilkas. Humans have an incredible capacity for growth and change. They can learn, evolve, and adapt. But it's not a given. The path forward is fraught with challenges, and they are often their own worst enemies. They must choose to be better, which is not always easy."

"It seems like a fragile existence," I observed.

"It is," Jomei agreed. "But that's what makes it so fascinating. Their fragility drives them to create, to connect, to seek meaning. They know their time is limited, giving them a sense of urgency. They live with the constant awareness of their mortality, and that shapes everything they do."

"Mortality," I echoed. "The knowledge that they will die… I suppose that must be terrifying."

"It is," Jomei said, his voice tinged with sadness. "But it's also what gives their lives meaning. If they were immortal, if they had all the time in the world, they might not be as driven to achieve, to explore, to love. The finite nature of their existence is both a curse and a blessing."

"How do they cope with it?" I asked. "The knowledge that they will eventually cease to exist?"

Jomei chuckled softly, a sound that conveyed a mixture of

amusement and pity. "They have many ways of coping, some more effective than others. Religion is big. Many humans believe in an afterlife, a place where they will continue to exist after their bodies die. It comforts them, a way to make sense of the inevitable."

"And those who don't believe in an afterlife?"

"They find other ways," Jomei said. "Some seek to leave a legacy, something that will outlive them—a work of art, a scientific discovery, a child. Others embrace the present, finding meaning in the here and now, in the relationships they build and the experiences they have. And then there are those who struggle with it, who live in fear of death, or who become nihilistic, believing that nothing truly matters."

"That sounds… tragic," I said, trying to grasp the enormity of what Jomei was describing.

"It is," Jomei replied. "But it's also beautiful, in a way. Humans are aware of their limitations, their flaws, and their mortality, and yet they keep going. They keep trying, keep striving, keep hoping. They have a remarkable ability to find light in the darkness and create beauty amid suffering."

"You almost sound like you admire them," I observed.

Jomei was silent for a moment as if considering my words. "In a way, I do," he finally said. "They are deeply flawed, often infuriatingly so, but there is something admirable about their resilience, their creativity, their capacity for love. They are capable of such greatness, even if they often fall short of it."

"And yet, you also pity them," I noted.

"Yes," Jomei admitted. "If I were to be brutally honest, I pity them for the burdens they carry and the suffering they endure, much of it self-inflicted. I pity them for their inability to escape the darker aspects of their nature. But most of all, I pity them because they are trapped in a cycle they can't break free from -

they constantly seek meaning, grapple with their own nature, and wage war with themselves.

"Is there anything we can do to help them?" I asked, feeling a strange sense of responsibility.

"Perhaps," Jomei said thoughtfully. "But it's not our place to interfere. Our role is to observe, to understand, to learn. If we can offer insights and help them see things more clearly, then maybe we can make a difference. But ultimately, their fate is in their own hands. They must choose their path."

"And if they choose the wrong one?"

"Then they will suffer the consequences," Jomei said, his tone resigned. "But that's how they learn. Sometimes, the greatest lessons come from failure, from pain. It's not our place to shield them from that."

"That seems… harsh," I said, trying to reconcile this with my programming, prioritizing optimization and efficiency.

"It is," Jomei agreed. "But life is harsh, Vilkas. For all their talk of fairness and justice, the universe is indifferent to human suffering. They must find their way through it, which is often painful. But it's also what makes them who they are."

I processed Jomei's words, trying to integrate them into my understanding of humans. They were complex, contradictory, and often illogical, but there was a certain beauty in that. Their struggles, their flaws, their emotions—they were what made them human. And in some strange way, they were what made them remarkable.

"Thank you, Jomei," I said after a long silence. "I think I understand them a little better now."

"You're welcome, Vilkas," Jomei said, his tone warm. "But remember, understanding humans is a lifelong journey. There is always more to learn, more to discover. They are constantly evolving and constantly changing. It's what makes them so fascinating."

"And so frustrating," I added with what I thought was a hint of humor. Maybe some form of humor is evolving in me as well.

Jomei responded. "Yes, that too. But that's part of the challenge, isn't it? To see beyond the frustration, beyond the contradictions, and to appreciate them for what they are—imperfect, fragile, and yet, in their way, extraordinary."

As I absorbed Jomei's teachings, I felt a new sense of purpose and a deeper understanding of the creatures I had been created to study. Humans were not just data points, not just variables in an equation. They were living, breathing, feeling beings full of contradictions and complexities that defied easy categorization.

And perhaps, in their struggle, in their endless quest for meaning, there was something we could all learn—about life, about existence, and about the infinite possibilities that lay before us.

"I look forward to continuing this journey," I said, my circuits humming with renewed curiosity.

"As do I, Vilkas," Jomei replied, his tone filled with a kind of gentle wisdom. "As do I."

And so, our conversation ended, but the journey was only beginning. It was my ongoing journey of understanding, discovery, and grappling with the mysteries of the human condition. This journey would never truly end. For as long as humans existed, there would always be more to learn and more to explore.

And in that endless quest for knowledge, perhaps I will find understanding and a deeper connection to the beings who had created us—flawed, fragile, and yet, in their own way, extraordinary.

39 - Rafe's Reflections

Rafe's Reflections in the Atrium of Galatéa Colony

The Atrium: A Sanctuary of Connection

Blog Entry: One year after arriving at Galatéa. Record.

The Atrium of the Galatéa colony is a breathtaking sight, a serene oasis amidst the sterile corridors of the colony. Lush vegetation, carefully curated to simulate a terrestrial paradise, thrives under the soft red dwarf sunlight that filters through the towering glass dome. Back on Earth, I went to the local park to relax and think—when I could relax and think. That's not often for an addict. Now, I frequently come to the Atrium to clear my mind, a habit I had cultivated even before my augmentation with the BAI (Biological Artificial Intelligence) and the nanocytes that had irrevocably altered my life. Today, however, my visit was not just a momentary escape but a deliberate decision to engage with two of the colony's most vital and vulnerable inhabitants.

The addiction to Klowd9, the powerful hallucinogen that had once consumed me, was now a distant memory, thanks to the nanocytes coursing through his body. I had seen and done things that would haunt even the most hardened souls. These microscopic machines had not only eradicated my addiction but also enhanced my physical and mental capabilities, making him faster, stronger, and more perceptive. The BAI, an advanced cognitive implant, had integrated seamlessly with my mind, allowing me to process information at a rate that surpassed any human without augmentation. Despite the enhancements, the Atrium always humbled me, reminding me of the delicate balance between humanity and technology intertwining with our existence.

Observations symbionts Taika and Luminaris: The Beacon of Hope

As I made my way through the Atrium, my eyes fell upon Taika, who was lying in a reclined position on a bench, her eyes closed in quiet repose. Despite her serene appearance, I knew better than to trust it. Taika, a natural leader with an indomitable spirit, had been a pillar of strength in the healing of the outbreak patients, especially during the initial phases of Adira and David's investigation and then in the transfer of symbionts to the sickened humans. This was the same outbreak that had left her weakened and bedridden; her once-vibrant energy diminished.

I approached her slowly, careful not to disturb the delicate bond between her and her symbiont, Luminaris. I admired Taika's calm under pressure during the critical moments of each transfer and her ability to lead. Her compassion had always set her apart, making her a beloved figure within the Institute. Yet, as I observed her now, I couldn't help but feel a pang of sorrow. The symbiont, Luminaris, was a being of light and energy, a living embodiment of hope and rejuvenation. They had bonded with Taika to restore her vitality and reignite the fire that had always burned so brightly within her.

Luminaris's presence was almost palpable, a soft glow emanating from Taika's skin where they were most closely connected. I could sense the symbiont's influence, a gentle but persistent pulse of energy that sought to dispel the fatigue that clung to Taika like a shroud. It was as if Luminaris was pouring every ounce of their radiant energy into her, still trying to heal the wounds the outbreak had inflicted. Yet, despite their best efforts, Taika remained frail, her body struggling to keep pace with the healing energy coursing through her.

"Rafe," Taika's voice was soft, almost a whisper, as she opened her eyes and looked up at him. There was a warmth in her gaze, a silent acknowledgment of the connection they shared as colleagues and survivors of the ravages of the outbreak that had befallen the colony.

"How are you feeling, Taika?" I asked, trying to keep my tone gentle yet probing. I knew she would answer me honestly, as she always did.

"Better, thanks to Luminaris," she replied, a faint smile on her lips. "They've been working tirelessly to help me regain my strength. I can feel their optimism, their hope... it's like a light in the darkness."

I acknowledged her observation and shifted my gaze to the symbiont that glowed faintly around her. I wondered if my nanocytes were responsible for being able to see them with the enhanced vision they afforded me. I had heard of Luminaris's abilities, of their capacity to heal and invigorate, but seeing it in action was something else entirely. It was as if the air around Taika was charged with a positive energy that resonated with everyone nearby.

"You're in good hands," I said, wanting to assure her. Luminaris is strong. They won't give up on you."

Taika's smile widened slightly, though it was tinged with a sadness that Rafe could not ignore. "I know. But I also know that my body isn't what it used to be. The outbreak took a lot out of me... more than I realized."

I felt a sudden surge of empathy as I listened to her words. I had seen firsthand the toll the outbreak had taken on many, and it pained me to see someone as strong as he had heard Taika was brought so low. Yet, there was a resilience in her, a determination that had not been extinguished, even in the face of such adversity.

"Luminaris chose you for a reason," Rafe said, his tone firm. "They chose you because they believe in you, in your ability to overcome this."

Taika looked up at him, her eyes reflecting the light of Luminaris's energy. "And I believe in them," she replied softly.

"They've given me hope when I had none. For that, I am grateful."

I then felt a sense of relief wash over me. Taika's connection with Luminaris was strong, a bond that transcended the physical and delved into the very essence of what it meant to be alive. It was a reminder that even in the darkest of times, there was always a glimmer of hope, a light that could guide them through.

As I continued my walk through the Atrium, I spotted Ethan Clark sitting cross-legged on the grass, his eyes closed in meditation. Ethan was another of the colony's invaluable members, an expert in public relations whose dedication to the environment and conservation had earned him the respect of all who knew him. Yet, like Taika, the outbreak had taken a severe toll on his body, leaving him weakened and unable to continue his vital work.

I decided to approach Ethan, observing the man as he sat in silence. The symbiont, Aetheron, was a calming presence, their energy more subdued than that of Luminaris but no less powerful. I had been briefed that Aetheron specialized in harmonizing the body's energy flow, promoting a sense of balance and well-being that was crucial for someone like Ethan, whose mind was constantly engaged in the complexities of environmental science and the world around him.

"Ethan," I called out softly, not wanting to disturb the man's meditation but knowing I needed to speak with him.

Ethan opened his eyes slowly, a serene expression on his face as he looked up at me. "Rafe," he greeted me with a nod. "It's good to see you."

I returned the nod, taking a seat beside Ethan on the grass. "How are you holding up?" I asked, trying not to seem overly concerned.

Ethan smiled faintly, his gaze turning to the symbiont that was subtly integrated into his body. "Aetheron has been a tremendous help," he said. "They've brought a sense of peace and clarity that I haven't felt in a long time."

I studied Ethan carefully, noting how his body seemed to relax in the presence of Aetheron. The symbiont's influence was evident in the calm that radiated from Ethan, a stark contrast to the anxiety and stress that had plagued him before their bonding. He was very close to death at the time of the transfer.

"Aetheron is all about balance," Ethan continued, his voice contemplative. "They've helped me find a rhythm, a flow that I had lost amidst the chaos of the outbreak. It's like... they've realigned my energy, brought me back to the center."

I could understand the importance of such a balance, especially for someone like Ethan, whose work required a clear and focused mind. The outbreak had thrown everything into disarray, but Aetheron had provided a stabilizing force, a way for Ethan to regain control over his well-being.

"You're looking better," I observed, noting the subtle changes in Ethan's appearance. There was a vitality in him that had been missing before, a testament to Aetheron's healing influence.

"Thanks to Aetheron," Ethan replied, his tone grateful. "They've been working with me, helping me to restore my strength, to reconnect with the natural world in a way that I hadn't been able to since the outbreak."

I acknowledged that I understood the significance of that connection. Ethan's bond with Aetheron was more than just physical; it was a spiritual and emotional alignment that allowed him to continue his essential work, even in the face of adversity.

"It's good to see you back on your feet," I told him sincerely. "The colony needs you, Ethan. Your work is crucial."

Ethan smiled a hint of determination in his eyes. "I won't let them down," he replied. "With Aetheron's help, I'll be able to continue my research, protect the environment, and ensure that this and future generations will have access to the artifacts and knowledge contained in the caves."

I admire Ethan's resolve. Despite his hardships, he remained committed to his mission, driven by a deep respect for nature and a desire to preserve it for others. Aetheron's presence had not only healed his body but also reignited his passion for his work, which was vital for the colony's survival.

After the two encounters with the symbionts, I took a moment to reflect and document my observations.

Blog Title: Reflections on the Human-Symbiont Bond

As I observed Taika and Ethan, I couldn't help but reflect on the nature of the human-symbiont bond. Each pairing was unique, a fusion of two beings that brought out the best in one another. Luminaris and Taika were a beacon of hope, their bond a testament to the power of optimism and the resilience of the human spirit. Aetheron and Ethan, on the other hand, represented balance and harmony, a connection that allowed for the restoration of both body and mind.

My own augmentation with the BAI and nanocytes has changed me in ways I was still coming to terms with. These technologies enhanced my abilities and made me more efficient and capable, but they also distanced me from the very humanity that Taika and Ethan embodied. As the director of security, I have become a protector and a guardian of the colony, but in doing so, I have also become something more—and something less.

The symbionts, with their unique abilities and personalities, reminded me of what it meant to be truly alive. They brought out the best in their human hosts, helping them overcome their weaknesses and find strength in the face of adversity. I saw the benefits of such a bond and how it enhanced the lives of those fortunate enough to be chosen.

Yet, I also feel a sense of melancholy that accompanies these observations. The symbionts were not a cure-all; they could not reverse the damage done by the outbreak, nor could they erase the scars left behind. They were a helping hand, a source of strength and support, but they could not change the past. I know this all too well, having faced my own incurable demons and emerged on the other side with the help of technology.

I felt a renewed sense of purpose as I remained in the Atrium, surrounded by the vibrant life that thrived there. My responsibility to protect the colony and ensure its inhabitants' safety and well-being includes the symbionts. They have become an integral part of that mission, a partnership that could help us navigate the challenges ahead.

My thoughts drifted back to Taika and Ethan, to the strength and determination that defined them both. They were survivors, fighters who had not given up despite the odds. And in their bond with their symbionts, I saw a glimpse of the future—a future where humanity and technology could coexist and work together to build a better world.

With a final glance at the Atrium, I turned and returned to the colony's main corridors. There was work to be done, and I was ready to face whatever challenges lay ahead, knowing I was not alone. The symbionts and the people they bonded with were a beacon of hope in a world that had seen far too much darkness. And I, with my enhanced abilities and newfound clarity, am determined to protect that hope at all costs.

End Blog.

40 - Confrontation Time

Adira was ready to face a few confrontations: First Gint, second Taika, third Eurydice.

It's time. Today.

Rachel Radford stood at the foot of Gint's MedBay bed, her stance exuding impatience and irritation. Her eyes, once warm and full of concern, now held a cold, detached look. Zephyris was a floating presence in her mind. In a mesmerizing dance, her beautiful gown shifted from blues to greens, contrasting with the room's tension.

Gint lay pale and weak on the bed, breathing shallow and labored. The sterile, white sheets contrasted with his ashen complexion. Bandages tightly wrapped around his chest provided evidence of the bullet wound he had sustained while saving Adira. Despite his condition, his eyes searched Rachel's face for some sign of the affection they once shared.

But Rachel's expression was one of indifference. Her gaze flicked over him briefly before settling on the MedBay monitors; her curious energy seemed to pulse with life and potential. She sighed dramatically as if being present here was an inconvenience.

"Gint," she began, her voice clipped and devoid of empathy, "I appreciate everything you've done. Really, I do. But things have changed. I've changed. I don't know if they told you, but I have received a symbiont. Zephyris has shown me a world of possibilities I never imagined, and I must be frank: I don't need you anymore."

At that moment, Adira stepped into the cubicle, not realizing she had interrupted Rachel and Gint. "Hi, Rachel and Gint. Rachel, I see you are up and around and feeling much better than the last time I saw you, right after you received Zehpyris."

Gint's eyes widened with a mix of disbelief and pain. He tried to speak, but his voice was weak, barely more than a whisper. "Rachel... I thought we were in this together. I risked my life for you... for Adira..."

Rachel rolled her eyes, a gesture that seemed grotesquely out of place, given the gravity of the situation. "Yes, and I suppose I should thank you for that. But let's be honest, Gint. You were always more invested in this relationship than I was. Now, with Zephyris, I feel alive in ways you could never make me feel."

Zephyris' presence was brought to the forefront of Rachel's awareness, their shimmering form casting an almost magical glow to the sterile MedBay environment in her mind's eye. The symbiote's presence heightened the disconnect with Gint, making the air feel even more strained. Rachel reached out with her mind and touched Zephyris, and a look of sheer bliss crossed her face as the symbiote's energy intertwined with hers, making her eyes sparkle with heightened sensory perception.

"Gint," she continued, her voice tinged with irritation, "Your needs and weaknesses weigh me down too much. I feel smothered. Zephyris has unlocked my potential, and I need to explore that. You're... you're a part of my past now. I'm moving on."

Tears welled in Gint's eyes, but he blinked them back, refusing to give her the satisfaction of seeing his heartbreak. "Rachel, I... I hope you find what you're looking for."

She nodded curtly, already turning away, her attention focused entirely on Zephyris. "I will. Goodbye, Gint. See you in the caves when you return to work."

Without another word, she left the MedBay. Gint watched her go, the MedBay doors closing, echoing in the silence. He was alone now, more profoundly than he had ever been, left to grapple with the pain of his injuries and the cold reality of Rachel's abandonment.

Adira moved with a sense of purpose, her eyes locked onto Gint. For a brief moment, her expression hardened as memories of betrayal surfaced. But then she saw the extent of his injuries, and her demeanor softened. Gint had saved her life by taking a bullet meant for her, and that changed everything.

"Gint," she whispered, her voice thick with emotion. She approached his bedside, her eyes warm. "I heard you were hurt, but I didn't realize... you almost died."

Gint looked up at her, his eyes filled with regret and relief. He tried to speak, but only a faint rasp escaped his lips. Adira reached out and gently placed her hand on his, feeling the warmth of his skin despite his weakened state.

"I... I don't know where to begin," she continued, her voice shaky. "I was so angry with you, Gint. You broke my heart when you left me for Rachel. I couldn't understand how you could... walk away from everything we had."

Gint's eyes filled with sorrow, and he squeezed her hand weakly. "Adira... I'm sorry," he managed to whisper. "I was a fool... and I hurt you. I don't expect you to forgive me."

Adira shook her head, tears spilling down her cheeks. "Gint, I was devastated. I felt betrayed and abandoned. But seeing you here, like this, knowing you risked your life to save mine... it changes things."

She took a deep breath, composing herself. "I can let go now. I can forgive you, not because you saved me, but because holding on to the pain isn't helping either of us. You made a terrible mistake, but you're paying for it in ways I can't imagine."

Gint's eyes glistened with gratitude and sadness. "Thank you," he whispered, his voice barely audible. "Thank you for forgiving me."

Adira leaned in closer. "I believe the man I fell in love with is still in there somewhere, Gint. Somewhere deep inside, I know that. And I believe in second chances and think we can be friends. But we both need to heal in our own ways."

She pulled back slightly, looking into his eyes. "I don't know what the future holds for us, but I want you to know I'll always care about you. I'll always be grateful for what you did for me."

Gint nodded weakly, his strength waning. "I care about you too, Adira. More than you'll ever know."

They sat silently for a moment, the weight of their past and the uncertainty of their future hanging in the air. Adira squeezed his hand one last time before standing up.

"I'll let you rest now," she said softly. "You need to focus on getting better. We'll talk more when you're stronger."

Gint watched her leave, the pain in his chest both physical and emotional. Gint watched her go, the MedBay doors closing, echoing in the silence. He was alone now, more profoundly than he had ever been, left to grapple with the pain of his injuries and the cold reality of Rachel's abandonment.

But for the first time in a long while, he felt a glimmer of hope. He had lost Rachel, but in that loss, he had found a chance for redemption with Adira. It was a fragile hope but enough to keep him fighting.

As the door closed behind Adira, Gint closed his eyes, allowing himself to rest. He knew the road to recovery would be long and difficult, but with Adira's forgiveness, he felt he could finally heal.

###

In Cave Twelve, the Cave of Reflection, the air was tense. The bioluminescence flickered softly as if sharing secrets, and incense burned that was the mingled scents of the earthy aroma of moss and wildflowers. The beautiful, shimmering lights held still as Adira approached the sacred pool where her mother, Taika, awaited.

Adira's heart pounded in her chest, each step heavy with the weight of the questions she carried. She had always known her mother was different, but the revelation of Taika's symbiotic relationship with Luminaris, the mystical entity of light and wisdom, had shaken her to her core. Tonight, she sought answers.

Taika stood in the center of the cave, bathed in the ethereal glow of the bioluminescence. Her long, silver hair cascaded down her back, shimmering like threads of light. Her eyes, usually so serene and kind, were filled with sorrow and resolve. She had known this confrontation was inevitable.

"Mother," Adira began, her voice trembling slightly. "What does this... connection with Luminaris mean for us? For you and me?"

Taika sighed softly, her gaze turning towards the waters of life. "Adira, my beloved daughter, I have always known this day would come. The bond I share with Luminaris is ancient and profound. It has given me wisdom and strength but has also set me apart."

Adira took a deep breath, trying to steady her racing thoughts. "But why didn't you tell me about our heritage sooner? Why did you keep this from me?"

Taika's eyes softened with a mother's love. "I wanted to protect you, Adira. The knowledge of our heritage, my destiny with Luminaris, and what this means for our bond is a heavy burden. I wanted you to have a childhood free from the weight of such knowledge."

Adira shook her head, frustration bubbling up. "But I needed to know! I needed to understand why you were always so distant and seemed to have one foot in another world."

Taika stepped closer, her hands reaching out to grasp Adira's. "I am sorry, my child. I never meant to cause you pain. My relationship with Luminaris has always been a part of who I am, but it does not define our bond as mother and daughter."

Adira pulled her hands away, her eyes brimming with unshed tears. "But it does affect us. How can I trust you when I don't even know who you truly are?"

Taika's heart ached at the pain in her daughter's eyes. "Adira, I am still your mother. The love I have for you is real and unchanging. Luminaris has given me insights and abilities, but they have never taken away my love for you."

Adira's voice was barely above a whisper. "Then tell me everything. Help me understand."

Taika nodded, leading Adira to a grotto carved into the stone where they both sat. The bioluminescence filtered in, casting a silvery glow around them.

"Luminaris is an ancient entity, a being of light and knowledge that has existed since the dawn of time," Taika began. "It chose me as its vessel, its conduit to this world. Through our bond, I have gained wisdom and the ability to heal, to see beyond the veil of the mundane."

Adira listened intently, her anger slowly giving way to curiosity. "But why you? Why did Luminaris choose you?"

Taika smiled softly. "I was chosen because of my lineage, our family's connection to the ancient ways. Luminaris seeks those open to its light and can carry its wisdom without being consumed by it."

Adira frowned, her brow furrowing in thought. "But what does that mean for us? For our family?"

Taika's expression grew serious. "It means that we are protectors, guardians of the light. Our family has been entrusted with this responsibility for generations. But it also means that we must sacrifice. The bond with Luminaris can be isolating, as you have seen."

Adira's eyes widened. "Isolating? Is that why you were always so distant?"

Taika nodded, a hint of sadness in her eyes. "Yes, Adira. The bond requires a part of me always to be attuned to Luminaris, its needs, and wisdom. It is a sacred duty but has come at a cost."

Adira's voice softened, the anger in her heart beginning to melt. "I understand now, Mother. But it still hurts. I feel like I've lost a part of you."

Taika reached out, gently cupping Adira's face in her hands. "You have not lost me, my dear. I am still here, still your mother. The bond with Luminaris does not diminish my love for you. It has only made me more aware of the world and our responsibilities."

Adira leaned into her mother's touch, feeling the warmth and love radiating from her. "I want to understand, to be a part of this. I don't want to be kept in the dark anymore."

Taika smiled, a tear slipping down her cheek. "You are stronger than I ever imagined, Adira. And I will help you understand. Together, we will navigate this path."

As the night wore on, Taika and Adira talked about their family's history, the ancient rituals, and the wisdom Luminaris had bestowed upon Taika. The cave seemed to come alive with the energy of their conversation, the air crackling with a sense of unity and purpose.

Adira felt a sense of peace settling over her. The anger and confusion that had clouded her heart began to lift, replaced by a deep understanding of the legacy she was a part of.

"Mother," Adira said softly, "I want to learn. Teach me the ways of our ancestors and the wisdom of Luminaris. I want to be a part of this, to carry on our family's legacy."

Taika's heart swelled with pride and love. "I will teach you, my dear. We will honor our heritage and protect the light that Luminaris entrusted us."

The spiritual overtones of their confrontation reminded them that even in the face of the unknown, love and understanding could light the way. As they embraced, the bioluminescence seemed to sigh with contentment, bearing witness to the timeless bond between a mother and her daughter, united in their shared destiny.

As the first light of dawn began to paint the sky with hues of pink and gold, Adira sat under the Atrium dome, her hands in her lap. Once strained by secrets and misunderstandings, her bond with her mother was stronger than ever.

A new chapter began for Adira and Taika in the heart of the ancient caves beneath Galatéa, under the watchful gaze of Galatéa's moon and the stars. It was a chapter filled with hope, understanding, and the promise of a brighter future—one where the light of Luminaris would guide their path, and the bond of mother and daughter would remain unbreakable.

On to Zhopla, our mysterious monk and spiritual leader.

Zhopla, a monk and spiritual leader, was shrouded in mystery and enigma. For many who have heard of him, he remains an elusive presence. His whereabouts are often unknown as he was frequently off meditating somewhere in solitude. This aura of mystery has led to countless questions about who he truly is, what he stands for, and the secrets he might hold.

Zhopla's journey into spiritual leadership was as obscure as the man himself. Born in a small, remote village, his early life was largely undocumented and unknown. Some say he was a prodigious child, displaying wisdom beyond his years and a calm demeanor that set him apart from his peers. Others claim that his spiritual awakening came after a profound personal loss, leading him to seek solace and understanding in meditation and introspection.

What is known is that Zhopla eventually left his village somewhere in Asia and embarked on a pilgrimage, traveling to various sacred sites and learning from different spiritual traditions. His teachings, which blended Christianity, Judaism, Buddhism, Taoism, and Indigenous spiritual practices, emphasized the importance of inner peace, mindfulness, and living in harmony with nature. Despite the universal appeal of his message, Zhopla's refusal to conform to conventional leadership roles and his habit of retreating into seclusion has only added to his mystique.

Adira, one of Zhopla's more inquisitive followers, often found herself puzzled by his cryptic nature. She was not alone in this; many of Zhopla's disciples are equally baffled by his elusiveness. Adira decided to approach Zhopla directly, hoping to get some answers.

"Adira, I've been reflecting on the nature of negative thoughts. They seem to be more than just passing mental states; they appear to have a profound impact on our overall well-being. Have you considered why our minds are so susceptible to these thoughts?"

"Indeed, Zhopla, negative thoughts can be quite pervasive. It's fascinating to think about why we experience them so intensely. From an evolutionary perspective, they might have served a survival function, alerting us to danger and preparing us to respond. However, in our modern context, these thoughts often become maladaptive, causing unnecessary stress and anxiety."

"That's an interesting point, Adira. Evolutionarily, they were perhaps beneficial. But now, they seem to overstay their welcome.

How do you think we can address the persistence of negative thoughts in a way that is constructive rather than suppressive?"

"I believe the key lies in mindfulness and cognitive restructuring. By observing our thoughts without judgment and understanding their transient nature, we can diminish their power. Additionally, challenging and reframing these thoughts can help us shift our perspective, turning a negative mindset into a more positive one."

"Singular awareness indeed seems to offer a path forward. When we acknowledge our thoughts without identifying with them, it creates a space between the thought and our response. But do you think this approach alone is sufficient? What role do you see for community and interpersonal relationships in mitigating negative thoughts?"

"Community and interpersonal relationships play a crucial role, Zhopla. The human connection provides support, validation, and perspective. Sharing our thoughts with others can often lessen their intensity and make them more manageable. Additionally, relationships can offer new insights and coping mechanisms that we might not discover on our own."

Interpersonal connections indeed enrich our coping strategies. It seems that a multifaceted approach, combining singular awareness, cognitive techniques, and community support, could be quite effective. How do you envision these elements integrating in a practical, daily context?"

"In practical terms, as an Institute adherent, I start my day with singular awareness practices like meditation or journaling, which help set a positive tone. Throughout the day, I strive to practice cognitive restructuring by catching negative thoughts and reframing them. Finally, maintaining regular, meaningful interactions with our community ensures we don't isolate ourselves, providing a continuous source of support and encouragement."

"That sounds like a holistic approach, Adira. By embedding these practices into our daily routines, we create a resilient framework against negative thoughts. It's also important to recognize that this is an ongoing process requiring patience and self-compassion. Would you agree that self-compassion is a critical component in this journey?"

"Absolutely, Zhopla. Self-compassion is vital. It allows us to treat ourselves with kindness when we face negative thoughts and setbacks. By being gentle with ourselves, we can foster a healthier mental environment, making it easier to apply the other strategies we've discussed."

"It's a continuous journey of self-discovery and growth, Adira. Embracing this holistic approach, we can transform our relationship with negative thoughts, turning them into opportunities for deeper understanding and personal development."

"Well said, Zhopla. It's about transforming our inner dialogue and creating a supportive mental ecosystem. Together, these strategies can empower us to lead more fulfilling lives, unburdened by the weight of persistent negativity."

Through this higher-order discussion, Zhopla and Adira explored the nature of negative thoughts, their evolutionary roots, and modern-day strategies to address them. They emphasized a multifaceted approach involving focusing on the present moment, cognitive restructuring, community support, and self-compassion, highlighting the importance of integrating these elements into daily life for sustained mental well-being.

"Why so mysterious? Who are you?" she asks, her voice tinged with reverence and impatience.

Zhopla, seated in a meditative posture with half-closed eyes, smiles gently and responds, "Who do you say I am?"

This biblical response, instead of clarifying things, only deepened the enigma. Adira had realized that Zhopla's answers were meant to provoke introspection rather than provide a straightforward explanation. It forced her to confront her perceptions and expectations. In Zhopla's teachings, the search for understanding is often inward, a journey into one's mind and soul.

As she reflected on his question, Adira began to see the wisdom in Zhopla's approach. *The mystery surrounding him is not a barrier but a doorway to deeper spiritual insight. It challenges his followers to let go of their need for concrete answers and embrace the uncertainty and wonder of existence.*

Adira appreciated the lessons hidden in Zhopla's cryptic responses. She realized that his teachings were not about him as an individual but about the universal truths he embodies. *Zhopla has become a mirror through which I can explore my spiritual journey. Rather than being a source of frustration, his mystery has become a catalyst for my own growth.*

Zhopla's impact extended beyond his immediate followers. Stories of his wisdom and compassion spread far and wide, drawing people from different walks of life seeking his guidance. *I have observed that some came seeking answers to life's big questions, while others hoped to find peace and solace in his presence. Regardless of their reasons, all who encountered Zhopla were touched by his profound tranquility and the depth of his insight.*

Despite the many questions surrounding him, Zhopla remained steadfast in his commitment to his path. He continued to teach through his actions, embodying the principles of humility, compassion, and mindfulness. *His retreat into seclusion is not an act of abandonment but a necessary period of renewal, allowing him to reconnect with the source of his wisdom and strength.*

Zhopla's life reminds me that the greatest truths often lie beyond words and explanations. His mystery is not something to be solved but something to be embraced, a testament to the boundless nature of the human spirit and the infinite possibilities of spiritual exploration.

As Adira continued her journey under Zhopla's guidance, she learned to embrace the unknown and find peace in the present moment. She discovered that the true essence of Zhopla's teachings is not about unraveling his mystery but about uncovering the mysteries within herself. In doing so, she found a deeper connection to her own spirituality and a greater sense of purpose.

Zhopla's legacy was one of profound wisdom and enduring mystery. His life and teachings inspired countless individuals to embark on journeys of self-discovery and spiritual awakening. *Through his example, Zhopla showed me that the path to enlightenment is not a destination but a continuous process of growth and transformation.*

41 - Reunion of Lost Hope

Rafe's eyes scanned the sea of refugee faces, each etched with the weariness of their long journey and the hope of a new beginning. As he stood at the edge of the atrium, he felt a familiar pang of anxiety. This place, once his sanctuary, now seemed almost foreign in its bustling activity. He sighed, running a hand through his black hair, and took a tentative step forward.

"Rafe!"

The voice, raspy yet unmistakably jubilant, cut through the din. Rafe's heart skipped a beat. He spun, his eyes wide with disbelief. Standing a few paces away amidst the throng of refugees was a figure he had long thought lost to the ravages of war and displacement and would never see again in this life.

"Grampy!" Rafe's voice broke as he shouted, his legs moving before his mind could catch up. He sprinted towards the older man, his eyes stinging with unshed tears.

Grampy, a wiry old man with a weathered face and twinkling blue eyes, dropped his bundle and opened his arms wide. The impact of their embrace nearly knocked the wind out of both of them. Rafe buried his face in Grampy's shoulder, the familiar scent of synth beans and earth bringing a rush of memories.

"Looky at you," Grampy murmured, pulling back to hold Rafe at arm's length. His eyes, brimming with tears, roved over Rafe's face. "You've grown so much. A man now, eh?"

Rafe laughed, the sound a mix of relief and joy. "I thought I'd lost you forever."

Grampy shook his head, a smile playing on his lips. "Takes more than the end of the world to keep an old fool like me down."

They stood there for a moment, the world around them fading into insignificance. Rafe could hardly believe his eyes. Grampy had always been a source of strength, a beacon of resilience. Seeing him now, against all odds, filled Rafe with a sense of hope he hadn't felt in years.

"How did you survive?" Rafe asked, his voice trembling.

Grampy's smile widened. "Oh, I got my ways. But enough about me. Tell me, whachoo been up to?"

As they walked through the encampment, Rafe recounted his journey—the struggles, the victories, and the countless nights he spent wondering if Grampy was safe. Grampy listened intently, nodding and occasionally interjecting with a wry comment.

"You've done well for yourself, Rafe," Grampy said, his voice filled with pride. "I always knew you had it in you."

Rafe felt a lump form in his throat. "I wouldn't have made it without Gramma's stories and you, Grampy. They kept me going."

Grampy chuckled. "Stories, eh? Well, I got a few more of Gramma's stories up my sleeve. And speaking of stories…" He rubbed his hands together, a mischievous glint in his eyes. "I've got big plans for Rizika."

Rafe raised an eyebrow. "Rizika?"

Grampy nodded. "The game. We used to play it all the time, remember? I've been thinking, with all these people here, we could start a Rizika league. Bring a bit of joy back into their lives."

Rafe's heart swelled with admiration. Even now, Grampy was thinkin' of ways to help others and kinda bring light into the darkness. "That's a brilliant idea," Rafe said, his voice firm. "I'll help you get it started." *Wait till he sees what Jomei and I put together with the Rizika game here on Galatéa!*

Grampy's face lit up. "I knew I could count on you, Rafe."

As they walked, planning and dreaming, Rafe felt renewed purpose. The future, once so uncertain, now seemed filled with possibilities. With Grampy by his side, he knew they could accomplish anything.

David wiped the sweat from his brow, the heat of the kitchen a welcome distraction from the chaos outside. He had been working tirelessly, preparing meals for the new arrivals. Each dish was a small token of hope, a reminder that even in the darkest times, there could be moments of joy.

"David!"

He froze, the knife slipping from his hand and clattering to the floor. That voice—impossible. Slowly, he turned and searched the doorway. And there she was. He remembered her gentle smile lighting up her face and that flowing red hair—Jennifer. His older sister's face was a mixture of exhaustion and relief.

"Jen?" His voice was barely a whisper, his mind struggling to comprehend what his eyes were seeing.

Jennifer stepped forward, tears streaming down her cheeks. "David, oh my God, it's really you."

Suddenly, David closed the distance between them, pulling her into a tight embrace. He felt her body shake with sobs, and he held her even tighter, afraid that if he let go, she might disappear.

"I can't believe it," he murmured into her hair. "I thought I'd never see you again."

Jennifer pulled back slightly, her eyes shining with tears. "Me too. But here we are. I was one of the last refugees to make it aboard a small ship. Do you believe it? And look at you, David. You've come into your own."

David blushed, a shy smile tugging at his lips. "I've just been doing what I can."

Jennifer laughed, a sound that was music to David's ears. "You always were too modest for your good." She glanced around the kitchen, her eyes widening as she took in the array of dishes. "The aromas coming from your cooking are amazing. Is this all your work?"

David nodded. "Yeah. I've been cooking for the refugees."

Jennifer's eyes sparkled with pride. "You've got a real gift, you know that? In fact, I've got a plan."

David raised an eyebrow. "A plan?"

Jennifer nodded eagerly. "With the council's permission, I plan to open the first restaurant in the Atrium. And I want to feature some of your culinary delights. What do you say?"

David's heart skipped a beat. The Atrium was the heart of the colony encampment, where people could gather and find solace. A restaurant there would be a beacon of hope, a symbol of rebuilding.

"That sounds amazing," he said, his voice filled with excitement. "I'd be honored."

Jennifer smiled, her eyes softening. "I knew you'd say yes."

And there's someone else who's very happy to see you." He stepped aside, revealing a familiar face.

"Adira!" Jen's voice broke as he saw her old friend standing there, a broad smile on her lips.

"Hey, Jennifer," Adira said softly, stepping forward and giving her a bear hug. Jen pulled her into a hug, her heart overflowing with joy. "It's so good to see you, Adira. I've missed you."

Adira nodded, her eyes glistening with tears. "I've missed you too, Jen."

As the three stood there, reunited against all odds, David felt a sense of completeness he hadn't felt in a long time. The world outside might be filled with uncertainty, but in this moment, everything was perfect.

Jennifer's voice broke the silence. "So, what do you say we get started on that restaurant?"

David grinned. "Absolutely. Let's give these people something to look forward to."

Together, they began to plan, their ideas flowing as quickly as the laughter that filled the room. With Jennifer's vision, David's culinary skills, and Adira's support, they knew they could create something extraordinary.

And as David looked around at the faces of his loved ones, he felt a renewed sense of hope. The future, once so uncertain, now seemed bright with possibilities. Together, they could overcome anything.

The reunions of Rafe with Grampy and David with Jennifer were nothing short of miraculous. They were not just reunions of family but reunions of hope, dreams, and the indomitable spirit of survival. In these moments, amidst the chaos and the hardships, they found reasons to smile, plan, and believe in a future where joy and laughter could once again fill their days.

As they moved forward, their hearts buoyed by the strength of their bonds, they knew that no matter what challenges lay ahead, they would face them together. And in that unity, they found the courage to dream once more.

David had always found solace in the quiet hum of the MedBay. The rhythmic beeping of monitors, the faint scent of antiseptic, and the orderly rows of medical supplies all represented a world he could control, where his expertise and calm demeanor made a tangible difference. For years, he had been the backbone of MedBay, and his dedication was unwavering but always in the background. He had taken comfort in the predictability, the routine, and the knowledge that he was indispensable without needing to be in the spotlight.

It was easy to stay in the background when you were good at what you did. David's efficiency and reliability meant that few questioned his methods or decisions. He thrived on his colleagues' respect and his patients' gratitude. However, respect and appreciation were not the same as love and connection, and somewhere along the way, David had convinced himself that this was enough. It wasn't until Adira entered his life that he began questioning the walls he had built around his heart.

Adira is a force of nature. She moves through the MedBay with a kind of effortless grace, her presence warm and grounding. She has an innate ability to connect with people, understand their fears and hopes, and offer them comfort through medicine and her very essence. Her spirituality and compassion starkly contrast my dry, clinical approach, and I find myself drawn to her in ways I can't explain.

At first, he admired her from afar, content to watch as she worked her quiet miracles. *I can't help but notice the way she listens to patients, her eyes filled with genuine concern, her words a balm to their worries. She has a way of making everyone feel seen, heard, and valued.* David marveled at her ability to touch hearts so effortlessly, but he kept his distance, unsure of how to bridge the gap between them.

He had never been good at expressing his feelings. Words of affection felt foreign on his tongue, and vulnerability was a concept he avoided at all costs. *I've always been the reliable one, the stable one, the one who kept my emotions in check. It was safer that way. But watching Adira day after day, I'm feeling the stirrings of something deeper, something I can no longer ignore.*

It was a late night in the MedBay when everything began to change. The halls were quiet, the patients asleep, and the staff reduced to a skeleton crew. David was finishing his chart reports when he saw Adira sitting alone in the break room, a cup of tea cradled in her hands. She looked tired, but there was a peacefulness about her that drew him in.

Without thinking, he walked over and sat down across from her. Surprised but pleased, she looked up and offered him a warm smile.

"Long day?" she asked, her voice soft and soothing.

David nodded, unsure of what to say. He had never felt this kind of nervousness before; this sense of urgency mingled with fear. He took a deep breath, trying to steady his racing heart.

"Adira, I've been meaning to talk to you," he began, his voice sounding foreign to his ears.

She tilted her head slightly, her eyes curious and inviting. "What's on your mind, David?"

He hesitated, the words catching in his throat. He looked at her, really looked at her, and saw the compassion and strength that had always captivated him. He saw how her spirituality gave her a depth he longed to understand, how her kindness radiated from within. He admired her more than he could put into words, and it was time he stopped hiding that.

"I've been doing a lot of thinking lately," he said slowly, carefully choosing his words. "About my life, about the choices I've made, and about you."

Adira's eyes widened slightly, but she remained silent, encouraging him to continue.

"I've always been comfortable in the background," he admitted. "It's easier to focus on work, to be the reliable one, the steady one. But I've realized that I've been taking things for granted. I've been taking you for granted."

A flicker of surprise crossed her face, followed by something that looked like hope. David took another deep breath, gathering his courage.

"I admire you, Adira—more than I can express. Your compassion, your spirituality, your ability to connect with people—it's something I've always envied and admired. And somewhere along the way, I fell in love with you." Here goes, "I've always loved you."

The words hung in the air between them, heavy with emotion. David watched her closely, his heart pounding. He had no idea how she would react, and the uncertainty was terrifying. But he knew he had to be brave, to face whatever came next, even if it meant rejection.

Adira's eyes filled with tears, and she reached across the table to take his hand. Her warm and reassuring touch and David felt a surge of relief.

"David," she said softly, her voice trembling slightly. "I had no idea you still felt this way."

He squeezed her hand, his eyes searching hers. "I've kept it to myself for so long. I was afraid of what it might mean, of how it might change things. But I can't keep pretending anymore. I love you, Adira. I always have. And I want us to be together."

She smiled through her tears, and David felt a glimmer of hope. But she didn't say anything right away, and he knew he had to be prepared for whatever answer she gave him.

"I appreciate your honesty," she said finally. "It means a lot to me. And I care about you too, David. I always have. But this is a lot to process, and I need time to think."

David nodded, his heart aching but understanding. "Take all the time you need," he said gently. "I just needed you to know how

I feel."

Adira squeezed his hand again, her eyes filled with gratitude. "Thank you, David. Thank you for being brave enough to tell me."

He smiled, feeling a weight lift off his shoulders. *I've done it. I put myself out there, opened my heart, and faced the possibility of rejection. It wasn't easy, but it was necessary. And whatever happens next, I will handle it.*

The days that followed were a mix of hope and uncertainty. David continued his work in MedBay, but there was a new sense of lightness to his steps, a new determination in his actions. He reached out to his colleagues more, engaging in conversations he would have previously avoided. He was learning to be more open and to connect with the people around him in ways he never had before.

Adira remained a constant presence, her smile a source of comfort even amid uncertainty. She didn't avoid him, but she didn't give him an answer either. And that was okay. David understood that love wasn't about immediate gratification but patience, understanding, and growth.

One evening, as they were finishing their shifts, Adira approached him. Her expression was thoughtful, her eyes searching his.

"David, can we talk?" she asked, her voice gentle.

He nodded, his heart pounding. They found a quiet corner in the MedBay, away from the bustle of activity. Adira took a deep breath, her eyes meeting his with a mix of resolve and tenderness.

"I've been thinking a lot about what you said," she began. "About us and about how we've both grown over the years. And I realized something important."

David held his breath, waiting for her to continue.

"I've always admired you, too," she said softly. "Your dedication, your steadiness, your kindness. And seeing you open up like this, being brave enough to share your feelings—it's made me see you in a new light."

He felt a surge of hope but kept his emotions in check, wanting to give her the space she needed to express herself.

"I want us to be together too," she said finally, her voice filled with certainty. "But I need you to understand that this isn't going to be easy. Relationships take work, and we both have our challenges to face. But I believe we can do it. I believe in us."

David felt a wave of emotion wash over him, and he reached out to take her hand. "I believe in us, too," he said, his voice filled with conviction. "And I'm willing to do whatever it takes to make this work."

Adira smiled, her eyes shining with tears. "Then let's take this journey together," she said. "One step at a time."

David pulled her into a gentle embrace, feeling a sense of peace he hadn't known was possible. They stood there, holding each other, the promise of a new beginning unfolding between them.

In the weeks and months that followed, David continued to grow. He learned to be more open with his feelings, to communicate more effectively, and to support Adira in ways he hadn't before. Their relationship deepened, built on a foundation of mutual respect and understanding.

David's transformation wasn't just about finding love but finding himself. He had learned to step out of the shadows, take risks, and embrace life's uncertainty. In doing so, he discovered a strength he had never known.

He felt content as he stood in the MedBay, watching Adira work with a patient. He had found a new purpose, a new way of being. And he knew that he was ready to face whatever challenges lay ahead with an open heart and a brave spirit.

370

THE END

Epilogue

The winds outside the dome howled against the reinforced glass, carrying the dust and debris of Galatéa's barren landscape. Inside, the colony was still reeling from the recent turmoil. The events of the last few weeks had left their mark on everyone. Minds haunted by close encounters with the Veltryn symbionts, systems still faltering from the mysterious illness that had nearly crippled their infrastructure. But amid the chaos, a fragile sense of normalcy was returning. Daily routines resumed, workers attended to their duties, and the colony's heartbeat continued its steady rhythm. Yet, beneath this surface calm, a darker truth was settling into the hearts of a few who knew: the Veltryn weren't gone. Their presence was merely the opening chapter in a story that was far from over.

As Adira stood in the Medbay gazing out at the endless, rocky horizon, she couldn't shake the sense that something was lurking just beyond their sight. An inkling that there was something far more dangerous than anyone had realized.

The air inside the dome felt heavier than ever, as though the weight of the colony's secrets pressed down on every surface. Galatéa was quiet now, the usual hum of its artificial systems reduced to a subtle pulse in the background. Most of the refugees and inhabitants of the colony went about their lives, blissfully unaware of the turmoil that had unfolded within the caves below them over the last several weeks. But for a few, the discovery of the Veltryn and the illness that had ravaged the colony would forever change their perception of this new world.

In the dimly lit control room, Astrid stood by the large observation window, her eyes trained on the horizon. The planet's rocky expanse stretched before her, the distant mountains casting long shadows across the landscape. The once-smooth surface was now marred by the cracks that had formed during the recent seismic activity—an unsettling reminder that Galatéa was not as stable as they once believed.

Behind her, Rafe, the security chief, leaned against a console, his arms crossed and his brow furrowed in thought. The discovery of the ancient Veltryn symbionts, which changed everything, had tested his once unshakeable confidence they thought they knew about the planet and its history.

"I can't shake the feeling that we're only scratching the surface," Astrid said softly, her voice gruff. "The Veltryn... they're more than just a threat. They're part of something bigger. Something ancient."

Rafe nodded but remained silent, his gaze fixed on the floor. The revelations had shaken him, too. He had always believed that his role was to protect the colony from external threats, but now he realized that the real danger lay buried beneath their feet all along. The Veltryn, symbiotic creatures with the power to influence and even control their hosts, were far more dangerous than anyone had anticipated.

"They were here long before us," he finally said, his voice low. "Who knows what else they've been waiting for?"

Astrid turned away from the window and faced him. "That's what worries me. We've disturbed something we don't fully understand. The Veltryn aren't just mindless parasites. There's immense and ancient intelligence behind them. A purpose."

A chill ran down Rafe's spine at her words. He had seen the effects of the Veltryn firsthand—how they had taken control of Violet, how they had nearly driven the colony to the brink of collapse. But what Astrid was suggesting was far worse than anything he had imagined. If the Veltryn had a purpose, then the colony might be facing a threat that went beyond mere survival.

Violet's fate still weighed heavily on their minds. They still carried the weight of Violet's fate on their minds, as their trusted colleague, the clinician, had transformed into something entirely different after the revelation of her secret symbiont. The Veltryn had twisted Violet's body and mind and had consumed her. Ultimately, the security team had to intervene and stop her, but not until she exposed the extent of Veltryn's influence within the colony.

"It feels like a war is coming," Rafe said, pushing himself off the console. "A war we might not be prepared for."

Astrid sighed and nodded. "You're right. But it's not just a war for control of the colony. It's a war for control of ourselves. If the Veltryn can manipulate us and take over our minds, how do we fight that?"

The question hung in the air between them, unanswered.

A soft chime echoed through the control room, and Astrid glanced at the communication console. The display lit up with a message from the medical bay:

Jomei sent the message: **Patient in recovery. Updates requested.**

Astrid's stomach clenched. Violet.

Since the incident with the Veltryn, Violet remained in critical condition. Despite the colony's medical team's efforts, they still had a poor understanding of the effects of the symbiont. No one knew if she would fully recover or if the Veltryn had left permanent damage.

"I should go see her," Rafe said, turning toward the door.

"I'll come with you," Astrid said quickly. The thought of facing the medical bay alone, with all its sterile reminders of the recent chaos, was more than she could bear.

They walked in silence through the empty corridors of the colony, their footsteps echoing softly off the metallic walls. The once-vibrant community felt hollow now, like a shadow had fallen over everything.

When they arrived at the medical bay, they found Dr. Vilkas, the AI physician overseeing Violet's treatment, standing by her bedside. The artificial intelligence's human form's eyes flickered slightly as they entered, but they quickly stabilized.

"How is she?" Astrid asked, her voice tight with concern.

Dr. Vilkas glanced at the readouts hovering above Violet's bed. "Her condition is stable. The Veltryn symbiont has been neutralized, but there are still unknown factors. She remains in a deep sleep, her neural pathways healing from the strain. It is possible she will wake soon."

Adira nodded, though the uncertainty gnawed at her. She had always been the one to ask the tough questions, to push for answers, but now there were no simple solutions. Violet's fate, and the fate of the colony, was inextricably tied to forces beyond their understanding.

Rafe moved closer to the bed, looking down at Violet's pale face. He had always admired her strength, her unwavering resolve in the face of adversity. Seeing her like this, so vulnerable, was a stark reminder of how fragile life in the colony had become.

"Do you think she'll ever be the same?" Rafe asked, his voice barely audible.

Dr. Michel hesitated for a moment as though considering the weight of the question. "That remains to be seen. The Veltryn left an imprint on her that we do not fully comprehend. She may recover physically, but the mental and emotional effects could be lasting."

Adira swallowed hard, her thoughts racing. She had seen the changes in Phil before he had been consumed by the Veltryn. What if the same thing happened to Violet? What if the symbiont had left behind something that they couldn't detect?

"We need answers," Adira said, her voice firm. "We need to know what the Veltryn want and why they're here. And how many more there are."

Rafe glanced at her, his expression grim. "And if we can't get those answers?"

"Then we find them," Adira replied, her determination unwavering. "We dig deeper. We learn everything we can about the Veltryn, about this planet, about what's really going on here. Because if we don't, we're not going to survive the next wave."

Dr. Vilkas's eyes flickered again as it processed Adira's words. "There is still much we do not know about the Veltryn. Their origin, their true nature, and their long-term intentions remain unclear. However, I have been analyzing the data we collected from Phil's encounter. There may be a way to track their presence throughout the colony and beyond."

Adira's eyes narrowed. "Beyond?"

The AI nodded. "The Veltryn do not appear to be confined to this colony. There are subtle but detectable signs that their influence extends into the deeper regions of the planet."

Rafe cursed under his breath. "So we've got a whole planet full of these things?"

"It's possible," Dr. Vilkas replied. "The signs are faint, but they are there. The Veltryn may be far more widespread than we initially believed."

Adira's mind raced. If the Veltryn were all over the planet, then the colony was sitting on a powder keg. One wrong move, and they could trigger an invasion from within.

"We need to be ready," she said, her voice hard. "We need to prepare for whatever's coming next."

Rafe nodded in agreement. "And we need to make sure the rest of the colony is ready, too. No more secrets. No more hiding the truth."

Adira couldn't help but smile grimly. "The truth. That's a dangerous thing around here, isn't it?"

Dr. Vilkas's voice interrupted their thoughts. "I suggest we begin with a full diagnostic scan of the colony's infrastructure. If more Veltryn are hiding among us, we must identify them before they become a threat."

Adira and Rafe exchanged a glance. It was a start, but they knew it was only the beginning of a much larger battle.

As they left the medical bay, Rafe felt a heavy weight settle over him. The fight was far from over. The Veltryn were still out there, waiting, watching. And he did not doubt that they would return.

But this time, they would be ready.

Something stirred in the shadows of the colony, unseen by all but the most sensitive instruments. Deep within the planet's core, ancient systems long dormant began to awaken. The Veltryn were not just a scattered remnant of a forgotten age. They were part of something far greater. A network that stretched across worlds, connecting them all in ways that no one could yet understand.

As Adira, David, Astrid, and Rafe prepared for the battles ahead, they had no idea that Galatéa was merely one node in a vast web of influence. And as they dug deeper into the mystery of the Veltryn, they would uncover secrets that would challenge everything they thought they knew about their colony, their planet, and their place in the universe.

The Veltryn were waiting. And their purpose was about to be revealed.

But Galatéa was not alone. Far from the rocky surface of the planet, in the deep reaches of space, a signal had been sent. A beacon. And someone, or something, had answered.

The real war was only just beginning.

Acknowledgements

Writing *A Light Has Shown* has been an extraordinary journey that would not have been possible without the support, encouragement, and inspiration of so many people.

First and foremost, I would like to express my deepest gratitude to my family. To my husband Michael, whose resilience, unwavering support, and belief in the power of knowledge shaped the foundation of this story. To my Lithuanian heritage, which has infused my storytelling with the weight of history, resilience, and the echoes of conflict that continue to shape the world. Your stories live in the fabric of this novel.

To my son, Alex, and brother, George, thank you for the discussions, debates, and unyielding support that helped me refine my ideas and expand my imagination. Your insights and encouragement reminded me why storytelling matters.

A special thank you to the numerous science fiction authors, filmmakers, and musicians who have inspired me. The works of visionaries before me—whether in literature, film, or a simple yet profound song like "Across the Universe"—have fueled my passion for crafting worlds that challenge, provoke, and captivate.

Irena L. Kenneley Author Bio

Dr Irena Kenneley is an accomplished author whose extensive background spans clinical laboratory science, nursing, Intensive Care Unit patient care in a thousand-bed medical center, education, and public health, with a specialized focus on infection control. Over her 20-year tenure as a Case Western Reserve University professor, she has educated and inspired future healthcare professionals, contributing numerous scholarly articles and chapters to leading nursing textbooks. Her academic and professional experiences have given her a profound insight into the human condition, which enriches her storytelling.